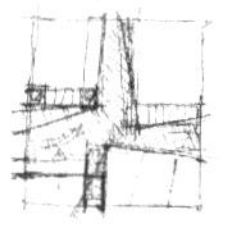

Secret Paths Editions presents

The Cloud Catcher

Alan McCluskey

First published in June 2021
Secret Paths Editions, Mureta 2, CH-2072 Saint-Blaise
Copyright © Alan McCluskey
Cover illustration by Alan McCluskey
Print Edition ISBN 978-2-940553-26-6

Other books by the author

Stories People Tell
Local Voices

Chimera

Boy & Girl Saga
Boy & Girl - Book One
In Search of Lost Girls - Book Two
We Girls - Book Three

The Storyteller's Quest
The Reaches - Book One
The Keeper's Daughter - Book Two
The Starless Square - Book Three

Coming soon
Bursting With Life

1.

Fran reined in her pony and stared up at the sky. Great wispy clouds curled in long tendrils, turning pink as the sun set. A single darker cloud to the West stood out, solitary and intriguing.

The countryside was deserted. Traffic rarely travelled that road, certainly not in the evening. Her father's farm was over a mile away. Being Friday, he'd normally be in his study, the door locked, curtains drawn. Fran shuddered, shoving away unwelcome memories. Today was not such a day, she reminded herself. Her parents were away, gone to stay in her father's hunting lodge on the other side of town. From all accounts, it was a dull place. She couldn't understand why they'd been so excited about going there.

Only the faint rustle of the breeze could be heard. Fran enjoyed being out alone. She found the peace and quiet profoundly moving. Sitting still in the saddle she drank in the silence, long and deep, imagining it could wash her soul clean. As if that were ever possible.

Sighing, she was about to nudge her pony forward when a muffled moan at the horse's feet had her looking down. In the gloom under a solitary walnut tree, a girl her age sat barefoot in an old-fashioned nightdress and nightcap, her back against the tree trunk, crying softly.

Dismounting, Fran tentatively offered a hand, saying, "You shouldn't sit too long on the ground, it can get very damp when the sun sets."

The girl stared up at her, her expression blank. Fran took a step closer, meaning to help her stand, but the girl shied away, fear in her eyes. Fran let her hand fall to her side and looked the girl over. The skin on her face was drawn tight over her bones as if she hadn't eaten in days, possibly months. Her legs and arms were all flesh and bone. As for her nightdress, it was stained and torn in places and her feet were filthy as were her hands. Goodness only knew what ordeal she'd been through.

"I'm not going to hurt you," Fran said, trying to keep her tone soothing. The girl urgently needed help, but Fran was at a loss what to do.

Thinking food might do the trick, she rummaged in her saddle bag and drew out a ham sandwich. She'd brought it in case she felt peckish. When she offered it, the girl snatched it and sniffed it warily, her nose wrinkling in disgust, then she ripped the slices of bread from the ham, tossing them onto the grass and stuffed the meat in her mouth, desperately trying to swallow the piece whole.

Within seconds, she was choking, coughing violently. With her mouth wide open, Fran could see only gums and no teeth. No wonder she was starving. When a violent cough sent the meat flying in Fran's direction, she deftly caught the slimy lump. Her turn to be disgusted.

She wished she had her penknife. At least then she could have cut off small pieces and handed them to the ravenous girl. What on Earth had happened to her teeth? Her mouth was like a baby's. A baby. Yes. That would work. She'd seen a mother do it. That was all very well with a baby, but this girl was her age. Her saliva in the other girl's mouth. She couldn't. Yet there was something uncanny about the girl that made refusing difficult. A kind of unspoken 'Yes' that forced itself on Fran.

Steeling herself against her disgust, Fran lifted the lump of meat to her lips and bit into it. The other girl began trembling with rage. If she'd had the strength, she'd probably have flung herself at Fran. Had she had teeth, she'd have bitten her. Through it all she made no sound. Fran was beginning to wonder if she wasn't deaf and dumb.

Having chewed the meat to a pulp, she took it between her fingers and offered it. At first the girl didn't react, as if she didn't understand. Then she grabbed Fran's wrist and plunged meat and fingers into her mouth.

In her alarm, Fran tried to recover her hand, afraid the girl might seek to swallow it, but, for all her weak appearance, the girl had a grip of steel. So Fran stood still and let the girl lick and suck her fingers, surprised and embarrassed at the way the slobbering sent waves of pleasure coursing down her spine. In a distant corner of her mind, she heard her pony shift uncomfortably, whinnying softly.

When the girl finally released Fran's hand, she felt bereft, a sinking feeling of loss in the pit of her stomach, her fingers cold and dissatisfied in the evening breeze. Bringing the remainder of the ham to her mouth, she bit off a further piece and set about chewing. She did so several times, till all the meat was gone. Unable to resist the waves of pleasure, Fran would not have pulled her hand free even had doing so been possible. Her whole attention was riveted on her fingers.

When the girl took hold of her empty hand and slid the fingers back into her mouth, Fran wondered if the girl was trying to torture her. But she dutifully licked between her fingers and sucked each one in turn. Fran couldn't help moaning as a delicious shiver shuddered down her spine and lodged deep in her stomach. She finally pulled her hand free, her lungs heaving as she sucked in breath after breath trying to get a grip on her rampaging emotions.

Fran turned back to her pony and rested her forehead against the cool of the leather saddle trying to recuperate. She closed her eyes. The strong smell of the animal mingled with the characteristic odour of the grease used to treat the leather were reassuring.

Who was this girl? And what had she just done? Fran had never felt such a violent upheaval in her body. She dragged her thoughts away from the memories as they set off renewed shivers coursing down her spine. She was afraid she might shatter if the experience were to repeat itself.

Gathering her courage, she opened her eyes and turned to face the girl, bent on getting answers to her questions. To her shock, the girl was gone. Disappeared. Only a faint depression in the grass hinted that anyone had been there. Fran hurried to check behind the pony. No girl hid there. No one was behind the tree either. She'd only just met the girl, yet the feeling of disappointment and loss was acute.

Fran stood in the near dark, her arms tightly clasped across her chest, struggling to reassure herself. Surely she hadn't imagined it all. She brought her fingers to her nose. They were no longer wet, but there was a faint odour that was unfamiliar.

She tentatively pressed a finger against her lips which remained pursed, resisting the temptation, as if knowing she was asking for trouble. Don't be ridiculous, she told herself. Relax. She let the tip of her finger ease between her lips. A red hot bolt shot through her body, coming to rest in her belly where it pulsed in time with her racing heart. Alarmed, she withdrew the finger. Had the girl bewitched her? Witches were no longer in fashion, but how else could she explain what was happening?

Casting one last lingering glance at where the girl had sat, Fran mounted and trotted off. The sun had long set although it was not completely dark. Above, the strange little cloud had gone and the pink wisps of clouds had been replaced by more solid dark grey masses that hung heavy in the sky. Not rain clouds. Nor those promising thunder either. Yet sinister, all the same. The world remained quiet, but it was no longer peaceful. The all-embracing silence had been replaced by an expectant lull, like an in-drawn breath. Something was about to happen.

Nothing did. The ride back to the stables was uneventful. In its stall, Fran removed the saddle and brushed down her pony, all the time wondering about the girl. She must have been distracted, because the pony nudged her to draw her attention back to the task.

"I know," she said. "I'm sorry. I'm a little preoccupied." She flung her arms around the pony's neck and hugged it, burying her nose deep in its coat, savouring the reassuring odour. Horses had such a characteristic smell. Nothing like dirty runaways.

None of the girls at school were anything like the one she'd just met. Sure. They could be a laugh, they fooled around a lot when the nuns weren't around, they shared many things, although rarely with her. But they'd never have sucked another girl's fingers in such a sensual... No way! Feeling the telltale stirring in her gut, she cut off that train of thought before it could blossom into hot uncontrollableness.

With her parents away - her mother had insisted they wouldn't be back before Sunday evening - she grabbed a bite in the kitchen, carefully avoiding the ham - would she ever safely eat it again? - and climbed to her room. It was Friday evening and her homework was already done. She had extra chores about the farm to cover for her parents, but otherwise she had the weekend to herself.

As an only child in a large farmhouse, she not only had her own room, but an adjacent bathroom and a small study where she had her desk and schoolbooks. Her father repeatedly bemoaned she didn't deserve such luxury. Above all, he begrudged her the limited privacy it offered.

In the small hall that served as entrance she hung her riding hat on a peg next to the riding crop and sat on a bench to pull off her boots. She removed her socks too, planning to change into pyjamas and read a book. She pulled her pullover over her head as she entered her bedroom, almost stumbling over a pile of books she'd carelessly left in the way as she navigated blind. Finally free of the pullover, she turned her back to her bed and tossed it in the direction of the bathroom. Her jodhpurs followed, the two forming a crumpled heap near the bathroom door.

Dressed in only her underclothes she turned to the bed meaning to get her nightdress from under her pillow and screamed. She screamed so loud the windows rattled. Had any normal person been in the house, they would have come running, thinking she was being murdered. But her parents, especially her father, were not normal and would surely have savoured her screams.

There, seated at the foot of her bed, was the waif, completely unperturbed at having Fran scream. Under the scrutiny of the girl's implacable gaze, Fran blushed at being caught in only her underwear. Apart from her father, nobody had ever seen her half-naked, not even her mother or the school doctor. Her hands flew to cover herself, a futile effort. Two hands were not enough. The ridiculousness of her reaction was quick to strike her. She ceased screaming, although her body continued to scream long after her voice had stopped.

However had the girl got in? The doors had been bolted. Could she manipulate locks or was she able to walk through walls? And how had she known that this was Fran's home? Or that this was her room? Was she some sort of mind-reader? And what did she want? Fran shuddered. Was she out to play with her fingers again? The thought filled her with both desire and dread.

As if to make things worse, the girl pulled back the sheets and blankets and was about to crawl into bed. Fran shuddered. "No!" she shouted. She couldn't have the filthy girl in her bed. She might have lice or God knew what. The girl seemed unperturbed at the refusal.

Scooping her up - Fran was alarmed at how little she weighed - she carried the girl into the bathroom. She'd expected resistance, but got none. The girl was alluringly compliant. She'd also expected to be overpowered by the stench, but the girl smelt surprisingly pleasant, mouthwateringly in fact.

Needing to set some distance between her and the girl, Fran sat her on the toilet, hoping that didn't give her any ideas, and went to run the shower. Once the water was the right temperature, she turned back, half expecting the girl to have disappeared. But she was still seated there, her eyes following Fran's every move.

"You should get undressed," she told the girl, only to elicit the same blank expression as earlier. "You can't shower with your clothes on," she pointed out. To no avail. There was not even a flicker of a smile, or a tight-lipped sign of stubbornness, just a perplexed stare.

There was nothing for it, she'd have to undress the girl, but could she trust herself to do so? A part of her was worryingly eager to see the girl naked. She dreaded the idea she might have become her father's daughter. Even if she could get the girl's clothes off, she had no idea how to persuade her to stay under the shower and wash herself. She had comic visions of chasing a dripping girl around her room.

Sparing use of water was a lesson her parents had drummed into her, so constant running water had her feeling guilty. Unable to wait, she scooped up the girl and stepped into the shower with the girl in her arms and clumsily pulled the curtain closed behind them.

2.

Warm water gushed over their heads and streamed down their bodies soaking their clothes as the girl clung to Fran, her breath coming in short, sharp gasps. Fran was acutely aware of the other girl's chest heaving against hers. The same confused mixture of desire and dread drove a wedge through her. What was she playing at? If her classmates were to see her... Gently prising the girl's fingers apart, Fran loosened her grip and pushed away, reaching for the soap.

Lathering the cake of soap in her fingers, she took hold of the girl's hand and began rubbing soap into the palm. She then placed the cake of soap in the girl's hand, but the girl made no move to wash herself. Taking back the soap, Fran began rubbing it down her arms, hoping the example would help the girl understand. When she handed her the soap again, the girl just stood there unmoving.

Reluctantly Fran took the soap and began lathering the girl's arms and legs, paying particular attention to her filthy feet. She tried to adopt a clinical attitude as if it were a scientific experiment in which she wasn't really involved. She knew she should wash the rest of the girl, but baulked at the thought. For once the girl took the initiative, struggling with her dripping nightdress, she pulled it up and over her head and dropped it at her feet.

Fran sucked in a watery breath and turned the girl round. Starting with her back seemed the safest option. The girl was so skinny there was almost nothing between Fran's soapy fingers and the girl's bones. Touching such a starved body sparked a mixture of disgust and anger and pity that made her stomach churn. Reaching the small of the girl's back, Fran had no difficulty convincing herself she didn't need to be thorough, so she skipped washing her backside. Straightening up, she was alarmed to see the girl turn, as if expecting her to wash the front too.

When Fran moved to turn the water off, the girl grabbed her wrists and placed Fran's hands on her chest. Lack of food must have stunted her growth, because she had very little in the way of breasts compared to Fran. Standing there with her wet hands unmoving on the girl's chest, Fran sensed a strange feeling of detachment creep over her. She wondered how much longer they would have warm water. The boiler would soon be empty. It would take ages to warm up again.

The girl had relaxed her hold so Fran was able to free her hands and turn the water off. Reaching for a towel, she handed it to the girl and, taking a second one, she wrapped it round her shoulders. With the girl not reacting to words, Fran mimed how the girl should dry her hair and skin. Despite her efforts, the girl stood unmoving, dripping on the bathroom floor. "Enough!" Fran said, and loosely wrapping the towel around the girl's shoulders, she gave up on miming and went in search of clothes.

To her dismay, the girl trotted after her threatening to soak the carpet. Having shooed the girl back into the bathroom, Fran hastily closed the door and, making the most of being alone, she pulled off her wet underclothes. Drying herself as best she could, she hurriedly pulled on her nightdress then rummaged through her drawers in search of a second nightdress. She found an old one buried under her pants and bras. It would be too large, but she had nothing else.

Sucking in a calming breath, she opened the bathroom door, the nightdress clasped in her hands. She steeled herself at the thought of finding the girl standing there, dripping like a bedraggled duck. But she found no one. The bathroom was empty. The girl had flitted back to where ever she came from, taking the towel with her.

Disappointment rivalled with relief as Fran sank onto the bed, her fingers still tingling from lathering the girl's skin, her heart racing. She lay back, dazed, and stared up at the ceiling, her mind blank. From time to time she furtively glanced around the room to make sure the girl hadn't returned. But she was alone and, for once in her life, she didn't relish the prospect.

Tomorrow would be a busy day. With her parents absent, she had a lot of additional chores and would need to get up even earlier. She should go to bed, but she was too perturbed to contemplate sleep. On a normal day, if she couldn't sleep she'd go down to the kitchen for a quick snack. It generally did the trick. Although she had to careful to dodge her father's groping paws.

But the thought of making her way through the dark, empty house spooked her. Damn it! The girl could move through solid walls. However did you keep her out? Or in, a wicked little voice whispered as she drifted off to sleep.

Ah, there you are. I've been looking for you everywhere. It was the girl, but it was not the girl. Gone we're the hollow cheeks and the gaunt figure. Gone were the spindly arms and legs. Her complexion was no longer pale and sickly, but rosy pink. She looked strong and healthy. And happy too, if her smile was any indication.

She was wearing a pretty floral dress that flared out from her waist but was so short as to be more of a smock. It was made of no material Fran had ever seen. It had a metallic sheen to it, mirroring the lights around, yet it moved like silk over the girl's body.

But the most striking thing about her was her hair, or rather the lack of it. She was completely bald. As if to accentuate the fact, her scalp had been oiled making it shine in the light. The sight of that smooth surface had Fran yearning to run her hands over it. The thought had her shivering.

The girl's ears, which struck Fran as abnormally small, were adorned with a coiling band of silver that snaked round her ear and disappeared into its depth. No wonder she had difficulties hearing.

I'm glad you came, the girl said.

So she could talk. But in that strange place it wasn't really talking. Her lips didn't move. Maybe that was because it was a dream. At least, Fran hoped it was. How else could she explain what was happening? She'd been nearly naked in the shower with the girl and felt how thin her body was. This smiling nymph couldn't possibly be the same person. Maybe her wish to see the girl healthy was colouring her dreams.

I'm Xristy, by the way.

Fran wanted to tell Xristy how glad she was to see her well, but no matter how hard she tried, she couldn't say a word. She knew she used to be able to, but it was as if she'd forgotten how. The dream had turned the tables. Now she was the one struck dumb. But at least she could hear ... of sorts.

Let me show you round, Xristy said, grabbing Fran's hand, her touch warm and inviting as she pulled her forward. A section of the wall slid open with a meaningful hiss and let them through. They stepped into a vast, well-lit atrium filled with a great variety of plants and bushes, most of which she didn't recognise. Above a giant glass dome suspended from a latticework of girders covered the whole space. Beyond she could just make out a swirling mass of clouds.

We can't live outside. The atmosphere is too hostile, Xristy explained. *So we grow everything we need inside.*

Fran wanted to ask why the atmosphere had become unbreathable, but she couldn't pronounce a single word. It was so frustrating she wanted to stamp her feet. Only the thought of appearing childish stopped her.

Xristy led her across the atrium, weaving a path between various cordoned off areas each with a different mixture of plants. It reminded her of allotments except these were round, not square. The colours of the flowers were violently vivid. Looking at them was like being punched in the gut. But it was the scents that were the most striking. The fragrances were so potent her head began to spin as they burrowed deep into her being. The world blurred and she wistfully wondered if the dream was over as she began to fall.

If Xristy hadn't caught her, she would have flattened one of the plant patches. *I fainted*, she wanted to say by way of apology, but was condemned to silence, her head lolling to one side as Xristy jogged along the path. It was then, in Xristy's arms, as she felt a breeze about her thighs, that Fran realised to her dismay that she was wearing only her nightdress.

Still feeling woozy, Fran closed her eyes and let herself be cradled by Xristy. She heard the whoosh of another door opening and, as it closed, the overpowering scent of flowers diminished.

I guess it was the flowers, Xristy said. *I imagine they're overpowering if you're not used to them.*

Where the hell did you pick her up? a girl asked. Despite the antagonism, her voice was even more melodious than Xristy's. *You do realise she can't stay.*

I know, Xristy admitted with a sigh.

Fran cracked open her eyes, curious to know who Xristy was talking to. The beauty she saw took Fran completely by surprise. Despite being bald like Xristy, the girl literally made Fran's mouth water. Hopefully she wasn't drooling. Sure. She was surrounded by girls at school. Not surprising, it was an all-girls school. But she'd never been attracted to any of them. Not like she felt drawn now. Come to that, she hadn't been much interested in boys either. But then, she knew so few of them. And her twisted ties to her father had soured any desire to be with boys.

I've no idea where she was. All I saw was that they venture outside and get around on large four-legged animals. They live alone in large boxes and have so much running water they stand for hours under it. Oh, yes. And they can't talk and I don't think they can hear either. I tried several times to communicate with her, but she didn't react.

Fran was flabbergasted at this warped vision. She wanted to

set Xristy right and would have done so had she been able to. As for communicating, that was a lie. The girl had never tried. It was the other way round. Fired by indignation, she opened her eyes wide. They were in a small cubicle and, protruding from one wall, was a bed on which she was lying. A glass-fronted cupboard was set in the opposite wall containing shelves on which sat a wide assortment of little bottles and flasks. A doctor's surgery, she guessed.

The two hadn't noticed she was awake. They pursued their discussion as if she weren't there, presumably thinking she couldn't hear. *You shouldn't give her that potion,* the girl was saying.

True, Xristy replied, although she didn't sound so sure. *Who knows what effect it might have on someone from another world,* she mused.

Is she a good kisser? the other girl asked, some of her antagonism giving way to curiosity.

No idea. I didn't get a chance.

Who were these people? They were so strange. Did they go around judging a girl by how well she kissed? She had to giggle. She imagined having examinations in kissing at school. An all-girls school at that. Her giggling, however, had attracted the attention of the two girls who stopped talking and came to lean over her. For one terrible moment she was afraid they were going to try her skills at kissing. Instead they continue talking about her.

Her ears are so big, the other girl said. *They're quite ugly, don't you think?* The girl leaned closer, inserted her little finger in Fran's ear and squealed. *There's a hole,* she blurted out. *She's got a hole in her head.*

Suddenly it dawned on Fran. They had no ears. Well they did, but ones that didn't work, not like hers. That was why they couldn't hear. But they communicated all the same, having developed some kind of talking between minds. For some reason she could hear their thoughts, but she couldn't project her own.

She burst out laughing causing both girls to look at her in

alarm. Presumably they couldn't hear her laughter but they could see the expression on her face. It was at that moment she felt a strange tugging on her mind and wondered if she was finally going to be able to communicate. But everything went black. When she could see again, she was back in her room.

3.

Wow! Telepathy. She sprang to her feet, excited at the prospect, only to realise it was pitch dark. Glancing at her bedside clock she saw it was only three. In three hours, she'd have to get up and begin her chores. Reluctantly she lay down, not expecting to be able to sleep.

The next thing she knew her alarm was ringing. It was six and time to get up. Stiflingly a yawn, she clambered out of bed, took off her nightdress and went to have a shower. She almost slipped on a puddle of water. She'd completely forgotten to clean up after the girl.

It suddenly struck her that she'd seen no boys in Xristy's world. Were there only girls? The idea appealed to her. But how could that be possible? Maybe they didn't need to have children. Maybe they had something like test-tube babies. Or perhaps they lived for ever young. Who knew?

Washed and dressed she went down to fix breakfast. With her parents away, nobody had lit the range. She shivered and pulled her shawl tight around her shoulders. The temperature always fell at the beginning of September just in time for the return to school. She decided to make herself porridge rather than her usual muesli, at least that might warm her up.

She'd just spooned the steaming porridge into a bowl and was about to turn back to the table and eat, when she felt another presence in the room. Sure enough, glancing over her shoulder, she saw Xristy seated at the table looking at her. This time, the girl had come in clothes from her world which looked all the stranger in their old-fashioned kitchen. Her colourful dress was surely far too flimsy for such cold weather.

Do you want some? Fran asked, indicating the porridge. She didn't actually say the words, only thought them as loud as she could.

So you can talk, Xristy exclaimed, beaming.

Sure, Fran answered. *At first I couldn't understand what was happening. In this world we communicate using our mouths and ears, not our thoughts. Once I understood what was happening, I realised I might be able to talk to you the way you do. So, do you want some porridge?*

Clearly the girl didn't understand, so Fran handed her her bowl with a spoon and went to cook some more. *Careful, it's probably too hot.*

Xristy tried a very small piece and made a face.

Hold on a moment, Fran said. Heading for the fridge and bringing out a bowl of fresh cream, she poured a little on the porridge and sprinkled brown sugar on top. *That should be better. Try.*

Xristy dipped her spoon cautiously into the mixture and brought it to her mouth, sniffed cautiously, then ate. A smile spread across her lips. *Mmmm! This's good.*

Once her portion of porridge was ready, she joined Xristy at the table and the two ate in silence. They'd just finished when one of the farm's cats, a large tabby, slunk into kitchen and rubbed itself affectionately against Xristy's legs. It had sensed there was cream in the offing. Xristy screamed, flinging back her chair as she jumped to her feet and clambered onto the table. The cat sat back on it haunches and stared up at her with doleful eyes, as if to say, What's the matter with that one.

It's what we call a cat, Fran said, scooping up the cat and scratching behind its ears. *We keep them as pets.*

Pets? Xristy asked, clearly unwilling to get off the table.

Animals that live with us. They often stay with us in our house and keep us company. In return, we give them shelter and food.

Xristy finally climbed down, but kept her distance from the cat. *We have no such animals,* she said. *We have neither the food to feed them nor the room to house them.*

Fran put down the cat, which wandered off, and set a kettle on the cooker to heat water. While she made tea, she explained what the drink was. The girl preferred water, so Fran gave her a glass of tap water.

Xristy marvelled at the sight of the liquid running freely from a tap. *Water is so rare in my world,* she explained. *It's a real pleasure to drink freely.*

Tell me... Fran began, cupping her hands around her mug. Despite the porridge, she was still cold. She should have lit a fire in the range. Plucking up her courage, she blurted out, *What's all this about kissing?*

Xristy grinned then licked her lips. *It's one of the things we girls enjoy most.*

Between girls? Fran was a little apprehensive about the answer.

With who else?

Boys, Fran replied incredulous.

Boys? Xristy replied, her expression perplexed. *We haven't had any of them in our world for centuries. So you have boys here?* The possibility didn't seem to excite her. If anything, she seemed disgusted.

Fran nodded. So she'd been right. There were only girls in Xristy's world. Another question troubled her. *How come you have ears but you can't hear?*

Your question is so strange. I don't think we've ever been able to use our ears. No one ever mentioned it to me.

And why do you shave your head? Fran asked.

Shave? Clearly the girl did not know the word.

Fran pointed to her hair and mimed cutting it.

We've never had hair on our heads. The only place we have hair is between her legs.

Fran spluttered at her candid answer. Maybe in a world

peopled with only girls you could talk about such things openly. She imagined mentioning the subject at school. It would cause a scandal. But then girls at her school were particularly prude, at least publicly, which was to be expected in a girls school run by the church.

While they were on the subject of 'down there', something else troubled Fran. *Without boys or men, how do you manage to have babies? Do you use some form of artificial insemination?*

The girl had no idea what that was. Instead she said, *Well, there shouldn't be babies. None of us can have them. Something to do with the air. I've only ever heard of one. A number of years ago.* She hastened to add, *it was hushed up and the baby got rid of.*

Horrified, Fran burst out, *You killed it?*

No, Xristy replied, absently. *I believe it was given to someone to look after.* There followed a thoughtful pause. *I imagine, if babies were required we'd find some way of making them.*

The possibility was so self-evident, she couldn't understand Fran's confusion. *Here, two girls can't make babies,* Fran said. *You need a boy for that.* Which raised questions about the one baby they did have.

How terrible, Xristy exclaimed. She sounded genuinely shocked if not disgusted. Clearly she had no idea how that one baby came about. Or if she did, she wasn't letting on.

Fran was tempted to push her to explain, but she feared an enquiry might lead to a practical demonstration, so she kept quiet. Instead she washed the dishes and prepared to go outside. The hens were first on her list. If Xristy was afraid of a cat, how would she react to a clucking mass of hens?

I've got work to do outside, would you like to come?

Outside? Xristy sounded apprehensive.

Sure. Outside is safe here.

Xristy looked bleak. *I can't. All my life I've been told going outside is synonymous with dying. Maybe another time.*

But we first met outside. Surely you remember.

How could I forget? I almost died.

It was true, she'd looked dreadful. Why had the girl been so sick when, only hours later, she was perfectly healthy? How was that possible? Fran began to wonder if an overdeveloped mind might make a body ill simply by thinking it.

I can't force you, she said. *But, like the porridge, I really encourage you to try.*

Xristy closed her eyes and sat stock still. At first, Fran imagined she was contemplating her choice. It must be frightening. The girl was convinced she'd die. When the moment lasted, Fran wondered if it wasn't rather a bout of mute stubbornness. A refusal to take the risk. A childish tantrum without the waving of arms and the stamping of feet.

After a while, the lack of movement became disturbing. She was like a lifeless statue. When the grandfather clock in the hall struck the hour and it was time to go, Xristy still hadn't moved, Fran shifted closer, trying to make out signs of life. Judging from her placid expression, it was almost as if the girl were waiting for something to happen, but Fran had no idea what.

Closeup the girl smelt faintly of flowers from her world. The mixture of scents was enticing. Made braver by Xristy's continued lack of movement, Fran stepped nearer, till her nose was only inches from the girl's head. It was the oil. The oil rubbed into her scalp. The smell was delicious. As if entranced, Fran had a wild desire to kiss that smooth skin. To taste the oil. To press her lips against her skull.

Tentatively, she puckered her lips and brushed them feather-light over the surface. Now the oil was on her lips sending a shiver down her spine. She wanted more. Much more. She planted her lips on the crown of the girl's head and pressed firmly till her lips parted and her tongue brushed the skin. The taste of the oil was intoxicating. It penetrated her brain and set fire to her thoughts.

Renouncing all caution, she began licking Xristy's scalp, like a starving cat lapping up milk. Somewhere, in a distant corner of her mind, a terrified schoolgirl, her hands clasped in prayer, was screaming at the devil to stop tempting her. Fran shoved her rudely aside as she moved to licking Xristy's forehead, her nose, her cheeks, finally halting only inches from her lips. Even the faint breath from those lips smelt of flowers. It drew her in.

Kissing was their greatest pleasure, Xristy had said. Yes. It was easy to believe. And she wanted to, so badly. As if her whole life had been leading up to that moment. Leaning in closer, she pressed her lips against Xristy's and plunged into a wild, warm world, completely lost in a kiss that she prayed would never end.

As if the kiss had awoken her, Xristy's fingers roved through Fran's hair, pressing their lips even tighter together. Her tongue darted out, boldly exploring Fran's mouth. A faint moan escaped her lips. Which of them had moaned was unsure. Both probably. It didn't matter. Then, with a deft movement, the girl pulled Fran astride her lap and laced her arms around her waist, pulling their two bodies so close that the line between them blurred. Even their minds were kissing.

You're insatiable! Fran exclaimed, breathless, afraid she'd dissolve for ever in the girl if they went any further.

I know, Xristy purred. *The thirst won't be quenched.* She licked Fran's nose. *No matter how wild the love-making. It's never enough.* She ran her index finger around Fran's ear tracing its contour, ending by tugging her ear lobe. *Being incomplete drives me mad. I've roamed so many worlds, but no answer was to be found.* She tightened her grip on Fran as if to underline her desperation.

Then, from one moment to the next, Xristy was gone and Fran, teetering on the verge of a cliff, sat urgently kissing empty air. She wanted to fling herself into the void. She wanted to reclaim the half of her that had flown away with Xristy. She wanted to give back the part of Kristy that now wriggled inside her. How could she possibly go on alone, having known that blurring of beings?

Feeling decidedly diminished, she pulled on her wellies and headed out to the chicken coop, head bowed, a wicker basket in hand. She fed the chickens and went in search of eggs. Some hens laid in the most ridiculous places. She'd once found an egg months later. It had exploded when she moved it, showering her in stinking goo. It had taken ages to rid herself of the smell. At least it'd kept her father away.

The mention of smells, whether good or bad, had her sniffing her fingers. Yes. Xristy's scent still lingered. The oil must have been drugged. It had driven her crazy. She'd acted like a wild animal in rut. Not even a stud would have behaved like that. She shuddered at the thought. What if someone from her school had seen her licking the girl's bald head, not to mention them slobbering over each other, their lips glued together. She felt her face burn. The humiliation. She'd surely be ostracised, if not expelled. Thank heavens Xristy didn't pop up at school. Not yet, a little voice purred.

4.

Much to Fran's disappointment, but also relief, Xristy hadn't reappeared all weekend. Finishing her chores with time to spare, she'd taken her pony through its paces for more than an hour. With the imminent return of her parents, she brushed down the pony, showered and tidied up, all the time wondering if Xristy hadn't been a figment of her imagination. Yet the girl had seemed so blazingly real. Fran couldn't believe herself capable of dreaming up such delicious antics. The very mention sent wave after wave of shivers down her spine.

She had absolutely no prior experience making out with girls. The thought of kissing a girl had never crossed her mind. She knew some girls did, or at least bragged they did. She'd always imagined they vaunted their exploits with girls only because it was forbidden. She'd never been interested herself.

If she'd had a doctor she could trust, she might have sought advice. Maybe her feverish state and the wild hallucinations were a known illness and there was a cure. But the family doctor, old Peterson, would probably drool over the story, coaxing out every juicy detail, then promptly inform her father and maybe even the headmistress, if not the police. Talk about the villain calling the others villainous!

She was expecting the arrival of her parents to be an awkward moment. They'd surely notice something odd about her, some telltale sign that she'd done things she shouldn't, but in reality her mother was so full of their weekend, she wouldn't even have noticed if Fran had her head shaved like Xristy.

She was obliged to sit through a particularly long evening meal during which her mother enthused about how exciting the weekend had been without once going into details. Fran nodded at all the right places and asked the necessary polite questions to show how pleased she was for them without appearing to pry, but all the time she looked at her parents as if seeing them for the first time.

Her mother, who must have been attractive at some time, was considerably past her best. Traces of grey hairs were a sure sign, but it was the wrinkles across her forehead and beneath her eyes that singled her out as being on the decline. Fran had never noticed before. Neither had she paid any attention to the folds of skin forming under her chin. When she began wondering what her mother would be like without any hair, Fran hastily looked away and unwittingly caught her father's eye.

His blues eyes sparkled in anticipation as he held her gaze. He'd fared better than his wife, although he was considerably older. His weatherbeaten skin from years spent outdoors made him look almost younger. Stretching across the table to grasp the water pitcher, his hand brushed hers causing her to shudder in disgust. Fran tore her eyes from his, hoping to get support from her mother. Hopeless wish. The presence of his wife had never deterred her husband's barely concealed advances. Her mother looked weary. Bone weary. And resigned.

Deliberately glancing at the clock, Fran said, "You must be exhausted after your weekend and tomorrow's an early start..." How odd to handle her parents like that. Had her encounter with Xristy changed her that much?

Her father stifled a fake yawn as her mother rose with a sigh to clear away the dishes. "Don't worry about that," Fran told her. "I'll do the dishes. School starts later on a Monday morning." Not waiting for her mother's agreement, Fran began piling plates in the sink.

A worried look flitted across her mother's face as if she suspected Fran had other motives in hurrying her off to bed.

"Thanks," she said, yawning again. "I could do with an early night." Her father shot Fran a lecherous glance over his shoulder before he turned and strutted after his wife. He clearly believed Fran had chased off her mother to be more readily available. She'd have to shunt the dresser against her door again, although he was deaf to the message.

Can I be of any help? a silky voice asked in her head. Spinning around she discovered Xristy sitting at the table, smiling at her. She'd forgone her short metallic dress and was now dressed in a blouse, jacket and skirt, but they were still very clearly from her world.

Fran held a finger to her lips saying, *Shhhh. Don't wake my parents*. It was a silly thing to say seeing as they were talking mind-to-mind.

Parents? Xristy asked, looking perplexed.

However did you explain such a self-evident concept? *The man and woman who brought me into the world and raised me. I am their child.* Xristy continued to look perplexed. Fran shrugged and gave up. *They are my guardians. They tell me what to do, and what not to do.* The whole thing was weird when you said it like that. Why did being her parents give them the right to order her about?

They wouldn't be very happy to find you here. As churchgoing people, they'd probably be furious about her frequenting a girl who, judging from the outrageous way she was dressed, was probably some sort of loose hussy. Privately, though, her father would be thrilled and would be scheming to corner Xristy at the first opportunity. *They'd demand all sorts of explanations. I've no idea how I'd explain. I don't understand myself.*

Do you wanna come with me? We're having a party. Fran's look must have been incredulous, because Xristy added, *Only if you want.*

I can't possibly come, I've got school tomorrow.
School?

The question was inevitable. Fran should have known Xristy would have no idea what school was. *A place to learn.*

Why do you need a place to learn? Can't you learn everywhere? I do. We do. Every occasion and every place is a chance to learn.

It suddenly struck her she'd never wondered what school really was. *It's a place where specially trained people, called teachers, help us learn. They've traced out a path of what we need to know and lead us down that path, testing us often to see if we've understood.* Far too often, Fran thought.

Xristy chuckled. *You can't be serious. How can one person tell another what they need to learn? It's different for each person.*

Fran couldn't argue with that. In truth, she'd probably learn more by going with Xristy to her world than by struggling through hours of maths or English, stuck at her desk, forced to listen to a boring teacher. Most of the time lessons just went in one ear and out the other. She had to admit, it was hard to memorise the unmemorable. *Okay. I'll come. But only for a short time. I need to get some sleep. But I must clean up here first.*

Judging from Xristy's behaviour, Fran expected a party in her world to be more like an orgy. She'd heard about such things. Apparently the Romans were very fond of them. With such unChristian thoughts in mind, Fran was disappointed when Xristy told her they were going to climb to the roof of their world.

You can't go dressed like that, she said. *This is a very special occasion and special occasions require special clothes.*

Fran had changed out of her work clothes that still smelt from mucking out her pony that morning. But the clean clothes she'd donned to greet her parents were nothing fancy. Just jeans and a pink blouse. Wearing clothes that were the slightest bit alluring when her father was around was asking for trouble. How was she to know she was to be invited to a special ceremony?

Once in Xristy's world, the girl led Fran into a small room along each wall of which hung hundreds of dresses in all manner of iridescent colours. They reminded her of exotic butterflies.

Before she could object, Xristy had pulled off Fran's blouse as if that were the most natural thing to do. She halted at the bra, fascinated. Fran couldn't understand why. It was nothing special, just a plain sports bra. *Why do you wear that?* Xristy asked.

Another one of those questions Fran was at a loss to answer. *It's reassuring*, she finally said. *All girls my age wear one.* She cupped her hands protectively over her breasts, hoping that would discourage the girl from trying to remove it.

Xristy shrugged and went to work on the zip of Fran's jeans. That proved to be more of a challenge. Apparently such things didn't exist in her world. Fran unzipped her jeans, but then stood still, letting Xristy do the rest. It was a game, a daring but delicious game, that caused goose bumps to form on her arms and legs.

When Xristy reached out to pull down her underpants, Fran objected. *We don't wear such things*, Xristy insisted. She made a move to hike up her dress to prove it, but Fran stopped her. *I believe you.*

Xristy shook her head. *What a strange little thing you are*, she said, gifting Fran a winning smile. *Let's chose you a dress. The others are waiting for us.*

The others turned out to be a group of five girls her age who looked sufficiently similar to Xristy that Fran wondered if they weren't sisters. She felt uncomfortable in her borrowed dress whose unfamiliar material chaffed her skin and left her feeling exposed. She rarely wore a dress and never so short. Experience had taught her to avoid even the slightest thing that could be construed as an invitation when around her father.

Her dress echoed the iridescent colours of theirs. No two were the same, but the distinct air of family about their clothes, recalling that of their faces, made her feel all the more out of place. Never before in her life had she felt so alien. Yet for all that, the others seemed to accept her, albeit somewhat formally, politely asking questions about her world, questions, unfortunately, she was at pains to answer. Her inability to explain the familiar, which to them was unknown and alien, only underlined her feeling of otherness.

Amongst the group was the girl she'd spotted on her earlier visit. Duffni was her name. Glancing frequently in Fran's direction, she joked with her friends about Fran's swooning fit only to insist, in exaggerated tones, that there'd be no such flowers where they were going. Despite the obvious taunt, Fran was reassured, guessing it was oil from those flowers that had driven her to slobber all over Xristy. Maybe there'd be no orgy after all.

With Xristy, who'd taken to holding her hand, they followed the others into a small room with sliding doors. The room was devoid of furniture and had only a small light set in the middle of the ceiling. There were no other doors and no windows, leaving Fran feeling claustrophobic as the doors slid closed behind them. Then, as if the floor were falling away beneath them, the room shot up. Fran couldn't help squealing, a fact that passed totally unnoticed as clearly none of the girls could hear.

A lift! They were in a lift. She rarely used lifts. At school it was all stairs. At home too. Not even the town library or the local theatre had lifts. But in the few lifts she'd ever been in, none were as large and as rapid as this one. And it kept shooting up.

Fran glanced at Duffni who must have felt her eyes on her because she shot her a penetrating look. *Are you ready for the adventure?* the girl asked, still taunting, only to add dismissively, *Of course you're not. But there's no need to be afraid, as long as you hang on tight.* The obvious glee and the barely veiled threat was hardly reassuring. So, wherever they were going, there were dangers.

Don't pay any attention to Duffni, Xristy said. *She enjoys scaring newcomers. It's her favourite sport.*

Newcomers? Do you often have visits from girls like me?

No. You're the only one. I meant girls who are new to our group. Each girl has to come on this journey at least once.

Do you go all the time? It was the impression Fran had.

No. But we are the designated Cloud Catchers. You'll see. She wouldn't say more.

The name was intriguing. It had Fran's imagination running wild. She saw the girls cavorting across clouds with giant nets scooping smaller clouds into a basket. The image was so comical, she had to laugh. Her mirth went unnoticed in the ambient deafness.

When the lift finally slowed to a halt, Fran had become so accustomed to its breakneck speed, she staggered and almost fell, only to be caught by both Xristy and Duffni. For a brief moment there was a tussle between as to who would help her. She imagined them in a heated conversation that only they could hear. Then Duffni relinquished her hold and bowed her head almost imperceptibly. So Xristy was the leader. Good to know.

The doors slid open and light flooded into the dimly lit room. Squinting out, Fran was so astonished and alarmed at what she saw, she was afraid she'd swoon again. She gasped, her lungs battling to get air. There was a whooshing in her ears as the light gently faded and her legs buckled beneath her.

5.

You fainted, Xristy said. *It's the altitude and lack of oxygen. Try this*. She gently pushed a couple of leaves between Fran's lips. *Chew*, Xristy said. It was bitter, so bitter Fran shuddered and made a face. *I know. But it'll help you breathe. Above all it'll help you get over the vertigo.*

Xristy helped Fran to her feet, handing her a pair of goggles attached to a larger contraption. *These will allow you to see better. The light is so bright, if you're not used to it, it can be blinding.* These were no ordinary goggles. Not only did they work as dark glasses, but there was a mask that came over her mouth and nose attached to a bottle of oxygen that she was to carry on her back.

Xristy helped her fit the device over her mouth and nose and attached the goggles over her eyes. The world abruptly went dark causing her to falter. *Don't worry*, Xristy said, *you'll need them once you get outside.* When Xristy help her don the backpack, she was astonished how light it was. Xristy pressed a knob at the top of the backpack and air rushed into Fran's lungs. She was surprised at her relief. She hadn't realised how difficult breathing had become.

When Xristy had donned a similar headgear, they headed for the door. Nothing could've prepared Fran for the shock she had when she looked around. They were outside - Yes! Outside! - standing on an open platform that towered above the world. Clouds rolled away at their feet like a sea of fluffy waves, constantly changing form and colour.

Welcome to the Cloud Catcher's domain, Xristy said with a flourish.

Fran stared wide-eyed at the landscape of clouds. It was so beautiful, it almost hurt. *I thought you couldn't go outside*, she exclaimed.

Up here the air is different, and, anyway, we all have oxygen masks. Xristy took her hand and led her across the platform to where the other girls were grouped round what looked like scooters without wheels. A dreadful suspicion crept over Fran. Surely they weren't going to ride those things over the clouds. She shuddered, imagining herself falling off and plunging to her death miles and miles below. She morbidly wondered what would happen to her body back home...

We call ourselves Cloud Catchers, Xristy said, so caught up in her story she was oblivious to Fran's distress, *but in fact we are more like shepherds herding sheep.*

Why ever would you do that? Fran exclaimed.

Apart from the fact that it's the most exhilarating experience I know, even more than kissing you, Xristy replied, a grin in her voice, *we do it because the clouds are our only source of water. No rain can penetrate the dome. Without our work the settlement would have no water and everyone would die.*

How odd that a whole settlement should depend on such a small group of young girls for their survival. In her world, girls that age were corralled in school, unable to venture out of an evening without parents' permission, let alone do anything useful for society.

Here, Xristy said, brandishing a harness that she strapped around Fran's waist then buckled over her shoulders. When Xristy pulled a strap between her legs and attached it to the back of the harness, Fran held her breath, wrestling with a surge of troubling feelings. *To avoid any accidents,* Xristy explained.

Do accidents happen often? Fran asked, her mental voice trembling.

No. Never. Xristy said. *We're always very careful. But better to be sure.*

The other girls had climbed onto their scooters and, with a mental whoop, sailed off the platform and skimmed over the clouds. *I can't possibly fly one of those things,* Fran exclaimed, taking a step back.

And no one expects you to. Xristy suddenly sounded very serious. *It takes years to learn to skim clouds. If ever we had to take a new recruit, she would be allowed to fly solo only after a very long apprenticeship. No. You'll be flying with me. I am the most experienced of the Cloud Catchers. I've been at it far longer than any of the others.*

So Xristy was the leader of the group and to think she'd taken her for a frivolous child whose libido ran wild.

Climb on, Xristy said. *I'll ride behind you.*

What about the harness? Fran asked, clinging desperately to the straps as if her life depended on them.

They'll be attached to the scooter.

But what if the scooter breaks down?

That's never happened. Anyway, they're programmed to fly back here if ever there's a problem. I understand you're apprehensive, but I can assure you, it's well worth it.

If she hadn't been so preoccupied with thoughts of plunging to her death, Fran might have seen the kiss coming. She ought to have wondered why Xristy pulled both their oxygen masks aside. She vaguely hoped it meant Xristy had given up on the flight. As it was, Xristy's lips on hers took her completely by surprise and when the girl pushed the tip of her tongue between Fran's lips, she just had time to register the now familiar taste of plant oil swirling in Xristy's mouth than the wild passion set in. An errant thought about how the girl had managed to hold so much oil in her mouth flew into tiny nonsense fragments as her mind went up in flames.

Long before she'd had her fill, Xristy replaced their masks, letting welcome oxygen into her lungs, and lifted Fran bodily onto the scooter still in throws of raging desire. She cuddled in behind with one arm tight round her waist and the other latching onto the strap that ran between her legs, and they were off with a mighty Whoop! Fran opened wide her mouth and let out her own wild whoop that no one else would hear.

How Xristy managed to fly the craft with both hands clinging onto her, Fran had no idea and frankly didn't care. She was consumed by the excitement of skimming from cloud to cloud. That her legs were cold and wet was of little import. The rise and fall of the craft had Fran flinging out her arms to embrace the passing clouds. God! Yes! She could do this all day long, all life long.

Up ahead, Fran spied a second tower that looked like a giant trumpet pointed upwards. No, more a flower open to the heavens than a trumpet. Skimming round it, the other girls were nudging smaller clouds near the orifice, only to see them drift lazily inside. She could have sworn she heard a sigh as each cloud disappeared.

Why do you have to do that? Fran asked. *Wouldn't they just get sucked in anyway?*

Clouds are clever. They know to avoid the collector if they can. We have to trick them into sailing too close. Clouds like to jostle each other. They try to do the same to us. That's how we catch them.

Heightened as her senses were, Fran felt the shudder go through Xristy. *What's wrong?* she asked. Xristy pointed mentally away beyond the cloud collector. There, in the distance, huffing and puffing like a disgruntled old man, roiled an angry cloud. She recognised it immediately. Cumulus nimbus. The lightning cloud. And, sure enough, lightning ricocheted inside it and, shortly after, repeated claps of thunder assaulted her ears. The detonations were deafening.

Back to the tower, she heard Xristy call out to the others, her words urging them to hurry, and they sped back the way they'd come. No skimming now. Just headlong flight. The effects of the oil were beginning to wear off and Fran felt a surge of fear course through her veins. So much for safe passage. Glancing over her shoulder, the angry cloud seemed much bigger. It was gathering clouds on its way, growing in height and strength as it did.

She could make out sheets of rain slanting diagonally within the cloud as it loomed over them, arrogant and sure of itself, clearly bent on revenge. How dare these upstart girls poach in its domain. It'd make them pay.

Glancing forward, the tower was now in sight and racing towards them. The moment their feet touched the platform, the cloud was on them, lashing them with bitter wind and icy rain. Violent shivers wracked Fran as Xristy hoisted her off the craft and ran with her in her arms towards the entrance. The crashing of thunder so close hurt Fran's ears making her cry out in pain as lightning struck all around. Despite the violent onslaught, they managed to dive inside and mercifully the doors slid shut behind them.

Xristy called out the names of all the girls and relief washed over them as all answered 'present'. Judging from the fear still thick in the air, they were not yet safe. They dashed to the lift and their descent had hardly begun when a shock rippled through the tower and the walls of the lift glowed a steely blue. Bright blue sparks crackled across the ceiling and Fran could have sworn a deep voice rumbled, "Don't think you can escape me!"

Despite the storm, the lift continued to descend, although its speed was dreadfully slow. When she complained, wishing it would go faster, Xristy told her, *It's a safety precaution*, as she cuddled a shivering and soaked Fran in her arms.

Fran squealed when three hot white sparks arced across the lift, speeding in her direction. The first burnt a brand in the back of her hand held protectively over her heart. The sting was so painful, she burst into tears. The two others sank deep into her chest causing her to cry out, not in pain but in joy and exultation. Her whole being responded as if she'd been touched by god. God? Despite the hypocritical fervency of her churchgoing parents, or maybe because of it, God was a concept that was alien to her, yet she had no other word for it.

There, the deep voice rumbled, *it is done.* To her surprise, in those words was not only satisfaction but benevolence. The other girls clearly didn't see it that way. Their mental gasps were filled with fear and awe. Someone, somewhere whispered, *It's her!*

Mission achieved, the cloud ceased its rumbling, the crackling fizzled out and the blue light faded giving way to the true colour of the walls. In response, the lift began to descend more quickly. Only the stinging burn on the back of Fran's hand and a joyful stirring in her chest remained to remind her what had happened.

Reaching the bottom the girls formed a congratulatory huddle with Fran watching on. Hardly a few seconds had gone by than she was pulled into the huddle and found herself in its middle. Gentle kisses rained down on her head and shoulders and her cold and wetness were completely forgotten. She felt accepted and welcome. It was a heart-warming feeling. Never in all her time at school, surrounded by so many girls, each dressed alike to mask their differences, all different and proud to be so, had she felt she belonged. Not like that. It made tears well in her eyes.

Time for the bath, Xristy announced as the huddle broke apart in excited chatter.

Bath? Fran asked, perplexed. *I thought you had no water for such things.*

Not water. Silly. Clouds, Xristy replied, taking Fran by the hand and leading her after the others. *It's a special privilege for Cloud Catchers. Fresh clouds. You'll love it.*

Bathing was a ritual. First they ceremoniously stripped off. Of course they did. Fran should have known. These girls didn't have the slightest modesty. Maybe it was the remaining effects of the oil that made her less reticent about undressing, but when it came to rubbing oil all over her partner's body she faltered. She had visions of writhing in calculated oblivion.

It's not the same oil, Xristy reassured her, massaging oil into her tense shoulders and working her way down her back. Whatever was in the oil, she felt herself relax. In fact, she was so relaxed, rubbing oil into Xristy was no problem with a little help and guidance. She'd never explored another's body before, it was an eye-opening experience.

What Fran saw in the giant bath tub took her breath away. The bobbing clouds were pretty shades of pink and tasty yellow, glowing as if they'd retained the light of some no longer visible sun. Fran had only one desire, to fling herself in amongst them.

That said, she did have misgivings about climbing into a tub full of naked girls. After all, she wasn't a Cloud Catcher. Several steps led down into the bath the surface of which had been cunningly carved to avoid slipping. To her surprise, the clouds curled around her in a welcoming embrace and continued to huddle close as she made her way after Xristy to the centre. Their presence set her body tingling all over, even in the most secret places. A giggle burst from her lips.

I warned you, Duffni said addressing Xristy. *She shouldn't be here. Look at those clouds cosying up to her.*

Fran wanted to ask what she was talking about, but Duffni grabbed her arm and hurried her out of the bath. Without the clouds surrounding her, Fran felt cold and abandoned. Duffni gave her no time to complain, marshalling her to a nearby bench, she said, *Let me look at your hand.*

Clearly the girl meant the one struck by the cloud. But Fran couldn't resist checking her breasts to see if the bolts of lightning had left a mark. They hadn't. Unlike the back of her hand, the skin on her chest was as virgin smooth and unblemished as it had always been. It was only inside that she felt the difference. A wispy presence, almost spirit like, uncurled and frolicked within her.

In answer to Duffni's request, she held out her hand, noting, to her amazement, that the wound had already healed leaving a white scar. It might be a pure coincidence, but she could have sworn the scar resembled a fluffy cloud.

6.

"That's an ugly scar you've got there," her mother exclaimed. "However did you get that?" She suddenly gasped in horror. "You haven't had one of those ghastly tattoos, I hope. You know we don't approve." Her mother leaned close to get a better look. "And you've been using perfume, a cheap, distasteful floral perfume. Go upstairs and wash your hands immediately. I'm going to talk to your father about this."

Fran grabbed an apple, and, abandoning her unfinished breakfast, left the kitchen without a word. She didn't go up to her room as her mother had ordered, but donned her blazer and pulled her satchel over her shoulders. She'd get hell when she returned, but she was in no mood to pander to her mother's whims.

Since she'd returned from Xristy's world, the presence in her chest had remained calm but she could sense it at all times. Despite its tenuous nature, it infused her with a solidity and a determination she had not known before. She struggled to explain the change. The best she could come up with was that she was more ... there.

Her bike was propped against the wall outside. The ride to school was mostly downhill, which was fine going, not so good returning. She let the bike go at its own speed and stared up at the clouds. They were quite different from those in Xristy's world. They seemed bigger and more sluggish. Xristy's clouds were young and frisky. Except the massive grandfather cloud that was solid and imposing, but no less quick.

A few 'younger' clouds flew much lower, skipping along like little lambs discovering how to use their legs. A couple even seemed to be keeping pace with her. She waved and called out mentally to them. One ducked down and swirled briefly around her head before darting off to rejoin the others.

She locked her bike in the bicycle rack and steeled herself for the hostile reception. The headmistress and several other teachers hovered around the entrance, inspecting each girl in turn. They were very strict about the dress code.

"Francesca!" When the headmistress called you that meant trouble. The woman would have been imposing had not her head been far too small for such an immense body.

"Yes Sister Stroon," Fran dutifully replied. How she hated it when they used her full name. Francesca went to school. Fran skimmed the clouds. She preferred the latter.

"Show me your hand!" the woman snapped.

Taking a considerable risk, Fran chose to show the other hand. The headmistress slapped it away. "The other one, dimwit."

Fran held out her hand, palm up. The woman grabbed it by the fingers and flipped it over, none too kindly. "What's this?" You'd have said a policewoman interrogating a murderer.

"I burnt my hand," Fran lied.

"It's ugly," the headmistress spat, wrinkling her face in disgust. "Looks more like a devil's mark if you ask me." Nobody asked you, miserable quacking penguin, Fran silently replied. Thank heavens the woman couldn't hear her thoughts. "Go to the infirmary. If they can't get rid of it, have them cover it up with a plaster. And take two hours detention for impertinence."

Fran knew better than to challenge the nun. Instead she turned her back on the woman and marched into the school, her head held high, to the sound of the woman muttering that there were ever more badly educated girls.

The nurse in the infirmary, a wiry little nun with piercing eyes and a sharp tongue, insisted on applying a foul-smelling ointment to the scar even though it was clearly healed. She then scotched a large skin-coloured plaster over the top before shooing Fran off to class. The bell had rung some time ago. Entering class late she'd probably get punished again.

In for a penny... she thought, not that pennies existed any more. She might as well arrive even later if she was going to be punished anyway. She slipped into the girls' bathroom, ripped off the plaster and wiped the foul cream on a towel leaving a sickly green mark for all to see. Since when had well-behaved Francesca been a rebel? She knew the answer only too well. Since she'd partaken of the Devil's oil. She grinned at herself in the mirror and was about to leave when the door burst open.

Maria Gonzales strode in, her prefect's badge glittering importantly on her oversized chest. "Francesca McKenzie, why aren't you in class?"

"I could ask you the same question," Fran shot back, deciding she had nothing to lose.

Maria faltered, no doubt unused to anything but docile submission. Then her cheeks turned bright red and puffed up as if she were about to explode.

"Careful," Fran ventured. "You'll hurt yourself..." She didn't get any further. Maria flung herself at her, all claws extended. Following some primal instinct, Fran sidestepped, only to see the lumbering prefect sail by and crash headfirst into the door of the toilets. The crunch of skull on wood was alarming, but not as much as seeing the girl collapse to the floor, her eyes open but only the whites to be seen.

"What have you done to Maria?" the nurse asked, stepping into the room closely followed by Sister Stroon. Both nuns stared accusingly at Fran. "Well?" Stroon asked.

"She did that to herself," Fran pointed out. "I had nothing to do with it. She ran headlong into the door." The trouble with telling the truth is that it is often more unbelievable than lies.

"Tend to her," the headmistress ordered the nurse and dragged Fran by the arm out of the bathroom. The woman towed her all the way to her office and made her stand with her hands on her head while she rummaged in a cupboard in search of her cane.

Fran had never been caned. She'd heard that other girls who'd been punished had bruises on their backsides for weeks. Sitting down had apparently been torture. And how was she to explain it to her parents? They'd never believe her version either. Of course they'd side with the headmistress. Not only was she a figure of authority, but as a nun she represented the highest authority of all, God.

Sister Stroon flexed her cane, which she'd finally found, and ordered Fran to bend over and lift up her skirt. Fran did no such thing. Instead, she hoped Xristy would hear her plea and whisk her away to her world. When that didn't happen, in desperation she called on the clouds for help. She felt that presence within her stir, but it was outside that the response came.

To her surprise the windows rattled violently as a crash of thunder shook the building. Only minutes earlier, it had been sunny and good weather had been forecast for the whole day. Now dark clouds were bearing down on the school and peals of thunder battered the building. She heard screams from nearby classrooms as lightning struck the grounds of the school, felling several trees and setting fire to a bush.

Sister Stroon had gone pale and her hands were clutching a trembling cross. "Make it stop," she pleaded.

Fran was tempted to say, "Only if you forget all that nonsense about Maria." But doing so would amount to admitting guilt. As if to underline her thoughts, one of the windows shattered and icy cold air rushed into the room. Fran could feel the cloud that entered swirling protectively around her, although nothing was visible.

Sister Stroon broke down and began to cry. It was an ugly sight. What could have been a moment of triumph left Fran with serious doubts. She was setting foot on a dangerous and lonely path. By putting everyone's back against her she would make life extremely difficult. Taking a step forward, she placed a hesitant arm around the sister's bulky shoulders and led her gently to the oversized armchair that was reserved for her. "You've had a shock," Fran said. "Sit down and catch your breath. I'll make some tea."

At her words, the storm began to abate and Fran whispered a mental word of thanks. The cloud that surrounded her reluctantly withdrew leaving a distinct impression it was disappointed. It would have enjoyed wreaking more damage.

An electric kettle stood next to a small washbasin in one corner. Fran heated water, returning frequently to the nun's side to make sure she was okay but, above all, to ensure she didn't scarper. It was unlikely. The woman could hardly stand, let alone run. Fran had never seen Sister Stroon run. Tea in hand, Fran offered it to the nun who took the cup mechanically. The woman was still in a state of shock, staring blankly at the broken window.

"It might be good to check on the damage," Fran suggested, aware she was pushing her luck. Sister Stroon nodded but continued to clutch her cup, making no move to go and investigate. "Drink your tea," Fran urged her. "It will do you good." The woman raised the cup to her lips like a sleepwalker and sipped noisily.

"Would you like me to check for you?" Fran asked, not sure leaving the woman was a good idea.

"Yes," the nun said, her voice weak and shaky. "Tell them I sent you."

With that 'laissez-passer' mentally in hand, Fran hurried off. The library next door was in a shambles, several windows had been broken and books lay strewn on the floor. The librarian was seated at her desk, her head in her hands, sobbing. The classrooms further down the corridor had all been abandon but any damage had been done by panicking girls not the storm. Fran wondered where everybody was. She found out soon enough. The gym was crammed with noisy girls, for many of whom the chaos was like a hyped-up trip to the zoo.

One of prefects tried to grab Fran and wrench her into the gym, but she ducked away, raising a hand to silence the girl who was using language not suited for a prefect in a church school. "I'm here on Sister Stroon's orders to survey the damage and report back to her."

The girl stared at Fran incredulous. "You're joking."

Fran shook her head. "Is anybody injured?" she asked, imitating Sister Stroon, her voice firm and full of authority.

The prefect was clearly confused. She must have sensed something was amiss but she couldn't spot the flaw. "No. Only bruises and scratches."

"Have you called the roll?"

The girl looked scared. She clearly hadn't. "See to it, then," Fran said, enjoying her new role. "I'll tell the headmistress you're busy doing it." The girl sighed with relief. "Do we need to call a doctor?"

The prefect shook her head and hurried away promising to call the roll.

When Fran finally made it back to the headmistress, the nurse was flapping around her, all semblance of calm professionalism gone. "Get out," she snapped at Fran.

Fran ignore her, planting herself in front of the headmistress. "I did as you instructed," Fran said, knowing full well she'd suggested it herself. "The girls are all in the gym. Nobody is seriously hurt. Only cuts and bruises. I suggested the prefects call the roll and they were doing so as I left."

"Thank you," the headmistress said, her voice still weak. "You did well? Can you fetch the caretaker? We need to clear this up."

Looking up, Fran saw the nurse furtively glancing from her to the headmistress and back, her expression perplexed. "Excuse me," Fran said, pushing past the woman as she headed for the door in search of the caretaker or his wife.

By the time she set off for home, Fran had been promoted to unofficial assistant to the headmistress. She'd been running errands all day. So much for school and lessons. Her new responsibility had left her tired, but satisfied. Labouring back up the hill her mood shifted as she remembered with dread how she'd walked out on her mother that morning. She was in for trouble.

Fran had barely stepped inside than her mother flung her arms around her and clung on tight. "Are you alright?" the woman asked, sounding hysterical. Such behaviour was so out of character, it worried Fran. Surely her mother hadn't imagined Fran was so upset she'd try to end it all? She was about to reassure her mother when the woman blurted out, "I heard it on the radio. How terrible. Was anyone hurt?"

Talk about being confused. She'd never before noticed how muddled her mother's thinking was. "I'm fine. Nobody was seriously hurt. Just a few windows broken." And a lot of panic, but that she didn't say.

"I tried to phone," her mother said, relinquishing her hold on Fran. "But all the lines were down. I'd have come myself, but Bess went into labour and was on the point of having her calf..."

"How is she?" Fran asked, glad to get off the subject of her school. Her mother went into great details about its birth while Fran sat down and relaxed. It was then her mother noticed the scar.

7.

Fran was confined to her room. Mother's orders. The woman had very little imagination when it came to punishment. But Fran preferred confinement to beating, although she might not be spared that when her father returned. He'd gone to see about a second-hand tractor and spending money always put him in a bad mood.

She'd been half expecting Xristy to visit, hoping, longing even, but maybe the girl was free to come only on weekends. The thought was ridiculous. She could hardly imagine weekends being important in Xristy's world. Whatever the explanation, she was disappointed.

She rubbed the back of her hand. The scar itched. She hadn't noticed that before. Maybe the nurse's ointment contained some form of irritant or poison. She wouldn't put it past the bitch. Holding it closer, she studied the white mark, running a finger around the cloud-shape. It sent a thrill shooting though her. In the fading light the scar seemed to glow. She hadn't noticed that before either.

She couldn't resist sniffing the back of her hand. Yes. She sighed. It was there. She breathed in deeply, sucking the smell of Xristy and her oil deep into her lungs where it jostled with that other presence that now inhabited her. The urge to kiss was overwhelming. To her embarrassment, she found she was drooling. Worse, she suspected she'd wet her pants. Why did it have to be at that moment her mother called her down for evening meal?

Having splashed cold water over her face - to no avail - Fran steeled herself to confront her parents. As she'd expected, her father was in a foul mood, so much so he asked her to say grace which was normally his unswerving prerogative. "For what we are about to receive..." she intoned without conviction, wondering how she could possibly be grateful for the coming beating. Rather she sent a silent prayer to old man cloud that he not intervene like he had at school. The presence within her remained unresponsive.

The meal was eaten in silence as it invariably was. If storm there was to be, it would break after dessert. Sure enough, hardly had he laid down his spoon, than her father cleared his throat and launched into an angry tirade. "You know we do not condone those who mark their skins with outrageous tattoos." It was like an abbreviated trial in which guilt had unequivocally been determined prior to the event and only the sentence remained to be pronounced and the punishment meted out. "That you, our daughter, should sink so low, is profoundly disappointing. Not only does it besmirch you, but it drags the rest of the family down with you..."

As he went on and on, working himself into a cold rage, readying himself to beat the hell out of her, literally, Fran felt eerily detached. It was as if she floated, not unlike a cloud, above herself, unconcerned by the prospect of a beating and dreamt of skimming the clouds with Xristy. A distant roll of thunder brought her back to reality. Please, she thought to the clouds, you'll only make things worse. But the clouds were having none of it. A flash of lightning closely followed by a mammoth crash shook the house and the lights went out.

Her father cursed and stumbled to his feet in search of a candle. He knocked over several chairs in the dark till he finally located the candle by the range and lit it with his lighter. His features distorted by the flickering flame, he looked like the incarnation of the devil himself. Planting the candle on the table, he was about to pursue his tirade when a bust of wind blew open the kitchen door and extinguished the flame. If Fran had cursed like he did then, she would have been beaten black and blue.

He rose to his feet, upsetting yet another chair as he raged against her and the storm like they were one. If only he knew. Rounding the table, he clearly intended to grab her. What exactly he planned to do will never be known because the kitchen windows shattered at that moment and an angry cloud surged into the room to the screams of Fran's mother. Seconds later, her father screamed too, only to cease abruptly with an ominous thud. As in school, the cloud curled lovingly around her shoulders before exiting by the window with a parting clap of thunder.

Thanks, she thought, wondering if clouds understood irony. With her father groaning somewhere on the floor and her mother snivelling nearby, Fran was the only one capable of doing anything. She was about to go in search of a torch when the lights snapped back on, revealing the chaos. But neither the upturned chairs, nor the flour and pasta and oatmeal scattered everywhere, nor even the kitchen utensils empaled in the walls held her attention. She saw only the heap that was her father, lodged between the range and the sink.

She tried to gauge if he was still a danger or if she dared get closer and see if first aid were possible. It was hard to tell. At least he made no attempt to grab her when she moved closer, instead he snarled and bared his teeth. That was warning enough. She left him to his anger and went into the hall to dial for an ambulance. Returning to the kitchen she finally noticed her mother seated at the kitchen table, her expression blank. She was tempted to make the woman tea as she had for the headmistress, but her mother drank neither tea nor coffee. As for herbal teas, she wanted nothing to do with them because that was the stuff of witches.

Not knowing how to help, she left them to their misery and went to stand in the porch waiting for the ambulance to arrive. Five minutes they'd said over the phone. The flash storm had cleared as fast as it had come, leaving the sky clear. A feast of stars shone down, but, despite their breath-taking beauty, they could not raise her spirits. She felt completely abandoned. Never before had it been so evident how mad her parents were. Especially her father. She shivered. He could well have killed her, had he managed to get his hands on her.

On the road into town she made out headlights snaking up the hill before she heard the approaching siren. Two male nurses climbed out and hurried towards her. "A freak storm,..." she explained. "Her father injured ... her mother deeply distressed..." Stretcher in hand they went inside. Fran couldn't stomach seeing her injured father and hoped to spare herself his inevitable accusations, so she remained on the porch staring at the stars.

Whatever was happening inside took a very long time, time enough for Fran to begin shivering in the cold night air. She snatched a scarf from the hat stand in the hall and wrapped her school blazer around her shoulders. When the men emerged they carried an unmoving figure on the stretcher to the ambulance. "He's not...?" she began when they came back.

"No, no. We had to sedate him he was so agitated. He has broken ribs and a broken arm and there may be internal damage. We can't tell without a scan."

"What about my mother?"

"In shock. We couldn't get any sense out of her. She kept mumbling they'd been visited by the devil. We'll take her with us for observation."

"Will you be alright here on your own?" the second man enquired. "You can come with us, if you want."

"No. I'll be alright. And anyway, somebody's got to look after the animals."

The man scrutinised her with a mixture of pity and admiration, then joined his colleague who was leading a hesitant but compliant mother towards the ambulance. Fran was unable to look away as the ambulance doors closed on the shreds of her parents. She stood for a long moment sheltered under the porch watching the ambulance disappear amid the lights of the town.

Alone in the farm, Fran sat at the kitchen table, her head in her hands in the ruins of her parent's kitchen. It would be so easy to stare off into the distance, absent like her mother, and give up. "I'm not my mother," she told the empty room. Her voice, echoing in that void, didn't sound convinced. "I'm not her," she insisted.

Knowing there was no way she could sleep after such a nightmare, she set about clearing up the mess. When everything that could be was back in place, the floor had been swept and a fawning cat fed, Fran heated herself porridge. Through the broken kitchen window, the first rosey glimmers of dawn outlined the farm buildings, an enchanted beginning to a disenchanted day.

At the smell of porridge, Xristy's reaction sprang to mind. Fran decided this was very definitely an occasion for cream and sugar. The Demerara sugar was buried at the back of a cupboard behind the empty biscuit tins. Her mother discouraged the use of sugar and cream had been reserved for her father, allowed only because he had to work so hard. The freedom to eat what she pleased was a small triumph.

As she spooned porridge dripping with cream into her mouth, she drew up a mental list of all that had to be done. If she had to maintain the farm in the absence of her parents, she certainly wouldn't have time for school. All the better. School was a waste of time any way. Had not Xristy said you learnt far more from life than school? Those weren't her exact words, but the meaning was there.

Talking of Xristy, Fran wondered why the girl hadn't visited. Since their first encounter under the tree, Xristy had been a regular visitor. Hopefully nothing had happened to her and her fellow Cloud Catchers. Fran regretted not knowing how to call Xristy or to travel to her world. She had no way of finding out if all was well.

There was another reason for wanting to see Xristy. She needed to understand what was happening with the clouds. She couldn't continue letting them lay waste around her every time she was threatened. Sooner or later, people would start to see the connection. It would make a good story in the tabloids. The girl who commanded the winds, a prelude to a modern-day witch trial with her on the pyre.

By the time she'd tended to her pony, fed the hens, checked on the goats, and looked in on their cow and its calf, she was exhausted and ready for a second breakfast. Instead she phoned the school, explaining that her parents had been taken ill and for the foreseeable future she'd have to forgo school. The headmistress was not happy - was she ever? - but as Fran was eighteen, the woman couldn't force her to attend.

She was dozing, her head rested on her arms at the kitchen table after a second bowl of porridge, when the phone rang in the hall. It was the hospital. "Is that Francesca?" the doctor asked? When she said yes, the woman continued. "I have some bad news for you. Unfortunately, your father did not survive his injuries."

Fran sank into the chair in the hall. "Did he suffer?" she asked. It seemed the right thing to say.

"No. He never regained consciousness and the police, who wanted to question him, were unable to do so. They'll probably want to ask you some questions."

"And my mother?"

The pause that followed was not a good sign. "She's a little 'disturbed'."

Fran could hear the inverted commas around the word. Nuts. Wacko. Bonkers. Off her rocker. It seemed a fitting end for someone who'd been slavishly complicit with her fanatical and violent husband.

"We've transferred her to Stonyfields," the doctor confirmed. It was the local psychiatric clinic, reputed to be one of the most old-fashioned institutions in the region, if not the country. Electric shocks. Forced isolation. Psychotropes. The works.

"Can I visit her?" She had to ask, even if she had no desire to do so.

"That might not be such a good idea. She's agitated and

is convinced you are to blame for everything. Your seeing her would probably make her worse. Better to wait till the treatment has had some effect."

"Thank you for informing me." Fran felt she had to say something, although she was acutely conscious that this was probably not the right thing.

There was another short, embarrassed pause before the doctor asked, "Do you have anyone to turn to, someone who can guide and support you in these difficult times?"

The truth was a resounding No!, but Fran imagined the woman wouldn't be happy with that answer. "Oh yes. Teachers, parents of friends, all sorts of people."

As she hung up, she was acutely aware of the daunting task that faced her. She had rarely enquired about the workings of the farm and had no idea of the state of her parents' affairs. Now she would have to look after it on her own. More than anything, she wished Xristy were there, if only to hold her hand.

8.

The longer Fran went without news of Xristy, the more concerned she got. Something must be wrong, seriously wrong. If only she knew how to travel to Xristy's world. Not that she had much time to worry about Xristy. She had to field one visit after another. There was the undertaker, a smarmy guy who looked at her as if sizing her up for a coffin.

Of course the police came. That was more tricky. She showed the women the broken windows, the marks where kitchen ustensiles had been impaled in the walls and even a tree outside uprooted by the storm. She told them the whole story. Well, most of it. They seemed particularly interested to know if her father had ever been violent. She hesitated. Could they be trying to incriminate her? Getting her to admit to defending herself against him? Then killing him. Finally she showed them some of the bruises.

Spotting the scar on the back of her hand, one policewoman asked, "Did he do that?"

"No." Luckily her embarrassment fit the story she was about to tell. "Silly really. I wasn't fully awake. I burnt myself cooking breakfast."

They wanted to know if she'd been hit the day he had his accident. "He was away all day," she explained. "He arrived back just in time for the evening meal. We'd hardly finished than the storm struck..."

The two policewomen couldn't understand why she or

her mother hadn't been hurt too. "It was weird," she replied, pausing to call up the images of the cloud's attack. "I know it must sound wacky but you'd have said the storm was after him and him alone..." The women were sceptical but didn't question her further, saying they might have to come back.

A lawyer, who apparently worked for her father, and her father's banker came knocking. Fran didn't trust either of them. They looked like crooks. That they'd worked for her father was excuse enough not to like them. They explained that, given that her mother had been sectioned...

"What does that mean?" She'd never heard the expression before.

"Officially designated as mad and, as such, no longer legally responsible," the banker told her. His blunt assessment bore witness to an utter lack of empathy.

"That means not only do you inherit your part of the estate,..." the lawyer continued, licking his lips. It was a nasty habit that made him look like a lizard. "...but you also control all your mother's fortune." He went on to talk of the will. Apparently her father had appointed him executor of the testament. All funds remained blocked till the will had been sorted out.

He enquired if she had enough money to get by. Not wanting to admit her ignorance, she replied, "Sure. No problem." She resolved to go through her father's papers as soon as possible to find out what he had, not trusting the men to keep her informed.

"I need to digest what has happened - it's been so sudden - before I make any decisions," she told them, showing them to the door. "It wouldn't be wise to rush things, would it?" They nodded their agreement although the banker replied, "I wouldn't wait too long." His words were almost a threat. Neither seemed willing to leave, but she wished them good day and closed the door on them.

As if all that hadn't been enough, she had a visit from the child protection agency. "As you are over eighteen," the young woman said, studying a file grasped in her hand, "you're not strictly our business." What an odd expression. How could she possibly be anybody's 'business'? "But we've had an anonymous tip that your father mistreated you..." she let the sentence hang as if inviting a reply.

"Listen," Fran said, rounding on the woman. "My father just died. My mother has been locked up, certified mad. And I am left to look after the farm and all their affairs. It's hardly the time to grub around in my father's past looking for signs of abuse. Let him go. That's what I'm trying to do."

The woman stared at her, her mouth slightly open as if she wanted to reply but couldn't find the words. "Well. Yes. I understand," she finally managed and handed Fran her card. "If ever you need help, don't hesitate to contact me." And with a stiff bow, she was gone.

There were two rooms in the house Fran avoided entering, her parents' bedroom and her father's study. So it was with trepidation that she pushed open her father's study door only to be driven back by the stench. The air was stale and fetid. For someone who'd worked all his life on the land, it was odd he'd apparently never opened the windows.

Above all, it was him at his worst, when, in a bout of fury, sweating profusely, he'd mete out vergence. The odour brought back painful memories that had her shuddering. Cupping a hand over her nose, she hurriedly flung open the windows, leaning out to gasp for fresh air.

Her father's miserly attitude went hand in hand with an almost obsessional drive for order. Documents were neatly stocked in files, each duly labelled according to its content. His desk was completely free of papers as was the table under the window.

At some time she'd have to go through everything and decide what to keep and what to burn. For now she was only interested in the bank accounts. And the mortgage. She had no idea how long it was for and what monthly payments were due. If the worst came to the worst, she'd sell off the farm and buy herself a small flat in town, although the thought of having to abandon her childhood home and her faithful pony brought tears to her eyes.

Opening the cupboard, the file pertaining to the bank was right in front of her, almost as if her father had wanted it to be seen. She couldn't bring herself to sit at his desk, so she carried the file to the table under the window and drew up a chair. Everything was there. And, to her horror, everything was very little. The total assets in the bank were ridiculously low. How could that possibly be? She'd always imagined her father hoarding money, not splashing out. If that was all there was, she wouldn't survive very long. So much for living it up in a flat of her own. She'd have to go to work and earn a living.

She returned to the cupboard, and went through the files in the hope of finding another bank account. But there was nothing. A horrible suspicion crept up on her. She went back to the files and desperately looked for documents about the mortgage. What if the farm was not all paid up? She wouldn't even be able to get much out of the sale of the place. She wasn't one to curse, but she cursed her father for being so clumsy and careless in his handling of money.

Slumped in the chair at the table by the window she stared off into space feeling lost and forlorn. There was nothing she could do. Absentmindedly, she ran the back of her scarred hand under her nose in search of solace. The cloud - she was pretty sure it was a cloud inside her, however odd that might sound - stirred at her touch but she didn't insist. She had no way of controlling it and she didn't want it wreaking havoc amongst her father's well-ordered papers.

The faint trace of Xristy's oil lingering on her fingers jolted her back to reality. She sat up straight and looked intently around the room. There must be more. She couldn't believe that someone so miserly could have been so dissolute.

Having found nothing in the cupboard, she began systematically searching the rest of the room. Not that there was much to search. Apart from crucifix on the wall behind the desk, most of the rest of the room was bare. She peered under the desk, she rummaged through it, she even pulled out the drawers and looked behind them, but found nothing. Could he have stashed the papers somewhere else? Only one other place came to mind.

Getting to her feet, she bounded out the door, ran up the stairs and burst into her parent's bedroom. If her father's study stank of him, her parent's bedroom reeked of her mother. Not that she ever wore perfume. She didn't. But there was a cloying something in the air that epitomised Fran's mother. Twisted? Ugly? Unhealthy? Perverse? Vicious? Whatever.

Two beds stood as far from each other as possible, a pair of slippers neatly aligned by the respective bedsides. So her parents no longer slept together. It didn't surprise her. She'd never seen the slightest display of affection between them.

Two wardrobes faced each other across the room. The first was her mother's, filled with skirts, blouses and dresses. Many she wore about the farm, but there were also those she wore to church. To Fran's surprise, hidden at the back, were a bunch of pretty dresses she'd never seen. Had Fran ever dressed like that, her mother would've been furious and her father would've beaten her senseless.

She closed the door. Her father would never have hidden anything in there. That was women's territory. He'd rather have burnt in hell than be tainted by 'that'. To her disappointment, his cupboard was locked. She tried to force the lock, but it wouldn't budge. This would require more radical means. A crowbar, fetched from the tool cupboard in the barn, made quick work of the door leaving it hanging aslant on one hinge. She shuddered. If her father had seen what she'd done to his cupboard, he'd have gone spare.

Like his wife, work clothes and Sunday best hung side by side, but beneath, half hidden by a raincoat, was a stack of glossy magazines depicting naked women. Fran burst out laughing, unsure if she was amused or hysterical. So this upstanding member of the church community, who railed at any hint of sex on the telly, who beat his daughter if she so much as bared a knee, had porn stashed in his bedroom. The laughter had her bent over double, a stitch forming in her side, tears welling in her eyes, till the tears gave way to sobs that wracked her body and she cried bitterly. The sadist had beaten her for contravening rules he'd invented, only to retreat to his bedroom seeking relief in glossy women spreadeagled across well-fingered pages.

When she could cry no more, she blew her nose, dried her cheeks and, avoiding touching the magazines, rummaged under the clothes in search of anything else hidden there. All she found was a brief case. More porn, she guessed, or worse. She didn't want to know, but she had to check. It might just be the deeds to the farm.

Once she'd forced the lock thanks to the crowbar, it turned out to be much more. Not only were there the deeds to the farm, the mortgage of which, to her relief, had been completely paid off, but also a letter from a bank in a nearby town. Apparently there was an account, although she had no idea how much was on it.

Returning to her room, the briefcase under her arm, she got on all fours and slid it beneath her bed. She almost banged her head on the bed frame when a knock rang out at the door. It was her nearest neighbour, a farm owner called Thomas, come to offer his condolences. She hardly knew him. Not surprising. She couldn't recall him ever visiting the farm. She offered him tea and had to put up with barely veiled hints that he'd willingly take the farm off her hands for a good price.

Hardly had she got him out the door, than a new knock announced the arrival of the priest come to offer a prayer for her father's soul. It would take a lot more than that to save him from hell's fires. Rather than make a rude comment, Fran limited herself to an 'Amen'. The priest was seen on his way without the slightest drop of tea. She knew there'd be no stopping him if he started on the iniquity of today's youth. He was so fixated on the young, Fran vaguely wondered if he too had a stash of glossy magazines locked in a cupboard in the rectory.

There followed a steady stream of people, many of whom seemed more interested in glimpsing the inside of the farm they'd never dared visit when her father was alive. Some brought flowers, others came with enquiries about her future and, of course, there were the would-be benevolent buyers.

When their inquisitiveness got on her nerves she set up a makeshift shrine in the barn with the flowers she'd received and the crucifix she was glad to remove from the house. She found no photo of the man, but a certificate ensuring he was a trusted customer of a pesticide company suitably took its place. She even found a wooden box about the size of a coffin and draped it in a large piece of sacking that had been gathering dust. She kept visitors out of the house, letting them say their goodbyes amongst bales of hay, next to a rusting tractor, the scene suitably shroud in the stench of the nearby dung heap, serenaded by the constant buzz of flies. A fitting setting to see off such a specimen.

9.

Tuesday was market day, although, by the time Fran biked down to town, most of the stall owners were folding away their stands and selling off any remaining perishables. She hadn't checked if she needed anything, but imagined there were sufficient stocks in the farm. She strolled around the square enjoying the bustle of human activity. Despite all the visits that morning, she felt alone and isolated up on the hill.

Her main reason for venturing into town was to see if she could withdraw a small sum of money from the bank. The idea of asking the banker for an advance so soon after shooing him out of the house was less than appealing, but she had no alternative. She'd found no cash hidden amongst her parents affairs.

Not in any hurry to reach the bank, she sauntered along the pavement peering into the windows of shops, many of which she hadn't known existed. She'd never noticed how drab the town was, as if it had stood still for a couple of decades while a thick layer of dust settled on every surface. Resigned to going to the bank, she spotted a notice pinned to a door between two shops. Jakob Branson: lawyer with experience in the management of properties, it read. Why not? He couldn't be worse than those her father had befriended.

On the narrow landing at the top of steep stairs, a single door stood ajar. She knocked. "Come in," a voice called out from within.

Pushing open the door, she found a young man on all fours

rummaging under the sole desk. "I'm looking for Mr Branson," she said, wondering who this youth was. An assistant, maybe? Or a cleaner.

He clambered to his feet, clutching a wad of paper, "Found it," he said triumphantly. "Been searching for it for ages." Then, dropping into the swivel chair behind the desk, he asked, "What can I do for you?"

"Is Mr Branson in?"

"Yes," he replied grinning at some joke she didn't get. "I am he."

Fran blushed. "I'm sorry," she stammered. "I thought..."

"Don't worry, a lot of people mistake me for the caretaker's son." He chuckled. "I look a lot younger than I am. Genes, I suppose. My mother looked much younger than she was too. So, what can I do for you?"

When she looked around for a place to sit, he sprang to his feet and removed the stack of books cluttering the sole other chair in the room. "Sorry. Do take a seat. Coffee? Tea?"

She shook her head. "If I drink another mouthful of tea, I might wet myself." Realising what she'd just said, she blushed for the second time. "I mean..." But there was no taking it back.

"Tea does that to me too," he said affably. "I do have smarties, if that would help." He pulled a bowl filled with the sweets from the top drawer of his desk and planted it invitingly in front of her. "I find munching them helps concentrate." He scooped up a handful and began popping them one at a time into his mouth. He was weird, but she liked him. "So what's the problem?"

Where to begin? "I need to be sure that what I tell you will remain between us."

He got to his feet, downing the remaining smarties in his hand and closed the door. "Yes," he assured her. "Whether I take on your case or not, confidentiality is ensured."

Leaning forward, she tentatively took a couple of smarties from the bowl and slipped them into her mouth. "My father just died," she began. It seemed deliciously inappropriate to break the news chewing sweets, something he would never have permitted. "And my mother has gone crazy. She's been - what's the word? - sectioned."

He nodded to indicate he'd understood and pushed the bowl of smarties closer to her, but said nothing. She took two more. "I am left with the entire responsibility for the farm and all the lands around."

"I'm sorry for your loss..." he began.

"Don't be," she interrupted, her words sharper than she intended. "He was a violent bastard." She drew in a deep breath trying to calm her anger. "The world is better off without him. And my mother was not much better. She was accomplice to all his excesses." Never before had she told anyone of the hell she'd endured. To do so now had tears springing to her eyes. Angrily brushing them away, she forged on. "They told me nothing of their affairs. I was completely in the dark about the finances..."

The lawyer straightened in his chair and suddenly appeared older and more serious, but he made no comment.

"His banker and lawyer visited me, encouraging me to hear the will and settle the estate. According to them, the banker was appointed executor of the will." She described their visit and her refusal to be hurried. "I don't trust them." She explained about the accounts she'd found and her surprise at how little money there was in the bank. "I did find the deeds of the farm..." She pulled a wad of papers from her satchel and handed them to the lawyer.

He studied the deeds, munching smarties as he did. "Help yourself," he said. "I have loads more in the cupboard." When he'd finished, he handed back the document, saying, "If nothing else, you have the value of the property, which, according to the deeds, was worth several million when it was bought."

The sum had Fran reeling. She instinctively scooped up a handful of smarties and shovelled them into her mouth, causing her to cough violently. The lawyer produced a glass from a drawer in his desk and poured fizzy water into it. She took a welcome sip. Disappointingly, the fizz had gone out of it.

"There's a WC just down the corridor," he told her.

She blushed for the third time.

"These deeds are good news," he added, "but we would need to see the will before we celebrate."

"There's more," she said. "Hidden in the same place I found this." She handed him the letter from the bank which he read twice, frowning.

"It's tempting to speculate," he began. "But I prefer to investigate first. Have you got any other revelations, while we're at it?" He punctuated his question with a grin. "Good," he said when she said no more. "I think we've got plenty to go on for now."

"So what do we do?" Fran asked.

"Well, first of all, I think we should go and see that banker of yours. I'll accompany you, if you agree. Having a lawyer at your side will give more weight to your arguments. What exactly do you want from him?"

Once she'd explained, he slipped into the room next door, saying he had to change. When he returned, she gasped at the sight of him with his smart suit and tie. He looked a completely different person.

"The clothes help," he explained, glancing briefly at how she was dressed. She was still wearing the stained skirt she'd worn to feed the chickens and tend to her pony. And her blouse was crinkled from setting up the shrine in the barn. "Let's see if we can do something about that," he said enigmatically.

Out on the street, he took her by the arm and led her to a fashionable shop for women's clothes.

"I have no cash," she muttered. He knew that. Getting money was the main reason for seeing the banker. But she wanted to avoid the inevitable embarrassment in the shop.

"Don't worry about that, I'll put it on my expenses for the case. You'll pay me back when we sort all this out."

In the shop, he was greeted by a grinning salesgirl whom he addressed by her first name. "Let's find something to suit Fran," he said. She was pleased he didn't call her by her full name. She vowed never to use it again. It would be buried with her father. "A suit, maybe," he said. "Something serious, but not too..."

Trousers for women were another thing her father had not approved of. What a sick joke. When you saw what he drooled over in private. As for suits, he'd have thrown a fit seeing her dressed like a young man as she strode towards the bank. The clothes really did give her added confidence, one of the things, she suddenly realised, her father hated most in women.

The lawyer paused at the entrance to the bank. "I don't mean any disrespect, but I suggest you let me do the talking," he said. "I know how to deal with this sort of person. They tend to look down on young women. As for girls, forget it. It's sad, if not annoying. But that's the way things are in this town. What counts, for now, is getting him to do what you want. We can deal with entrenched misogyny later."

The banker's office was all green leather and cigar smoke. She imagined only the best customers got to sit in the leather armchairs. If she'd come alone, she'd never have got past the barren office down the corridor where they were first received. As for the cigar smoke it was suffocating and made her cough. She had a wild desire to fling open the windows, but was unsure she could get away with it and didn't want to disrupt the efforts of the lawyer.

As it was, her friend the cloud, with a wind in tow, flung open the windows for her. The banker, who'd been trying to appear cool and collected, sprang to his feet, terrified, no doubt remembering what had happened to her father.

"You might as well leave them open," Fran said calmly, unable to keep quiet. "It brings welcome fresh air."

The banker shot her a sour look and sat down. "If you have decided to hear the will, I should call your father's lawyer," he said reaching for the phone.

"My father's dead, sir," she said, holding his gaze. "He no longer has a lawyer. Mr Branson here is my lawyer." So much for letting her lawyer speak for her. With the cloud curling softly around her neck, keeping silent was hard to do.

"We would like to discuss the state of my client's late father's accounts," the lawyer began. He forced a very reluctant banker to reveal the details. To Fran's surprise, there was more than the single account she'd discovered in his files. Several other accounts hid considerable sums of money. Mr Branson insisted on Fran having a copy of the accounts. After all, she was now in charge of the estate. When the man promised to have it delivered within the week, the lawyer insisted it be handed over immediately.

Having been given the banker's copy, the lawyer raised the question of access to cash. "The law permits a portion of the inheritance to be paid in advance to cover expenses. A thousand pounds should be sufficient."

Fran nearly choked at the sum, but was able to dissimulate her surprise with a cough. What on Earth was she going to do with so much money?

The man made a brief call and a bank clerk appeared carrying an envelope and a form. He handed the form to Fran to sign, but offered the envelope to the lawyer. Mr Branson waved him away. "It's not my money, but that of my client." The clerk reluctantly handed the fat envelope to Fran and promptly left. "You might like to count that," the lawyer suggested. So Fran emptied the envelope onto the edge of the desk, much to the disgust of the banker, and counted the notes, totting up the total in her head. "It's all there," she announced.

Once outside, Fran turned to the lawyer and asked, "Why so much?"

"Partly because finalising the succession can take time, but above all because you'll have expenses like the funeral..." he paused, grinning "...and an advance for your lawyer."

10.

On the lawyer's advice, she'd bought a leather pouch she could hang around her neck and hide under her clothes in which she kept the bulk of the money. They then paused in a teashop frequented mostly by old ladies to discuss what to do next. Never in her life had she had tea and cream buns in such a place. So much had changed in the short time since she first met Xristy. She missed the girl and worried something was seriously wrong. She resolved to ask the cloud to help her reach out to her friend at the first opportunity.

Her father's former lawyer scowled at the sight of Mr Branson at her side as the two entered his office. "So you've come to read the will," he said.

When Fran nodded, he took a document from the drawer in his desk and began to read. "I hereby leave all my estate and my belongings to the charity named Bonjon's home for stray cats."

When he stopped reading, Fran looked at him aghast. "Is that all?"

"I'm afraid so," the lawyer said.

"Let me have a look," her lawyer said. Having read the document, he pulled out his phone took a picture and then started typing on the touchscreen. Fran wondered what he was doing. Surely it wasn't the time to be sending messages.

"When exactly was this will written?" Fran asked.

When the man didn't answer, Fran continued, "Did my father ever write a will?"

"Interesting," her lawyer said, looking up from his phone. "According to the trade register, Bonjon's home for stray cats is owned by none other than yourself and my client's father's banker. I think this might be a matter for the police. I'm sure they'd be intrigued to know how this came about."

Mr Branson leant forward and took the will from him and slid it into his briefcase. "Unless of course, you were to give me the other two copies."

The man begrudgingly opened a drawer, pulled out a folder and handed it to Mr Branson. "I think we can assume that my client's father never wrote a will," her lawyer said, looking directly at the other lawyer. "Wouldn't you agree, colleague?"

"That was neatly done," Fran told her lawyer once they were outside.

"Now all we have to do, is follow up on that other bank and make sure your father wasn't being pursued for tax evasion," the young man said.

"Surely not."

"Judging from what I've seen, he almost certainly was avoiding paying taxes with the complicity of his banker and lawyer. We need to be careful about those two. They could well try to tip off the taxman just to spite you for not letting them walk away with your money."

"God! It's all so complicated. How do rich people manage?"

"They employ crooks like those two."

"I bet some of them employ people like you," she retorted, unwilling to believe all rich people were crooks.

"I'll take that as a compliment," he said, grinning. "Although I could be bribed if you were to offer me lunch."

She halted mid-step and starred at him, only to realise he was joking. "Unfortunately, bribes are not on the menu today. And anyway, with all the smarties you've eaten you can't possibly be hungry." She smiled at him. "What's more, I have to feed the hens and tend to my pony, not to mention the goats and cow. Another time."

"I'll hold you to that. I'll organise a meeting with that bank and let you know the date and time. We can take my car, if you want."

She thanked him and they parted. She couldn't possibly cycle home in her new suit, so she returned to the shop intending to change back into her old clothes. The shop assistant, who was still as charming, even without the handsome lawyer as incentive, showed her several neat skirts as well as pairs of shorts. Finally she opted for jeans, one of the many clothes forbidden while her father was alive. She also bought a pale blue blouse and matching bra - another forbidden accessory - as well as a darker bluejeans jacket.

Dressed in her new attire, she climbed onto her bicycle as the shop girl promised to have her suit and older clothes delivered to the farm before evening. As she approached the farm, she had an uncomfortable feeling something was amiss. The front door stood wide open and crashes could be heard inside. She abandoned her bike by the barn and, armed with the handle of a pick axe, she headed for the house.

Moving stealthily, she slid into the building and crept along the corridor towards the noise. Instinctively she called on the cloud and was reassured to feel it wrap its presence about her neck. Peering round the door frame, she saw two men shoving silver into a sack. "Stop!" she said in the loudest voice she could muster. The men froze. But when they turned to see who was there, their expressions changed from fear to an evil grin.

"Put down the bag," she ordered, "and leave. If you do, no harm will come to you."

One of the men burst out laughing. The other said, "D'you hear that Jock. The little girl wants us to leave." He sneered at her. "As if we'd be afraid of some stuck-up girlie."

"You ought to be," Fran said, feeling the cloud increasingly restless. "This is my last warning."

No doubt thinking he'd had enough of her histrionics, one of the thugs took a threatening step towards her. He didn't get any further. A great force flung him against the wall down which he slithered till he landed in a heap on the floor. "I warned you,"

Fran said. "Your friend was not very clever. Maybe you can learn from his mistakes."

The second man flinched but held his ground, drawing a gun from his pocket. She'd warned him, but the silly man was too blind. A bolt of lightning shot across the room and slammed into his hand. The man's scream was deafening. Fran plug her ears and closed her eyes, but she couldn't shut out the stench. A second clap of thunder cut short the scream and a ringing silence fell.

Opening her eyes, she immediately wished she hadn't. Next to the unmoving heap of the first man lay the charred remains of the second. What was left of the cream bun in her stomach lurched upwards, threatening to splatter over the two bodies. No! Not that! She wrapped her arms tight around her chest and gritted her teeth.

What a disaster. How was she to explain two more bodies to the police? *Friend cloud*, she thought, still unsure how to address it, *can you get rid of the bodies and dump them far away?* A roaring wind raced through the house chasing the bodies before it, leaving only a blackened mark where the second man had fallen. *Thank you*, she called after the cloud as it disappeared out the front door.

The cloud had no doubt saved her life, but she wished it hadn't killed the men. There must be some way to rein in its brutal strength. Not for the first time she wished she could ask Xristy. The girl had so much experience coaxing clouds, she might know.

Having scrubbed the floor clean, Fran decided to burn the bag the thieves had left behind. Better not to leave evidence lying around. While she was at it, she'd also burn her father's dirty magazines. A bonfire would have been good, but she didn't want half-consumed naked ladies floating away on the breeze. She opted to use the incinerator. The one her father had bought was rudimentary, consisting mainly of a metal barrel covered by a grid.

Donning protective gloves, she went in search of the

magazines and carried them down at arms' length as if they might contaminate her. Having placed them in the incinerator, she fetched all his clothes which she'd decided to burn as well. Finally, anything and everything that could burn that reminded her of him was piled into the barrel, including the cane he'd used so often to beat her. Snapping it in two was little consolation, but she did so all the same.

She was about to set fire to the lot when she thought of one more item to burn. She hurried up to her room and fished out her school uniform, underclothes included, and added them to the pyre. School should have offered a temporary refuge from her father, but it had rapidly become just another face of the violence she was subjected to. Good riddance. Wanting to be thorough, she added her school books and those terrible report cards that had provoked so many beatings.

She could have gloated over the painful memories going up in smoke, but instead she turned her back on the roaring flames and headed for the sitting room to tidy up the silver scattered across the floor. The thieves had forced the front door which would no longer close properly and several windows had been shattered in the kitchen when the cloud had forced its way in. It would be easy for would-be burglars to break in. How could she imagine sleeping in such an insecure place? She couldn't do the repairs herself and she had no idea who to ask

The answer was obvious. Pulling his card from her trouser pocket, she dialled Mr Branson. "Sorry to disturb," she said and explained her problem.

"I'll have someone come over and fix that in the next hour," he assured her.

Realising she'd only eaten a cream bun since breakfast, she grabbed an apple and some cheese and took her frugal late lunch out onto the veranda at the front of the house. If anyone drove up to the farm, she'd see them from miles away. Cheese and apple eaten, she leaned back on the cushions and closed her eyes.

It was the familiar smell that alerted her Xristy was there. She would recognise the scent of that oil anywhere. *Xristy,* she gasped, opening her eyes. *At last! Where've you...?* She didn't get any further. Her mouth fell open in horror. It was Xristy alright, but she looked far worse than the first time Fran had seen her. She was so gaunt, her face little more than skin over bone. Dark patches sagged under her eyes and her lips were dry and cracked.

We need your help, Xristy croaked. She convulsed, her eyes rolled back in her head and she collapsed to the floor. Fran screamed as she sprang to her feet, desperate to help her friend, but she was too late. Xristy had already disappeared, leaving only a faint trace of her perfume muddled with a much less pleasant smell like rotting flesh. *Xristy,* Fran called out, tears streaming down her cheeks. *How can I possibly help if I'm stuck here?*

It was red-eyed and wet-cheeked that Mr Branson found her, curled up on the floor of the veranda, sobbing. He helped her up and sat her on the rocker. He sent the carpenter, who was accompanying him, to make tea and sat down next to her. "What's going on?" he asked.

"It's terrible," she managed to say. How could she explain? He'd think she was mad. He probably thought she was mad anyway, blubbering on the floor as she had. "It's all been too much. The death of my father. The madness of my mother. The will. The bank. And now this robbery..." And the problems with Xristy, she added silently. Above all, the problems with Xristy.

The tea arrived at that moment. He poured her a cup, enquiring if she wanted sugar or milk. She didn't. The carpenter stood nearby, shifting uncomfortably from one foot to another. He seemed eager to get on. "We should give our man here instructions so he can get to work. Do you feel up to accompanying us?"

She took a sip of her tea and got to her feet, albeit shakily. "Let's survey the damage," she said. Not only did they look at the front door and the kitchen windows, but they toured all the doors to see how security could be heightened. Once every thing was sorted, Fran returned to her tea and the lawyer accompanied her.

"I imagine it must be very lonely here, in this large building all on your own," the lawyer said, pouring himself a cup of tea. "Especially in the current circumstances." He paused, as if hesitating over what to say. "My parents have a large house on the other side of town. I've spoken to them and they'd willingly welcome you for a few days if you'd prefer to have company."

The idea appealed to her, but she couldn't possibly go when she might have to leave at any moment to join Xristy. "That's really kind. Please thank them for me," she said. "But I can't possibly leave now. There's so much to do on the farm."

He quickly dissimulated his disappointment but she'd seen it and he knew she had. "Oh well," he said with a sigh, "I tried." He put down his tea and turned to face her squarely. "Know this. If ever you have the slightest problem, don't hesitate to call."

"Thank you," she said.

11.

Fran walked the circuit, checking every possible way in. The doors and windows were as secure as possible in such an old house. As the carpenter had pointed out, real security would require a considerable investment. He'd made some suggestions and had offered to make an estimate, if ever she was interested.

The two men had diven off together chatting amiably leaving Fran with the impression they were good friends. An errant thought crossed her mind. Did men friends kiss fervently like she and Xristy did? She had no idea. The little she knew about men was probably biased. In her experience they were unpredictable and violent, constantly on the look out for signs a girl was willing, capable of imaging such signs if they were not forthcoming, lashing out if they felt in the slightest bit threatened or insecure. Blast the man. He haunted her even once he'd gone. She forced her thoughts to turn to food.

Her mother had always decided what they ate and when they did and she'd done all the cooking, so having to do those things herself was a novelty. In fact, it was unnerving. It would have been so much easier to accept Mr Branson's offer and go stay with his parents. There was no guarantee the call from Xristy would come. If it didn't, she'd have to spend the whole night in that empty house alone. Hold on a moment. She was no child. She ought to be capable of weathering a night there. It was home, wasn't it? She straightened her back, and went in search of something to eat.

Amongst the things she'd tossed into the incinerator in her righteous purge had been her school cookbook. Silly mistake. She could use it now. She recalled her teacher's facetious remark about girls needing to know how to cook if they were to satisfy their husbands. She wondered how many of the other fathers beat and groped their daughters to get their satisfaction. The angry growl that resonated deep in her throat took her by surprise.

"Concentrate," she told herself. Cooking and cookbooks. She didn't think her mother had books about cooking. In fact, she doubted her mother had any books at all. Her father despised women who read. He even mocked Fran for going to school. Girls didn't need an education, he would intone. She shook herself. She was getting distracted again and by what? By the sick ideas of her father. He was dead, for God's sake, why couldn't she let it be.

She'd have to buy a cookbook next time she was in town. The realisation that she had the means to do so was comforting. She opted for pancakes, a recipe she'd learnt at school. Well at least school had been useful for something. To her relief, she found all the necessary ingredients in the otherwise empty larder. She was going to have to buy food too.

Her mouth watered at the sight of the stack of pancakes waiting on the table. She was just about to sit down and eat, congratulating herself on her newfound cooking ability, when a sharp rattling at the front door had her spring up in alarm. Picking up the axe handle which she kept close at hand, she padded silently towards the entrance. The rattling had stopped, but it started again as soon as she moved closer. If someone was trying to force an entrance, they surely wouldn't have done it like that.

"Who is it?" she asked. The only answer was a low, drawn out moan. The sound sent shivers shooting down her spine. It was inhuman. At the thought, she suddenly realised who or rather what it was. Could it be old man cloud, the king of the clouds? She unlocked the door, cracked it open and a rush of air came whistling in. Not curling comfortingly around her neck like it usually did, it shot past and rumbled into the kitchen where it moved around in a disjointed, agitated fashion.

"What's up?" she asked, sure it's agitation had something to do with Xristy. Not that there was any way it could answer. A deep rumbling was all she'd ever managed to get out of it. A small swirl of air separated from the rest of the cloud and pushed the plate of pancakes in her direction as if saying, "Eat." Having spread marmalade on a pancake, she chewed as she watched the cloud toy with the utensils hanging along the kitchen wall. She'd always thought of the cloud as old, but seeing it play, she wondered if it weren't younger. A child may be. A girl even. The thought pleased her.

She'd almost finished the stack of pancakes and was feeling satisfyingly full, when the cloud slid the plate out of her reach. A mother then, she thought with a wry smile, not a child. She'd just grabbed one more pancake when the cloud began winding itself tighter and tighter around her. A bossy mother, at that. It surrounded her in a swirling white mass that finished by alarming her. The kitchen was no longer visible. She was lost in a cloud of white. When the whiteness finally dissipated, she was not in her kitchen, but by a bed in which Xristy lay groaning.

You made it, the girl said, her voice weak and broken.

Xristy looked starving. Glancing around, Fran saw nothing to eat. Then she realised she still grasped a pancake. Ripping off a small piece, she slid it between Xristy's lips, causing the girl to cough violently. She lacked the strength to chew. So Fran took the food in her own mouth and chewed it before feeding the mushy paste to the starving girl. She had visions of a bird feeding its young. Water would've helped. But there was none in the room.

Clouds were water, weren't they? Maybe the cloud would relinquish some of itself so that Xristy could drink. She didn't even need to ask. An odd feeling of being squashed ran through her as if she were a lemon being squeezed and a puddle appeared in a dip on the worksurface nearby. Unsure how to get the water to Xristy - she had no bowl or spoon - she opted to dip the pancake mush in the water before feeding it to the girl.

Whatever was in the water, it had an immediate effect. Xristy regained some of her colour and looked less like a starving wretch. Intrigued, Fran dipped a finger into the puddle and sucked. It was sweet and nourishing and delightful. It brought a smile to her lips. She whispered a word of thanks to the cloud who responded by cuddling round her neck.

By the time she'd finished the pancake and the puddle was almost spent, Xristy was looking much, much better. *I wanted to come,* she explained to the girl. *But I had no idea how. It was the cloud that helped me.*

The cloud? Xristy asked, sounding confused.

Yes. The cloud that follows me around and helps me when I'm in trouble.

Xristy's look was troubled. *A cloud?* she asked in a whisper.

Yes. The one that gave its water for you to drink.

I drank water from a cloud? She sounded horrified.

It's alright, Fran tried to reassure her, seeing the girl get more and more agitated. *I drank it too. It's delicious. I think it was the water that revived you.*

Xristy looked stricken.

I don't understand, Fran said. *Why are you so frightened of clouds and their water?*

In the lore of Cloud Catchers, she who partakes directly of a cloud will become a cloud herself and bring about the downfall of our world.

Well, I'm no cloud. Look at me.

No. But you have a cloud in tow and you can communicate with it.

Is it possible your lore got it wrong? After all, doesn't your drinking water come from clouds?

That's different, Xristy retorted. *The water is filtered through many layers of special earth. No. That lore can't be wrong. Our whole life is built on it.*

Fran couldn't bring herself to contradict. She helped the

girl to her feet and followed her out of the room. What she discovered there was dreadful. Instead of well-ordered gardens, long gouges left paths in shreds, bushes and plants had been crushed and saplings had been torn up and flung haphazardly across once neat patches. To add to the feeling of disaster, an unpleasant smell hung in the air like rotting corpses, the very smell Fran had sensed when Xristy had briefly appeared in her world.

What happened? she asked.

I can't tell you here. We're not safe.

Not safe? What an earth was going on? She loved the place. There may not be playful, laughing girls skipping along the paths between the well-ordered gardens but it was a haven free of boys and men. It was as if some brute had thrown a temper and smashed anything and everything in sight.

Xristy heaved aside a fallen branch with Fran's help, revealing a trapdoor. The effort had Xristy gasping for breath. *Pull. Open.* Xristy managed to say. *Don't. Have. Strength.* Once open, Fran helped Xristy down a ladder. The girl had to pause at the foot having no force to go on. Fran looked around. They stood at the beginning of a long, straight tunnel dimly lit at floor level.

She glanced at Xristy, who was bent over double, wheezing. They'd never make it with the girl in her state. Abruptly, Fran realised her friend would die if she did nothing. As Xristy straightened up, on an impulse, Fran planted her lips on the girl's - to Xristy's surprise and alarm - and kissed her firmly, despite Xristy's feeble efforts to stop her. She drew on a giant, swirling force she discovered in her depths and let it flow through her mouth and into Xristy's, filling the girl with warmth and strength.

When Fran finally pulled away, Xristy stood in front of her, restored to her pristine form. She looked so beautiful, so full of life, Fran was tempted to kiss her again. Only one thing marred the moment, the scowl on Xristy's face. *What's the matter?* Fran asked.

What have you done? The question was almost a wail of despair.

Fran didn't understand. Had she not just saved Xristy's life? *You were going to die*, Fran said, sounding almost as desperate as Xristy. This world and its people were much stranger than she'd imagined.

Better to die, than be taken over by a cloud. Xristy spat the bitter words like an accusing finger pointed at Fran. *Be gone!* the girl roared, her words, like a curse, flung Fran out of her world.

Fran found herself slumped on a chair in the farm kitchen, the remainder of the uneaten pancakes cold in front of her. A sob of anger and incomprehension and hurt burst from her lips. How incredibly stupid. How could anyone be so rigid as to refuse desperately needed help? She'd been confronted by such stubborn shortsightedness every day at school, at home and in the church. Had she been so misguided to hope she could escape it in Xristy's world?

She shivered, feeling at a loss. She'd got it all wrong. From the moment she'd met Xristy, she'd thought she'd found a way out. A way to dodge the violence of her father, to get away from the suffocating presence of her mother, to avoid the straitjacket that was school and the narrow moral dictates of the church. Xristy's world had seemed like the paradise she'd never dared dream of, a place where she could finally be herself.

Only days later, her father was dead, her mother was in a mental hospital and school was no longer an option, all because of her. Instead, she bore the crushing responsibility of a working farm. As for Xristy's world, she'd been banished. Banished from her dream, refused the prospect of love and happiness, cut off from her real self.

A gentle wind stirred around her shoulders and ruffled her hair, as if the cloud were trying to console her. She sprang to her feet in fury, shaking her fist, and screamed, "Get out of my life. You've destroyed everything. Be gone. I want nothing more to do with you."

With her words a vital part of herself was ripped from her chest. The pain was excruciating. She cried out and sank to the floor, her arms outstretched in a desperate attempt to cling on to God-knew-what. Her heart? Her hope? Her soul? Where the cloud had once been, she found only lifeless void. All the joy had bled from the world. She burst into sobs and sank forward till her forehead rested on the cold flagstones and let despair take her.

12.

A gentle hand shook Fran's shoulder. "Leave me alone," she muttered. She didn't want to wake. She was dreadfully cold. Every bone in her body ached. The hand persisted. Cracking open her eyes, she found she was curled up on the flagstones under the kitchen table. Not only did she feel bruised as if she'd been battered all over, but her eyes stung from crying and her throat was sore.

"Let me help you up." It was young Mr Branson. Surely it couldn't be time for their appointment.

"Not yet," she mumbled.

He insisted, placing a firm hand under her arm and lifting her up. When she collapsed the moment he let go, he scooped her up in his arms and sat her on a chair, keeping a firm hold on her shoulder to stop her sliding off. "I'd offer to make some tea," he said, "but you'll have to promise to stay on the chair and not flop to the ground."

Paying no heed to his request, she asked, "Is it time?"

"Time for what?" He sounded genuinely perplexed.

"For our appointment."

He chuckled. "That was ages ago. When you didn't turn up, I was worried..."

"What time is it?"

"Three."

"Three!" How could it be mid afternoon? No wonder she ached. She'd been lying on the stone floor for aeons. Then she remembered. Xristy. The cloud. Her friends. Gone. She burst into tears.

He didn't try to take her in his arms. For that, she was grateful. He kept a respectful distance, one hand poised ready to catch her should she fall. But fall she did, although he probably didn't see, and nothing he could do could stop that fall. She was falling apart.

She felt tern and flat and acutely empty. It was alarming. Something vital was missing, as if she weren't all there. In chasing away her cloud, she'd extinguished a flame, a beautiful, colourful flame she hadn't even known was hers. Rather than a presence, she'd become an absence. Instead of being alive, she was seized by a painful yearning for life, that, in itself, was a yawning hole that refused to be filled.

After a while, he pulled a packet of tissues from his pocket and handed her one. She blew her nose, noisily, and was about to hand back the used handkerchief when she realised what she was doing. She pocketed the thing and said, "You can go make the tea. I can't fall any more." The truth. Nothing but the truth. She'd fallen so low, there was nowhere else to fall.

To fall no more. An odd expression. Maybe that explained his look, so full of doubt and concern, but he shifted away and went to heat water. As he bustled about the kitchen in search of tea - an unfamiliar figure in a painfully familiar world - she got unsteadily to her feet and headed for the door. At his look of alarm, she said, "Gotta pee," and stumbled out.

When she returned, he was seated at the table with two mugs of tea steaming in front of him. "You should get something to eat," he said, that constant note of concern in his voice.

"I'm not hungry," she replied. In fact she was ravenous, but nothing material sustenance could satisfy.

"I insist," he said. "You can't go and visit a banker on an empty stomach." He offered her no chance to refuse, so she agreed with a sigh and ate half-heartedly a breakfast they prepared together. The whole time, she absently rubbed the scar on the back of her hand. It no longer glowed and when she touched it, she felt no answering tingle stirring in her chest.

He looked like he wanted to question her, but refrained. She appreciated his restraint and respect. Like her, he ate very little. When they'd finished, they set off in his car, riding a long time in uncomfortable silence.

"I don't like cars," she finally said. When he glanced at her in surprise, she went on, "They go too fast. Such speed is not natural. Give me a horse any day." That said, she'd have to check on her pony the moment she got back.

He chuckled. "I don't think the banker will have stables for your horse. Do you have many? Horses, I mean."

"Just the one," she replied. "My father would never have let me have that one if I hadn't promised to pay its keep with my pocket money. He was always looking for excuses to get rid of it." She glanced out the window at the passing fields, worried about her pony. She'd been neglecting it. "Do you ride?"

"You trying to flog me a horse?" He was concentrating on the road, but a broad grin spread across his face.

"Lord. No. I'd never sell my pony. Just making conversation."

He snorted. "I appreciate your frankness. It's refreshing."

She blushed. "At school they always scolded me for being so direct."

"Of course they did. School teaches girls to be modest, obedient and to keep their thoughts to themselves."

"The only place I liked at school was the library. My father hated books so we had nearly none at home. He hated girls and women that read even more. I've often wondered if he knew how to read. I had to be very careful where and when I read. The library was the only place I could get my fill of books without fear of being beaten. I would have spent hours there had I not been obliged to attend their stupid classes."

"Here we are," the lawyer said.

He parked the car outside a shabby building from which hung a faded sign announcing, Handels Bank. "Doesn't seem the sort of place you'd leave your money," Fran remarked.

"Depends whether you want people to know about it or

not," the lawyer said wryly.

"So my father was dodging taxes?" Fran asked.

"Seems likely. If he put his money in a dump like this."

"Will I get into trouble if I use money he kept from the taxes?"

"No. But Inland Revenue might try to take some of it away."

There was no receptionist at the reception. Ringing the bell that sat on the otherwise empty desk, had a squat little man hurrying out from an inner office. "How can I help?" he asked, an ingratiating smile plastered across his face.

"My client and I have come about account number..." He pulled a paper from his briefcase and reeled off the number.

"Yes. You telephoned, I believe."

The lawyer nodded. "My client has recently lost her father..."

The man mumbled condolences. Fran didn't even bother to acknowledge.

"...and would like to know the state of the account. And the conditions under which you keep her money."

"I need you to prove your identity of course," the banker said. "We can't have anyone just poking their noses into our customers' affairs."

Fran had no passport. She'd never travelled. Her father would never have allowed it. But the lawyer had prepared for such an eventuality, bringing with him her birth certificate as well as a letter from the local administration stating she was her father's daughter. He also produced a copy of the death certificate.

The banker studied the documents for a long moment. Fran wondered if people often tried to get access using fake documents. "Good," he finally said, leaning back in his chair apparently satisfied. "Come with me." He got to his feet and led them through a side door into an office which had only a large table in the middle. "Stay here. I'll bring it to you."

"Bring what?" Fran asked, the moment the banker was out of the room.

"A deposit box probably."

The banker returned almost immediately, wheeling a small trolley on which a large box was placed. If the size was anything to go by, there must be a considerable fortune inside, unless her father was playing a farce. If her father had anything to do with it, he'd probably have put a large mouse trap inside.

"Your father, may God bless his soul, came from time to time to add material to the box. I believe he kept a tally of its contents. The list should be inside." He handed Fran a key.

Unsure, Fran glanced at the lawyer, who nodded in encouragement. Turning the key in the lock, she lifted the heavy lid. It wasn't immediately apparent what was inside because a velvet cloth covered the contents. Only a small scrap of paper full of scribbled figures was visible. She picked up the paper and attempted to decipher it. Her father was not much better at writing than reading. At first she couldn't believe what she read. The quantities were far too large to be correct. But when she removed the velvet, the wads and wads of banknotes confirmed the figures she'd read.

"You should check the total tallies with the contents," the banker advised.

With Mr Branson's help, she laid out the wads of notes in rows on the table till the whole surface was covered and they had to continue on the floor. They counted the contents of each wad, noted the total on a note attached to the wad and finally added the totals. It was long and arduous work. Fran muddled her numbers several times and had to begin again. The banker left them, saying he would return in a couple of hours with refreshments.

They were squatting on the floor, counting the last wads when the lawyer said, "While we're alone, we should talk about what you want to do with this money. You could leave it here, it seems quite safe. But you might want to invest a portion of it."

"How much do I owe you?" she asked.

"You want to pay me off already?" he replied, grinning to show he was joking.

"No. I wanted to settle my debts. In fact, I wanted to know

if you'd accept a retainer so we can continue working together."

"Retainer? I was thinking more of a business partnership..."

He didn't get any further. The banker arrived accompanied by a young woman carrying a tray of drinks. The girl - she was more a girl than a woman - couldn't have been much older than Fran. She was scantily dressed in a short skirt and an over tight blouse and looked weary and downtrodden. Fran knew the look. There were days, those when her father was on a rampage, that the girl with the dark shadows under her eyes and the tense lines around her mouth who stared back at her from the mirror wore that expression.

Moving to free a place for the drinks on the table, Fran kept a constant eye on the girl. As Fran piled wads of notes back into the box, she remarked how the girl shifted away whenever the banker got too close. She couldn't help noticing the man's clumsy attempts to touch her as he made a show of helping lay out the glasses and the revulsion that flitted across the girl's face every time he did.

Seeking a pretext to engage with the girl, she deliberately knocked several wads of notes off the table at the feet of the girl, who bent down to pick them up. "Good," Fran said, squatting down next to her. "I was looking for someone to give me a hand."

The girl shot a nervous look at the banker, who frowned but didn't refuse. She began hurriedly sweeping up piles of notes. "Take your time," Fran whispered, their eyes meeting briefly. "I think we can manage here," Fran said to the banker. "I'm sure you have important things to do. We'll call if we need help."

The man didn't appreciate being dismissed. He liked even less having to relinquish his hold on a girl he clearly considered his property. Her father had had similar proprietary claims over her. The banker hung hesitant, glancing frequently in the girl's direction, undecided what to do. It was Mr Branson who made up his mind for him. Slinging an arm around the man's shoulder, he led him to the door, saying, "We'll soon be finished here and you'll be rid of us.

Once the man was gone, Fran turned to the girl and asked, "What's your name?"

"Nelly," the girl whispered.

"Well Nelly, how would you like to work for me?"

The girl shot Fran an incredulous look that screamed, 'Me? Why me?' Fran answered the unspoken question. "Because I suspect you have potential that is wasted here. But above all, I can see you are being mistreated. I personally know how terrible being abused can be. So I want to offer you a way out." Turning to Mr Branson, she asked, "Do you agree, partner?"

He looked at her gravely, and replied, "I agree, wholeheartedly."

"This incident has convinced me to remove my money from this bank. I won't trust it to the hands of someone who abuses young girls."

The girl gasped at her words. True, it was the sort of thing people kept quiet about. But it had to be said.

"You should check the man hasn't got more of your father's money stashed away in a forgotten corner," the lawyer suggested.

"He has," Nelly admitted. "At least one more box like that." She pointed to the box on the floor which was now closed and locked.

"Take the box to the car," the lawyer said, handing her his coat. "Wrap it in this. And take Nelly with you. I suspect she won't be safe here. I'll deal with the banker."

13.

Fran was deep in conversation with Nelly, questioning her about her story, when a sharp rap at the window had her look up in alarm. A scrawny man with a toothless grin and a scar across his left cheek gestured for her to unlock the door. She heard Nelly gasp. She herself was seized with terror. If only the cloud had been there. *Please, please, I need you*, she said in a fervent prayer that went unanswered.

The man grabbed hold of the door handle and tried to tear it free. His efforts rocked the car. When Fran refused to open, the man drew a gun and pointed it at her. Nelly whimpered, cowering away. *It's now or never*, Fran said, her words run through with urgency and authority. Not that it did any good. Even clouds could be stubborn. With shaking fingers, she unlocked the door. What else could she do?

Abruptly the man's eyes rolled back in his head and he slumped forward, his face crashing against the window with a sickening crunch and slithered, almost comically, to the ground, revealing Mr Branson standing behind him, a large metal box grasped in his hand, a grim expression on his face.

While the lawyer stowed the box in the boot along with the first one, Fran did her best to comfort the girl. The sight of violence had sparked wave after wave of uncontrollable trembling. Fran took Nelly in her arms and cuddled her close, whispering words of comfort and reassurance, "It's over. We're safe now. I'll look after you..."

By the time they'd reached the motorway, Nelly was calmer and Fran went to unclasp her arms, but the girl clung to her. "Nelly has no close family," she explained to Mr Branson. "That filthy pig of a banker..." disgust and hatred making her almost spit the words, "...had granted her lodgings in his house as part payment for the job and in return for her compliance. You can imagine the rest..."

"I guessed as much," the lawyer said. "That man had a distinctly unhealthy air to him. You did well to withdraw your funds. Although we need to find a safe place for this wealth. All that money attracts scum, as you saw."

Fran shuddered, a shudder that was echoed by Nelly. "Got any ideas?" she asked. Maybe she was wrong to trust him. Large quantities of money seemed to transform even the most normal of people into monsters. Yet she was confident. He'd stuck by her so far and had given good advice.

"Well, yes. A man called Bryant. He's manager of a small, independent bank in town, affiliated to a larger national bank. He handles my meagre fortune," he chuckled, one-handedly indicating how small it was, "and he's always been very understanding and helpful."

"Let's go see your Mr Bryant."

Two hours later, all three were seated around the kitchen table in the farm, relieved to be free of the cumbersome boxes and their wealth of bank notes. Mr Bryant had opened an account in her name and the money had been duly counted and accredited to her. She had the opening balance on paper to prove it. So much money. To think they'd lived in near poverty while her father hoarded all he could. And to think, he'd complained bitterly about having to replace their sole tractor that was falling to bits with a second-hand model!

Together they had rummaged through her mother's meagre supplies and come up with an improvised, albeit strange meal. "I'll have to go shopping tomorrow," Fran said. Nelly was eager to go with her.

As they laughed and joked preparing the meal, she glanced

at the lawyer helping Nelly peel potatoes. It seemed odd to continue calling him Mr Branson or her 'lawyer' and him always referring to her as his 'client'. "My name's Fran," she said, startling him with her outstretched hand awaiting to be shaken. "This is Nelly. Who are you?"

A broad smile lit up his face as he took her offered hand and said, "I'm Jakob, with a 'k'. Pleased to meet you." And - her turn to be surprised - he pulled her into hug. Seeing Nelly standing off to one side, Fran reached out to pull the girl into the huddle but Nelly stepped out of reach.

The girl was initially reluctant to take part as they made plans while they ate. A return of the carpenter to improve security. A room for Nelly. That suggestion finally had the girl reacting as she squealed with delight. Fran realise Nelly was little more than a child. A visit to Mr Bryant about investments, with Jakob's help. Improvements to the farm. Jakob had ideas about that too. By the time they'd cleared up, Fran's head was reeling.

"I need to tend to my pony," she said, abandoning a reluctant Nelly in the hands of Jakob. "I won't be long," she added, trying to reassure the girl, but Nelly insisted on accompanying her. Fran unclasped the girl's hand that clung to her sleeve, saying firmly, "Stay here." She needed a moment alone. Events were happening so fast, she'd had no time to think things over.

She found a disgruntled pony awaiting her in the stables. Not even an extra helping of mash could placate it. Finally a long hug and a good brushing won over the animal that nudged her lovingly with its head. "At least I've still got you, faithful friend," she told it. When she'd finished, she realised it was late and she'd left Jakob far too long coping with a scared Nelly. So much for thinking things over. Handling her pony had taken all her attention.

A tense atmosphere greeted her in the kitchen. The length of the table separated the two who sat in brooding silence. Fran went to the sink to wash her hands, saying, "Any tea left?" Jakob got to his feet, visibly relieved to be able to do something and set about making more tea. Fran chatted about her pony as she sipped her tea. When Nelly yawned several times, Fran took the hint, saying, "Let's find you a place to sleep."

Not wanting to use her parent's bedroom, Fran made the girl a temporary bed on the floor next to hers. Leaving her to try on a nightshirt, Fran accompanied Jakob to the front door. She would have felt safer if he were to stay. After the attack, she had visions of ruffians breaking in while they slept. But she was afraid an invitation to remain would give the wrong idea.

In the end, it was him that suggested it. "I'd feel reassured," he began, "if I could stay this night to make sure there's no trouble."

She was relieved he offered. They'd all be able to sleep in peace. She was about to say so when he leant forward and kissed her lightly on the cheek. Despite his gentleness, there was an urgency to his embrace that repulsed her. It was nothing like being kissed by Xristy. There was none of the mutual understanding of like with like. None of the melting together in a red-hot fire, spurred on by Xristy's devilish oil. His lips were coarse in comparison and he smelt so different, so unappealing, so alien. A man. An image of her father rose to taunt her. Not that Jakob was anything like him, but she couldn't help cringing. "Don't," she said, holding up a hand to ward him off.

She needn't have bothered.

"I'm sorry..." he stammered, taking a step back, his expression miserable. "...I thought..,"

"You thought wrong," Fran said, not so much angry as sad and resigned. "I've enjoyed your company. I really have. I appreciate all you've done for me. You're a wonderful person. But I can't. I won't. Not that. Not after all I've been through."

"I'm so, so sorry," he repeated, his head bowed and he turned to go.

His abrupt departure had her in panic. "Don't go," she said, grabbing his sleeve. "Please."

He looked back at her, his expression one of pained confusion verging on accusation. "Are you playing with me?"

His words shocked her. "No. Never. I'd never do that," she said, pained herself now. "Partners, we called ourselves." She tried to smile at the memory, but could only manage a grimace. "I want us to stay partners, to stay friends." She finally managed a smile. "But not that sort of partner..." She shuddered at the thought of herself in bed with him, his hands roaming over her naked body. "You're a sensitive man. Surely you can understand that I've been hurt in ways that make all intimacy with a man unthinkable."

"It was so selfish of me. I didn't think."

"I don't blame you. You've shown you're really considerate." She imagined herself in his place. "It must be unbearable to continually have to keep in mind the violent reality that has been my daily life. Lord knows, it's bad enough that I have to suffer the constant reminder, without inflicting it on you."

"I feel a great deal of tenderness and affection for you," he said, clearly struggling to express what he felt. "I believe my kissing you was more an expression of that tenderness. It's a bit like listening to beautiful music and wanting to sway or dance. You move me, literally. I am moved to kiss you, to hold you in my arms, to protect you. I would be dishonest if I denied I don't desire you as well. I do. You're an attractive young woman..."

"Are you alright?" they heard Nelly call out from above, her voice trembling. Looking up, Fran saw the girl leaning out of her bedroom window, her long hair ruffled by the breeze. Fran reminded herself the girl had her own reasons to be wary if not scared.

"All is okay," Fran called out, glancing at Jacob as she did. The man blushed with embarrassment. "I'll make you a bed on the sofa," she told him, "if you agree."

He still seemed undecided, then, after a long hesitation, stepped back into the house and followed her into the living room. "Don't worry about it," she said, pulling blankets and a pillow from a cupboard. "We'll figure it out."

Having said goodnight, she climbed to her bedroom where Nelly was perched on the edge of her bed waiting for her. "He didn't...?" Nelly asked, sounding anxious.

"No. Just a misunderstanding," Fran said as she stripped off. It was only when she was completely naked that she realised Nelly was staring at her. Pausing a moment, she tried to gauge that look. There was evident interest but also apprehension, if not fear. Pulling her nightdress over her head, she asked, "What's the matter?"

The girl blushed. "I... errr..."

"Have you never seen a naked girl before?" Fran asked, climbing between the sheets.

Nelly shook her head.

What with Jacob wanting to kiss her and Nelly staring at her as if she were a three-course meal, this new life was full of unexpected experiences. "Well, now you have," Fran said, a little harsher than she intended. "It's time to sleep. We've got a lot to do tomorrow, so why don't you lie down."

They could only have been asleep for a few hours when Fran was awoken by Nelly tossing and turning as she battled with her covers. "Don't!" the girl moaned in her sleep. "Please don't."

"It's alright," Fran murmured. "You're safe. I'm here." Her words didn't seem to calm the girl who continued to toss and turn. Then, abruptly, Nelly sat bolt upright. "Where am I?" she asked, her voice distant, her eyes still closed.

"You're in my house," Fran said.

Blinking open her eyes, the girl stared at Fran for a long moment uncomprehending. Then she whispered, "Can I get into bed with you? I'm so scared."

Fran sighed. She was beginning to regret having invited the girl, but she patted the bed next to her, turned over and closed her eyes, saying, "If you stop me sleeping, I'll kick you out of bed." Being next to her must've calmed Nelly because she slept soundly the rest of the night.

When she awoke, Fran turned to get up but found she was trapped. Nelly had slung a leg across her thigh and had an arm wound around Fran's waist. Gently trying to push her off proved unsuccessful. The girl clung on too tight. "Wake up, Nelly. I need to get up." The girl groaned but didn't release her. When nothing else worked, Fran shoved the girl with all her might. That worked. Nelly freed her but rolled over and promptly fell off the other side of the bed. Her scream would have woken the dead. As it was, it awoke Jakob who came bounding up the stairs and burst into the room.

The man stood in the doorway, a look of incomprehension on his face. What he must have thought, she couldn't imagine. There she was seated on her bedside in her nightdress, her head in her hands, while Nelly flailed on the floor on the other side of the bed, still screaming, her nightshirt up around her waist.

"It's a long story," she told him, wearily. "Suffice it to say nobody is in danger and nobody was hurt."

"Speak for yourself," retorted the girl. "You flung me out of bed."

Fran blushed. Having refused to go to bed with him - or something along those lines - he now saw she'd spent the night in bed with the girl. "I allowed you to get into bed with me, Nelly, because you were so afraid," she said, going to pains to straighten things out with Nelly but also to give Jakob the right message, "but I warned you I'd kick you out of the bed if you stopped me sleeping. I should also have warned you I'd kick you out if you stopped me getting up."

Nelly had finally managed to right herself and was more or less decent in her nightshirt, although she didn't look in the slightest contrite. As for Jacob, his grin couldn't have been wider. "What are you laughing at?" Fran asked. "Have you made our breakfast?"

Still grinning, he bowed stiffly. "No, my lady. I was led to believe the larder was bare."

She grabbed her pillow and tossed it at him.

14.

Having nothing for breakfast in the larder - she could have gone in search of eggs, but there was nothing to eat them with - Jakob took them to a tearoom in town. Settled comfortably in the small alcove which gave them some privacy, they were enjoying a full English breakfast. Not something Fran had ever had before, such was the frugal existence her father held them to. She'd just finished her bacon and eggs and was about to start on a slice of toast when she felt a strange whistling in her ears. She wondered if it meant the cloud was back and readied herself to greet it. But as the sound grew louder, she found she was drifting away and could no longer clearly see either Jacob or Nelly who were fading fast into a mist.

No. This was no cloud's doing. It was her being pulled into Xristy's world. She braced herself against a torrent of abuse, expecting the girl to take up where she'd left off. Instead, only silence welcomed her. She stood in an empty room. The very one where Xristy had laid ill. Nobody lay there now.

She moved to the door, which obligingly slid open, whooshing at her as it did. Outside she had hopes the chaos had been righted, but she discovered the same destruction she'd seen last time. Threading her way along the broken path, she came to the entrance to the underground tunnel.

Climbing down, she half expected to find Xristy waiting for her. It was not Xristy, but Duffni, Xristy's friend, leaning against a wall, her hands in her pockets. *You took your time,* the girl snapped. *Surely you must have realised it was urgent.*

How was I to know? Fran retorted, indignant at the unfriendly greeting. *Last time I was here Xristy banished me. She wanted nothing to do with me.*

Doesn't surprise me, the girl replied, looking down her nose at Fran. *I can't see you being able to satisfy her. Not even I could do that.*

So that was it. Jealousy! *It wasn't like that...* Fran began.

Ignoring her indignation, Duffni pointed an accusatory finger. *Not only have you consorted with clouds, you've done something to Xristy that has put her life in grave danger.* She sprang forward her hands outstretched, reaching for Fran's neck. Fran stood her ground although she was terrified the girl would try to strangle her. Instead Duffni grabbed her by the collar and shook her violently. With the girl's face only inches from Fran's, she could see tears welling in the her eyes. *You must do something to save her,* the girl pleaded.

I ask for nothing better, Fran replied. *But I can't.*

Why ever not? Duffni exploded, shaking Fran furiously a second time.

Because I no longer have the cloud with me, Fran said, giving voice to her own despair as she let the girl's desperate anger wash over her. *When Xristy banished me, I was so hurt and angry I banished the cloud. Without it, I can do nothing.*

Duffni looked stricken. She stood there staring at the ground for a long moment, then, as if coming to a decision, grabbed Fran's arm, saying, *Come with me.*

Where? Fran demanded, digging in her heels.

To see the Council. They'll know how to make you save Xristy. Tears were flowing freely down the girl's cheeks. Such desperation! Such profound attachment to Xristy. Had the girl been Xristy's lover? Fran had been so engrossed in her passionate encounter, it had never occurred to her that there might be another girl in Xristy's life. She had no time to unravel the knot of feelings the realisation had formed. They'd arrived.

She'd expected the Council to consist of elders, but what

she got was a group of girls barely older than herself seated in the circle. Duffni shoved Fran into the middle and went to join the others. For a long moment they stared at her, their expressions both grave and disapproving. No one spoke. Then, one of the girls, who looked remarkably like Xristy but without the smile, got to her feet and said, *You have been found guilty of consorting with clouds. There can be no higher crime. What do you have to say for yourself?*

I did not choose to be linked to a cloud..., Fran began.

Several Council members frowned, others looked frankly hostile. *As we suspected,* the leader butted in, *you are nothing but a pawn.*

Fran opened her mouth to object, but the girl cut her short. *Show me your hand,* she ordered. With a sigh, Fran held out her hand, the cloud mark uppermost. The girl examined it closely, rubbing her thumb roughly across the scar. It stung painfully when she did, as if angered at the girl's touch.

You are clearly still under its sway, the girl said, abruptly shoving Fran's hand away as if it were tainted. *The clouds are behind this. You may appear responsible, but you are nothing. It is the clouds that are attacking Xristy.*

Although Fran was glad they didn't think she was to blame, she intensely disliked being told she was nothing. She was on the verge of answering back, but a part of her advised caution. She heeded the warning and kept quiet.

I don't like it, the girl continued, *but I see no other solution than to send you to intercede on behalf of Xristy.*

There was a gasp from the other girls. When Fran glanced around, she could see horror and worry etched on their young faces. *Okay,* she said. *I'll do it.* She'd survived one encounter with an angry cloud. Surely she could survive another.

I don't think you understand, the leader said. *You'll be escorted to the base of the tower, but from there you'll be on your own.*

Fran was flabbergasted. Despite their hostility, she'd expected them to accompany her like Xristy had done. *But I can't fly those scooter things,* Fran pointed out.

I doubt you'll need that. The clouds will surely come to you. After all, you are their pawn.

Fran didn't believe she was anybody's pawn and she intensely disliked being sneered at. She was about to object when the girl turned on her heels and headed out of the hall, imperiously calling out, *Follow me!*

When they were beyond the scrutiny of the Council and Fran's indignation had subsided, she asked, *How's Xristy?*

Gravely ill, the leader replied, her face pinched with in-held grief. *I fear she'll not last the night.*

Xristy is your sister, Fran said. It was not a question, rather a sudden realisation.

Not exactly. The girl halted, staring off blankly into the distance. *I was her protégé. You could say she adopted me. Like a sister. When our former leader Narie passed away some fifteen years ago, Xristy should've been our leader. She was the natural choice, being the eldest. But, like Narie, she was constantly restless and driven to roaming far and wide. She refused the role, claiming her heart was not in leading.*

After a pause, she resumed walking. *Xristy had always been different from the rest of us, but the more time went by, the more she was beset by incomprehensible ideas, like hunting you down and bringing you here. Nothing I could say would dissuade her... As a cloud catcher, maybe that close proximity to clouds finally drove her over the brink...*

So you were chosen instead?

Unfortunately. The word was almost a sigh of resignation. A brooding silence followed lasting till they reached the tower. As they did, the grumblings of the clouds beyond the bubble were getting ever louder.

I must go, the leader said, staring up at the menacing clouds swirling around the top of the tower. She lent closer, causing Fran to catch a whiff of the oil so characteristic of Xristy, and startled Fran by planting a kiss on her lips. The girl kissed as well as if not better than her sister. For a brief moment Fran forgot all else, carried away by the passionate onslaught. Then, as abruptly as it had begun, the girl broke off and coldly spat out the words, *Save my sister.* At which she turned her back on Fran and stomped away.

Although Fran felt bereft in the aftermath of that kiss, the kiss, or maybe it was the oil, had given her courage. She stepped into the lift and the door hissed closed behind her.

The ride skyward brought back terrifying memories of wild storms and ear-splitting thunder claps not to mention blinding lightning strikes, but above all the searing pain at being branded by the cloud. The leader had insisted there would be no second branding. *Once branded,* she'd said, *always branded.*

The lift halted and Fran climbed to the windswept platform. Unlike her last visit, the tiny, frisky clouds were nowhere to be seen. The sky was dark with towering clouds that billowed angrily upwards, hissing and spitting as they did. She could imagine Xristy fervently advising her not to venture out.

A bolt of lightning struck the platform not far from her, sending a blue light shimmering across the whole surface. Turning to face the oncoming clouds, Fran moved away from the scooters, clearly having no use for them. The clouds were coming to her. And anyway, the scooters were surely associated with those who trapped young clouds and she didn't wish to antagonise the older ones. She needed all the good will she could get.

All around clouds rolled over each other in their rush to reach her. So many nuances of grey, topped with plumes of brilliant white that curled round the tips like uncontrollable sprites. They came to rest in a tight but continually moving circle around her. And above and through them all, one immense cloud reaching far higher than she could see. Not rushing, him, but moving sedately forward with the inevitability of a judgement about to fall.

You have been very foolish, daughter, the cloud boomed, each word like a clap of thunder in her mind, shaking her to the core. His voice weighed on her existence, shot through with millennia of knowledge. It could snuff out her flame without a thought. Yet she felt no anger radiating from it, only concern and incomprehension. She sank to her knees and prostrated herself. *What made you think you could deny your very nature?* Her teeth rattled with each word echoing inside her skull. *You cannot drive out you heart with impunity.* There was a rush of wind that sighed through her. *What are we to do with you?*

As its breath swirled inside and outside her, making nonsense of the notion of skin, of boundaries, of individuality, she felt the immensity of clouds, their inhuman strength and their alarming fragility. She was a part of it, no, she **was** that immensity, aware that it filled her with undeniable life. She knew with a knowledge akin to that of clouds, that her cloud had been restored, that she was whole again and she wept.

The clouds must've transported her into the lift and sent her down, because when she opened her eyes she found herself lying at the foot of the tower. As she struggled to her feet, she was acutely aware of her body, of her skin, of the limits that contained her and made her who she was. The immensity of being a cloud, being connected to all clouds, to the whole universe, was only a distant memory. What had the cloud said? *You are our bridge to the world, a presence were none of us can go. Use it well.*

Staggering along the path towards the centre of the bubble, she encountered Xristy's sister, apparently waiting for her. *Is she still alive?* was Fran's first question.

Barely. No thanks to you.

Take me to her.

The girl led Fran into an adjacent building where Xristy lay curled on a bed, her face ashen, her breath coming in short, sharp bursts. There seemed to be little life left in her. Then, abruptly, the wheeze of her breathing ceased, causing Xristy's sister to cry out in distress.

At her bedside in a flash, Fran lent forward and kissed Xristy on the lips, letting the cloud in her surge up and flow from lips to lips, bringing life to Xristy's dying body. Rather than flooding her with the cloud, like the first time, Fran fed her just enough to bring her back.

Xristy stirred and opened her eyes. *You!* she said, spotting Fran, and growled. *I banished you ...* With an imperious wave of her hand she dismissed Fran.

Your sister... Fran began, but broke off at the evident anger in Xristy's expression and the certain knowledge she was being driven out...

Stay, Xristy's sister pleaded, but the girls' world was fading fast.

The taste of bacon and eggs was disconcerting when her nose was still thrumming to the memory of Xristy's oil and her mind reeling at the sting of being rejected, yet again. Looking down, she held a knife poised to spread butter on toast. A small bowl of marmelade stood nearby, a spoon protruding from it. Relaxing her grip, she let the knife clatter to her plate and looked up. Both Jakob and Nelly were staring at her, worried expressions on their faces.

"Are you alright?" Jakob asked. "You look unusually flushed."

A gentle breeze rippled through her, the all-too-familiar caress of a cloud, in response to Jakob's voice. Not so much his voice, as the breath it rode on. It would be so easy to get lost in that breath. It called to her. She tried to shrug it off and ran a trembling hand across her forehead. Beads of sweat had formed leaving her fingers moist.

"I'm fine," she managed, although her voice didn't sound fine. She rubbed her thumb absently over the scar left by the cloud. "I'm not used to such a rich breakfast."

"Would you like me to drive you home?" Jakob asked.

"No. I'll be okay. Maybe they have some chamomile tea. That would help."

Waiting for her herbal tea to be brought, she struggled to concentrate on the conversation, but she was constantly distracted by the shifting of the cloud inside her. Its presence was far more pronounced than before. Back then the cloud had been more like a visitor swirling around her. Now it was a living part of her with a mind of it's own.

When she failed for the third time to answer a question Jakob had asked, he said, "I really think I should drive you back."

"Yes," Fran said. "It's not very sociable of me, but I'd like to be alone for a while. I've got a lot to think about. I'll go for a ride on my pony. I haven't taken it out for a while."

15.

A doleful whinnying greeted Fran as she entered the stables. Understandable. Their daily outing had been a ritual. Since the advent of Xristy, she'd ridden her pony only once and it was intent on reminding her that was unacceptable.

As she saddled the animal, Fran absently wondered if she returned to that spot under the walnut tree would she find the girl waiting for her. She snorted at her silliness. She missed Xristy and would willingly have returned to that time of playful discovery before Xristy decided she was the cloud's devil. Wishful thinking indeed. For all she knew, Xristy might well be dead. Heaving herself up, she straddled the pony and they trotted out.

Glancing up at the sky, she was struck by the ribbed structure of clouds high above. A strong wind must be chasing them across an otherwise blue sky. On the ground there was barely a breeze. Thinking of clouds and winds had the cloud in her stirring, like a cat pricking up its ears, suddenly attentive in its apparent slumber, it unrolled and stretched, flexing its muscles. Her pony stirred under her as if sensing the change.

The pony was the sole luxury her father had allowed her and then only because he believed she'd bring home prize money from competitions. She hadn't. Neither she nor her pony were cut out for it. Her father had gone on and on about how useless the pair were. Several times he'd threatened to get rid of the animal, complaining about how much it ate. She'd had to hand over her meagre earnings from odd jobs to help buy mash. That didn't stop her returning from school everyday with a sinking heart and check her pony was still in the stables. To her relief, it always was.

Selling off the pony would probably have been the last straw. It might well have driven her from her father's grip, causing her to flee and spill the beans to the authorities. And he knew it. Maybe the fear of being denounced was why he never went beyond threats.

The winding track broke from the wood after about a mile and ran along a ridge high above the town. Thursday. Market day. The square would be packed. She peered down. From that distance little was to be seen, lest it be patches of bright colour where the square should have been.

She generally avoided the press of people that the market entailed, preferring to be outside, on her own, in the wind and wild. Sensing her mood, the cloud unfurled from around her neck where it had been basking in her presence and let itself be carried up and away by the wind. For a brief moment Fran panicked, fearing it would be torn from her, but reaching out she could sense it still solidly linked to her.

She halted the pony and, sitting still in the saddle, closed her eyes and concentrated on the cloud and its contortions. It had caught an updraft and was joyfully soaring skywards in search of other clouds. Participating in that headlong upward rush was exhilarating. When the cloud flowed in and through others she got a shock. It was as if her being were dissolving, as if she had no limits, that all clouds were in her and she in them.

Her shock was even greater when a distant voice brought her abruptly back to earth, shouting, "Hey, Miss." The words wrenched her from high above, from boundless existence to a limited body astride a pony. She opened her eyes to see a man in his fifties, coattails trailing in the wind, bearing down on her on a stallion at a gallop. The cloud reacted immediately, forming a protective ring around her that bristled with disapproval. She had to struggle to calm it, not wanting another dead body on her hands.

Fran winced for the poor horse when the man wrenched it to an abrupt halt only feet in front of her. "I've been looking for you everywhere," he said, not bothering with greetings. She'd never seen him before. He had nothing of the thug who'd tried to rob them the day before, but there was a predatory air to him that warned her to be cautious. It might have been his thin, pinched mouth or the overly pointed nose, but more likely it was the greedy light in his eyes as he looked her up and down.

Rather than engage in conversation, she waited for him to explain. "Come quick," he said. "You're needed at the farm."

"Why?" she asked.

"There's been an accident."

It seemed unlikely. Not only had Jakob and Nelly gone into town to shop at the market, but this man was a complete stranger. How could he possibly know? "Did Martin send you?" she asked, trying to catch him out.

"Yes. He said to hurry."

Gotcha! she thought. "Go ahead. I'll follow in a moment."

He shook his head. "I can't do that. I was given strict instructions to accompany you."

"I'm sure you were," she replied, surprised he didn't spot her sarcasm. "And who gave those instructions?"

"Why, Martin of course."

"Who's Martin? I know no one of that name."

A moment of confusion swept across his face, but he quickly recovered, saying, "Smart." When his right hand slid to his pocket, she knew exactly what was coming next. That would be the second time in a day someone had pulled a gun on her.

"I wouldn't do that if I were you!" she said almost amicably. "You'll regret it."

The trouble with men was that they thought girls were stupid and defenceless. True, men's violence, even in subtle, almost imperceptible forms, did render many young girls unable to think and left them weak and helpless. That was not Fran's case. She'd twice confronted the leader of the clouds, a terrifying figure, who spat bolts of lightning for breakfast. This puny man just didn't make the cut.

His stallion shifted skittishly, whinnying as it did, no doubt sensing the cloud curled around its hooves. Oblivious to the warning signals, the man drew the gun from his pocket just as the horse reared up and flung him backwards out of the saddle. A shot rang out, causing the stallion to bolt but no one was hurt, apart from the man himself who bashed his head on a convenient rock. The gun had flown out of his grip and was now careening down the hillside gathering a host of small stones to its cause. Fran hoped it wouldn't start a landslide.

She turned to look at the man. A trickle of blood ran down his cheek and onto his neck. A large bruise was forming on his temple. He hadn't moved from where he'd fallen, but he still seemed to be breathing. She would have ridden off and left him there, but he began gasping for air as if he were being strangled, his hands struggling to free himself from whatever invisible assaillant grasped his throat.

Enough, Fran said to the cloud. *We can't go around killing everyone who tries to do us harm, even if they want to kill us*. She was pleased to see the man cease his struggle and his breathing return to normal. *Thank you*, she said to the cloud. Then she rode off.

She approached the farm cautiously, having dismounted at a distance. If the man had intended to bring her there, someone else might be waiting in ambush. It wasn't exactly communication, but she sensed the cloud wanted to go ahead and scout the place. An intuition, she called it. She held back amongst the trees, riding with the cloud as it flowed around the farm, exploring first the barn and the outhouses before entering the house itself.

Sure enough, two men lounged at the kitchen table chatting amiably as they downed a glass of beer. They must have found her father's stash. Not that there was much else they could steal. She was glad the money was safe at the bank. The cloud paid no attention to their conversation, but did convey a sense of smug self-confidence and distain. They clearly felt at home, as if the place were already theirs.

Spending so much time riding the cloud, Fran was getting a better understanding of what it could do and was beginning to have an inkling of its 'thoughts', if they could be called that. *Yes*, she thought, *fill the kitchen with a dense fog and make sure they can't move from their seats.*

By the time she reached the kitchen, the two men had been yelling to be set free for at least five minutes. They sounded hoarse and not a little frightened. "Gentlemen," she said, remaining hidden by the fog. "How good of you to make yourself at home. I trust the beer is to you liking." She decided to scare them even more. "I had it specially laced with strychnine, knowing you were coming. You should be feeling the effects soon. I gather it stimulates first then kills afterwards. I've heard it's a delightful, but excruciating way to go."

Both men made strangling sounds. She was unsure if they were imagining their imminent death or simply suffocating from fear. The cloud was restless as it swirled in ever tightening circles around them. She sensed it's thirst for blood. It wanted to be done with the two. *No*, she insisted. *No killing unless absolutely necessary.*

"I met your colleague," she said. "He had an unfortunate accident but before he was 'incapacitated' he was able to explain why you wanted to see me. I was intrigued. Unfortunately, his explanations were rather garbled. Not surprising really with that hole in his head. Maybe you could explain it better." She heard them gasp in horror. Despite the gravity of the situation, she was having fun. The strange mix of feelings was almost inebriating, much to the horror of a distant part of herself.

When neither of the men spoke, Fran suggested the cloud make it a little more difficult for one of the two to breathe. The cloud did so with a blood-thirsty relish that should have warned Fran something was not right. As it was, the gurgling death rattle was quite dramatic and had the desired effect.

"No. Don't," the other man pleaded. "Not me. We were sent by..." he mentioned the name of the owner of a nearby farm, the one who'd come to buy the farm. In accosting her, they were to frighten her into selling the place for a pittance.

When she instructed the cloud to release its strangle hold on the other man, it was not happy, demonstrating its displeasure by knocking over several chairs and rattling the windows. "Thank your employer for his offer but inform him my answer is No! You can also tell him I'll send a representative over in the next few days to reclaim retribution for the damages you and your colleagues have caused.

Having retreated into the shadows, she ordered the cloud to release them and lift the fog. If the cloud was unhappy before, the idea of letting the two go made it furious. Instead of releasing them, it tightened its hold. When Fran insisted, it flung them to the ground, soaking them with a sudden downpour that would have inundated the kitchen had she not grappled with the cloud to get it under control.

The last she heard as the two scampered out, bedraggled and terrified, was them screaming the house was haunted. She had no wish to remain in the kitchen. It was as if their presence had irremediably tainted the place. She sensed the cloud wanted to blow through the house to chase away the smell of the men but, instead, she cleared the bottles and glasses the men had used and mopped up the puddles the cloud had left on the kitchen floor.

Having wiped the table and chairs with disinfectant, twice - she was surely overreacting, but she had to make sure they were gone from her home, from her life - she made herself a tea and sat down to have a think with the cloud coiled comfortably around her neck.

She was worried. It was as if the wild, ruthless nature of the cloud was seeping into her. She shuddered at the glee she'd felt at torturing the two. She could so easily have had them killed. Was life worth so little? Another terrifying suspicion crossed her mind. With the demise of her father, had she finally become his heir? The idea was sickening. She dismissed it, trying to concentrate on the cloud. But it left an acrid taste.

Clearly, not only did she have to battle to keep the cloud

under control, but she also had to rein in its influence on her. Okay. She'd accepted it was wild. Being wild was good. Seeking to tame it would be equivalent to ripping the life from it. Yet she was not wild. She could not both live in society and let herself go wild. There was no place for a wild girl that broke the rules, that didn't hesitate to kill when it suited her.

A crash at the front door had her fearful more men had come to taunt her. The cloud reared up, readying to defend her, only to sink back at the sound of Nelly's excited chatter. Jakob and the girl bustled into the kitchen and dumped heavily laden baskets and carrier bags on the table. Nelly looked flushed as she rummaged through the shopping in search of something, oblivious to Fran. Jacob, in comparison, was staring at her, a worried look in his eyes. "What happened?" he asked.

16.

"I don't understand," Jakob said, scratching his head. "How did you manage to chase away two men, not to mention the man on the hill? I mean, I know you're strong willed, but surely no amount of will can defeat a fully grown man."

"She's got magical powers," Nelly said, lovingly fingering one of Fran's scarves she wore around her neck. It annoyed Fran that the girl helped herself to her things as if they were hers.

Jakob scoffed. "Why do people always turn to magic when they can't explain things?"

"'Cause it's true," Nelly said, pouting.

The girl's unbridled adoration was worrying. She had no tangible reason to suspect Fran. Yet she insisted. "Nelly is right," Fran said, grinning, hoping humouring the girl would diffuse her interest, even if it wouldn't placate Jakob. "I have a guardian angel who watches over me."

"I told you so," Nelly exclaimed, triumphant.

"And this guardian angel is able to chase away two thugs?" Jakob asked, not bothering to hide his scepticism.

Fran could feel the cloud urging her to show off. She resisted. "You're going to have to take my word on that."

In a huff, the cloud dived under the newspaper lying on the table and sent it's sheets scattering around the kitchen floor.

Nelly squealed, wide-eyed, and clutched her chest as if trying to contain her elation.

"Your guardian angel?" Jakob asked, ignoring Nelly's

antics.

"Yes. He's not very happy," Fran said, a wry smile on her lips. "He'd rather I showed him off more."

Jakob must have taken it as a joke because he shrugged. He wouldn't give in that easily, but apparently he'd decided now was not the time. "So what are you going to do about your neighbour?" he asked. "I think you should tell the police."

"No," Fran said, to his surprise. "I trust nature to sort things out." She wasn't going to mention the apocalyptic storm she had in mind.

Jakob shook his head. "Such fatalism on a sunny day."

Nelly, in comparison, ceased her insistence but kept eyeing Fran knowingly as if she were privy to some great secret. The girl's behaviour was alarming. She couldn't possibly know, yet she acted as if she did.

Once they'd put all the shopping away, Fran prepared a salad with one she found in the garden along with a couple of hard-boiled eggs fresh from the hens and a slice of ham. They ate in companionable silence. Nelly looked tired and, as for Jakob, he was thoughtful. "I'm going to have a lie down," Fran said. "All this fighting with men is tiring."

Jakob snorted. True, it might seem comical after all she lived through with her father. Judging from his frown, he didn't find it funny. "I have to go to the office," he said. "I'll be back at the end of the afternoon. Will you be alright?"

"As right as rain," Fran said, smiling at her oblique reference to the coming storm.

"I'm exhausted too," Nelly said, aping Fran's yawn. "All that shopping has worn me out."

"You can use my bed," Fran said. "I'll rest down here in an armchair." When Nelly objected, saying they could easily share the bed, Fran insisted, saying, "It's no problem. I can sleep quite well in an armchair." She'd often had to do so when hiding from her father.

Once Jakob had driven off to his office, Nelly climbed reluctantly to bed after one last attempt to convince Fran to join her. Fran listened at the foot of the stairs to be sure the girl had gone into her room. When the bedroom door clicked shut, Fran slipped out the back door and, rather than take her pony, climbed on foot to the top of the hill overlooking the neighbour's farm.

The farm was considerably larger than hers. The man had quite a herd of cows requiring additional sheds to house them in. From her perch high above she could see the bustle of activity as the farmhands prepared to go out and harvest potatoes. A late crop. The potato harvester idled in the farmyard.

She glanced up at the sky. Not a cloud was in sight. It was an ideal day to get the potatoes in. Well that was going to have to change. She nudged the cloud that soared up into the sky. It was amazing how far away she could still feel its presence. It felt like riding on its back.

Despite the apparent absence of clouds, she could feel clouds potentially everywhere, although, unlike her cloud, they were tame and docile, as if no one had woken them. Her cloud chased them out of their torpor, forcing them to take shape, and, whipping up a wind, herded them back in the direction of the farm. By the time the men had reached the field, a dark, heavy mass of clouds hung over the farm. She saw farmhands glancing nervously up at the sky but they continued their work, driving the harvester into place.

Fran felt the moment the cloud let go and released its rain. It was an odd sensation, rather like wetting yourself, but without the shame. First there were a thousand timid trickles that quickly transformed into a deluge nothing could stop. Within minutes the field of potatoes was waterlogged. Farmhands scurried for shelter, abandoning the harvester where it is stood.

It was clear what the cloud had in mind. The more it rained, the more the field would turn to a giant sea of mud and begin to slide inexorably down the hill towards the farm, overturning the potato harvester as it did. Following every track left by farm vehicles, the mudslide would gain speed as it hastened greedily onwards, gathering ever more mud and stones as it did. Fran could imagine the screams of the farmhands as they fled the farm, closely followed by a stampeding herd of cows bellowing their dismay. Refusing to be deterred by the flimsy outhouses, the mudslide would sweep through, flattening everything in its wake.

Enough! she told the cloud. *This was meant to be a warning not a hecatomb.* No answer was forthcoming, lest it be a rumble of thunder, but she felt its stubborn reluctance. *I said STOP*, she insisted, pushing with all her presence against its ill-tempered resistance. After a long moment, the tension between them relaxed and the cloud gave way. The rain eased and the sun burst through the clouds producing a brilliant rainbow that arced across the sky.

Thanking the cloud, Fran turned to go only to discover Nelly standing right behind her, a broad grin on her face. She'd been so absorbed by the cloud, she hadn't noticed the girl creep up. "What are you doing here?" Fran exclaimed in a tone that would have cut through any sensitive person.

"I followed you," Nelly said, unable to conceal a sly smile. "I suspected you might do something after what you said about the other farm. I knew you'd use magic. And now I've seen it with my own eyes. How do you do that? Can you teach me?"

"Let's go have some tea," Fran said, shivering. "I could do with a warm drink." The cloud had returned damp and cold and, wrapped around her neck, it wasn't making her any warmer.

As they trudged back down the hill in silence, Fran wondered what to do with Nelly. She'd taken the girl in, believing she'd found a kindred spirit, but Nelly wasn't at all what she'd expected. They might both have been abused by a violent man, but the more she got to know Nelly, the more irritating she found the girl, especially when she tried to ape Fran. Then there was the insensitiveness of the girl insisting on sleeping with her. The shallowness of her reactions. The superficiality of her comments. And now spying on her and loudly insisting Fran did magic. The cloud was eager to mete out justice but Fran opposed her veto. But one thing was sure, she had to do something. The girl was becoming a liability.

I can't just eliminate her, she told the cloud. *Imagine how terrible the world would be if I snuffed out everyone who annoyed me or who frustrated my plans!* She pictured clouds swallowing each other up without the slightest qualms. Boundaries and identity were different for them. That said, her own cloud must be at odds with most clouds, attached as it was to her. It had an identity and couldn't lose itself so easily in the mass. *I wish you could talk,* she told it. *I'd dearly like to know how that feels.*

Tea made, Fran poured a cup for Nelly and herself, then sat down across from the girl. "What would you like to do with your life?" Fran figured they'd best start with plans for the future rather than speculating about imagined magic.

"Be like you," Nelly responded immediately, smirking.

"I don't think you'd like that," Fran said, frowning. Did the girl have any ideas of her own? "Imagine I weren't here, what would you do?"

"I'd be back working with that filthy banker, stuck there for the rest of my life."

"But you're not there." Fran found it difficult to keep the irritation from her voice. The restlessness of the cloud made it worse. "A whole load of other possibilities are open to you. What would you choose?"

The girl shrugged. "I'm quite happy with the way things are."

"Imagine I gave you a sum of money and a train ticket, where would you go? What would you do?"

"I'd put the money in the bank, sell the ticket and come straight back here."

Fran got to her feet, downed the last of her tea and took a step away from the table, determined to shock the girl to her senses. "Go upstairs Nelly," Fran ordered, deliberately hardening her tone. "You have five minutes to pack. I'm sending you away. It's for your own good."

The girl looked at her aghast. "Surely you don't mean that."

"I do. I'm sorry, but your future is not here. You have to make it yourself, separate from me."

"What about my room?" she whined. "You promised. I've never had one of my own."

Fran wanted to reply that she'd have a room the day she had an identity to go with it. Instead she said, "That'll come, no doubt. You're a resourceful person, I'm sure some day you'll have one."

"But you promised..."

Her strategy was not working. The girl was so entrenched in self-pity that no amount of threatening could get through to her.

"Calm down, Nelly. I have no intention of sending you away." Fran softened her tone. "I apologise. I thought my threats would make you realise you can thrive on your own. I was wrong. All the same, I do suggest you go upstairs and think over what just happened."

The girl was reluctant. No doubt imagining she might be banished all the same. "It'll do you good," Fran encouraged. "Take time to think things over then come back down and tell me about it." The girl finally accepted when Fran agreed she could try on one of her dresses. But only one.

When the girl didn't come down after ten minutes, Fran climbed the stairs, only to find her bedroom empty. Nelly's clothes lay discarded on the bed and the girl's tiny hold-all had been overturned. Even the pocket money Fran had given her was strewn across the floor. Checking the cupboard, Fran found one of her dresses missing. Had the girl fled after all? It didn't seem likely. Rather, it looked as if there'd been a struggle. Could Nelly have been kidnapped? She checked the windows. All firmly shut. No one had got in that way.

Where ever had the girl gone? Fran searched the whole floor but found no sign of her. What alarmed her most was that the cloud was nowhere to be found either. She called, but could only feel its nebulous presence a considerable distance away. Damn the thing. Had it abandoned her too?

Back in the kitchen, she brewed another pot of tea and waited for Jakob to return. He'd know what to do. He always had good ideas. She snorted, irritated at herself. Why should she have to depend on a man? In Xristy's world they'd done away with men and boys - although God knew how - and life was much better without them. She remembered Xristy's kisses and those of Xristy's sister and licked her lips in anticipation. A fat lot of good that would do her. She was still banished. Getting to her feet, she stomped the kitchen, periodically aiming a kick at the dustbin as she walked past.

The sound of a car driving up put an end to her angry rant. Refusing to rush to greet Jakob, she opened a novel she'd just begun - another pleasure her father had deprived her of - and plunged into the story. But instead of Jakob breezing into the kitchen, a knock rang out at the front door. Without the cloud to protect her, she was reticent about answering. The person knocked again, insistant.

Peering round the doorframe, she spotted the silhouette of the priest about to knock again. "Coming!" she called out and hurried to open the door. She deeply disliked the man, but she couldn't leave him stranded on the doorstep. Doing so would condemn her to a prime place in his next sermon. She could just imagine. Something about the faithless turning their backs on God's message.

She showed him into the kitchen and offered him tea. She was glad she'd put away the biscuits. The man was fat enough without her help. Not mincing his words, he launched directly into the subject of his visit. "You can't continue to live in this large house all alone. A young woman, unmarried, without close relatives and no one to care for you..."

His words sparked such a fury, she was glad the cloud wasn't present. She'd have sent the priest back to his church with a raging storm up his backside. She was wondering what to do with him before his self-righteousness exploded into a full-blown witch-hunt when she felt the cloud return. Rather than reassure her, it's presence only heightened her annoyance, as she continued to listen to the priest's tirade in stormy silence.

In mid phrase, the priest abruptly halted, looked up at the ceiling a long moment, uncomprehending, then down at his lap, his face red with embarrassment. Stumbling to his feet, his hands clutched protectively over his crotch, he rushed for the door muttering apologies as he went.

"What on earth was that about?" she asked the empty room. Getting to her feet she went to examine where he'd been sitting. Nothing could be seen on the ceiling, but the seat of the chair was wet and a large puddle had formed under it. Had he wet himself? Surely not. Then she remembered the cloud. *You did this, didn't you? You made him think he'd peed himself.* She burst out laughing and could have sworn the cloud was grinning with self-satisfaction.

17.

"Where's Nelly?" Jakob asked, glancing around the kitchen. "Surely she can't still be asleep."

"I threatened to send her away," Fran said, surprised at how dismissive she sounded. She hadn't planned to be so blunt. Embarrassed, she ducked down to take the casserole out of the oven? She'd prepared a stew.

"You did what?" Jakob exclaimed, clasping his head between his hands. "Tell me your joking."

"No. I suggested she leave." She placed the casserole on the table. "I thought the threat might shake her out of the slavish way she imitates me. But now she's really gone."

"Gone? Where?"

"No idea. She just disappeared."

"I worry about you. Why on earth did you do that?"

She ladled stew into their plates, saying, "Eat. It's better hot."

Getting no answer, he asked, "When are you going to send me away?" He sounded bitter.

A little voice in her head whispered, 'Now!', but she resisted the urge. Could the cloud be up to its mischief again or was this all her? She couldn't keep shoving people away every time they tried to get close. That was what Xristy was doing to her. "I have no intention of sending you away," she said and the moment the words were out of her mouth she realised it was partly a lie.

Jakob didn't look reassured. She had the impression he was

struggling with a desire to get up and walk out. All of a sudden she wondered if he'd become so attached to Nelly he'd prefer to run off in search of her. The thought stung. Could he prefer the girl? Jealousy! She didn't want to go down that road. With a sigh, she said, "I have a secret to tell you..." Talk about fleeing one difficulty right into the arms of another!

At the declaration Jakob looked alarmed. What could he possibly be imagining? Better to get it over with. But where to begin? "I..." No. Not Xristy and her world. That would be too much. "I said I had a guardian angel," she felt the cloud perk up in anticipation. "I was not joking." The expression on Jakob's face was unreadable. Was that fear? Or resentment? Or anger even? It was incredulity, for sure. "My guardian angel takes the form of a cloud that is always with me..."

He burst out laughing. Only to halt immediately, his hand over his mouth. Had he realised how hurtful that laughter was? "My apologies," he muttered. "It's just that what you say is ... so hard to believe."

"If I show you, I'm afraid I won't need me to tell you to leave. You'll dash out the door and never look back."

"Try me," he challenged.

She was about to get the cloud to demonstrate its abilities when Jakob shot her a penetrating look. "A cloud you say? Did you have anything to do with that sudden downpour at the neighbour's farm?" His question was clearly less of a suspicion and more of an accusation. "The whole town is abuzz with the news. A freak storm wiped out a whole crop. The farmer's gone mad. He's running around shouting you're using witchcraft to kill him. Last I heard they'd lugged him off to the clinic."

He paused to study her, troubled thoughts visibly flitting across his face. "You did say you'd let nature do its work... What did you mean by that?"

Hell! What a disaster! Cornered! And all her own doing. "I will tell you the whole story. You probably won't believe me, but at least hear me out." He nodded. She drew in a deep breath and began. "I was out riding one evening..." She told him about Xristy's visit but tiptoed round the kissing. By the time she reached the encounter with the old cloud, Jakob was getting restless, disbelief clearly visible in his frown.

She showed him the scar which he examined at length. Physical contact seemed to reassure him. When he didn't let go, she continued her story, acutely aware of his touch. "It was as if the cloud had adopted me and in doing so a part of me had become a cloud."

"Where is this cloud of yours?" he asked, finally relinquishing hold of her hand. "I don't see anything."

"It's coiled around my neck. That's where it generally stays when it's not off somewhere." She felt the cloud unfurl and watched fascinated as it settled on Jakob's hand. He looked down at his hand in alarm. He clearly felt its touch even if he couldn't see it.

Fran continued her story. Skipping over the episode at school, she headed straight for the confrontation with her father. "So you killed your father in self-defence?" Jakob surmised.

"No. At the time I had no control over the cloud. It reacted instinctively to protect me, not understanding the transitory nature of life. Clouds are always present even when we can't see them. When they do become visible, they flow in and out of each other, losing themselves in the mass then reappearing. They have no identity of their own. So they have a very limited understanding of death." She was letting herself get distracted.

Leapfrogging from one key moment to the next, she halted at the man on the hill. "When he drew a gun, the cloud jumped to protect me." She explained that she discovered the man was a messenger from the neighbour who saw her as a weakling who could easily be forced to sell her farm. "There were two more of his thugs waiting for me in the kitchen..."

The story of the mist in the kitchen had Jakob chuckling. A good sign, she hoped. Drawing her story to a close, she described the deluge on the neighbour's fields. "That was when I discovered Nelly spying on me. I don't think she had malicious intent. I hope not. She was just besotted. She was always trying to get into bed with me, to cuddle up close, to dress in my clothes, to be me. When I asked her what she wanted to be, all she could say was me."

She sighed, remembering the blind stubbornness of the girl. "I tried to scare her into changing. I threatened to send her away. It made no difference. She just pleaded with me to stay."

"So you had that cloud of yours get rid of her?"

"No! I did nothing of the kind." His suspicion sparked anger. "I suggested she take time to think. She went upstairs and I never saw her again."

"So she slipped away without a word?"

"I don't think so. If she'd left I'd have seen her go."

"So that's your story?" he asked.

She nodded, unsure from his noncommittal expression how he was going to react. "Now do you understand?" When he didn't respond, in desperation, she resorted to encouraging the cloud to convince him. It was a dangerous gambit. She had no idea what it would do.

Standing in the middle of the table next to the casserole was an empty fruit bowl. Jakob gasped when a tiny cloud formed in the air above it and began to rain into the bowl. A sudden miniature flash of lightning had the bowl split in two as a rumble of thunder rang around the kitchen rattling the windows. The water that spilled onto the table quickly froze as an icy wind whipped about the bowl and the rain was replaced by snow, dusting the table white. Then, just as suddenly as it had begun, the snow, the sheet of ice, the cute little cloud, everything was gone, leaving only a broken bowl in the middle of the table.

"Good Lord!" Jakob exclaimed. "That was amazing!"

Where all Fran's heartfelt words had failed to move him, a little theatrics from the cloud had done the trick. Fran was unsure whether to be grateful - after all only a bowl had been broken - or annoyed at being upstaged by a cloud.

Jakob bombarded her with questions while she slid the casserole back into the oven to heat up. Most of his questions she couldn't answer. He seemed bent on testing the limits of what the cloud could do. He was trembling in anticipation, such was his excitement, entirely invested in the potential of things, in the future, with little interest in the present. She wondered if his behaviour was typical of all men.

They had long finished their meal and were on the second cup of tea when Fran asked, "What exactly were people in town saying about that storm?"

Apparently another freak storm had hit the church school a few days earlier, although there had been much less damage. "Nobody was hurt thanks to the courageous efforts of a young girl, a pupil at the school." He looked questioningly at her. "Was that you?"

She shrugged. "I did what I could."

"You didn't mention that earlier..." he accused.

"So much has happened, I chose to give only the essential bits."

"What are you going to do now?" he asked. "That neighbour and his thugs were probably not the last to try to take advantage of your 'weakness'. It's a shame Nelly left. Having others live here might help stave off such forays."

"That reminds me, the priest dropped by this afternoon to let me know how unacceptable living out here on my own was." She chuckled. "He didn't stay long. He had an unfortunate accident and had to leave in a hurry."

Jakob looked alarmed. "What did the cloud do to him?"

"Made him think he'd wet his pants, or whatever priests wear under their cassock."

"That must have been very distressing for him," Jakob said, unable to conceal a grin. "About time someone put a stop to that man's arrogant pontification."

Jakob's words surprised if not shocked her. She'd never heard anyone criticise the priest so directly. Not surprising, maybe. The few people in her parents' circle had all been devout Christians who would have seen questioning a man of the cloth as a sin. At school the orthodoxy was even worse and, at home, if ever he'd heard her calling into question the words of the priest, God's voice on Earth, her father would have given her a severe thrashing.

"Did you not go to church when you were young?" Fran asked.

"Why do you ask?"

"Because you are so free with your condemnation of the priest, I wondered what your history with the church had been."

"Usual sort of nonsense. Altar boy. Choirboy. Bell ringer. You name it, I've done it. They even wanted me to go into a seminary to become a priest."

"Why didn't you? You'd have been much better than him. At least you've got something to say. All he does is spout what he's been told to say."

Jacob glanced around the kitchen, presumably looking for the crucifix.

"I burnt it," Fran said, shrugging. "Along with his dirty magazines."

Jacob whistled between his teeth. "Wow! Brutal. You're even more harsh than me."

"It's the hypocrisy I can't stand," she said. "That, and the violence in the name of the institution. To think my father would beat me with righteous indignation, quoting the bible as he did. And all the while, unbeknown to me, he drooled over pictures of naked women in glossy magazines."

"In comparison, my life was easygoing. My parents went to church regularly but they were not fanatical. When it was a question of me attending a seminary, they would have been delighted but didn't insist. I think I turned against religion at school. Unlike you, I didn't attend a denominational school. We had a French teacher who delighted in telling us stories about the horrors the church had committed. About witch hunts as a way to put women down. About the avidity that had churches decorated in gold while the faithful went hungry. And, above all, he warned us never to get trapped alone with a priest. So doubt was my daily diet."

A knock at the door had them looking up startled. Both were

on their feet and ready to run when the door cracked open. Then, to their surprise and alarm, Nelly staggered in, her dress torn, her face haggard, her eyes wild and confused.

18.

Nelly's legs buckled under her and she collapsed. She would have hurt herself badly had not Jakob dashed to catch her. He carried her into the neighbouring room and laid her on the couch. Fran followed, sliding a cushion under the girl's head. "What ever happened to you?" Jakob asked.

The girl stared up at him as if he were a complete stranger speaking a foreign language. Then her eyes darted to Fran and she flinched. "Keep away from me," she muttered, trembling violently.

"Can you make some tea," Jakob suggested. "She's in shock." When Fran turned to go, he added, "Put lots of sugar in it."

Leaning on the kitchen sink as the kettle came to the boil, Fran couldn't help feeling dismissed. Sure. If her presence frightened the girl, it would be better she weren't around. But that left Jakob alone with Nelly. He would surely question her and Fran wouldn't know what was said. That worried her. What if the cloud had been up to mischief. Someone had got her into that state. If it wasn't the cloud, who could it be? She was tempted to eavesdrop, but decided against it. If it couldn't be said to her face, better not hear it.

Not for the first time, she dearly wished she could talk to the cloud. *Do you know what happened?* she asked. *Of course you do.* Rather than cuddling around her neck as it usually did, the cloud seemed to be sulking in a corner. She closed her eyes and tried to think herself closer. There was resistance, considerable resistance. Whether it was hers or the cloud's, she wasn't sure. She tried forcing her way through the barriers, but the more she pushed, the harder the push-back.

Having paused to pour hot water over the tea, she returned to the challenge. She tried threatening the cloud. That sparked a rumble of thunder and a couple of nasty burns from a stab of lightning. She tried mentally walking backwards toward it, but not knowing where she was going was too alarming. She even tried sidling up to it as if intending to do something else, but the cloud literally gave her the cold shoulder. Only when she caressed it, did it finally let itself be approached.

Curling her fingers mentally into its cotton-like form, she let herself mingle with it as if she were a cloud. To do so, she had to momentarily relinquish her hold on her own body which bound her to one place, to one identity. She could have sworn it purred, or whatever the cloud equivalent of purring was. *What happened?* she breathed. Something stirred in the cloud akin to a sigh and she was sure it was about to reply, when Jakob called out, "Is that tea ready?"

"Coming!"

Nelly was sitting up, streaks of tears down her cheeks. Jakob sat next to her, his arm slung around her shoulder. Neither of them looked happy. "What's up?" Fran asked as she laid the tea things on the low table.

Jakob frowned. "It would seem your friend tried to abduct Nelly..."

"My friend?"

"The... cloud."

Fran stared at him, unsure what to say. True, she'd wondered if her cloud had been involved. But she doubted it would have roughed the girl up as someone clearly had done. "Are you sure?"

Nelly struggled to her feet, pointing a trembling finger at Fran. "I saw what your devilish friend is capable of. It wiped out a whole crop without a second thought. Well, it grabbed me and dragged me off like a rag doll. It had me out of the house and into the wood. I fought all the way. Then all of a sudden it dropped me as if it were no longer interested. I must have hit my head, because I can't remember anything after that."

Fran shook her head. "My cloud would never have done that."

"She saw no physical aggressor," Jakob said. "How do you explain that?"

Fran felt her shoulders slump. Was it possible? Sure it was. But she didn't want to believe it. She looked at Jakob pleading for understanding, but the only answer she got were tight lips and a closed expression.

"For Nelly's safety, she should get as far away from here as possible," Jakob said. "I've offered to take her to a place where neither you nor your cloud will be able to find her."

Fran wanted to object, it was unfair, but what was the point. His mind was made up. She'd been judged and found guilty.

"You mentioned giving her money," Jakob said. "Now would be a good time."

Fran nodded, feeling defeated. She pulled her purse from her bag and counted out a couple of notes and handed them to Jakob.

"Go upstairs and fetch your things," Jakob said to Nelly.

The girl hurried away, her earlier weakness forgotten. Seeing her eagerness, Fran was worried what she might take. Stepping round Jakob, who was standing in the doorway, she climbed the stairs after Nelly.

The girl was busy pulling various articles of Fran's clothing from the wardrobe. "Those are mine!" Fran exclaimed.

"Not anymore," Nelly spat.

All of a sudden, Fran wondered if the girl's story had been true. Could it be just a ruse to get vengeance by stealing Fran's things? She was loathed to use the cloud against the girl. It would confirm the girl's accusations. But she couldn't let Nelly get away with stealing her clothes. The girl was mad. She had some kind of mania, taking herself for Fran.

Entreating the cloud not to be too rough, she had it wind itself around the girl so that her arms were pinned to her sides. Seeing the girl about to scream, Fran had the cloud curl a wispy tendril about Nelly's mouth. With the girl unable to move, Fran pulled a tote bag from under the bed and lay in it the few possessions that really did belong to Nelly. She added a skirt and blouse of her own as a peace offering. Judging from the foul look the girl gave her, the offering was not appreciated.

The cloud released Nelly's arms, but forced her to climb down the stairs and enter the kitchen with Fran following close behind carrying the bag. "Your little protégée tried to steal my clothes," Fran said to Jakob as she handed him the bag. "However sorry I might feel for her predicament, I can't allow that. Take her away before she does any more damage."

She took one last look at Jakob and his angry face, trying to remember the dashing young man she'd seen the first time they'd met. "I'm very sorry this had to end like this. I don't believe Nelly is telling the truth. Although it is clear that something untoward happened to her. I will try to find out and if I do, I'll let you know, if you're still interested in knowing. Goodbye, Jakob."

The sound of Jakob's car faded in the distance and silence fell over the farm. Even the hens had ceased their cackling. Fran slumped at the kitchen table, her head resting in her hands as the cloud wrapped itself cautiously around her neck. *We have some talking to do*, she said. Not that she had any idea how. *I'm sure you know exactly what happened. And I need to know. So we're going to have to find some way for you to tell me.*

Fran shivered. She hadn't lit the range and was beginning to feel hungry. It was getting late and dusk was on its way. Rather than light the range, she went through into the sitting room and built a fire in the grate and then collected slices of bread which she toasted in front of the fire. It was the sort of thing she'd never done as a child. Her father had been against lighting a fire. Unnecessary and costly, he'd have said.

Fresh bread roasted on an open fire with nothing to mask

the taste was unbelievably good. The smell alone had her mouth watering. "Mmmm. Delicious," she said to the empty room and sat back in one of the armchairs. *You can do so many things*, she said to the cloud. *Surely you can find a way to talk to me.*

A long pause followed as Fran munched her toast to the sound of crackling flames. She'd have to tend to her pony, but that could wait. Her mind kept harping back to Nelly trying to steal her identity and the look of anger and disappointment on Jakob's face. She liked the man, even if she didn't like him in the way he wanted. She wondered how much of his anger had its roots in her refusal of him.

As for Nelly, she'd completely misjudged the girl. Here was not the fellow spirit she thought she'd found. The girl was clearly unhinged, although Fran had no idea what could drive a person to want to be in the clothes if not the skin of someone else. She was no psychiatrist. There was probably nothing she could do to help Nelly. All she could do was protect herself from any damage caused by the girl's craziness.

She was debating whether to fetch more bread when there was a subtle alteration in the air, like a shift in emphasis or a variation in the light or a change of key in music. It was accompanied by a sinking feeling in her stomach. Looking up she was startled to see an old man seated in the armchair across from her. With his ruddy complexion, his long white hair shooting off in every direction and his bushy eyebrows completely lacking in discipline, he looked thoroughly windswept. Yes. The word fit him well. That the man was a manifestation of the cloud was obvious from the disturbing hint of transparency about him.

Good evening, she said, guessing mind communication would suit him better.

Good evening Fran. His voice was delicious. It made her want more. Like a symphony in itself, swaying and swerving gracefully around the words, it danced a stately dance with her emotions.

How come you didn't show yourself earlier? she asked, her mental voice sounding flat compared to his rich overtones.

You have to understand that the predominant element of clouds is water. We also have an intimate relationship with air and sometimes we even flirt with fire. In contrast to you, we have little to do with earth, the fourth element. Earth is what gives you form and solidity. It anchors you to the ground. To appear before you I have to tap into your earth energy. That's not easy for clouds. In a similar way, you have to piggyback my affinity for water and air if you want to join me amongst the clouds. But I doubt you wanted a lesson on the differences between clouds and humans. You have other questions.

Yes. What happened to Nelly?

He smiled. *I'm going to have to tell you something of the world I come from. The young girls you met are not the only inhabitants. There are the men. The ones who live outside the bubble.*

But I thought no one could survive in that air.

That's what the girls believe. But the men survive.

I don't see the connection.

He smiled. It was like the sun bursting through the clouds, making her feel warm inside. *Patience. You will. The girls and the men have always been at odds. Most of the time they avoid each other. But occasionally they fight. Recently the men attacked the bubble.*

Is that why Xristy was so ill?

The man shook his head sending his white hair sailing out around his head like his own personal cloud. *I doubt the presence of men would make her ill, but that's what she believes and her illness is real enough. You saw for yourself. As for the effect of bursting the bubble, that's another matter.*

I know she was ill. I healed her, thanks to you. But she still sent me packing. She couldn't conceal her anger and hurt. The memory still stung. It was unjust.

I saw. You shouldn't be too hard on her. Her whole world is based on beliefs that are not always correct, but which are very hard to change.

Have you ever tried?

The man frowned, seeming perplexed. *Why ever would clouds do that?*

So you clouds never intervene?

That is the key question which brings us back to your Nelly. Generally we clouds are above such petty squabbles. He winked at her. What was that meant to mean? Was he joking? *But a few clouds side with the men and some favour the girls. It was those that side with the men who tried to kidnap Nelly.*

Why on Earth would they do that? Surely she's nothing to them.

True. Unless, of course, they mistook her for you.

Me? It didn't make sense. She had no quarrel with those men. *I have nothing to do with their 'squabbles' as you call them.*

Oh! But you do.

She shook her head in disbelief. *Do these men have some lore that lumps all girls together in the same basket?*

He shook his head. *Let me put it very succinctly. Xristy is the real leader of the girls and Xristy is in love with you.*

No way! That couldn't be true. Sure, they'd kissed passionately. But she'd kissed Xristy's surrogate sister too. Had Xristy not continually pushed her away? No. Fran couldn't believe it.

The cloud grinned another of his sunrises as if to say 'How could you possibly doubt me?' *And to make things worse, in the eyes of the men the fact that you've formed a bond with a cloud makes you a powerful, if not dangerous ally that could tip the balance in favour of the girls for a long time to come.*

19.

So, are they going to attack me? Fran asked, wondering if she'd fare any better than Nelly in trying to fend them off.

Not after I scared them away. If there's one thing they'll avoid, it's a conflict with me. He gave her a jaw-splitting grin that made him look much younger.

She had to remind himself this old man was just a form he'd adopted to talk to her. He could just as well have opted for a monkey or a young boy, although neither would have impressed her so much. *Are you stronger than them?*

Not exactly. Her question seemed to amuse him. *Comparing relative strengths doesn't make much sense. Fundamentally, there's only one Cloud and we are all part of it.*

Fran scratched her head. His words took some grasping. *But then how can there be renegade clouds?*

Judging from the old man's smile, he was pleased at her question. *You're right. There shouldn't be. But prolonged contact with humans has 'tainted' some clouds. They have started to think and act like humans. They consider themselves separate. They take sides. They have cut themselves off from the body of clouds. And in so doing they have lost not only much of their strength but also their wider awareness. They are unsure and fearful, worried that someone is going to attack them. That has driven them even further into the welcoming arms of a few men who certainly don't have the interests of the world at heart.*

The prospect was both alarming and reassuring. At least

their powers had been curtailed by rebelling. *But what about you?* Fran asked, her brain in overdrive. *Doesn't becoming part of me cut you off from the others?*

One of my biggest struggles is to remain connected to the great body of clouds while I'm linked to you. You could say I'm being torn apart between the consuming foibles of being an individual and the imperative of being an inseparable part of the great All. But I'll manage.

The concept was so challenging, Fran had the impression just thinking about it was tearing her apart. She had visions of the cloud as a gladiator spreadeagled between horses galloping in differing directions. A far cry from her memories of it joyously diving in and out amongst clouds above the farm. *It must be good to have the support of the clouds here?*

It shook its head sending a cloud of fine white locks swirling around it. *Unfortunately not. Clouds in your world are sleepwalkers. They are no longer free to move where they will and cannot think for themselves. They are driven hither and thither by the elements. They have lost all the deeper awareness clouds have. They are no longer connected to the great Oneness.*

She had never wondered how difficult it might be for the cloud to tie itself to her. In fact, at no time had she imagined herself in its place. The closest she'd come was soaring with it to meet other clouds and the alarm she'd felt at flowing into them. And even then, she'd been caught up in her own feelings. She had no idea what it felt, if it could feel at all.

It seemed amused at her unspoken musings. An alarming prospect crossed her mind. Could it read her thoughts? *You can't...?*

To a certain extent, it replied. *I am a part of you, after all.*

Does that mean I can...? She certainly hadn't been aware of its thoughts other than those it chose to share with her.

You might find it difficult to wrap your mind around my thoughts. They tend to be .... big.

Was that a smug smile she imagined on its face? The anger she felt was immediate and dangerously close to the surface.

She'd had her fill of men and boys telling her she couldn't understand because she was a mere girl.

You don't need to get annoyed, it said. *I didn't mean to belittle you. It's just that being aware of the Whole is something your brain is unaccustomed to. I promise to let you catch a glimpse, but not at the moment. We have other pressing preoccupations.*

Her anger was only partly assuaged, but she resolved to move one. *I need to explain this to Jakob and avoid Nelly doing too much damage. And what of Xristy and the other girls? I should try to help them.*

First of all, you should get some rest. It's almost time for bed and maintaining this form of mine is drawing on your energy, not mine. It is your will to talk to me that makes it possible.

It was loud hammering at the front door that awoke Fran. Judging from the light outside, she'd slept through the night, although she didn't feel either rested or refreshed. She'd had nightmares about men stalking girls through a luxuriant jungle full of dangerous creatures. She'd barely managed to escape but some of the girls had not been so lucky.

Hastily getting dressed she hurried down to open the door. Outside stood three policemen, arms at the ready, their expressions grim. Since when did the police carry arms? Where was the danger?

"We've come to take you in for questioning," the tallest of the three said.

She wished Jakob was there. As a lawyer, he'd know what to do. "On what grounds?" she asked.

"We have received a number of accusations of witchcraft..."

Fran had no idea witchcraft was still pursued as a crime. "What do you mean by witchcraft?"

"It is not for us to discuss such issues. Our job is to make sure you accompany us to the station."

"So you are arresting me?"

The tall policeman shifted uncomfortably from one foot to the other, but rather than answer took a step closer.

"Do you have a warrant?" she asked.

"We have not come to arrest you," a short, chubby policeman replied, "but to invite you to reply to some questions." He at least was a little more diplomatic.

"Good," Fran said. "Then I will come. But not now. I have just woken up and need to wash, dress and have some breakfast. I'll come this afternoon at three."

The taller policeman, who seemed to be in charge, was unhappy but his colleagues persuaded him to accept. "Just in case you're tempted to make a run for it, one of our number will stay to keep an eye on you." He turned to the one who hadn't yet spoken and indicated he should stay.

"I accept," Fran said. "But not him." She nodded towards the taciturn policeman, then she pointed to the one who'd been so diplomatic. "Him. If someone is to keep me company, at least let it be someone I can talk to." The man in question covered his mouth to conceal a smile while the taller leader scowled. He finally capitulated saying a car would be sent to fetch her just before three.

"You hungry?" Fran asked the policeman, once they were alone.

He nodded. "Didn't have a chance to snatch breakfast, what with getting the kids ready for school and helping my wife milk the few cows we have..."

"Busy man. What's your name, by the way?"

"Jock."

"Give us a hand, Jock." And they set about preparing breakfast with Fran enquiring about his family, his job and life in town.

Pushing away his plate, having eaten the lion's share of the meal, Jock looked up and said, "I don't understand. I can't believe you are the evil person people are saying you are."

"What do they say I've done?" Front asked.

He hesitated. "I'm not supposed to say. But you'll hear sooner or later anyway." He sighed. "Some say you wrecked a private school in the centre of town. And then there's that crop ruined by a freak storm that no one can explain. And finally there's that poor girl who claims you stole her identity. She reckons this farm is hers."

Fran burst out laughing, much to the alarm of the policeman. "So that's what she had in mind," Fran exclaimed.

"I don't understand," the policeman said.

Fran told the story of how she first met Nelly and how she'd taken pity on the girl because of the abuse she'd been the victim of. She described how the girl repeatedly wanted to wear her clothes and be like her or even be her.

"You might have some difficulty convincing people," Jock said. "The girl has been telling everyone her story and there are those who have a vested interest in believing her, like the headmistress of that school or the owner of the farm. Even the priest agreed with them."

"But I've been attending that school for years," Fran said, exasperated. "As for that farmer, he knows me well enough. He came to try to convince me to sell my farm. No doubt he thinks he'll get the farm on the cheap if Nelly is the owner." She made no mention of the priest. That ugly specimen could go to hell as far as she was concerned.

Jock shrugged. "It's your word against theirs, and you are all alone."

Not as alone as you think. If the worst came to the worst she could always resort to using the cloud or she might even go to Xristy's world and stay there. "I have to go and shower and get dressed," Fran said, getting to her feet.

"Go ahead," the policeman said. "I'll do the dishes."

The moment she was in her room, she pulled out her phone and dialled Jakob's number. He didn't pick up immediately and when he did, he sounded annoyed. "What do you want?"

"Your help," was all she said.

"And you expect me to help, after all you've done."

"So you believe that nonsense Nelly has been putting around?"

"Of course not. But some of what people say is true. You told me so yourself."

"If you remember what I told you, I was not responsible for what happened in the school. And as for the farm, let's call it divine retribution for the attempts to murder me."

There was a long pause and Fran wondered if he'd hung up. Then he spoke again. "That argument won't hold up in court. You have no proof that there were any thugs let alone that they tried to kill you."

"So, you'll help?" Fran asked, hopefully.

There was another long pause, punctuated by sighs, then Jakob finally asked, "Where are you?"

"At the farm. There's a policeman watching over me. I have to go down to the police station at 3 o'clock."

"Okay. I'll be there in about half an hour. I can't promise anything. Let's see what we can do. But no stunts with that cloud of yours."

She took a quick shower and was coming out of the bathroom naked towelling her hair when she found the old man seated in an armchair looking at her. She blushed and immediately covered herself with the towel.

Don't bother, he said. *There's nothing about you that I don't already know or haven't already seen.*

It was a sobering thought. He'd seen her in her most intimate and vulnerable moments. Even if he was supposed to be a part of her, she had come to see him as separate and as a man. That made all the difference. If Xristy had seen her naked that wouldn't have mattered.

So what are you going to do? the cloud asked. *We could lay waste to the whole town.*

She wasn't sure, but she thought she detected a smile on his lips. *You can't be serious,* she said. *If we did that we'd have the whole country down on us. You can't solve problems by trying to wipe them out.*

You could come back with me to my world. I'm sure we can convince Xristy to take you back.

The idea was appealing, although she wasn't sure she could go to Xristy's world and not have to leave her body behind.

No. We're going to have to find a way through without magical clouds or disappearing acts.

The old man vanished leaving only a vague trace of mist where he'd been. As he did, she believed she heard a faint 'Good luck'.

Thanks, she replied. *Useful,* she quipped, knowing full well the cloud had difficulties grasping sarcasm.

She got dressed and went down to join the policeman and wait for Jakob. She didn't have to wait long. Jakob was punctual. The presence of the lawyer brought a worried frown to Jock's face. Jakob sought to reassure the policeman, saying, "I'm here to accompany my client to the police station."

Fran was relieved to hear he saw her as his client again.

"If you don't mind," Jakob again, "I'd like to talk to my client in private, please."

The policeman glanced at Fran, and when she nodded, he got up and left the room. "You seem to have thing's well under control," Jakob commented. His tone was cold and distant. But at least he was there.

"We talked. When you can talk to people reasonably, it's not so hard to get on with them."

She might be talking about the policeman, but he clearly understood she was also referring to him. "You should've been a lawyer," he said. "I don't know why you need me. I'm sure you can defend yourself quite capably yourself."

"I'm not so sure. There are too many people coming at me from too many sides. I can't possibly fend them all off on my own. I'm really glad you came."

"Have you any news for me? Anything I don't know already?"

She briefly explained what the cloud had told her. "So you see, it wasn't my cloud that attacked Nelly."

"Unfortunately, that doesn't help much. None of that would stand up in court and certainly can't be told to the police. I'm not sure what to do. We'll have to play it by ear."

When it came time to travel to the police station, Fran

refused to go with the policeman, insisting she would go with her lawyer. All the way into town, one police car tailed them, weapons at the ready, as if the men were afraid the two were going to try to escape. Another police car led the way. When they arrived without incident, the armed policemen looked disappointed.

"This is not the police station," Jakob exclaimed, seeing where they were. "This is the law court. What are they playing at?"

The police must have given credence to the stories about her, because she was escorted into the building by an armed guard who nervously fingered the triggers of their weapons. They'd be terrified if they realised she was carrying the cloud wrapped around her neck, ready to strike. She wouldn't of course. She'd promised Jakob. But its presence was reassuring.

Rather than being led into a small room for interrogations, the police marched them into the large chamber that served as a court. A central table had been set up, behind which sat a number of people she knew only too well. The priest. The headmistress. The farmer. His wife. And of course, Nelly, dressed to look like Fran, although anyone that knew Fran wouldn't be taken in. The public benches were mercifully empty, but the walls were lined with armed police.

Fran was made to stand in front of the table, no chair having been provided for her or her lawyer. "This is like a trial," Jakob muttered, sounding furious. "Without a judge or jury." He spoke too soon. Everyone got to their feet as a door at the back opened and an elderly woman strode in.

"Judge Harriet Rainer," Jakob whispered to Fran. Raising his voice so that it rang strong and determined throughout the room, "This is a complete travesty of justice." He made a move to take Fran by the arm and head for the door when a flurry of guns swung up, aimed at him.

"Leave the young lady alone," the elderly woman said, adopting that voice that is convinced it will be heard and obeyed. "If you wish to leave, you may do so, but on your own."

Jakob made no move to leave. Instead, he shifted closer to Fran and whispered, "Maybe we're going to need the pyrotechnics."

20.

Fran had no intention of using pyrotechnics if she could avoid it. A show of force would invariably fling her into an uncertain exile full of flight and fear. What's more, she didn't want to lose her farm. She might have taken no interest in it when it was her father's realm, but now she was the owner, she had plans and hopes for it.

"Stand close to me," she whispered, "just in case."

Jakob obeyed. She was tempted to take his hand, but it probably wouldn't help her case.

"Keep them separate," Nelly wailed, waving her arms like a scarecrow caught in the wind. "They're up to their magic. Be careful."

The elderly woman held up an imperious hand to silence the girl who continued muttering as she was forced to sit by a policewoman. The judge was clearly having none of her nonsense. But the guards around the room heeded her warning and took a step closer, their guns aimed at the two.

"This is not a trial," the elderly woman insisted, waving the policemen back, "as you wrongly surmised Mr Branson. I may be a judge in other jurisdictions, but this is a public hearing that, exceptionally, I have been asked to chair. As you will have remarked there is no public. I judged the subject too sensitive to be discussed in an open session. It would seem the collective imagination is doing overtime."

"You honour, if I may," Jakob began. The woman nodded

her approval. "Why are so many armed police present? Surely that is not normal for a hearing?"

"The evidence, as I understand it, points to the possibility of violent forces at play. The presence of these guards was suggested by the head of police as a precautionary measure. I would not have gone to such lengths, but I agreed. Hopefully they won't be needed."

"I hope so too, your honour," Jakob replied.

"Before we begin," the judge said, "can someone bring two chairs. There is no reason why Mr Branson and his client should be forced to stand throughout the hearing."

A scowling clerk appeared bearing two foldable chairs and handed them to Jakob who promptly unfolded them and gave one to Fran. Not the most welcoming or comfortable choice, but at least it got the weight off her feet. "Thank you your honour," Fran said as she sat down.

The judge nodded in acknowledgement then, turning to the head of police, she said, "I gather you've been investigating this case, maybe you could lay out the evidence and present the people seated at the table."

The man stood, his feet firmly planted a distance apart as if ready for combat. Several medals gleamed on the chest of his impeccable uniform. "Your honour," he began. "This case revolves around a series of freak storms, all of which took place in the presence of this young lady." He pointed to Fran. "The first hit the school. Sister Stroon, the headmistress was at the centre of the storm. Maybe she can describe what happened."

The judge nodded to the nun and the headmistress struggled to her feet, leaning heavily on the table to support her weight. "I was talking to Francesca McKenzie in my office when the storm broke," she began.

What a lie! She'd been about to cane her. Fran wanted to object, but the storm might be seen as revenge if she admitted she was about to be punished. The nun went on to explain how terrifying the storm had been, claiming Fran had gloated over her fear.

"What do you remember of this event, Miss McKenzie?" the judge asked.

"I was terrified. I could hear screaming in nearby classrooms and lightning felled a tree close to the school, setting fire to it."

"Did you 'gloat' as Sister Stroon suggested?" the judge asked.

"Not at all. I was shocked to see the headmistress breakdown," Fran said, shaking her head at the memory. "I was unsure what to do. Seeing your headmistress cry is not the sort of thing that happens everyday. I tried to comfort her and offered to make some tea."

"Is that true?" the judge asked the headmistress. The woman nodded sheepishly. "Then what happened?" the judge pursued.

"I suggested it might be good to check on the damage and see if everybody was okay," Fran continued. "The headmistress agreed and entrusted me with the task. Luckily nobody had been hurt. I spent the rest of the day running errands for her."

"I think we get the picture," the judge said. "I'm sure there's more, but that will do for now." Turning to the head of police, she indicated he should continue.

"Then there was the unexplained death of the suspect's father."

"I object," Jakob said. "The statement is tendentious. Neither is the death unexplained, nor is my client a suspect, as yet."

"I agree," the elderly woman said. "You should refrain from calling Miss McKenzie a suspect. We do not yet know if anyone amongst those assembled here might be a suspect or not. Tell us, what were the circumstances of her father's demise."

"Her father was admitted to hospital after a freak storm hit their farm house. The sus...," he faltered over the word, scowling, "the young woman was present when the storm hit, although she was unscathed. Her father subsequently died of his injuries. Her mother, who became unhinged at the tragic demise of her husband, blamed her daughter saying she was in league with the devil. She had to be admitted to the mental hospital. As a result Miss Mckenzie has inherited the farm."

It seemed obvious to Fran the sergeant was insinuating she manoeuvred the whole thing to get the farm. Jakob, however, did not object.

"What happened according to you?" the elderly woman asked Fran.

"My father had been out all day and came home in a bad mood. He'd had to spend money, something he never likes doing. We'd just finished dinner and he began berating me..."

"Why was that?" the judge asked.

"I'm not sure. I think it was because of a scar on my hand."

"A scar?"

"He seemed to think I'd had a tattoo. He is fervently opposed to tattoos."

"Let me see," the judge said. Fran moved closer holding out her hand. The woman seized it in bony fingers, pulled a pair of spectacles from her robe and peered at the scar. "That hardly looks like a tattoo to me." Releasing Fran's hand, she waved her back to her place. "What has this to do with the storm?"

"It was at that moment that the storm broke. Lightning must have hit the transformer because the lights went out. Furious at being interrupted, my father cursed as he searched for a candle. When a gust of wind blew out the candle he roared with displeasure. I was afraid he'd beat me..."

"Did he often beat you?" the judge asked, frowning.

Memories of all the times he'd taken his frustration out on her reared up causing tears to well in her eyes. She nodded.

"Did he beat you during the storm?"

"No. The windows shattered and wind and rain surged into the kitchen. All was dark. I couldn't see what was happening. But I heard a sickening thud and groans from somewhere on the floor. When I found a torch, I discovered my father curled up on the floor."

"Was he unconscious?"the judge asked.

"No. I moved closer to see if he was badly injured, but he snarled at me and bared his teeth. So I went and phoned for an ambulance."

"And your mother?"

"The shock was too much for her."

"What is this business with the devil?"

Fran frowned. She couldn't accuse her parents of being crazy, although that was probably the case. "Both my parents were very religious. For them, everything was either black or white, good or evil. That involved blaming the devil for all they didn't like or understand. And anyone they didn't like was clearly in league with the devil. My father was not very fond of me." She almost choked on the understatement. "So he often accused me of being an ally of the devil."

The judge nodded, but said nothing. Turning to the head of police, she indicated he should proceed.

"The penultimate incident occurred near the farm of farmer Thomas." He indicated the farmer who was sitting on the edge of his chair. The moment everyone's attention turned to him, he sprang to his feet, anxious to say his word. "She did it," he accused, pointing a finger at Fran.

"Did what?" the judge asked, a model of patience.

"Destroyed my crop," the farmer blurted out.

"And how did she do that?" the judge asked.

"She conjured up a freak storm and flooded all my fields."

"I don't understand," the judge said. "How could this young girl conjure up a freak storm?"

"She called on the devil."

"Ah," the judge said. "Do you go to the same church as her parents?"

He nodded. Glancing at the others seated at the table, he added, "Most of us do."

"What do you have to say to this accusation?" the judge asked Fran.

Now was time to be careful. Surprisingly, the judge seemed to be on her side, but one wrong word could ruin it. "Just after my father died, Mr Thomas called to convey his condolences. He also expressed, in no uncertain terms, his desire to buy the farm. I told him I was not interested. Two days later when I was out exercising my pony, I was accosted by a man on horseback who insisted I go with him to meet people at the farm. When I refused, he drew a gun and raised his voice, threatening me. His tone must have spooked the horse because it reared and threw him. The gun went off before rolling down the slope..."

"Errr... yes. We found it during a patrol," the head of police said, clearly reluctant to the admit it. "We were wondering where it came from. One round had been fired."

"The fall had dazed the man," Fran continued. "His horse had bolted. I checked to see he wasn't seriously injured, but he refused my help, saying I'd have to give in to Mr Thomas sooner or later. As he didn't want help, I left him to fend for himself. Forewarned, I approached the farm cautiously. Two men had helped themselves to beers and had their feet up on the table waiting for me."

"I decided to trick them. I told them the beers were laced with strychnine as a protection against thieves. I brandished a bottle saying it was the antidote. It wasn't true but it scared them so much they didn't try to attack me and even did as I told them. They admitted Mr Thomas had sent them. Apparently, he thought he could bully me into selling the farm. I sent them packing, having administered the 'antidote'."

"Which was?" the judge asked.

"A potent laxative we use for horses."

The judge covered her mouth to conceal her smile. "Mr Thomas, if what we've heard is true, you made a grave error of judgement. Miss McKenzie is far more resourceful than you thought."

"And my fields?" he bleated.

Fran shrugged. "No idea. Maybe nature really did pay you back."

"Indeed," the judge said. Turning to the head of police, she added, "You have one more incident..."

"Yes," he said, springing to his feet. "The unfortunate case of this young girl." He indicated Nelly. "She claims Miss McKenzie stole her identity and, in reality, the farm and everything in it is hers." Clearly the head of police was being cautious. Having had all the other cases dismissed, he didn't want to be proved a fool by this one.

"Young lady," the judge addressed Nelly. "What have you to say?"

The girl's face was flushed as she got to her feet and her eyes were alarmingly wide. "I took in that young woman," she began, nodding to Fran, "out of pity. She was in a sorry state. She'd been ill treated by her employer and I thought I could help her. Unfortunately, she's gone a little crazy and pretends to be me, dressing in my clothes, imitating what I do..."

Jakob burst out laughing, only to say, "My apologies."

"You have something to say?" the judge asked.

Jakob hesitated. "Well, yes." He described their visit to the banker and their encounter with Nelly. He explained how Fran had suspected the girl was being abused and offered to take her in. "Nelly has completely inverted the story. She is the one who has crazy ideas that she is Fran and tried to steal her clothes so she could be like her. If you have any doubts about Fran's identity, remember that none of the witnesses here mistook Nelly for Fran. I suspect she is in serious need of medical help."

"Thank you Mr Branson," the judge said. "It seems clear to me that the accusations of black magic or witchcraft are quite unfounded. That should be made publicly clear. I suggest a statement to the press. If there has been wrong doing in these cases, it is not Francesca that is to blame, she has acted in a mature and responsible way. That can hardly be said of some of you seated around the table. You need to think very seriously about your conduct. I leave it up to the head of police to decide if he wishes to press charges."

21.

"I said you should have been a lawyer," Jakob said as they drove to the restaurant. They'd chosen one in another town to avoid being overheard. The judge might have ordered a statement to the press, but that would take time to have an impact, if ever it did. Jakob chuckled. "That hearing was full of pitfalls and you steered clear of them like a pro."

The restaurant was a small affair, with few tables and even fewer customers. It served Thai food, something Fran was new to. Eating out was a sinful waste of money, her father always said.

"Is it very spicy?" she asked the waiter. On his reassurance, she ordered a red curry as did Jakob.

"So what are you going to do now?" Jakob asked.

"I don't know," Fran replied. "I'd like to make changes to the farm, but my ideas are not very clear." Uppermost in her mind, although she couldn't say so, was the need to help Xristy. But she had no idea how.

"Maybe you could convert part into lodgings and use it for bed and breakfast. Many have done that," Jakob said.

Fran was uneasy about admitting strangers. But living isolated was surely another legacy from her father. It was an alarming thought. The bloke was just as present now he was dead as when he'd been alive. "That's an interesting idea," she replied, not wanting to appear dismissive, "but I feel uneasy about having people I don't know wandering around the place."

"There are ways to create lodgings separate from your private space." He sounded both knowledgeable and particularly enthusiastic.

"Maybe you could suggest an architect and possibly help me get things right. I imagine there are all sorts of planning requirements to be fulfilled."

The food arrived at that moment putting an end to their conversation. When the owner came to ask how their meal was, he stopped and stared at Fran. "You're the girl that was on the news," he said.

She cringed. So everybody knew. "What news?" she asked.

"The girl that caused all those freaks storms," he said, clearly surprised she hadn't heard the news. "I gather she was to be tried for witchcraft. Wouldn't like to be in her shoes. That said, being friends with her might turn out useful if you've got enemies."

"We don't have television at home," Fran said, having got over her initial shock. "I wouldn't trust all you hear on the box. I bet half of it is made up. They have to fill the news somehow. How long have you been running this restaurant?" She could've sworn she heard Jakob chuckle, but she kept her attention on the owner.

"I know. I know," Fran said as she climbed into the car. "You still want me to be a lawyer."

"I didn't say anything," Jakob laughed. "But you did handle a difficult situation rather well. We'll really have to do something about the press and public opinion."

"I suspect we'll have a hard time persuading the man in the street to change his mind."

"Of course, you could always capitalise on this by calling your bed and breakfast The Witch's Lair."

"You have some very strange ideas, Mr Branson. Did you fall on your head as a baby?"

"No. But I'm dyslexic which caused all sorts of problems at school. They say dyslexic people have a lot of imagination and tend to think out of the box. That didn't help much at school.

Although maybe that's why I so readily accepted your claim to have a cloud as a companion."

It was well and truly night by the time they arrived back at the farm which might explain why they didn't see the lorry parked outside the building until the last moment. Splashed across the side in bright red letters were the words Outside Broadcast. As they drew parallel they discovered a camera crew facing the front door which was flooded by spotlights as if a play were about to be staged.

"Oops!" Fran said. "Now what?"

"Time to exercise those diplomatic talents," Jakob said, halting his car alongside the lorry.

"Can't we run away instead?"

The camera crew had spotted them and were training their camera, the lights and the microphone on Fran and the car. "I think they've noticed us," Jakob said.

Fran open the door and stepped out. "Gentlemen, ladies," she began "What can I do for you?"

"Are you Francesca McKenzie?" the reporter asked.

Fran nodded. "What brings you out so late?" Before they had a chance to reply, she added, "It's cold, would you like a cup of tea? I promise not to slip you any magic potions." She grinned at them which didn't seem to reassure them. Maybe you shouldn't joke about such things when you had a reputation for being a witch.

She ducked past the camera and headed for the house with Jakob hard on her heels. Over her shoulder she asked, "Milk or sugar?" They still hadn't answered when the front door closed behind her. She went straight to the kitchen and put the kettle on. Laying out the tea things, she could hear the crew struggling through the front door. "You can leave your stuff in the hall," Fran called out. "You won't need it in the kitchen."

Judging from the muttering coming from the entrance, they weren't happy about receiving orders. Apparently being a television crew gave them all the rights. Maybe that was why they trundled their equipment into the kitchen and blithely set it up, transforming the room into an improvised studio. How to turn everyday life into a television show.

The journalist was a young woman. All the rest of the crew were older men. The woman was hesitant about sitting at the table and Fran had to encourage her several times before she finally sat. Neither the journalist nor the crew dared drink the tea laid out for them. Fran picked up one of the cups, taking it for herself, and sipped. "There. You see. It's not poisoned."

It was the young woman who dared first, gingerly sipping a tiny quantity of tea. When she didn't keel over, she took a second sip and swallowed, nodding to her colleagues that they could go ahead.

"I'm amazed that the very idea of someone being a witch is enough to terrify adults," Fran commented. "Is the belief in witches still so alive and kicking?"

"Are you a witch?" the journalist asked, taking another sip of her tea.

Fran laughed. "Good Lord no. If I'd been a witch, my parents would've had me exorcised four times over. No. There's been a misunderstanding. Apparently the idea of witches still haunts people. So much so, they are inclined to see a witch whenever anything inexplicable happens. The attitude of the church doesn't help. It sees the devil in every dark corner."

"You're against the church?" the journalist asked.

"Not at all. Many churchgoers are the mainstays of the community. It's just that the church sometimes gets it wrong."

"So the church is not infallible?" the journalist asked. "Does that mean that God also makes mistakes?"

"I have no idea," Fran replied. "You'd have to ask him ... or her. But I'm sure you didn't come here to have a philosophical discussion about God."

"No. You've probably heard that you've been accused of witchcraft. What do you say to that?"

"You should ask the judge who chaired the hearing this afternoon. She'll set you straight. Have you spoken to her?"

"I plan to do just that, but I wanted to see you first. I'm

intrigued. How does a girl like you, who apparently wasn't very good at school, develop such far-reaching, radical ideas?"

"First of all, it's not because your school sees you as worthless, that you necessarily are. Sometimes it is the school that is worthless, not the pupils. As for those far-reaching ideas you mention, I love reading. My father banished books from the house, but I was able to read extensively at the library. I also write a lot. I did so in secret because writing was frowned on at home."

"So what do you say to all those who reckon you are a witch?"

"I am no witch. 'Witch' is a label. An oversimplification. A way of belittling someone, of dismissing them. Women and girls in particular. A label coined by men and their allies. A label used for those women they can't understand or control. Rather like my father. He used to say I was the devil. Another label. Not because I had any affinity to Satan. I didn't. But because he hated women and me in particular. I suspect he was afraid of me because I was different. He beat me. Maybe he thought he could beat that difference out of me. How arrogant. Everyone is different. Who's to say which 'difference' is the right one? In reality, I think he would rather have eliminated me..."

"So you eliminated him instead...?" the journalist shot back, hopeful.

"You have a lot of imagination," Fran responded. "No. I did not kill my father. If you had been at the hearing this afternoon you would know that." Fran got to her feet and fetched some biscuits. "Now turn off the lights and the camera. Enough of interviews. Tell me something about yourself."

The young woman looked startled at the idea, but suggested her colleagues pack away their gear which they did begrudgingly. Only the camera remained, placed in the middle of the table. Jakob, who'd been keeping to the sidelines, spoke from the shadows, saying casually, "The camera is still recording."

"That's very unfortunate," Fran said, fixing the journalist. "To think I mistakenly thought I could trust you. There goes our friendly conversation. Shame." She busied herself removing the biscuits before anyone had had a chance to eat one.

"I'm sorry," the young woman said. "I regret too. There's something about you that is compelling." Fran discretely sniffed the back of her scarred hand, wondering if this was Xristy's oil at work, but she could smell nothing. "I would have enjoyed getting to know you better," the journalist continued. "I like the clear way you approach things." She shrugged. "But I have my work to do."

"You do," Fran replied, giving the woman a wry smile. "Time to get on your way. Far from me to stop you doing your work."

No hands were shaken. No goodbyes were exchanged. The whole crew turned and left, backs stiff, expressions hardened. It was only once Fran heard their lorry drive away that she noticed the girl had left her visiting card on the table. Turning it over, she found the name Annie scribbled hastily and a phone number. An opening after all. Fran pocketed the card without comment.

"Thanks," she said to Jakob. "I hadn't noticed."

"It's beginning to look like you have a weakness for untrustworthy girls," Jakob commented, taking one of the biscuits from the packet.

"And you, Sir, have a weakness for biscuits," Fran replied. They both laughed. That he also had a weakness for young girls in distress flitted across her mind.

"You need to be careful with the media," Jakob said, his expression serious again. "They could well edit your interview to make you say quite the opposite. That's why I filmed the whole scene with my phone. Just in case."

"You are very..." Fran never reached the end of her sentence. There was a sound like rushing wind that took away her breath, her vision blurred and her legs gave way as she sank to the ground. She was vaguely aware that Jakob caught her, his arms strong about her, but, struggle as she would to regain control, there was nothing she could do. She was slipping away, ripped from her body by an immense force that wouldn't take no for an answer.

22.

"Bloody hell!" Fran said as her hip hit the floor so hard it rattled every bone in her body. Wherever she was, there was no Jakob to break her fall. Cracking open her eyes, she glanced around. A stern ring of girls stared unforgivingly back. She was lying in the middle of the Council. No point in swearing at them, they couldn't hear. She swore all the same, for the sheer joy of it.

You called, she said, her words laced with derision as she bowed, parodying a servant girl cum genie.

Do people from your world ever take anything seriously? It was Xristy's adopted sister that spoke.

Sure we do, Fran shot back. *Far too often. But you've never given me any reason to take your situation seriously, lest it be my fear for Xristy's well-being. Maybe you should begin by explaining what's going on.* That she should answer back in such an insolent manner brought scowls to the faces of most of those present.

Don't look at me like that, Fran said. *If you want me to help, you're going to have to tell me what's going. Wild men, is it?*

A roar went up from several members of the Council who sprang to their feet, fists clenched. They would have pounced on Fran had not their leader ordered them to be seated. They begrudgingly resumed their seats muttering colourful oaths.

Holding up a hand for silence, their leader said, *There are some subjects we do not talk about.*

Well that's going to have to change, Fran said, surprised at her own boldness. *How do you expect to repel these savages if you refuse to acknowledge their existence?*

She's right, one of the youngest members of the Council dared say, producing hisses of disapproval from most of the others.

If she'd known how to, Fran was tempted to jump back to her own world and let them get on with it. But she was worried about Xristy and didn't want to see her world destroyed. She did have one joker up her sleeve, the cloud. She checked. Sure enough, it was still with her.

As if I'd abandon you! it exclaimed, surprising her by talking in her head. *Yeah. I seem to have got the knack of it. I no longer need to take the form of one of you to talk to you.* She sensed its excitement, although she wasn't sure if it was because it had managed to talk to her or because it was back on home ground. She also sensed its anger at these stubborn girls.

Gently, she warned it. A sudden bolt of lightning shot across the room, curving low over the girls' heads only to crash into the wall opposite leaving a dirty black scorch mark. Several girls screamed, most ducked their heads under their arms, as if that would protect them. Only their leader sat still, defying Fran.

I have no wish to hurt you, Fran said. *But I'm fed up with your obstinate silence. Get your heads out of your arses.* So much for diplomacy! Where was the reserved schoolgirl she used to be? *Stop that!* she muttered to the cloud, suspecting it was tampering with her emotions again.

Who me? it replied, its words underscored by a smug smile.

Men exist, Fran's continued, wrenching her attention away from the cloud's antics. *They're attacking you. If you pursue your blind beliefs, that'll be the end of you. So who's going to have the courage to tell me what's going on.*

The young girl who'd spoken earlier got to her feet. *I'll tell you.* The reaction of the others was tumultuous. Fran was afraid they might kill her but no one moved.

Does it take the youngest and the smallest amongst you to

have the courage? And all you can do is threaten her. If I were your leader, I'd make her my second and send the rest of you packing. Fran's comments caused a new uproar. She ignored it, taking the young girl by the hand, saying, *Is there somewhere we can talk in quiet?*

Much to Fran's surprise, Xristy's sister joined them, a scowl etched on her face. *Someone's got to make sure you do no more damage,* she muttered.

So where do we go?

My room, the leader snapped.

Where's Xristy? Fran asked as they walked the underground passages.

Her sister took a long time answering. *Taken hostage by wild men.*

And you weren't going to tell me? Fran exclaimed, stopping in her tracks. *I don't understand you lot. Have you tried to get her back?*

We can't. The men have taken her out of the bubble. We can't survive out there.

By that token, neither could Xristy.

The leader's room was nothing special, a double bed with ruffled sheets that looked like they'd been the site of a battle, a bedside table, but none of the books you might have expected, only a few rickety chairs. No artwork on the walls. No abandoned clothes littered on the floor. The only thing out of the ordinary was the pervasive scent of Xristy's oil. It had Fran's heart pounding. She had to keep a firm grip on her emotions not to fling herself at the nearest girl and ravage her. How did the two manage to talk casually, seemingly indifferent to its potency? Focus! She was there to save Xristy.

My name's Fran, by way. I didn't catch yours. Both stared at her as if she were mad. Was not sharing names another of their weird quirks?

We don't usually tell strangers our names, the leader confirmed, her tone resembling that of a girl attending the posh school in town. As if Fran were an underling and talking to her required more effort than the girl was prepared to invest.

Fine, Fran retorted. *I'll give you a name then. Let me see. The sister of Xristy is called ... Zanu. How does that sound?*

The girl made a face that was a mixture of disgust and surprise. *Close. Zamia.*

Fran nodded. *And you?* Fran asked the younger girl.

Trixie.

Good. So, Zamia, what's going on between you girls and those wild men outside the bubble? Why are you always fighting?

It's easy for you to talk, Zamia said, her voice trembling as she spoke. *You haven't lived for millennia and thrived on unspoken traditions. You can't begin to imagine how difficult it is to talk about.*

You'd be surprised. I do understand, Fran said. *Where I come from, everyone used to believe the world was flat and at the centre of the universe. Anyone challenging those beliefs could be put to death. It took some very brave people to change the accepted vision of the world. No external threat forced them to change. It was science against theology. In the end science won. Your case is very different. Your very existence is in danger. If you can't come to terms with the changes, in a short while there'll be no more girls in this world. Or certainly not girls as you know them.*

It was Trixie that spoke first, much to the annoyance of Zamia who was visibly struggling to grasp Fran's words. *History tells us we're alone in this world. That must sound absurd when you know we're periodically attacked by men. History also tells us we cannot survive outside the bubble. Maybe that's why we don't believe in these men because they couldn't survive.*

Yet cloud catchers travel outside, Fran pointed out.

True, Zamia hastened to add before Trixie could respond. *The air up there is more breathable.*

But how do you understand the attacks? Fran asked.

We don't, Zamia replied. *Those people that believed your world was flat, how did they react to the suggestion it was round?*

Anger, incomprehension, denial, confusion,...

Well that's how we react to the idea that men could live outside the bubble, Zamia said.

Okay. I understand, Fran said. *But surely someone kidnapped Xristy. You said so yourself.* The two girls nodded. *Now let's have a look at who these people are. Could they be rogue girls from your own world?*

Both girls shook their heads, looking shocked. *That's impossible,* Zamia said. *We have a code of honour that's been drummed into us for centuries. Betrayal is a terrible crime.*

So whoever kidnapped Xristy came from outside.

The two sighed, but nodded reluctantly.

You've admitted these people are wild men. How do you know?

We just know, Zamia said, looking confused at her own words. *Maybe some long-lost memory.*

As Fran was about to pursue the idea, she realised it was not so important, not at the moment anyway. *Do you know anything about these men?* It was a silly question, but she had to ask.

Both shook their heads.

What do they do when they come into the bubble?

You saw our gardens, Zamia said. *They wreak havoc, tear up plants, pull down trees, break windows...*

They sound angry, Fran said. *Why would they be angry?*

It was Trixie that replied. *From what we can see, the world beyond the bubble is in bad shape. There are no plants or trees or wildlife. If there are people, I don't know how they survive.*

Fran wondered why the world outside was so devastated, but knowing the answer was not a priority. *How did they get in?*

How should I know? Zamia said.

Well let's go have a look, Fran suggested.

Both girls paled at the idea. *Remember,* Fran said, *we have a powerful cloud on our side.* Neither girl seemed reassured. Seizing Trixie by the hand, she pulled her out the door with Zamia trotting after. *Show me the way,* she said.

To Fran's disappointment, Zamia had no idea where the

men had broken in. Fortunately Trixie had. *I went exploring and found where they broke in. Follow me.* At the news, Zamia stared at the girl, perplexed, as if seeing her for the first time.

The council chambers and the girls' lodgings were situated near the centre of their world, so reaching the wall of the bubble entailed a considerable walk. Fran relished the chance to move. All that siting made her feel uncomfortable. But the two girls were quickly tired, as if they were unused to walking. If she'd been their leader, she'd have obliged them to get more exercise.

The closer they got to the walls, the more damage they encountered. Judging from the chaotic way the men had meted out their anger, she guessed this was no coordinated attack. The wall of the bubble had not actually been breached. There was an airlock, a bit like in a space station, presumably to keep contaminated air out, except that the door had been wrenched off its hinges. Examining it closely, she saw this was no sophisticated break in. Someone had battered the door till it'd given up and let them in. The same went for the second door on the far side which lay on the ground, broken in two.

Standing in the doorway, Fran looked out on a scene of sheer desolation. No living thing was in sight. Just scorched earth and giant boulders. The sky was heavy with clouds and an intense smell of burning and chemicals filled the air. A narrow path, no doubt worn by the passage of men, meandered amongst the rocks. Turning to speak to the two girls, she was surprised to find she was alone. Looking back, the two were just visible on the far side of the airlock, peering round the remains of the first door, their expressions terrified.

When waving for them to join her had no effect, she retraced her steps and took Trixie by the hand, tugging the girl through the airlock. She figured if the young one went, the leader would be obliged to follow. So much for well laid plans. At the sight of the girl outside the bubble, Zamia began to tremble violently. *Can't you see you're killing her,* she wailed as her legs gave way under her and she sank in a heap on the ground.

For all her doubts about the girls' beliefs, Trixie was visibly astonished at finding herself unaffected by being on the wrong side of the bubble. However, seeing Zamia collapse, she broke free of Fran's grasp and ran back to the fallen girl.

With Fran's help, Trixie heaved Zamia's head onto her lap and produced a tiny flask from her pocket which she opened and wafted under Zamia's nose. *The attacks are getting worse,* she mused.

Clearly Trixie was referring to Zamia's fit and not the depredation caused by the men. *So this has happened before?* Fran asked.

Yes. Every time something challenges a long-held belief. Her attacks have been occurring more and more often, as if they were building up to some sort of climax.

In a world of rigidly held beliefs, Trixie stood out as different. *You don't sound like a believer?*

It's not really a question I've asked myself. You'd think I'd be one seeing as I'm a member of the council, but then almost every girl is nowadays. There are so few of us left. Yet I'm not very active in the discussions. I don't always get the point. Their logic seems odd if not alien. I prefer to spend my time looking for new herbal remedies and taking care of those girls who occasionally get sick.

While they talked, Xristy was in the hands of violent men. The longer they tarried, the more chance there was the girl would come to harm. *We should go, if we want to save Xristy.*

You go. I have to tend to Zamia, Trixie said. Judging from her disappointment, the girl was not making excuses. She wanted to go.

Okay, Fran said. *Wait for me here. I'll bring Xristy back if I can.*

Are you sure you can handle those men? Trixie asked glancing at the shattered door.

We have men in my world, Fran retorted. *Some of them can be violent, very violent.* She thought of her father. *I would be untruthful if I said they didn't frighten me, but there are ways of dealing with them.* So saying, she stepped through the airlock and headed down the path.

23.

Fran had been walking for nearly half an hour without encountering any sign of life, lest it be some spoils torn from within the bubble only to be discarded along the way. Despite the absence of life, she had an uncomfortable feeling she was being watched.

You do well to trust your intuition, the cloud informed her. *Several people are moving near us. But they're too weak to be dangerous. Do you wanted me to get rid of them?*

No! she replied, horrified at the emotionless way it talked of eliminating them.

Just suggesting, it replied, in no way repentant.

When a disheveled youth jumped out from behind a rock and stuck out his tongue at her, knowing they were there didn't stop her gasping in surprise. Where the girls were clean and colourfully dressed, this young man was coated in grime and his clothes, if you could call them that, hung in shreds about his meagre body. He was so thin, he looked like he could do with a good plate of bacon and eggs, or two.

He must have expected her to bolt, because he looked confused, if not alarmed, when she stood her ground. *Hallo*, she said mind-to-mind. *Can you take me to your village?* When her greetings got no reaction, she tried talking out loud. "Hallo," she repeated. Her one word elicited a grunt and raised eyebrows. Of course, none of other girls could talk or hear. And these youths apparently couldn't 'hear' mind-speak. How about that for a recipe for conflict. Fran burst out laughing, causing the youth to flinch and take a step back.

The moment he moved, she noticed the stench. It was so overpowering, she wondered she hadn't noticed before.

The wind was behind you, the cloud explained.

"Phew," she said, with newfound candour, "you need a wash."

Allow me, the cloud said, raining all over him in a shower that fell in a tight circle about him. The downpour was so sudden and unexpected - it clearly rarely rained there - the youth stood unmoving, his mouth fallen open in wonder, half drowned but clean.

"That's better," Fran said, taking a step towards him. "Now take me to your village."

Shaking off some of the water like a bedraggled dog, he scuttled away along the path, but not too fast she couldn't trot after. The increased effort quickly had her gasping. The air might not be poisonous, but it was certainly heavily polluted. The youth must be having difficulties breathing too, because he slowed to a walk.

She speculated if it was the pollution or the lack of food that had stunted his growth.

Both, the cloud said, eavesdropping on her thoughts.

She was unaccustomed to being taller and stronger than boys. It made her feel more confident. That, and having the cloud at her side.

Don't forget, the cloud said. *These youths have a couple of rogue clouds on their side. The ones that attacked your Nelly. Not that they could best me, but you should be wary.*

Along the way more and more youths jumped from behind rocks, each attempting to scare her with a gruesome grimace as they rivalled for who could stink the most, till Fran was accompanied by a silent but odoriferous guard of honour. The stench was overpowering and there seemed little hope of escaping it. *Rain on us,* she told the cloud. *I'd much prefer to be soaked than suffer this stink.* So it was that the group of a dozen youths escorting Fran arrived dripping wet but considerably less smelly in their 'village'.

Village? Is that what you call this huddle of dilapidated shacks, precarious tree houses and unsavoury burrows? the cloud asked. *More like a slum, if you ask me.*

The youths led her to a large canvas structure in the centre of the village that looked like a mammouth tent with its sides ripped off. Tables had been arranged higgledy-piggledy under the canvas along with chairs of all sorts and sizes. A number of youths lounged in the shade, all eyes turned to watch her.

The sagging canvas was held up by a number of wooden poles, the largest of which stood in the middle. Attached to it by cords knotted around her waist, ankles and neck drooped Xristy. *Are you alright?* Fran hastened to ask.

Do I look alright? Xristy responded, as belligerent as ever.

Is that how you greet the heroine come to rescue you? Fran replied with a grin.

I don't need your help, Xristy spat. *Go back to your world and leave me in peace.*

Remind me to give you a good spanking when I get you out of here, Fran said. She was joking, but it might be interesting to try. Xristy's only reply was a rude noise. Maybe not then.

"So gents, what seems to be the problem?" Fran asked, turning to address the gaggle of youths.

Some looked alarmed, no doubt worried at the prospect of a girl who could talk. And rightly so. One or two did whistle their approval. At least, she hoped that's what it was. The tallest amongst them, although still not taller than her, wove his way through the crowd to plant himself in front of her. Unfortunately he wasn't one of those that had been washed clean by the cloud. She held up a hand to halt his advance. "Keep your distance," she said, screwing up her nose in disgust. "You stink."

The expression that flitted across his grimy face went from astonishment to anger before settling in an amused smile. "You don't smell so good yourself," he retorted. "It's that oil."

Interesting. So Xristy's oil repelled boys. Could it have

kept her father at bay? Probably not. When he got mad, he was oblivious to everything. "Point taken," she said. "So why is my friend tied up?" she asked, nodding to Xristy.

"She's our hostage."

"What for?" Fran challenged.

Her question had him confused. He paused before answering. "What do you mean, what for?"

"People take a hostage because they want something. What do you want?"

"We're fed up seeing you lot lounging around in that bubble of yours, eating your fill and ignoring us."

She glanced at Xristy who was looking away, feigning disinterest. Of course, she could hear nothing of their exchange. Which was part of the problem. That and the fact that the girls insisted these wild youths didn't exist.

Good luck with sorting that out, the cloud said.

"What do you eat?" she asked, thinking tackling the food problem might earn her some goodwill.

"Nothing, most of the time." It was not so much an answer as an accusation.

She wanted to complain that their lack of food had nothing to do with either her or the girls. But pointing it out wouldn't help. "Show me where you get your food." She'd seen no plants or trees and no wildlife either, so it was no wonder they were starving.

The youth shrugged, as if showing her was pointless, but turned and led the way through the gathering and down a slope to what once must have been a river. Now only the dried up riverbed remained. Water was long gone. Behind them the whole community trailed, muttering to themselves.

Kneeling down on a sandy patch, the youth fingered the sand in several places then began scraping a hole with a flat stone to reveal damper sand beneath. Plunging his hand into the wet patch, he pulled out a wriggling creature that looked like an oversized shrimp. Brandishing it triumphantly in the air, he said, "We eat this, amongst other things." He ripped the shell covering from the thing, stuffed the remaining flesh, still alive, into his mouth and chewed with obvious relish. Bloody boys!

Fran turned away in disgust and glanced back at the crowd of youths staring hungrily on. "Are there enough to feed you all?" The youth shook his head. "What else have you got?" The youth led her away along the river bed. Round a bend, they came to a patch that had been cleared of stones in which a number of plants were struggling to grow. They looked a bit like carrots, but like the boys, their growth was stunted.

"There's too little water," the youth complained.

"I don't understand," Fran said. "You've befriended a couple of clouds. Why don't you get them to provide water?"

"We've seen them hanging around," the youth admitted, "but we have no way of asking them anything."

Are they nearby? she asked her cloud.

Yes. Two of them. But they're keeping their distance, afraid to come any closer.

Is there some way I can make my voice carry as far as them?

Sure. I'll magnify it.

Listen you two, she said, her mental voice taking on some of the authoritative rumble of old father cloud with the help of her cloud. *If you want to side with these youths, you should do something useful. Help them water their crops.* They didn't exactly reply, but she felt their acceptance. *Do so now, as a token of your goodwill,* she ordered. Rain began to fall, a light rain that wet the sandy soil but did not wash the struggling plants away.

A gasp went up from the youths, who, judging from the state of the land, might never have seen rain in their lives, except, of course, those who'd been dowsed earlier. *Enough,* she said to the clouds. *Well done. I appreciate the careful way you did that.* Turning to the leader of the youths, she said, "You might want to move your plantation out of the river bed. If there's more rain and the water rises, it could carry your plants away."

"How on earth did you do that?" the youth asked, his attitude almost reverential. "Could you teach me?"

"I could try," she replied, turning to head back up the hill to the village. "It might work. In the meantime, have you got any buckets?" When he nodded, she added, "Line them up by the tent."

He looked at her as if she were mad, but sent youths scattering in search of buckets. She made the most of the pause to voice her doubts. *I want to get a delegation of girls to come and meet these youths,* she said to her cloud. *Do you think that would work?*

I doubt it. To say the girls are set in their ways would be an understatement. Maybe if you could win Xristy over, she might convince them.

Fran groaned. She wasn't having much success with the girl. *Could you do me a favour and fill those buckets?*

The youths gathered round the filled buckets, their mouths agape at the sight of so much water. "I am going to try to fetch you food," she told them, "and while I'm gone, I want you to wash yourselves and your clothes thoroughly. You should also clean up this area," she waved at the tables under the tent, "and prepare to receive honoured guests."

There was considerable grumbling at her request. They were reluctant to part with their filth. She wondered if Wendy had had the same problem with the Lost Boys. Probably not. They had welcomed the older girl with open arms and treated her as their mother. It was easy enough to make that happen in a story. She doubted this lot even knew what a mother was. Not that she had any desire to play mother to the rabble. It'd be a life of slavery. Just that a less tense coexistence between girls and youths seemed desirable. If only she could bring the two sides together without them fighting, maybe some of their long-held beliefs could be safely challenged.

Can you keep an eye on them while I'm away? she asked Xristy, gifting the girl, who was still trussed up like a turkey waiting to be roasted, a broad grin. *Make sure they don't do anything stupid.* Judging from the string of abuse Xristy flung at her, she didn't appreciate Fran's humour. *No? Oh well. We'll just have to trust them.*

Turning to the leader, she said, "I'm Fran, by the way. What's your name?"

"Bruno," he said haltingly as if unsure of his own name. Apparently names were not much used amongst the youths.

"Well Bruno, I hope to be back in a couple of hours, although you'll need to be patient, what I am trying to do is not easy. I expect you to do your part while I'm away. And no mishandling of my friend while I'm gone. I don't think I need to threaten you. I'm sure you can imagine what would happen should my friend get hurt... That said, I don't advise untying her. She can be quite unpredictable when she's upset."

24.

Seeing Fran arrive, Zamia - apparently recovered from her attack - struggled to her feet, refusing a helping hand from Trixie. *You stink,* she said, wrinkling her nose. Pulling a small bottle from a pouch at her waist, Zamia was about to spray her when Fran held up an imperious hand.

Don't! Fran shouted.

The girl took a step back in mock alarm, as if she wasn't aware that using aphrodisiac oil was all about power and control. *Why ever not?*

Because that stuff drives me wild. One whiff and I'd be swarming all over you like... Words failed her.

Zamia gave her a calculating once-over only to grin mischievously. *I wouldn't mind.*

Kisses and the rest can wait till later, Fran replied, steeling herself against the prospect of unadulterated pleasure.

Zamia made a show of pouting, but stowed the bottle. *So? Did you find Xristy?*

Yes. I found her. She's in good hands. She had to smile, picturing the furious girl tied to a post, shooting daggers at her with her eyes as Fran walked away leaving her at the mercy of the youths. *We've got things to do,* she said, glancing at Trixie who was standing meekly by, watching the exchange in silence.

Like what? Zamia asked, reverting to her regal arrogance.

Prepare a meal.

Who for?

For some ten starving people.

Zamia looked shocked. *We ration our food very carefully. I can't allow that.*

Fran couldn't fault Zamia. She had no idea how much food the girls had in stock. Nor where they got it, especially with some of the gardens destroyed. By feeding the youths she might be putting all the girls at peril. She'd been blithely trying to force her ideas through without considering the consequences. If she wanted to succeed she'd have to change tactics. And she'd have to begin by getting to know this world better.

Now she had a dilemma. She'd promised the youths food and left Xristy as a token of her goodwill. Getting to know the world would take time she didn't have. It crossed her mind she might bring food from her own world. But that was not without dangers. She had no idea if it would suit people from this one. She had nightmare visions of bringing illnesses with her and spreading them in Xristy's world. She might even already be doing so. Then she had an idea.

Is there anything that grows here that you don't eat but which could be eaten by others? she asked.

Zamia frowned. *We have so little space, we only grow what we can eat.*

Made sense. But didn't help. There seemed to be no other solution but to risk bringing foodstuff from her world. Of course, to do so she'd have to learn how to travel between worlds. She'd only ever done so because someone else brought her.

Do you know how to? she asked the cloud. It gave her a mental nod. In asking, she realised, she'd assumed it was privy to her thoughts. She'd need to find ways of shielding thoughts she didn't want heard. *Do you know any reason why I shouldn't bring food from my world?*

Other than those you've already thought of, no. Its words were accompanied by a grin, confirming her suspicions that it could read her thoughts. How come she couldn't do the same?

I'll explain, it replied to her unspoken question, *some other time.*

If I can find food from somewhere else, Fran asked Zamia, *would you come with me to present it to the youths that are holding Xristy?*

I thought you said she was okay?

She is. But she's also a hostage.

Zamia was furious. *You lied.* She shook her fist at Fran, an empty gesture seeing that she clearly didn't have the strength to carry through with her threat.

No I didn't. I said she was okay. And she is. She's in no danger.

I refuse. The girl folded her arms across her chest and stuck out her chin in defiance. *You can't be trusted.*

Trixie, who'd been doing a good job of staying inconspicuous, stepped forward and said in a trembling voice, *I'll come. These youths intrigue me. I want to see what they're like.*

No, exclaimed Zamia, furious. *You can't. It's too risky.*

That's how leadership changes hands, Fran said with a chuckle.

Zamia gave both her and Trixie a filthy look and stomped off.

First, we have to go to my world to fetch food, Fran said. *Do you wanna come?*

The expression on the young girl's face was a confused mixture of emotions. Fear maybe, longing probably, but excitement also. *Yes,* she said, her voice unsteady. *I'd like that.*

I must warn you, Fran said, *people communicate differently in my world. You girls exchange thoughts directly mind to mind. Whereas in my world, we make sounds that we call our voice using our mouth and throat,* she pointed to each part of her body to help Trixie understand. *Those sounds we can hear with our ears. Because you've never used your ears, you can't hear what people say. Like people in my world, the youths in your world also communicate with their voices and their ears.*

It suddenly struck Fran how vulnerable the girls must be. They couldn't hear anyone sneaking up on them. But maybe they could sense the presence of someone because of their thoughts. She resolved to ask later.

No wonder we don't get on with those youths, Trixie exclaimed.

Indeed. Fran said. *Hold my hand.* Speaking to the cloud, she asked it to transport her and Trixie back to her world. *I'll learn how to do it some other time,* she told the cloud.

Their arrival was somewhat chaotic. She'd completely forgotten she'd collapsed into Jakob's arms just before being wrenched away, which is exactly where she found herself when she arrived back. Trixie, who was standing next to her, screamed at the sight of a fully grown man capturing Fran and scurried across the kitchen, upsetting several chairs as she tried to hide behind a door. Jakob screamed too, and in his surprise, let go of Fran who tumbled heavily to the kitchen floor.

No doubt imagining Fran was being attacked by Jakob, Trixie dashed across the room, shoved a surprised Jakob out of the way and stood protectively over the girl. *You're very brave,* Fran said, struggling to her feet with Trixie's help. *But this man is not attacking me. He's a friend.*

"What the hell is going on?" Jacob asked.

"Meet Trixie," Fran said. "You remember I told you about the world where Xristy lives, well, Trixie comes from that world. Like all the girls from there she's both deaf and dumb. So there's no point in trying to talk to her."

"How on earth do they communicate?" Jakob asked.

"Mind to mind."

Jakob looked at the girl with admiration. "I wish I could do that."

Trixie, this is Jakob, a friend of mine.

But he's a man, Trixie exclaimed, astonished.

In this world men and women, boys and girls, are not separated like in your world. At least not most of the time, Fran thought. Maybe they should be. It would solve a lot of problems. *And create many others,* the cloud added.

"Is she hungry?" Jakob asked.

It was a bit of an odd question given that, in this world,

they'd just come from the restaurant. Typical of Jakob. Ever-ready to jump in and help. *Are you hungry, Trixie,* she asked. The girl nodded shyly, clearly intimidated by Jakob. "Yes," Fran said. "She is."

"I'll make something," Jakob said. "Are there things she can't eat?"

Fran frowned. She'd never eaten anything in Xristy's world. She had no idea. Turning to Trixie, she asked, *Are there things you don't like to eat?* The girl had no idea either, having never eaten food from Fran's world. "Make her a number of small dishes so she can choose," Fran suggested. The girl's choice might give her some idea what to take to the youths.

"I'm gonna go check on my pony," Fran told Jakob. "I'll take Trixie with me."

She took the girl by the hand, led her out of the kitchen, through the hall and into the yard. The girl halted, staring up at the sky which was laden with stars. *There's no bubble,* she exclaimed.

No. We don't need one. Air is not so polluted here.

That's so beautiful, she murmured, leaning back to get a better look. *Do you think...* she halted, clearly at a loss for words.

Stars, you mean?

Yes. Stars. The girl savoured the word as if discovering a delicious new dish. *Do they exist in my world? There are always so many clouds.*

Probably. Fran had the impression the girl could spend all night staring at the stars. She took her by the hand and led her to the stables. When Trixie caught sight of the pony she screamed. Her scream spooked the pony which kicked at its box causing Trixie to scream even more. *Stop!* Fran said. How did you explain a horse or a pony to someone who'd never seen one?

We call it a pony, she told Trixie. *It lets us ride on its back, which means we can get from place to place more quickly.*

You keep it enclosed? Trixie asked, venturing a little closer.

Yes. We don't let it roam freely. It might wander off. We give it a stable to live in, like this one, and food to eat. That's what

I've come to do, feed it. Do you want to help?

Once the pony was fed and Fran had apologised to it for not taking it out for a ride, they headed back to the kitchen where Jacob had prepared a feast of tiny dishes that covered most of the table. Fran might have only just eaten in this world, but with all the time she'd spent in the other one she was quite hungry. "Mmm. That looks good," she said, encouraging Trixie to join her at the table.

Trixie sniffed the bacon and the eggs but wouldn't touch them. Apples and pears she adored. With yoghurt she hesitated but when Jakob added oats, she ate all the mixture. Cheddar she liked. Stilton she twisted up her nose at. *It's gone off*, she told Fran. Bread was her favorite, especially with butter and jam, more jam than butter. She liked the bread less when toasted, but with honey it was acceptable. Carrots and radishes were hard work. Apparently she wasn't used to chewing. But the freshness pleased her.

Fran, who'd explained to Jakob about feeding the youths, said, "We're going to have to take quite a selection. The boys might well prefer meat and eggs while Trixie avoids them."

"Do you think the girls will come too?" Jakob asked.

His question had a suspicion sneaking into Fran's mind. What if he hoped he'd have more luck with them than with her? He was a man. It was to be expected. "Maybe, if Trixie invites them. They're terrified of anything new. But some of the younger ones might follow her."

Trixie was enjoying herself so much that she didn't want to stop. *You'll make yourself ill*, Fran said. *You're not used to this food. That'll do.*

Sure enough, only a couple of minutes later, Trixie turned pale and Fran had to rush her to the toilet. No such fixtures existed in Trixie's world so Fran had to show her what to do. With much heaving and retching, the girl threw up at least half of what she'd eaten, but once her mouth was rinsed, she wanted to return and eat more.

"We're going to have to be careful not to give them too

much," Fran told Jakob. "Otherwise, they'll gobble it down only to throw it up straight afterwards."

"You talk as if I'm coming with you," Jakob said.

He seemed game, although Fran was reluctant to share Xristy's world. She might have revealed its existence, but going there remained her secret. She was also concerned how he would react when he realised she was enamoured of Xristy. Some men got quite violent about girls making out. Her father for one. Devil's spawn, he'd called them. A bit rich from someone who hoarded pictures of naked girls doing things together quite unsuited for Sunday school.

"Would you like to?" Fran asked.

Jakob grinned and, as if that was not clear enough, he nodded vigourously.

"Remember," she said, "you'll be able to talk to the boys, but not the girls." Seeing how Trixie had first reacted to him, she didn't expect Jakob would get anywhere near the girls. They'd be running away. Then again, with all the youths present, the dynamic might change.

He shrugged. "Maybe someone will agree to teach me this mind-speaking business."

It was a dig at her, of course. He'd hoped she'd show him. But she didn't want to. She was unwilling to give up the advantage it gave her. She could talk to Xristy, for example, without him being able to listen in.

25.

Backpacks crammed with food, the three stood in a tight circle holding hands as the cloud lifted them out of Fran's world and set them down by the broken airlock door. Fran heard Jakob gasp as he gripped her hand even tighter. She scanned the surroundings for danger. The only possible threat was a petulant Zamia who stood leaning against the bubble wall presumably waiting for them to return.

Trixie had spotted her too, because she broke from Fran's grasp and ran to embrace her leader. Zamia held herself rigid and didn't return the hug, much to Trixie's chagrin. *Don't be like that,* the little girl said, shaking Zamia's arm, unsuccessfully trying to get her attention. *We've just returned from a great adventure.*

How dare you bring that man here! Zamia told Fran, her voice cold and dismissive. *This is our world, not yours.*

Oh! You can see him, Fran replied, grinning mischievously. *I thought men didn't exist for you girls.*

Zamia crossed her arms over her chest, refusing to rise to the taunt. Turning to Trixie she said, *By the power invested in me as leader, I banish you from our world! You are no longer welcome here.*

Trixie looked at her in disbelief, shaking her head. *You never were a very good leader,* she said, not in anger but in sadness. *Shame your adopted sister refused the job.*

Zamia's reaction was immediate, her hand flew out to slap

the girl's face. It never connected. The cloud was faster. Zamia flew through the air and hit the transparent wall of the bubble with a sickening thud only to slide slowly to the ground in a heap. Trixie bounded across the space between them and knelt at Zamia's side holding the girl's hand.

Jakob released Fran's hand and hurried to join Trixie. "Is she all right?" he asked, forgetting Trixie couldn't hear him. "I've brought a first-aid kit. There must be some smelling salts in here somewhere," he said rummaging in the little bag.

Trixie pointed to his bag and shook her head. She rolled the unconscious Zamia on her side and struggled to open the tiny pouch that hung from the girl's belt. Pulling a bottle free she prepared to spray the oil up Zamia's nostril. *No!* Fran called out. Too late! Trixie sprayed, causing Zamia to jerk to life and throw her arms around the girl in a passionate and slurpy kiss.

Jakob jumped back, his nose wrinkled in disgust. "What a stink!" he exclaimed only to stare entranced as the two girls rolled over and over in wild lovemaking.

Fran took him by the arm, struggling not to give in to the call of Xristy's oil, and led him away, saying, "Let's leave them to get on with it. That could take a while."

He looked at Fran in disbelief. "What the hell's going on?"

"These girls have an oil..." she began.

"That stink I smelt?"

"It doesn't smell bad to girls. It's an irresistible aphrodisiac..."

"How come you didn't jump on her too?" he asked, glancing back at the two girls who were tearing at each others' clothes.

"With difficulty," she replied between gritted teeth as she tugged him further away.

"And you agree with this?"

She wasn't sure if he was disappointed or disapproving. "You bet! With the right person..." She paused, remembering Xristy's lips on her breasts and sucked in a shuddery breath. She couldn't entirely escape the effect of the oil, even at that distance. "...it can be exquisite."

He stared at her in disbelief. "So you are... you prefer..." She nodded. He looked profoundly disappointed as the truth caught up with him. Well, at least it wasn't anger. "Now I understand," he muttered. What exactly he understood he didn't say.

She glanced at the girls who were oblivious to the world. Fran would willingly have left them to their rapture, but she didn't have the time. She turned mentally to the cloud but before she could request anything, it replied gleefully, *With pleasure.* Whipped up by a sudden icy wind, a shower drenched the two girls in freezing water. Both screamed and sprang apart, cursing the cloud and, seeing Fran looking on, her too.

Fran was reminded of her father chucking a bucket of cold water over a couple of dogs trying their luck in the farmyard. The comparison was not flattering. *That wasn't very kind,* Fran scolded the cloud. *You could at least have used warm water.*

That would only have made things worse, it shot back.

She had to concede it was right.

Did you order that? Zamia asked furious, her teeth chattering as she struggled to get warm.

Not exactly. But we have to go. You two can play any time you like, whereas saving Xristy cannot wait.

Who are you to give me orders? Zamia snapped.

The stubborn arrogance of the girl annoyed Fran. *I'm not giving you orders,* Fran said coldly. *Why would I? You're the leader, aren't you? No. I was talking to Trixie. I wasn't aware you were interested. Of course, you can come if you want.*

Seeing Trixie shivering violently with wet and cold, Jakob stripped off his jacket and wrapped it round her shoulders. Fran handed the girl her backpack and shrugged her own onto her shoulders. "Ready?" she asked Jakob. He nodded, still visibly shocked by what had happened. They stepped through the airlock with Zamia gripping the door frame, watching them go.

Looking back over her shoulder, Fran called out, *You sure you don't want to come?* The girl pouted, hate in her eyes.

Shame, Trixie said, *Zamia can be a really good person, but sometimes she's just so pigheaded.*

"She doesn't want to come?" Jakob asked, surprised. Of

course, he hadn't been in on the conversation.

"No. As a leader, she doesn't think she should take orders from anybody else."

"Yeah. I've met people like that," Jakob said. "They don't stay leader very long, unless of course they use force."

"It's not her fault," Fran said, "she's just adhering to age-old traditions."

Things are changing much faster than she or the others can keep up with, the cloud commented. *It happens from time to time. The natural fabric of events suddenly buckles and the unexpected happens. There's no taming it. Yet, as leader, she feels obliged to hold things together when it looks like they're falling apart. The feeling of loss of control can be devastating.*

It's words reminded her of the headmistress who'd broken down when the cloud had laid waste to her school. The devastation had rendered her incapable of action. She'd behaved like a lost child, effectively reversing their roles. It had been a disturbing experience.

Unlike the headmistress you're thinking of, that girl's reaction will be different, the cloud added. *She'll probably try to regain control by force, fighting the natural flow of events rather than accepting them. The result is likely to be a disaster.*

Fran tore herself from the conversation in an effort to concentrate on the task at hand. She led the way along the winding path between the boulders. She wondered how long it would be before the first of the youths sprang out to greet them. And, sure enough, as if thinking about them made them appear, several jumped out in front of them. They looked considerably cleaner than before, but still not clean enough, judging from the smell.

"Meet the youths, I told you about," Fran said.

"We should've brought soap in addition to food," Jakob said wryly.

The youths seemed fascinated by Trixie, maybe because she was more their size. They chatted incessantly to her, mostly about how pleased they were to see her and other less savoury subjects that can't be repeated, but she just stared back blankly.

"You're wasting your time," Fran told them. "The girls can neither hear nor talk, so she has no idea what you're saying." Thank heavens, she thought to herself. "This is Jakob, by the way," she said. "He can both hear and talk. So be careful what you say."

As they entered the village, Fran tried to imagine how Jakob must be seeing it, with all its rickety treehouses, the tumbled-down hovels and what looked like giant rabbit burrows. It was a far cry from the neat semidetached houses that most of Jakob's clients must live in. From his face, she guessed he was both horrified and fascinated. "Interesting?" she asked. He nodded vacantly, as he continued to stare wide-eyed.

When they reached the centre, Bruno stepped out of the giant tent to greet them. He'd clearly made an effort. His face was washed and his hair might even have seen a comb. Around his waist he'd fixed what looked like a small towel that served as loincloth and over his shoulders he'd slung a curtain, rings and all.

"Meet Trixie," Fran's said, indicating the girl. "She's both deaf and dumb. So no point trying to talk to her. But don't misjudge her. She's not at all stupid."

This is Bruno, he told Trixie. *He's head of the youths.*

"And this is my friend, Jakob. He helped us fetch food for you." Turning to Jakob, she added, "This is Bruno, head of the youths."

The introductions over, Jakob and Trixie, who seemed to work well together despite not being able talk, set about cleaning one of the tables and laying out food. As for Fran, she had her hands full preventing the youths grabbing food before it was ready to eat. They were so starving the sight made them even wilder. Once she'd taken the time to explain the problem to Bruno, he sent the youths to fetch instruments. Apparently they made music on special occasions.

"Where's Xristy?" Fran asked, realising the girl was nowhere in sight. When Bruno looked perplexed, Fran added,

"The girl who was here before."

"She was getting on everybody's nerves," Bruno said, making a face. "She kicked up such a stink, we moved her to the river where she can shout as much as she likes. We tied her up to a boulder."

"Show me," Fran said.

Bruno led her down the path to the dried-up river bed. She didn't immediately spot the girl, hidden as she was on the far side of a boulder. When she finally caught sight of her, Xristy was slumped forward unconscious. Fran hurried forward and untied her. If she'd had some of that oil, she would've tried Trixie's trick to revive her, although she didn't fancy making out in front of Bruno.

"Have you given her anything to eat or drink?" Fran asked, cradling Xristy in her arms.

"Why should we? We don't have any for ourselves."

Good point. What she needed was a little food from the village. If only she could call Trixie. She had no idea if mind speaking could reach so far. *Trixie?* she called out, not holding out much hope.

Yes, the girl replied immediately, sounding surprised. *Where are you? We've been looking for you everywhere.*

Down by the river.

So far away! I didn't know we could talk over such a distance.

Apparently. Listen. We urgently need a little food and something to drink for Xristy. She's in bad shape.

I'd bring it, the girl said, *but Jakob and I have our work cut out stopping these youths gobbling all the food in one go. What a band of uneducated savages.* Trixie giggled. *They're a laugh though.*

I can fetch it, the cloud told her, *if it's wrapped in something.*

Wrap the food up, Fran told Trixie, *and put it in one of our backpacks. The cloud will come and fetch it.*

When the backpack came flying though the air, Bruno's hair stood on end and he clasped one hand over his eyes. The other he fisted and stuffed into his mouth to stop himself screaming.

"It's alright," she told him. "I asked my friend the cloud to bring it." Her words didn't reassure him. As Fran reached out and grabbed the bag, he cringed away as if it were enchanted.

Ignoring his antics, she extracted the package from the pack and unfolded it. Trixie had included a small goat's milk cheese wrapped in a vine leaf and a rosy-red apple. Remembering how she'd fed Xristy the first time they'd met, she broke off a piece of cheese and slid it into her mouth then bit a chunk of apple and began chewing the two till she had a delicious, soft paste. Pressing her lips against those of Xristy, she pushed the mixture into the girl's mouth with the tip of her tongue.

When it began dribbling back out, Fran was obliged to push even deeper into the girl's mouth. Finally Xristy swallowed and Fran was able to repeat the process until all the cheese and apple were gone. As she paused for breath, she caught sight of Bruno watching her avidly, a distinctly unhealthy glow in his eyes. She trusted the cloud would protect her if ever the youth got the wrong idea.

What made kissing the girl so exasperating was the constant smell of Xristy's oil that had Fran trembling with desire. She wanted nothing more than to plunge heart and soul into the girl and be swallowed up. But she couldn't. She had to resist. Although, in the heat of the moment, she no longer remembered why.

26.

That's the second time you've fed me like a fledgling, a breathy voice whispered in her head. The raspy sound sent shivers down Fran's spine.

Xristy, Fran exclaimed. *Good to hear your voice.* No more words were exchanged. They were too busy kissing... until a loud cough insinuated it's way between them. Bruno. "Excuse me," he said, "but..."

Fran pulled free of Xristy's embrace and hauled the girl to her feet, both standing unsteadily. *We have a diplomatic mission to fulfil,* Fran said.

A what?

Come and say hello to your captors, Fran joked.

Xristy stiffened, her expression darkening... until Fran kissed her again. *Come and meet the probable future leader of the girls,* Fran said, teasing.

Whatever happened to Zamia?

She failed to rise to history...

Stop talking in riddles. Has my adopted sister been replaced?

Not yet. But I'd wager she will be soon.

By whom?

Trixie.

Trixie! You must be joking. She's the smallest and youngest amongst us. That shy little thing couldn't lead a fly.

Come and see.

To their astonishment they found Trixie and Jakob in the

middle of a wide circle of youths, dancing a wild dance to the accompaniment of drums and fifes amid enthusiastic cheers of encouragement. Jakob was beaming. Fran had never seen him look so young and full of life.

Trixie broke off abruptly, much to the disappointment of the youths, the moment she spotted Xristy. The music faltered and stopped as all turned to face Fran and Xristy. Trixie took a step towards the older girl and, in so doing, seemed to shrink in stature till she became the shy girl she'd once been. Fran had a strong impulse to shake her, saying, 'You're so much more!'

Xristy, Trixie said in a tiny, almost apologetic voice. *You're safe.*

That's more than can be said for you, Xristy commented, sourly. The haughtiness and arrogance in her voice shocked Fran, who promptly let go of her hand.

You dance well, Fran said, hugging Trixie who seemed uncertain faced with Xristy's hostility. "You dance well, Jakob. Who'd have thought?" She chuckled, then, turning her back on Xristy, she walked Trixie and Jakob in amongst the youths who congratulated the dancers. The more the praise, even if she couldn't hear a word of it, the more Trixie rediscovered her new-found confidence.

Glancing briefly over her shoulder, Fran saw Xristy standing outside the group, her expression one of incomprehension. She had no wish to punish the girl further, even if her haughtiness, which resembled that of her sister, annoyed her. Leaving Trixie and Jakob to their accolades, she returned to Xristy's side and took her by the arm. *Come meet them,* she said. *At heart they're good people.*

Xristy scoffed, at which Fran gently shook her. *Now, now. None of that family haughtiness!* Fran said, planting a kiss on the end of her nose. *You're much better than that.*

Xristy shot her a confused look as if she couldn't decide between surprise at Fran's self-assurance and directness or anger at being confronted. Fran gave her no time to figure it out. Tugging her towards the group, she said, *Leave that tempting refuge of superiority for a moment and allow yourself to enjoy meeting new people.*

By the time night fell, Trixie had danced a wild jig with every single youth. Fran wasn't sure if the glow that surrounded the girl was due to the exertion or the proximity of so many eager youths. Even Xristy, who watched from the sidelines, was persuaded to dance by Jakob thanks to elaborate sign language and much trial and error.

Bruno had lots of questions about food. He was interested in growing some of the plants from Fran's world. The main problem was lack of rain and limited sunlight under a constant cloud cover. "You have a couple of allies amongst the clouds," Fran pointed out. "Why don't you ask them to help."

"Pretty idea," Bruno said. Fran wondered if he were making fun of her, but his expression was serious. "It's true, a couple of clouds do hang around, but I'm not even sure they're friendly. And we have no way of communicating with them."

Fran could've offered to intercede, but she was wary of interfering in local politics. They had to sort this out themselves. What's more, she was unsure what influence she could possibly have on the clouds. It wasn't because she'd inherited a cloud by some fluke, that she had a say in their affairs.

You're right to be circumspect, the cloud said. *Not because you can't influence clouds - you could - but because negotiating the entrenched positions of the different groups is full of traps.*

Fran was pleased to have her choice confirmed. At the same time, she was intrigued to know she could sway clouds even if she had no idea how.

"We should be getting back," Jakob said. "Before it gets really dark."

Fran agreed. Seeing Bruno walking nearby, she asked him "Have you got a lamp or something we can use to light the way?"

He shook his head. "Haven't seen a light for years and years."

Fran went in search of the two girls. She found Xristy

examining musical instruments with a youth who was showing her how to play them. *We should go,* she told the girl who jumped at the sound of Fran's voice, so engrossed was she in what she was looking at. *Time to go,* Fran repeated.

Be with you in a minute, Xristy said.

When Fran found Trixie, she was even less willing to leave. She was learning new dance moves from a couple of youths. *Can't we stay till tomorrow?* the girl asked.

No, Fran said. *We need to get back. There's no place for you to sleep here.* Of course, Fran was sure that any one of the youths would find her a space to sleep next to him. For all the apparent promiscuity of the girls, Fran wasn't sure this little girl understood what it meant to sleep with a boy. *You can come back another day.*

Trixie made a face and stuck out her tongue at Fran, before hugging each of the boys and dutifully following her back to Jakob and Xristy. "Can you grab the backpacks?" Fran asked Jakob. "We'll probably need them again."

Fran half expected Zamia to be waiting for them at the airlock, a pout frozen on her lips. But the place was deserted.

Trixie halted at the threshold, and refused to go any further. *I don't think we can go in,* she said.

Why ever not, Xristy asked. *This is our home.*

Zamia banished us.

She can't do that, Xristy exclaimed. *That's not in her powers. I'm going to have to have a word with my sister. She seems to have lost her mind.*

"What about me?" Jakob asked, excluded from their mute conversation. "If these girls dislike men so much, maybe I shouldn't come with you."

"I don't think I should go either," Fran said. "I may be a girl that understands their way of communicating, but I'm as much an outsider as you."

Wise choice, the cloud said. *Profound change is underway, but taking this man in there would be too much at the moment.*

I think we're going to have to leave this battle to you, Fran said. *I am not in Zamia's good books. She sees me as someone come to overturn her world. Jakob and I will return home.*

Trixie was disappointed. *How are we supposed to confront that crowd if we don't have your help?* she asked.

You'll manage, Fran said. *You two are by far the best of all the girls.* Trixie clung to her when she hugged the girl in farewell obliging Fran to prise the girl's fingers open to get free. Fran would have kissed Xristy much longer, but Jakob's cough reminded her they were not alone. *See you soon,* she whispered.

To Fran's surprise, Trixie hugged Jakob, who seemed overwhelmed by her gesture. Being unable to participate in the girls' conversations must have set him apart even more than being a man. So this sudden inclusion visibly touched him. No words were exchanged, but he lent forward and kissed Trixie briefly on the forehead like a father saying good night to his daughter before coming to stand at Fran's side.

Addressing the girls, Fran said, *Speaking between minds seems to work over considerable distances. Trixie and I experimented. If there's trouble, try calling me. Who knows? Maybe it'll work. If not, I'll be back tomorrow. May the goddess of girls watch over you and protect you.* She took Jakob's hand, nodded to the cloud and it whisked them back to a darkened kitchen. Night had fallen and a wind was rattling the window panes as if it wanted in to shelter from the cold.

Even with the lights on, the kitchen seemed empty and desolate without Xristy and Trixie. Jakob must have had the same impression, because he hurried to light a fire in the living room while Fran put the kettle on and went in search of chocolate biscuits. To her disappointment she found none. But she did uncover a packet of crumpets that Nelly must have bought on their shopping spree. Seated side by side on the carpet, their backs against armchairs, they toasted crumpets in front of the fire as they basked in the fire's warmth and sipped tea.

"So Mr Branson, how does it feel to have travelled to another world?"

Jakob didn't reply immediately. Instead, he stared at the

flames flickering round a log. "I feel like I haven't completely returned," he finally said, his voice distant. "As if I'd left a part of myself behind. I don't know. My heart maybe, or my soul."

"I know what you mean," Fran replied, seeking inspiration in the same flames. "For me it's not so much that I've left something behind, but rather that there's a powerful link that joins me to Xristy's world, a bit like an invisible ombilical cord that continues to nourish me."

"Your love for her?" It was both a question and an affirmation.

She liked to hear him say it, as if doing so implied an acceptance she longed for. "Not only. It's as if that world was somehow also mine."

"If that cloud is part of you and it comes from that other world, doesn't that mean a part of you really is from there?"

An intelligent man, the cloud said.

She mentally nudged the cloud that was comfortably curled around her neck. *You're biased,* she replied, a chuckle in her voice. Turning to Jakob, she said, "I've often wonder 'why me?' Why did the leader of the clouds pick me? I'm nothing special. Just a common schoolgirl with an unfortunate choice of parents."

"Unfortunate indeed," Jakob said handing her another crumpet. She shook her head, refusing. She'd eaten enough.

"When things got really bad," Fran mused, "I used to imagine they were not my real parents. That there'd been a mixup at birth. Or that I'd been secretly adopted. But dream as I would, I couldn't escape the violent reality that was mine."

"Not until that cloud came along," Jakob pointed out.

I told you he was insightful, the cloud quipped.

"Indeed," Fran replied, ignoring the cloud's remark. "It saved me. Literally. I think my father would have killed me that night if the cloud hadn't intervened." She shivered at the thought, stretching out her hands to the fire in search of warmth.

"I'm glad it did," he said, sliding an arm around her shoulders, pulling her closer.

She stiffened, intensely uncomfortable at his touch. It was

so difficult to distinguish between kindness or friendly affection and that which strove to be more. He must have sensed her disapproval, because he immediately withdrew his arm and sighed deeply.

"Please don't be upset," she said as he shifted to put some distance between them. "It's just that I find it hard to be sure what men's intentions are. My father would hit me with all his might. You'd have said he wanted to kill me. He probably did. As if I were the bad in him that he desperately wanted to drive out. Then, in the next breath, he'd run his fingers through my hair or pull me tight against him as if we were lovers. It was terrifyingly confusing. I wanted to be loved, of course I did, I craved it all the more that I was severely punished so often, but not like that, not by him..."

Jakob looked stricken. "That's dreadful. I can't comprehend how a man could do such harm. It pains me even to think it. But that's not me," he said, running a hand across his face. "I couldn't be further from your father. I'm not interested in THAT." There was disgust in his last word.

She couldn't conceal her scepticism. "First me, then Nelly, and I've seen you with Trixie..."

"Okay. I am attracted to young girls," he admitted, blushing. "I tried avoiding them - why do you think I have so few friends? - but it is stronger than me."

Fran tensed at the revelation, fearing the worst. What was it about her that attracted monsters?

"I like their company," he went on, sounding wistful. "But it has nothing to do with...well, you know, getting physical." He looked away, embarrassed. "It's as if being with them makes me whole." There was a long pause filled only by the crackling of the fire. Fran waited, sensing more to come.

"I had a twin sister," he said, his voice almost a whisper. "Her name was Esther. We were very close. We spent a great deal of time together, talking, playing, or simply just being with each other. I would have protected her with my life. But in the end I could do nothing to save her. She died of tuberculosis when she was twelve. To make thing worse, my parents kept me away from her for fear I'd get ill too. I wish I had. It'd have been easier to die with her than be left behind."

"Oh Jakob," she said, her heart rending at the sadness of his tale.

He laid his head on his hands, tears brimming in his eyes. "I flung myself into my studies, going on to read law at university. But no amount of studying could completely deaden the emptiness I felt inside. Meeting you, then Trixie, reawakened that impossible quest. I knew I'd lost her for ever, but I couldn't stop hoping."

27.

"I should go," Jakob said glancing up at the clock. It was eleven. They'd been talking for hours. The fire had died down leaving only dull embers that were no match for a draught bringing with it chill night air. Her father had been unwilling to install heating elsewhere in the house. The bedrooms were always glacial even in summer. She pulled the blanket tighter round her shoulders.

"No one could ever replace your Esther," Fran said, softening her tone as she did. "She was unique. It's surely not what you want to hear, but you can't expect anyone to measure up to her."

He sighed, getting to his feet.

Fran didn't want him to leave. A bond had formed between them during their frank exchange. What's more, the prospect of a night on her own in the deserted farm unnerved her. But she daren't ask him to stay. After all they'd discussed, it would surely give the impression she was taunting him. He didn't deserve that. He'd been so open with her she didn't want to be cruel.

Torn as she was, it was the prospect of affronting a night alone that won out. "If I ask you to stay," she said, not daring to look him in the eye, "after all we've discussed, I'm sure you'll understand it is no invitation to my bed, but a desire to have company?" She shuddered at her own bluntness, but she was not one to beat about the bush.

He nodded. "I understand." He seemed relieved, as if he too

didn't relish the idea of a night spent alone. "We could build up the fire and make two beds in here... Separately," he added with a chuckle.

Pleased that he could joke about it, she smiled and hurried off to fetch bed clothes while he tended to the fire. There were no spare mattresses and the carpet was not very thick, but using several blankets and cushions from the armchairs they were able to build two comfy nests.

Wrapped up in blankets that smelt of moth balls, they discussed changes to the farm till both were so tired they couldn't keep their eyes open. With the lights dowsed, Fran drifted off to sleep to the faint crackling of the fire.

The distant sound of her name roused her. She was annoyed at Jakob. Why had he woken her? Cracking open her eyes, little could be seen in the dying embers of the fire, but it was clear it wasn't him. He was fast asleep.

Someone's trying to call you, the cloud told her.

Then the name came again. *Fran.*

Yes, she replied. The voice was distorted as if coming from a great distance, but Fran thought she recognised it. *Trixie? Is that you?*

Fran, it's terrible... The girl got no further as she broke down and sobbed.

There, there, Fran said, trying to calm her. As words didn't work, she tried reassuring emotions. When the sobbing finally ceased, Fran said, *Tell me what happened.*

They locked us up and are going to execute us. At the word 'execute' she broke down and began sobbing again.

Is Xristy with you?

Yes.

Where are you?

In a prison under the middle of the bubble.

Can you reach them? she asked, consulting the cloud.

No problem, was its cocky response. *I told you Zamia would resort to force to control the uncontrollable.*

Know-all, she thought, ignoring a sudden urge to poke fun

at the cloud for its unfailing self-assurance. *I'm coming,* she called out to Trixie.

For a brief moment she thought of waking Jakob but dismissed the idea. Let him sleep. She could manage. She nodded to the cloud. *Take me to Xristy's world.*

It was the odour that hit Fran first. Old and rotten, as if the air was of another age. Opening her eyes, sight confirmed smell. The cell must've dated from a much earlier epoch. No finely chiselled surfaces here, only uneven stone stained by dark, dubious smears.

To her astonishment, she found the two girls shivering, completely naked. *What ever happened to your clothes?*

Confiscated, Trixie replied.

After hours of mistreatment at the hands of the youths, this latest blow had unhinged Xristy. She crouched shivering in a corner, her face tear-stained, dribble escaping from the corner of her mouth. Fran moved to console her, but Xristy cringed away, shame etched all over her face.

Fran pulled off her jacket and was about to slip it over Xristy's shoulders when the sound of footsteps could be heard outside. Fran grabbed Xristy's hand and, pulling her towards Trixie, she just managed to catch the other girl's hand when the door creaked open. *Get us out of here!* The cloud obeyed, dumping all three unceremoniously in front of a dying fire in Fran's living room.

The clatter of Xristy falling heavily on Fran's bed awoke Jakob with a start. He screamed, as did Trixie who desperately tried to hide her nakedness. "What the hell...?" Jakob asked, a hand clasped over his eyes.

"Emergency," Fran said none too helpfully. She spread a blanket over Xristy who lay spreadeagled on the pile of blankets that was Fran's makeshift bed. The girl was unconscious but breathing, albeit shallowly. Fran checked. Meanwhile, Jakob had tossed a blanket to Trixie whose tiny frame was completely swallowed by the dour tartan. Only her pale-skinned face peaked out, her eyes riveted on Jakob.

He offered her his bed, which she was hesitant to accept until he came to stand next to Fran. "What happened?" he asked.

Fran was unsure, but she told him the little she knew. It was barbaric! How could blind adherence to tradition lead them to kill the adopted sister of their leader and one of their most promising young members? "I don't get it. How could they be so inhuman?"

"Religion and dogma can do that," Jakob said, pulling two armchairs close to the fireside and inviting Fran to sit next to him. "It's as if ideas, be it God's word or the party line or some pseudoscientific theory, win out over life. People end up little more than numbers and numbers are expendable."

How could they possibly change such an unyielding system? Fran mused, thinking of Zamia's stubborn refusal to accept that men or boys existed, let alone live outside the bubble.

Systems do change or get replaced, although not so often, the cloud replied to her unspoken question. *It can take monumental upheaval and bloodshed. More rarely it starts with an apparently insignificant change that sets a cascade of transformations in motion till people awake to a completely different world.*

Its words had Fran thinking of the internet. Who would have thought it would so radically change the world in such a short time? Talking of time, it was late. She glanced at Trixie who was fast asleep on Jakob's makeshift bed. Xristy was out too.

"We can't house them here," she said, as much as she'd have loved to keep Xristy at her side. "This is not their world. They're likely to end up imprisoned, if not worse... People here have a nasty habit of locking up, excluding or even eliminating anyone who's different." Her father had been a prime example. He systematically voted for those who wanted to keep foreigners out and he'd have eagerly shot any stranger venturing on his property.

"True," Jakob said, yawning. "But we should get some sleep, we're going to need it."

Talking of sleep was one thing, getting to sleep was quite another. Fran leaned back in her armchair, her eyes closed, listening to the faint snoring of Jakob and the quiet breathing of the two girls.

Grandfather wants to see you, the cloud said, tearing her from her reverie.

Grandfather? She knew the name was a convenient fiction. Clouds didn't exist separately.

That's not quite true, the cloud replied, listening in on her thoughts as ever. *I know it's difficult to understand. While clouds can temporarily exist as separate entities, they always remain a part of the indivisible whole. You humans are also part of a whole, but the vast majority of you have become so fixated on your individual identity you've lost any sense of belonging.*

Connected, Fran said enigmatically.

Exactly, the cloud replied. *The one you see as the most powerful of clouds, the one you met at the top of that tower, the one who joined us together asked me to take you to it.*

She'd never been summoned before. Was it an honour or a sinister omen? *Do you know why?*

The cloud's chuckle was more like a distant rumble of thunder. *What makes you think it'd confide in me?*

Point taken. So much for connectedness. *Let's not keep 'Grandfather' waiting,* she said. The cloud was about to whisk her away when she stopped him. *Hold on a mo. I can't go dressed like this. I'll freeze to death.* Suitably dressed for an artic winter, not that she'd ever been there, she signalled she was ready.

She'd half expected to find herself perched on the windswept top of Xristy's tower. Instead she was floating in the middle of a constantly changing ring of clouds with nothing vaguely resembling solid ground to stand on. She suddenly realised how much she relied on the earth under her feet to make sense of her world. Suspended in mid-air with no visible means of support was like being stripped of a fundamental reference that made her who and what she was.

Child. The booming voice rattled every bone in her body as she sank to one knee and lowered her head, her eyes staring down into the void. Serious mistake. She almost threw up as vertigo had her reeling. *Stand.* Forces of inhuman strength heaved her to her feet and steadied her. *We have a task for you.*

She was unsure if she should groan or laugh. She felt insubstantial confronted with the immensity of the cloud's unbounded form. What had her father always said to her? She was insignificant, worthless, a girl, a nobody. The memory made her furious, defiant even. She wanted to stand up, assert her worth, insist she existed, show her strengths. But doubts dragged her down. What could she possibly do that the cloud couldn't? Yet it had chosen her to carry out a task.

We are sick of those people squabbling down there. We, who are already battling to keep them alive, are worn out by their skirmishes. The time has come for you to bring their bickering to an end. Judging from the imperious tone, it sounded like an invitation to slaughter. What if she didn't? What if she tried to negotiate and they refused to end their petty feuds?

It hardly seemed the moment to assert herself, but if she didn't begin now, would she ever? *I have two conditions,* Fran said, trembling at her own audacity. The angry rumble of the gathered clouds warned her she had overstepped the mark. Too late. *That you ease up and let the sun shine through from time to time and that you give them rain so plants can grow.*

I can do neither. The cloud was categoric. Blast these stubborn men. Did they always have to have their way? *First, if I let the sun shine, they will die. It has got far too hot for them to survive direct sunlight.* God Lord! It'd never crossed her mind that the constant cloud cover was a protection. *Second, the water we hold is toxic. Their ancestors did their best to destroy this planet with their pollution. Much of the filth they spewed into the atmosphere is trapped in us. If we were to let go, they'd die horrible deaths.*

How terrible it must be to be a cloud and never be able to rain, no matter how heavy or how polutted the water you carried. *But...* she began, hesitating about broaching the subject. *The Cloud Catchers ride amongst you and...* she was unsure what word to use *... milk the smaller clouds for their water. How* *come that doesn't kill them?*

Those who regularly ride amongst us end up immune, to an extent. As for the water they steal, it's only a very small quantity and we manage to keep the toxins out of it.

So they don't really steal it. You feed them only those clouds that are safe? She couldn't believe it. The whole situation was absurd. *Why on earth do you let them continue to believe you're hostile when in fact you've only got their best interests at heart?* Her incredulous outburst brought renewed angry rumblings from the surrounding clouds.

If you think it through, it replied, a hint of a smile in its voice, *our benevolent interest would hardly fit their world view.*

She had to admit it was right. *What about me?* she suddenly thought. *Am I not in danger being here amongst you?*

No. You are here with us only in mind, not in body.

But my cloud? It's always with me.

You are right. But your cloud, as you call it, is a part of you. If you are not toxic, then neither is it.

You mean I am part cloud?

A cloud nodding was an experience never to be forgotten. It was like a giant affirmation of self. She felt buoyed up by the 'Yes!' that momentarily banished all doubts.

So do you accept?

Fran hadn't known she had a choice. Could she refuse? If she did, would the clouds wipe out these people? And what if she failed? Doubts rushed back to cloud her mind as she struggled to decide. Indeed doubts were the dark clouds that had marred her short life. Enough! She wished she could conjure up a strong wind to chase them away, but they were tenacious. Instead she recalled the 'Yes!' of the cloud and, drawing herself up to her full height, she sucked in a deep breath and simply said, *I accept,* only to continue, *You who know them well, have you got any suggestions how I could do this?*

The mental smile the cloud gave her was like a burst of sun in the clouds that warmed Fran all over and gave her strength. *You're a resourceful girl, I'm sure you'll find a way.*

28.

Fran could just make out the farm buildings far below, dark against the surrounding countryside in the pale moonlight. The cloud was holding her afloat in midair at the limit of a bank of clouds. *Why aren't you taking me to the farm?* Fran asked, her only wish being to get to bed as fast as possible.

Look, the cloud said, *close to the farmhouse.*

Fran squinted, but all she could see was a blurry black mass.

Let me help, the cloud said. What occurred then was so strange, Fran wondered afterwards if it had actually happened. It was as if someone had slid a telescope in front of her eyes. Her vision zoomed in on the farmhouse and she could see all the details despite the darkness. There, lurking in the shadows along the side of the building, was a lorry. No. Not a lorry. One of those outside broadcast vans.

Fran swore. Damn the nosy blighters. What the hell were they playing at? She searched near the vehicle, looking for movement, and immediately spotted a couple of people sneaking along the wall, camera and microphone in hand.

I could blow them away, the cloud suggested.

Not helpful, Fran said. *Anything spectacular will only encourage them. They'll come back for more.* The two would soon round the corner of the building and head for the main entrance. *Set me down on the steps to the front door,* Fran said. As it placed her gently on the top step, she realised she had retained her night vision and could see almost as if it were day.

The two would not have her advantage, so she slunk back into a corner where she'd be hidden from view.

When they were almost on top of her, she said, "How nice of you to drop by." The woman screamed, or would have if she hadn't clamped a hand over her mouth. Fran was grateful for the restraint. She didn't want to wake the others. The last thing she wanted was the TV yobs to catch sight of Xristy and Trixie, especially if they were still undressed.

The man didn't scream, but he was so rattled, he let go of his camera which fell to the ground with an ominous thud causing him to swear profusely. He bent to pick it up but the cloud nudged the camera just out of reach. *Don't torment the poor fellow,* Fran told the cloud.

"Can I offer you some tea?" Fran asked in her most innocent voice, as if she'd just bumped into longtime friends in the middle of the afternoon. Convinced as they probably were she was a witch, they'd never touch anything she gave them. But you had to be polite, didn't you? Especially when your visitors were so terrified.

The man had given up trying to catch his camera and shied away from it as if it were cursed. As for the woman, she was clutching her microphone like a sacred relic that could ward off evil spirits. "Tell me," Fran said conversationally, leaning back against the door, "what brings you out so late, or should I say so early?"

"We saw that interview you gave," the woman said, struggling to pull herself together.

"What am I supposed to have said that got you out of your beds at night?" Fran asked, perplexed.

"You said your father called you a witch," the woman said. "And you spoke out against the church."

"Ahhh!" Fran said, suddenly realising what had happened. "I see that journalist, what was her name, Annie I think, has been meddling with my words. No wonder you were misled. If I were to speak to you, would you do the same?" She didn't give them time to answer. "Of course you would. That's what you do."

"So what did you say?" the woman asked. She'd relaxed her death grip on the microphone and looked less like a Sunday school girl who'd just met a devil.

"We have a recording," Fran said. "But that hardly seems important now my words have been travestied." She was tempted to send them away. They were no use to her. She glanced at the woman only to realise she was barely older than her. With her hair cut ultra-short, her bushy eyebrows and her fleshy lips, she would have been quite attractive were it not for the sour look on her face. "What's your name?" Fran asked, softening her tone.

"Celia," the young woman replied, looking a little perplexed at suddenly becoming the focus of the conversation. She was even more surprised when Fran stepped closer and traced the line of Celia's cheek bone with her index finger. Why not taunt her a little? She knew only too well her fingers must smell of Xristy's oil. She'd caressed the girl earlier that evening. Judging from the way the young woman leaned forward trying to prolong the moment, the oil was having its effect.

"It's late," Fran said, stepping away. "We should all go to bed." She couldn't helping smiling at the ambiguity of her words.

Stop teasing the poor thing, the cloud chided, echoing Fran's earlier words. *She's no match for you.*

It was right. She was letting herself be influenced by the Cloud Catchers and their cavalier attitude to intimacy. What would be acceptable and well understood amongst the Cloud Catchers, could be devastating in a world where relationships were mostly one-to-one with the other sex.

With a sigh, the young woman wrenched herself from Fran's company and stumbled back to the van. Fran waited at the top of the steps till the vehicle had driven away before entering the house. All was quiet. In the living room, the three slept on, apparently oblivious to what had happened. Fran eased into her armchair, pulled a blanket up to her chin and was about to close her eyes when Jakob whispered, "Where have you been?"

"Sorting things out," she said, too tired to embark on long explanations. "I'll tell you later."

"Are you alright?" he whispered. "You sound agitated."

His insistence annoyed her. Why couldn't he wait? "You'd be agitated if you'd just met the king of the clouds," she shot back. To be honest, it wasn't the meeting with the cloud that had her in a state, but flirting with the girl from the television. She must've been under the influence of the oil herself.

"Wow!" he said, mocking her. "A private meeting with the king in the middle of the night. Sounds exciting. Should I phone the tabloids?"

If she'd had a cushion at hand, she'd have thrown it at him. As it was, she turned her back and closed her eyes.

"Good night," he said. Despite her closed eyes, she could sense the smile on his lips. It made her smile too.

When Fran awoke, bright sunlight streamed in the windows. Day was well under way. Everybody was up with the exception of Xristy who lay unmoving on her makeshift bed. Worried that the girl might have passed away from sheer exhaustion, Fran was relieved to see her chest rising and falling in a steady rhythm.

She found Trixie in the kitchen with a blanket slung round her like a toga held in place by a giant safety pin. The girl was helping Jakob prepare breakfast as the two engaged in a faltering conversation composed of evocative gestures and comical grimaces. Fran kept to the shadows for a long moment observing the two who were clearly enjoying each other's company. Her thoughts harped back to her conversation with Jakob about his twin. With all the naivety of one who'd lived only amongst girls and had no expectations of men, Trixie would probably make a far more suited partner for Jakob than her.

"Come out Fran," Jakob said, winking to Trixie who screwed up her face trying to imitate him. "You surely don't believe we haven't noticed you there keeping an eye on us."

Fran nodded to Trixie as she came forward. Grinning, she said, "I didn't want to disturb. You were getting on so well together." Jakob must have understood exactly what she was alluding to as he blushed. *That blanket suits you,* Fran said, turning to Trixie, who was fiddling uncomfortably with the safety pin. Apparently the girl had noticed Jakob's blush and, although she probably didn't understand, she sensed his embarrassment.

"What's for breakfast?" Xristy asked, emerging from behind Fran. Wondering why on Earth Jakob covered his eyes, Fran glanced over her shoulder to find Xristy standing in the doorway completely naked. Fran burst out laughing. *I'm going to have to explain one or two things about this world,* she said, taking Xristy by the arm and leading her up the stairs to her bedroom.

The plan had been to find suitable clothes, but Xristy had other ideas. Fran should have known it wouldn't be so simple. She'd mistakenly imagined that, without her oil, Xristy might be a little less inclined to jump her. Wrong again! With a complete disregard for anything else, the girl tumbled her onto the bed and wrapped her arms and legs around her before planting her lips on hers. Fran might be eager and willing, but she was also confused, only yesterday Xristy had repeatedly rejected her.

Ten minutes later and completely out of breath, Fran struggled free of the naked girl and got unsteadily to her feet, wearing little more than Xristy. Taking a shower seemed like a good way to calm her hammering heart. It would have been, had not Xristy followed her into the bathroom and stepped into the shower with her. They were busy experimenting with soaping each other when Trixie appeared in the doorway. *Breakfast is ready,* she said, a broad grin on her lips. Fran half expected the girl to join them, but Trixie turned and left. At least it hadn't been Jakob standing there.

Enough, Fran told Xristy, gently unclasping the girl's hand from her breast. She turned off the water, stepped out of the shower and handed Xristy a towel. *I'm hungry. Let's go get some breakfast.* Xristy pouted, to which Fran replied, *Come off it! I can't believe all you do in your world is make out. I know for a fact that you spend a lot of time chasing clouds.* She remembered the seriousness and application with which Xristy led the Cloud Catchers. *I bet you do a great many other things too.*

Jakob and Trixie had finished eating when Fran finally made it down. "We were too hungry to wait," Jakob commented.

"Sorry," Fran replied. "Had some difficulty finding suitable clothes for Xristy." In reality, Fran'd given her the first pair of shorts and a t-shirt she'd found. Even dressed, the girl still managed to look provocatively underdressed.

Jakob glanced at Xristy then at his watch, clearly not believing a word of it. "Eat," he said, an impish grin on his lips. "With all that exercise you must be starving."

Fran had indeed been hungry. Xristy too, judging by the ravenous way she consumed slice after slice of toast and marmelade. "So," Jakob said, joining Fran at the table, "what's all this about the king of the clouds?"

With all the excitement, Fran had completely forgotten her visit to Grandfather Cloud. She should talk to Xristy and Trixie about it, they were the ones who might have advice, not Jakob. But he would only pester her if she said nothing. Of course, she could lie to fob him off, although that seemed pointless. She had no reason to keep her meeting secret. "I was summonsed," she began. "He ... it wanted to give me a task."

She paused, as her doubts surged anew. Why her? She was not cut out for such a mission. Was it possible she'd dreamt it all? The whole scene in the clouds did seem unreal. Surely Jakob would laugh at her if she told him. She glanced at him. His expression said, 'Well?' Shaking her head in denial, she said, "It asked ... no commanded me to make peace between the girls and the youths of that world."

Rather than burst out laughing, as she expected, his expression was serious. "That makes sense," he said. "You're the only one who can speak to both sides." She was about to list reasons why she was unsuited, but he went on. "You've already made a step in the right direction." When Fran looked perplexed, he added, "You took Trixie to meet the youths. And you would have taken the leader too, had she not been so stubborn."

She stared at him in disbelief. He was supposed to be the voice of reason who picked apart her wild fantasies. Not the one who shored her up and encouraged her. Her confusion, if not alarm, must have shown on her face, because Trixie asked, *What's up?*

I need to talk to you and Xristy. Xristy, who'd been rummaging in the cupboard looking for more marmalade, came and sat at the table carrying several unopened jars. Trixie got up, poured herself a glass of water and went and sat on Jakob's knees. Fran found the sight disturbing. Whatever happened to the girls-only tradition? Decidedly Trixie was not like the others. Fran was not tied by their traditions and she had no claims on Trixie, but she still felt a tinge of disappointment. At the same time, she was happy for Jakob seeing the broad smile on his lips.

Shrugging off her discomfort, she said, *The head of the clouds has given me a mission, to bring peace between the girls and the youths in your world.*

Xristy sprang to her feet knocking over a pot of marmalade. *You can't be serious?*

29.

Trixie moved to get up, presumably to clear away the sticky mess. Xristy was not making cleaning up any easier as she repeatedly ran a finger through the spilt marmelade, smearing patterns across the table before sucking the conserve from her finger with noisy relish. Fran gestured for Trixie to stay put, saying, *That can wait.* Finally, it was Jakob, barred from the conversation as he was, that went in search of a cloth and soapy water.

How do you plan to do that? Trixie asked, giving Fran her full attention, something that couldn't be said of Xristy who seemed unable to tear her eyes from the marmelade. It was almost as if the shock of Fran's announcement had driven her over the brink. Not surprising. Xristy had been teetering on the edge well before. All the same, Fran couldn't help regretting the girl's disinterest. She really liked Xristy and would have gladly had her at her side in this adventure. *No idea. What would you do?* Fran asked.

Trixie glanced at Jakob. There was a touching tenderness in her eyes that made Fran uneasy. Surely no girl could live up to the ideal Esther that Jakob had forged for himself. *Learn to speak to each other, so no one feels excluded.*

How would you do that? Without ears to hear, how could the girls possibly speak? As for the youths, it was doubtful they'd ever be able to hear thoughts.

Sign language, maybe.

Clever, Fran admitted. A third possibility!

Trixie waved a hand to catch Jakob's attention then

demonstrated a couple of signs they'd already invented. It was agreed they'd continue to develop signs. *It would be better if we worked with those youths,* Trixie mused.

Even better still, Fran said, *if we could convince a couple of girls to join you. You know of any likely candidates?*

Yeah. Maybe, Trixie replied, her expression thoughtful. *But I'd need to talk to them.*

That's all very well, Fran said, *but how can you sound them out if you don't dare approach for fear of being executed?*

Easy, Trixie said. *Bring them here.*

Fran looked at the girl in admiration. She had a knack of finding solutions to apparently impossible situations. *Can you do that?* she asked the cloud.

Sure. If you can figure out which ones I'm to bring.

Whoever you chose, Fran told Trixie, *they'll be important. Those who can communicate will have a considerable advantage. They'll probably be the future leaders at your side. The same goes for the youths. You should work closely with them. Get to know them. Win their trust.*

Xristy was slumped over the table, fortunately now free of marmelade thanks to Jakob. Her eyes were open but her expression was vacant. She looked awful. Could she be seriously ill? After all, on each previous visit to Fran's world she'd been taken poorly. Trixie, in comparison, seemed to be thriving, gaining confidence the longer she stayed. Fran was about to say that maybe it was not wise to bring the girls to this world for fear they'd fall ill like Xristy, when a sharp knock at the front door interrupted her.

Fearing trouble, Fran had Jakob usher the girls upstairs and out of sight. Waiting for him to hustle Xristy up the stairs with the help of Trixie, Fran went to answer the front door. On the doorstep stood a delegation of local dignitaries, the mayor whom she'd never met but recognised immediately, the headmistress of her school as sour-faced as ever, the priest and several other people she didn't know. She was relieved there were no policemen and no troublesome Nelly. "What can I do for you?"

she asked, deliberately blocking the way into the house.

The mayor stepped forward using his corpulence as if wielding the weight of his office, trying to force his way in. She stood her ground, refusing to be intimidated. "Let us in girl!" the mayor said, annoyed.

"Why?" Fran asked. "A number of you tried to have me convicted on false charges. What ever makes you think you'd be welcome in my house?"

The mayor snorted in a very undignified way, apparently convinced he had every right. He opened his mouth to respond angrily, when Jakob, who'd come up behind Fran, said, "Why indeed? It's a valid question."

"We have come to deliver an ultimatum," he said with the bluntness he was renowned for.

"Fire away," Fran said, defiantly planting her hands on her hips. Jakob came to stand at her side.

"Your presence is no longer welcome in our town," the mayor said, an angry spray of spittle accompanying his words, forcing Fran and Jakob to take a step back.

"Who says so?" Fran countered.

"We do," the priest chimed in.

"You have no authority to banish law-abiding citizens from the town," Jakob calmly pointed out.

"We have the moral authority," the headmistress said, clutching the heavy crucifix that hung around her neck as if it were authority incarnate.

You could spend all day arguing who has the right of it, but it would be pointless, the cloud commented. *They're set in their ways and will not concede. Nothing you could say will convince them.*

He was right, but a plan was beginning to form in her head. "Okay," she said to the surprise of everyone, including Jakob. "We'll no longer visit your town. But I predict that before six months are up you'll be wishing you hadn't banished us. I look forward to that day." With which she shut the door in their faces.

"Are you sure?" Jakob asked. "It's a risky strategy."

"I know," Fran said, "but how else was I to get rid of them? We can use the time to strengthen our position. You remember we talked about turning the farm into a bed and breakfast? Well, what if we bring together those girls from Xristy's world and those youths who are willing to help us build a new home here."

"So you plan to abandon the other world?" Jakob asked.

"Not necessarily," Fran said. "I'm trying to imitate Trixie's way of thinking. When the choice seems impossible between two alternatives, pick a third one."

"She's clever like that," Jakob said, a smile on his lips.

"I suspect you'd find anything Trixie did wonderful," Fran said.

"Come off it!" Jakob retorted, giving her a friendly shove.

"There's one thing I need to know before embarking on such a project," Fran said, making a show of rubbing her shoulder where he'd pushed her. She thought of Xristy's 'illness'. "I want to be sure our world doesn't make our guests ill."

"Like Xristy, you mean?"

"Exactly. She's been ill every time she comes here."

"It doesn't seem to affect Trixie," he pointed out.

Knowing why he was taken by Trixie didn't stop her being irritated at his pronounced interest in the girl. It was as if his whole world revolved around the youngster. "You might want to spend your days dallying with Trixie..." she began, abruptly turning on him. He blushed scarlet.

Jealous? the cloud asked.

It was teasing her, but, all the same... *Damn you,* she shot back. *Stop spying on my deepest thoughts.*

"Sorry. That was unfair," she relented. "This whole situation has me on edge, what with the meddling townsfolk and the stubborn girls in Xristy's world, not to mention the demands of the clouds." The latter was a dig at the cloud who responded by ruffling her hair in gentle reprimand.

"You two get on well together. I'm glad for you," she said and she meant it. Trixie was the perfect partner. "I'm happy for you, my friend." She smiled at calling him her friend. He was. A good friend. "But I still need to be sure none of the girls or boys we bring here fall ill."

They climbed the stairs in search of Xristy and Trixie. They found the two where Jakob had left them. Xristy lay asleep on Fran's bed while Trixie was thumbing through one of the few books Fran had managed to hide from her father, a prize won as a little girl at school. The typeface was large and there were colourful drawings. As a kid, it had been her treasure. *Can you read?* she asked Trixie. She doubted it. The girl was holding the book upside down.

Trixie looked perplexed. *Read?*

These are words, Fran said pointing to one. *Like the words you use to express your thoughts, they have meaning and can be used to communicate between people. Reading means understanding the words written on a page.* She wondered if the notion of 'word' made any sense to someone who neither read nor spoke, exchanging only thoughts. Better to be concrete. Turning the book up the right way, she ran her finger over the word 'cat'. *This one says 'cat'. And this one says 'dog'.*

Trixie giggled in delight, repeatedly running her finger over the two words.

Glancing at Jakob over her shoulder, Fran said, "Reading. Another thing we'll have to teach them." He grinned.

Fran wanted to share her project, but she needed Xristy to hear too. She laid a hand on the girl's shoulder and shook her. "Wake up Xristy." The girl, who lay face down, groaned but didn't move. Fran heaved her onto her back only to discover her skin was deathly white, as if all blood had drained from her. *Help me,* she pleaded to the cloud and leant over Xristy, pressing her lips against the girl's. Calling on the cloud in her, she blew energy into Xristy's lifeless body.

Xristy lay unresponsive. Was she too late?

Try again, the cloud said, *longer and deeper this time.*

She had to do so several times before Xristy stirred and groaned. Fran would have continued breathing energy into the girl, but the cloud stopped her. *Enough,* it said. *She'll be okay but if you continue to call on your essence you'll make yourself ill.*

Why does she keep falling ill? Fran asked the cloud.

There are some things it is not for me to reveal, it replied.

Come off it! she responded, annoyed at his coyness. *It's important.* But the cloud refused to say. It could just be the power of Xristy's imagination, Fran speculated, hoping the cloud might confirm her hypothesis. The girls' belief that they couldn't survive outside the bubble was so strong. Maybe her mind was inducing the sickness. Getting no response from the cloud, she turned to Trixie, asking, *Do you know why she keeps getting ill?*

Trixie sighed, seeming reluctant to answer.

What's wrong with you lot? Fran said both to Trixie and the cloud. *What's the big secret?*

When Trixie finally spoke, she said, *In the beginning, only two girls served as handmaidens to the priests, Narie and Xristy. Frozen for ever at a young age, they spent hundreds of years in service. When the priests began to leave, there was never any question of the girls leaving. Instead, the men decided to recruite new girls to look after the temple in their absence.*

Typical men, Fran thought, cowardly lack of responsibility.

Myself and the others were brought into the bubble, Trixie continued, *and subjected to the influence of its eternal youth. We were put to work tending the place. Our stay, compared to that of the first two, has been much shorter. Amongst the skills the priests taught Narie and Xristy was the ability to travel between worlds. Because it was deemed dangerous, it was never taught to the rest of us. The itch to travel was the downfall of Narie who fell ill each time she journeyed to another world. It finally killed her. It would seem Xristy is suffering the same fate.*

Her story made sense. *Can you remember what remedies you used for Narie?* Fran asked.

Sure, Trixie replied. *A complex herbal mixture.*

Where did you get the herbs?

We grew them ourselves. Her face glowed with pride at

some unspoken memory. *My task was to tend the herb garden.*

Do you think we could sneak in and pick some?

That won't be easy, Trixie replied, on the verge of tears. *It's one of the first things the youths ransacked when they attacked.*

Is anything left?

It's a complete shambles, but maybe we can save some plants. I don't know.

Aren't the girls trying to repair the damage? Fran asked.

Trixie shook her head. *With me gone, it can't be easy. And anyway, I have the impression they've given up. You have to realise that these attacks completely demoralised them.*

It made sense. Their bubble had burst, literally. They'd felt secure behind their walls, all the more so that they refused to believe anyone could live beyond.

They discussed a possible raid, with Fran acting as a relay between Trixie and Jakob. Fran would have liked to involve Xristy, but the girl was still very much out of it. They decided to make a quick foray without her.

You might do well to lock the other girl up, the cloud suggested. *For her own safety.*

Fran agreed. They decided to secure Xristy in Fran's bedroom.

The cloud set them down by the ruins of the herb garden. For once, the youths had been methodical. Fran wonder if they were aware of the strategic impact of their vandalism. Some plants had been ripped out of the ground, presumably those that looked edible, and carted off, while the remainder had been trampled. It was Trixie's job to gather those that could be saved, with Fran and Jakob carrying baskets to put the survivors in. All three kept close together in case they had to leave in a hurry.

The baskets were almost full when a cry shattered the silence, swiftly followed by angry shouts. *Thieves! Thieves!* The girls had spotted them. Grabbing the free hands of the other two, Fran glanced at the gang of girls gaining on them, their pretty faces contorted with hatred, before asking the cloud to carry them away.

Back at the farm, Fran led them to the greenhouse behind the barn. It'd been her mother's responsibility but she'd neglected it in recent years. The panes of glass were intact, but the flowerbeds were overgrown with weeds and cobwebs stretched between every vantage point. Fran helped Trixie and Jakob clear a space. She was glad they were reconstructing the herb garden, but she couldn't help feeling despondent. She pictured those girls' faces twisted in snarls of rage. They'd surely been far too optimistic in their plans. There was little hope of convincing any of the girls to join them. She wondered if winning over the youths would be easier.

30.

Maybe *we should wait till things settle before we try to get one of the girls to join us,* Fran suggested.

She'd just finished repeating her words out loud so Jacob could follow, when Trixie replied, *I don't agree. If we wait, that'll give the council time to spread false stories about us destroying the herb garden.* The girl signed some of her words to Jakob in their ever increasing vocabulary and Fran completed the rest.

"She's right," Jakob said. "The faster we move, the better. Maybe we should go immediately." Trixie nodded when Fran repeated Jakob's words.

A loud crash from behind the farm froze them mid-sentence. Fran swore and was on her feet in seconds. Jakob followed suit with Trixie, who couldn't hear, reacting to their alarm. Together they ran to the back door. The noise was coming from the other side of the barn, near the greenhouse.

Rounding the corner of the barn, they discovered three youths chucking stones at the glass. Luckily their projectiles bounced off. Fran's mother had had the foresight to use specially reinforced glass, saying that you never knew when a mob of foreigners might try to smash it.

She'd argued with her husband about what he called a sinful waste of money, their voices rising almost to a shout. Even with her door shut, Fran could hear every word. Her father was adamantly against. But, for once, her mother insisted. Finally it was her father's fear and hatred of foreigners that won him over. Fran wondered what they'd have said if they'd known not foreigners but a gang of local white boys would try to smash the once-treasured greenhouse.

Can you stop them? she asked the cloud.

With pleasure, he replied.

Don't kill them, Fran added as an afterthought. *They might turn out to be useful.*

The cloud pinned the youths face down in the mud while Fran went in search of a cord. By the time she returned, the youths were spluttering in a desperate attempt to breath. *I said don't kill them.* She rolled the boys over on their backs. Their faces were caked in mud as they struggled to claw the stuff from their mouths and noses. No doubt thinking it might be helpful, the cloud showered them, effectively washing away some of the mud, but almost drowned them in the process.

Trixie had fetched a tea towel from the kitchen and was trying to wipe the youths' faces, a kind gesture that was completely misinterpreted. No doubt thinking he was being attacked, one of the youths lashed out and grabbed Trixie's leg only to get whacked over the head by Jakob wielding a broom. He sank back, face down, into the mud.

What a debacle. Fran couldn't make up her mind whether to laugh or scream. "Enough!" she finally said, as Jakob was about to brain another youth who was bent on fending off Trixie's ministrations. "Help me tie them up."

Hands tied behind backs and linked together to form a chain, Fran led them towards the house. It was at that moment that Xristy burst from between two bushes, head down, breasts heaving, completely naked. *What's up?* Fran asked, handing the string of youths to Jakob. She slung an arm around Xristy's shoulder and led her out of sight of the ogling youths.

The door was stuck, Xristy managed between gasps. *I had to force it. And I couldn't find you anywhere.*

Fran had been so engrossed she'd completely forgotten Xristy. *We need to get you dressed. You can't walk around like that. You'll get us in serious trouble.* She slung her jacket round Xristy's shoulders and led the girl at the back of the group, out of sight of the boys. The girl seemed unaffected by the cold, despite her lack of clothes. In comparison, the three youths, who were sopping wet, were shivering violently.

While Jakob and Trixie led the youths into the kitchen, Fran took Xristy up to her room to find her clothes. Back in the kitchen, with Xristy more or less respectable, they found the three youths seated around the table sipping tea and talking to Jakob.

"So she's deaf and dumb?" one of the youths asked, his eyes alight with interest. Mud had caked his hair in a series of jagged spikes, making him look like a porcupine who'd had a bad shock. Fran vaguely knew the other two from around town, although, with their hair plastered flat and smears of mud across their faces, they were barely recognisable.

Jakob nodded in reply, signing the conversation as best he could to Trixie.

"Now you're all cosy," Fran said, joining them at the table, "maybe you can explain why you were trying to smash our greenhouse?"

Her question put an abrupt end to the conversation. All of a sudden, the content of their mugs was much more interesting. To add to the confusion, Xristy opted to sit on Fran's lap and slung an arm around her neck planting a kiss on her lips. The girl must've daubed oil on her neck because Fran felt herself losing control. *Now's not the time,* Fran said. When Xristy persisted, Fran shoved her away using more force than she intended.

Xristy lurched against the table, overturning the porcupine's mug before she bolted for the door slamming it after her.

"Sorry about that," Fran said, going in search of a cloth to wipe up the mess. "She's been a little disturbed since she got here." She poured more tea, then resumed her seat. "Where was I? Ah yes, the greenhouse."

"It's a long story," the porcupine youth replied. That said, he seemed disinclined to say more. It was the youngest who took up the story.

"I made a silly mistake..." he began. When Fran shot him a questioning look, he added, ducking his head, "Shoplifting."

"What does that have to do with our greenhouse?"

"The police promised not to press charges if I ran a little errand for them."

"Ah!" said Fran. "And what was that?"

The youth stared pointedly at the table. "Scare you."

"Well that worked well," said Jakob said, fixing the boy with a sardonic grin.

"And you?" Fran asked, turning to the others.

"Same," the porcupine youth replied. The other nodded.

"So it was the police that sent you?" Fran continued, glancing at Jakob. "I wonder how they justify that?"

He shrugged. "The word of three petty criminals pitted against that of the police wouldn't carry much weight."

"So what are we going to do with you?" Fran asked. "We can't hand you over to the police. They'd probably just send you back to cause more trouble."

"The police could just as well pack you off to Borstal until you're old enough to go to prison," Jakob said. All the youths cringed at the thought. "After all, you didn't keep your part of the bargain."

Trixie, who'd been more or less following thanks to Jakob's signing said, *Why don't you send them to my world for a stay with those youths? They'll sort them out.*

I'm not so sure, Fran said, shaking her head. *This lot are more likely to cause havoc if they don't get lynched.*

Lynched? Trixie asked, perplexed.

Strung up by their necks with a cord till they die of suffocation.

How barbaric!

Welcome to the outside world.

"Couldn't we stay here?" the youngest youth pleaded, glancing around the kitchen, his eyes lingering on Trixie.

Good luck with her, Fran thought. "How could we possibly

trust you?" she asked. "And anyway, what would you do if you were here?"

It was the porcupine youth that replied. "All three of us were apprenticed in the building trade. Scratch there, is an electrician," he said pointing to the youngest, "Wiggle is a plumber and I'm a carpenter. Maybe you've got some building you'd like done."

"Haven't you three got jobs to go back to?" Jakob asked.

All three shook their heads, their expressions grim. "The police made sure our employers knew we'd broken the law," Porcupine said, "and that was the end of that."

Jakob nodded. "Makes sense." Without work and a possible conviction hanging over their heads, the youths were completely at the mercy of the police.

Fran briefly explained to Trixie while Jakob questioned the youths about the work they could do. *I like the idea,* Trixie said. *If they help build the place, they're less likely to want to tear it down.*

"Jakob, what do you think?" Fran asked.

"It might work. Let's give them a probationary period, say a month or two."

They'd just began discussing the details, when there was a crash at the front door followed by the sound of a scuffle. The youths got to their feet as one, their expressions terrified. Jakob moved to protect Trixie and Fran turned to face the kitchen door. *Help!* Xristy called out.

The door burst open and two policemen shoved their way into the kitchen, dragging Xristy by her hair behind them.

"Let go of her immediately!" Fran said, furious.

"Not before we recuperate those three criminals you're harbouring," the largest of the two growled. Fran recognised him. He'd been at the hearing. A click behind her, had Fran turning to see Jakob taking pictures of the police with his phone.

"Stop that!" the policeman shouted, taking a threatening step towards Jakob.

"Violence against innocent bystanders is a crime," Jakob said, standing his ground. "Especially on the part of a policeman.

I'm sure you two don't want to spend time in prison."

The policeman let go of Xristy's hair and shoved her, causing her to stumble and fall heavily to the ground. The two clenched their fists readying themselves to attack Jakob.

Deal with them, Fran said to the cloud.

A look of sheer terror wiped the belligerent expressions from the faces of the two men as they gasped for breath, their fingers desperately clawing at their necks trying to free themselves from an invisible hand.

Xristy struggled to her feet, tears streaming down her face. She planted herself in front of the man who'd dragged her by the hair and slapped him with all her force, sending him reeling against the doorframe.

"Don't kill them!" Porcupine shouted, horrified. "We'll get blamed."

Xristy would have slapped the defenceless man a second time if Porcupine hadn't intervened. Furious, she turned on him and raised a hand to hit him too. The youth put up no resistance. Fran was impressed, but she couldn't let an enraged Xristy punish someone who was ultimately trying to protect her. *Stop that immediately!* she ordered.

The faces of the two policemen had turned an alarming green, their eyes wide with terror as they struggled and failed to breathe. *Ease up!* Fran ordered. The cloud obeyed, letting the two sink to the ground sucking in desperate mouthfuls of air. Porcupine, assisted by Scratch, led a bewildered Xristy by the arm and helped her to the table. At the sight of them taking such care of Xristy the choice was obvious. She would let them stay. All they had to do now was dispose of the two policemen.

What now? Trixie asked. Judging from their expressions, the same question was on the minds of all the youths, although, with the policemen present, they didn't dare voice it out loud.

Use the oil, Xristy said, surprising Fran. The girl might appear to be out of things, but she was clearly following what was happening.

" I thought it repelled men, Fran pointed out.

It does. But after a while it'll drive them mad with desire. How long?

Five or ten minutes, Xristy replied. Just the time for a trip into town, Fran thought.

"So what are we going to do with those two?" Jakob asked.

"I thought we'd try out the gelding iron," Fran said.

"The gelding what?" Jacob exclaimed.

"We use it for horses, you know, male horses, when we don't want them to make any more foals. The red hot iron must be a bit painful, I guess, but once it's done, you don't feel a thing I've been told."

Jakob stared at her in abject horror. The two policeman looked terrified. "You can't possibly..." one of the policeman said.

"Oh, but I could," Fran said, turning to Jakob and winking. She hoped he got the message. It would spoil the effect to have him intervene in favour of the policeman. "Of course," Fran pursued, "if you agree to keep quiet, we might just let you go."

"You can't do that," Jakob said, having guessed what was going on. "They'll surely blab."

The two were getting more and more agitated, although there was not much they could do. The cloud had a tight grip on them. "That doesn't matter," she said. "Xristy's got some home-made truth syrup. A spray of that and they'll never be able to tell anything but the truth."

Fran nodded to Xristy, saying, *Spray it into their mouths. They think it'll force them to tell the truth.*

As Xristy approached, the spray brandished in front of her, the two struggled desperately to get free, but the cloud held them tight. "Would you prefer I go and fetch the gelding iron?" Fran asked. Their struggling ceased immediately. "Open your mouth," Fran said. "If the spray gets in your eyes it'll hurt terribly." They dutifully opened their mouths as wide as they could and Xristy sprayed a dose of oil down their throats.

"Good," Fran said. She wanted to get the two as far away as possible before the effect kicked in. She had no wish to see the

two of them pawing each other. That was for the town's folk to
see. "Do allow us to escort you to your car."

31.

"Tell me," Jakob asked as he sat down at the table, his face flushed from helping the youths clear a spare room to be their temporary bedroom, "does such a thing as a gelding iron exist?"

"I hope not," Fran said, grimacing. "But you must admit it worked pretty well. Let's hope it's scared them off for good."

The kitchen door banged open and Porcupine burst in. "Quick! You wanna hear this," he said, beckoning. When he turned and ran, they hurried after, finding the youths hunched over an ancient wireless. Made of dark polished wood, it must've been lost amongst the rubbish for years. It was a miracle it still worked. Fran was so unaccustomed to the mellow, almost woody tones of the person talking it was as if the voice came from a different age.

"... the two policeman were discovered in their car outside the police station, their clothes torn to shreds, swarming over each other like wild animals in rut..."

"Wow!" exclaimed Scratch.

"Shhhhh!" hissed Wiggle.

"...It took four officers to pull them apart. Even then, according to those present, they tried to rip the clothes from their fellow policemen. The police have, as yet, not released a statement. Speculation is rife, however, that the two men were drugged. They had just returned from a mission to a farm outside the town, the owner of which has quite a reputation..."

So much for solving their problems, Fran thought, wincing.

"That's torn it." They'd managed to strengthen the poisonous image people had of her and the farm. Maybe fleeing to Xristy's world was the only solution.

"... Breaking news," the newscaster announced. "Apparently the two policeman had been dispatched to apprehend three escaped criminals who were taking refuge in the farm. We've just learnt the police applied for a warrant to arrest the owner of the farm for harbouring criminals. However, Judge Harriet Rainer refused to grant the warrant, arguing that the suspicions were based purely on supposition and that, until proof was available, she would not comply. Off the record, several people working in the station claimed the police themselves sent the three youths, ostensibly to cause trouble..."

"You should thank the judge," Jakob said. "That's the second time she's saved your skin."

"To Judge Rainer!" Fran said, raising an imaginary glass in toast. "Now let's go eat before something else happens."

Goulash! Her father would have been horrified. Nasty foreign food, he'd have said. Saps the Englishness from the best of us with its indigestible spices. The added pleasure of annoying her defunct father made the heart-warming dish all the more palatable.

Fran looked around the table. The three youths huddled together eating their goulash in near silence, eyes fixed on their plates, stealing the occasional furtive glance in the direction of the girls. Trixie and Xristy were oblivious to their attention, engrossed as they were in a silent conversation about the woes of their world.

That left Jakob, who sat next to Fran, plying her with questions about the future of the farm. She answered willingly, but his enthusiasm worried her. True. He was her lawyer and a good friend and confidant, but he spoke as if his future lay in developing her farm. Was that really how he saw things playing out?

"What's happening to your work?" she interrupted. "Have all your clients fled since you tangled with me?"

Whether it was her question or the piece of beef he'd just forked into his mouth, he almost choked. She thumped him repeatedly on the back with the flat of her hand. "Tangled?" he managed to say.

"I heard tell I was a dangerous woman who led good men astray..."

He shook his head. "You're impossible."

"You haven't answered my question."

He sighed. "You have a bad habit of asking awkward questions," he began. When she didn't react, he continued. "Okay. I've been neglecting my work. Is that what you want to hear?"

She shook her head. "No. I'm just worried the events here are distracting you from your career."

"Career." He said the word as if hearing it for the first time. "I don't think in terms of 'career'. Yes. I enjoy the challenges of working as a lawyer but I see getting this place off the ground as far more worthwhile than defending the interests of people who frankly don't deserve to be defended."

"But what about all the time and money you invested to get there? Wouldn't that be a waste?"

"I'm not saying I'll stop being a lawyer. I'm confident my training and practice will be put to full use keeping you and your friends," he glanced at Trixie, "out of trouble."

"I'm glad you see things that way," Fran said. "Your help..." she paused, hesitating over words that might be misconstrued, "and your friendship have been invaluable." The moment could have been embarrassing, but Jakob's attention had been caught by Trixie. Her conversation might have gone unheard by the men in the room, but her agitation was plain to see.

What's up? Fran asked her.

Something's going terribly wrong in our world, she gasped, tears overflowing down her cheeks. *So much pain and suffering. I can sense it.*

Had the clouds lost patience? If the girls and boys continued their skirmishes, wouldn't the clouds carry out their threat?

She'd promised to put an end to their warring yet she'd done very little to make it happen. If she didn't succeed, the clouds might get fed up waiting.

Not as far as I know, the cloud commented.

Jakob, seeing Trixie's distress, moved to her side and took her in his arms. The youths watched the unfolding drama uncomprehending, concern, if not alarm, etched in their faces. If Fran were to return to Xristy's world, what would happen to them? Could she leave them to defend the farm against the belligerent townsfolk? The prospect was worrying. Not because she didn't trust them, but because of the unpredictable if not violent reactions of the town. True. Little or no time passed in her world while she was away, but the incident with the police would surely have a sequel and it could unfold at any moment. On the other hand, if she took the three with her no one would protect the farm in her absence.

Can you be in two places at once? she asked the cloud. Surely that might be possible if clouds could be everywhere.

It doesn't work like that, it replied.

"We're going to have to leave you, for a short while," Fran said to the three youths. "We have to deal with a problem at Trixie and Xristy's home. Do you think you'll be able to manage here on your own?"

"Can't we come too?" Porcupine asked. "If there's trouble, maybe we can help."

Fran shook her head. "I need you to stay here, to guard the farm."

He looked sceptical. "I'm not sure what we could do if the police came," he said. The other two youths were clearly apprehensive too.

Fran was wondering how to convince them when Jakob spoke up. "I'll stay and keep you company."

His offer had her relieved. It was the best solution, the one she hadn't dared consider. "Are you sure?" she asked, hoping he wouldn't change his mind.

"Oh yes," he replied with a grin. "I mean, I might be able to use those lawyer skills you were talking about so much."

"I think I need a private word with you," Fran said, getting to her feet. He followed suit, winking to the three youths. In a dramatic aside, he whispered, "If you hear me scream, come rescue me." Having other males around had transformed his behaviour.

Outside, in the corridor, Fran stopped and turned to face him. "It was kind of you to offer. I hadn't been expecting it. I thought you'd want to stick with Trixie."

"Stick?" he asked, raising an eyebrow.

"You know what I mean. You're very protective. I wondered if you'd let her go without you, knowing the situation was probably very dangerous."

"Are you jealous?"

It was not the question she'd been expecting. She had some difficulty not blushing, even though there was no reason. "No. Why should I be? After the discussion we had and what I said about my father and you about your sister, how could you imagine such a thing? I know you like Trixie. I find it cute, although I worry a little about the difference in age, but if she's willing, why not?"

"I'm glad I've got your permission," Jakob said, a wry smile on his face.

"That's not what I meant," Fran retorted.

"I know," he said, "but you are very protective of 'your girls'."

The way he said the words made it sound as if they were a special category. He was right. They were. She felt responsible for them, not just because they were guests in her house, but because of the mission the cloud had entrusted in her. "I am. I wouldn't like anyone to hurt them. Not that I think you would."

"Thanks for your vote of confidence."

She huffed. Far from reassuring her as she'd hoped, the more they talked the more complicated things got. What's more it was taking too long. "I have to go," she told him. "Lives might depend on it."

Back in the kitchen, she addressed the three youths who looked up from their quiet conversation. "Take your lead from Jakob. Try to keep yourselves and the farm safe, but whatever you do, no heroics!" She half expected a show of bravado that often characterised boys, but their expressions were grave. "See you soon," she added as she led Xristy and Trixie away.

Upstairs in her bedroom, the three dressed in preparation for Xristy's world. They needed practical clothes that would offer more protection than the flimsy garments the girls usually wore, but that were still suited to a slightly warmer climate. Fran donned her riding gear and found trousers and t-shirts that fit the others. Trousers were a novelty, that caused some amusement despite the gravity of the circumstances, especially when Xristy put them on back-to-front.

Ready? the cloud asked, apparently impatient.

Hold on a sec! Fran replied. *Where are we going?*

To the Council, Xristy said.

Fran shook her head. That hardly seemed a good idea. Was it not the Council that had banished them and threatened to execute them? Trixie agreed. *I'd go for younger girls' quarters,* she said. *Let's find out what's happening and see if we can persuade some to join us.*

The younger girls' quarters it is then, Fran said, grabbing her riding crop.

You won't need that, the cloud said. *It'll only get in the way.*

She put it back on her dresser although she felt vulnerable without it.

How can you feel vulnerable with me at your side? the cloud asked.

Sometimes you can be more macho than a men, Fran commented, wondering why she'd never asked herself if clouds were male or female or neither.

Answering that would require more time than we have, it replied to her unspoken thought.

Did anyone ever tell you you were exasperating? Not waiting for an answer, she offered a hand to the other two and asked the cloud to transport them.

A strong smell of burning hit Fran hard the moment they arrived. The air was full of acrid smoke that stung her eyes and ran roughshod over her nose, throat and lungs. She coughed violently. Charred remains surged from the pall of smoke forming a forbidding landscape where ever she looked. Amid the crackling of the fire, muffled moans could be heard somewhere nearby.

What the hell's going on? demanded Trixie.

Xristy stared aghast. *How could they?*

Fran too wondered why the youths would have attacked. Last time she'd seen them, they hadn't seemed hostile. *Can you blow away the smoke?* she asked the cloud.

That'll only fan the flames, was its reply.

Renewed moaning nearby had them hurrying to see who it was. Rounding a corner, they were horrified to discover a twitching arm reaching out from beneath a smouldering beam. The stench of burning flesh was unbearable. Xristy let out a scream as she rushed forward. It was Zamia, her adopted sister, who'd been crushed. *Help her!* she called out in a heart-rending plea.

There was little they could do. The girl's eyes were closed, her face twisted in pain. A steady trickle of blood was seeping out of her mouth and running down her chin. The blow must've smashed her ribs and done considerable damage to her abdomen. *Can you lift the beam off her?* Fran asked the cloud.

The movement would probably make things worse, not to mention the additional pain it would inflict, the cloud replied. *Judging from the injuries, she's very unlikely to survive much longer.*

Xristy knelt at her side, tears coursing down her cheeks as she desperately tried to wipe the blood from the girl's mouth. Zamia's eyes flittered open and lingered a long moment on her as if trying to remember who she was. *Xristy,* she said, her mental voice barely a whisper. *You came.* She closed her eyes and there was a long pause as she gasped for breath. *Save the others*. And she was gone.

32.

Xristy let out an ear-piercing wail and would have flung herself on Zamia, paying no heed to the smouldering wood, had Fran not grabbed her and dragged her away. In her desperation, Xristy pummelled Fran's chest, but there was no force to her blows. Fran wrapped her arms around the struggling girl, drawing her into a tight embrace. The fury quickly went out of Xristy giving way to despair, her body sagged and she broke down and sobbed, her tears flowing freely down Fran's neck.

Fran glanced at Trixie who was staring upwards, her mouth fallen open. *It's gone*, the girl exclaimed in total disbelief.

What's gone? Fran asked.

The bubble!

Fran looked up. *Good lord! You're right.* The protective bubble, the very barrier the girls believed essential for their survival, had shattered.

We're doomed, Trixie whispered.

Doomed? Not necessarily, the cloud commented to Fran. *It might finally put a stop to their long-held, but erroneous beliefs.*

You're too hard on them, Fran objected. At least it made transporting girls to Fran's world all the more pertinent. Although, getting some boys to come with them might be compromised if they were responsible for the catastrophe. Disentangling herself from Xristy, Fran said, *Let's go search for survivors.*

Moving through the ruins was no easy task with Xristy leaning heavily on Fran for support. The paths were often blocked by twisted metal girders and they had to clamber over heaps of rubble. After half an hour, they'd come across no other victims, but they'd found no survivors either. *Where is everybody?* Fran asked.

Underground, Trixie replied. *They're probably trapped.* She pointed to a metal plate on the ground half hidden under a giant slab of stone. *That used to be one of the entrances.*

We can't go down there, Xristy said, backing away. *They'll kill us.*

They might try, Fran said, shrugging. *But I doubt it. They've got other things to worry about. The least we can do is attempt to rescue as many as possible.*

Judging from her resigned expression, Xristy had little hope.

Follow me, Trixie said, apparently not so sceptical. *I've got an idea.*

Amid the ruins, a stone arch stood defiantly intact, despite the onslaught of several girders that had fallen across it. Rummaging under the arch, Trixie uncovered another metal panel which they managed to heave open, revealing steps leading down.

It crossed Fran's mind she should've asked what weapons the girls had, if any, but Trixie was already halfway down. *Wait for us at the bottom,* Fran called out as she helped a reluctant Xristy negotiate the stairs. Their descent was lit by emergency lighting that had miraculously survived the disaster.

The smell of smoke was not so strong underground, but structures collapsing above had caved in tunnels requiring lengthy detours. Trixie led the way, cautiously advancing for fear they'd be attacked. Despite their fears, the tunnels were deserted.

Where are we headed? Fran asked after another long trudge to avoid a blocked passage.

The young girls' quarters, Trixie replied. *It's evening. Maybe some were there when the dome collapsed.*

Their hopes were to be dashed. The passageway to the quarters was badly damaged, heaps of rubble rendering access impossible. Fran was beginning to despair they'd find anybody alive when she heard a faint noise, like nails scratching on stone. She was about to ask Trixie if she heard it too, only to realise she was the only one who could.

I hear something, Fran told them. *Somebody is alive on the other side.* She turned to Trixie who was visibly straining as if willing herself to hear. *You know them,* Fran continued. *Try calling.* Trixie mentally spoke the names of the younger girls, her voice trembling with emotion as she did. A faint query came back like a distant echo, *Trixie?* It was followed by such a long pause, Fran wondered if she'd imagined it. Then the raspy voice spoke again, *Help!*

It's Yssel, Trixie said. *Coming,* she called back as she and Fran desperately tried to fray a passage. Even Xristy helped. It was slow going. They had to pick their way round chunks of masonry that were too big to move. When no further voice was heard despite several attempts to call, they quickened their pace, fearing the worst.

Can't you ask your cloud to help? Trixie asked, rubbing scratched hands on her trousers.

Can you? Fran asked it.

Not a good idea, it replied. *That kind of force would probably cave in this whole section. It's very unstable.*

Fran relayed the bad news and they toiled on. Several times the walls shook as distant rumbling announced another cave in. Mindful of the cloud's words, when they finally broke through, they were very cautious the roof didn't collapse. Trixie crawled through the tiny opening followed by Xristy. When it came to Fran's turn, the area shook violently and the rubble shifted, blocking the passage with much larger boulders. There was no way she could free a new passage and large sections of the ceiling seemed ready to give way. *I'm stuck,* she told Trixie and Xristy, staring in horror as a giant bolder rolled to a halt only inches away. *That was close!*

Use the cloud! Trixie urged. *To hell with the risk. Blow your way through.*

It won't work, the cloud insisted. *Only more rubble will come tumbling down and probably kill everyone.*

You're right, Fran replied. *But there might be another way. Take me home and bring me back on the other side.*

When they returned to the underground passages, she found Trixie kneeling at the side of a young girl whose face was smeared with blood. *Head wound,* Trixie told Fran as she knelt beside her. *Only shallow. She should be ok. Can you help Xristy?*

Xristy was struggling unsuccessfully to remove a large chunk of fallen ceiling that blocked a doorway. *There's someone trapped inside,* the girl said. Fran could see there was no way they could shift the obstacle. *Let's get Yssel to safety,* Fran said. *Then we'll come back for the others.* Once she'd explained her plan to Trixie, she had the cloud transport them to the farm.

Not wanting to use her bedroom as a hospital, she had the cloud set them down in the barn. Placing Yssel on a temporary bed of straw, Fran left Trixie to tend to the girl as best she could with Xristy staring on and went in search of Jakob and hot water. She found everyone seated around the kitchen table. The moment Jakob saw her dishevelled and covered in dust, he sprang to his feet, exclaiming, "What the hell happened to you?"

"No time to explain," Fran said. "Fetch hot water, bandages and a first aid kit. Take them to the barn. You'll find the kit under the stairs in the hall. Help Trixie. I have to go." Not waiting to reply to the barrage of questions, she called out "Hurry!" over her shoulder and ran back to the barn.

Jakob's on his way, she told Trixie. Grabbing Xristy's hand, she added, *We'll see if we can rescue any more.* Maybe she should have asked Xristy before dragging her off. She'd assumed the girl would want to rescue her fellows, forgetting that she'd had a terrible shock. Too late to take her back.

Landing on the other side of the blocked door, they discovered three exhausted girls prostrate on the floor. Apparently they'd been trying to shift the rubble that prevented them escaping. Xristy checked the adjacent rooms. They were empty. Meanwhile, Fran went from one girl to another, searching for wounds. They were all still breathing and didn't seem to be hurt, just exhausted. Glancing up, she saw ominous cracks streaking across the ceiling. Calling Xristy to her side, she said, *Let's get out of here while we can.* Making sure she was touching or touched by each of them, the cloud whisked them away.

Back in the barn, Jakob and the youths had set up a makeshift hospital ward with palettes and blankets while Trixie had cleaned up Yssel who looked much less alarming without her bloody mask. Smoke rose from an improvised brazier in the centre of the room and the air was thick with the smell of burning herbs.

Everyone joined forces to carry the three new girls to beds. Trixie, who'd adopted the role of head nurse, with the three youths running errands, examined each girl but found none were injured. They were dehydrated and exhausted, she said, prescribing a herbal tea.

Fran joined Jakob in the kitchen where he was brewing the tea for the new arrivals with ingredients Trixie had provided.

"Any idea what happened?" Jakob asked, pouring water on the leaves.

Fran shook her head. "At first I thought it was those wild youths who'd attacked, although I can't see why. They certainly didn't seem ready for out-and-out war when I was with them. And they could never have shattered the bubble that surrounded Xristy's world. It's been in place for hundreds of years."

"The bubble?" Jakob queried, his expression sceptical. "That was immense. How on earth could anyone survive such a collapse?"

"They live mostly underground," Fran replied, searching for cups. She told him how they'd found Xristy's adopted sister crushed under a girder. "She didn't survive."

"I'm so sorry," he said, lapsing into silence. After a long pause, he asked, "Could there be more survivors?"

Fran had been asking herself the same question. "I don't know," she replied. "We should check, but it's dangerous."

"If we get any more refugees, we really should start building like we planned."

"I agree. The sooner the better. I'd like to be involved," Fran said. "But if you could take charge of the building and move that forward..." He grinned and nodded his agreement. Of course he was delighted. The project had won his adhesion right from its inception. "You'd do well to consult the girls and youths," she suggested. "After all, they're going to have to live here."

"I wouldn't have done it any other way."

Fran helped him carry the tea through into the barn. Several of the new arrivals were awake and talking animatedly to Trixie. Fran was intrigued to know what had happened, but the conversation was all about their concern for the other girls. *We should go fetch them*, one of the girls called Vynia said.

Indeed, Fran said, taking her place next to Trixie.

Who are you? Vynia challenged, as if to say 'how dare you butt into our conversation'.

This is Fran, Trixie said. *She's the owner of this place. It's thanks to her that you are alive.*

Trixie's explanation didn't seem to placate the girl who braced herself for a fight. *I wouldn't do that if I were you,* Fran said, her tone quietly menacing as she let the cloud ruffle the girl's hair and push her gently back. Vynia gave out an inaudible squeal, a look of terror twisting her face as she turned even paler than she already was.

Who's coming with me to see if we can rescue any more girls? Fran asked. None of the girls, who looked terrified after her little display of power, volunteered.

I'd come, said Trixie, glancing at her 'patients', *but I think I'd better stay here.*

Fran looked to Xristy for support, but the former courageous head of the cloud catchers sat downcast, apparently still mourning the loss of her little sister.

Fran turned and headed out of the barn, planning to leave on her own when Jakob stopped her and asked, "What's up?"

"None of the girls are willing to accompany me in search of

survivors."

"I'll come," he offered.

Fran shook her head. "Not sure a man in an all-girls' world would be welcome."

"Their world is in ruins. Many of them are probably dead or dying. If they persist in refusing help from men or even denying we exist, on their heads be it!"

He was right. "Come then," she said, relieved not to have to go alone. "Let's tell the others we're going."

He caught her arm, stopping her. "That may not be a good idea. I don't trust those girls. They're afraid of you, but if they know you're not around they could cause mischief. Why don't you just tell Trixie."

True, Vyna had challenged her, but Fran wasn't sure the girls would cause trouble, amongst other things they were still exhausted, but now was not the time to argue. She nodded and called Trixie. *You're in charge while I'm away,* she told the girl. It was a silly thing to say. Trixie already was in charge. But delegating power seemed the right thing to do. *Better not tell the others I'm gone. Don't want them causing trouble.*

Seconds later as they emerged into Xristy's world they were greeted by an ominous cracking. Had Jakob not yanked her back, she would have been crushed to death by a giant girder that crashed were she'd been standing. Enveloped in a cloud of dust kicked up by the fall, Fran took refuge in Jakob's arms, shuddering violently.

33.

Her chest still heaving from fright, Fran freed herself from Jakob's arms and turned to stare at the girder. Dust continued to swirl where it had fallen. Thank heavens she hadn't come alone.

You're not alone, the cloud retorted.

Sure! Fran replied angrily. *Where were you when I was about to be crushed?*

I may be with you, it said, sounding annoyingly like a parent addressing a little child, *but I also have important obligations elsewhere.*

Like what? Fran snapped, her anger getting the better of her. *What could be more important than saving my life?*

The clouds were discussing how to react to the collapse of the dome.

I thought you folks could be everywhere at once, Fran shot back. *How come a part of you was not here protecting me?*

"Are you alright?" Jakob asked. "You look distraught."

Not distraught, she was tempted to say, furious. To think, the cloud cared little for life, hers included.

That's not true, the cloud cut in. If she didn't know that clouds had no emotions, she could have sworn it was upset at her accusations. Sad even.

I really don't get you, she told the cloud.

Being with you is just as confusing for me.

Jakob took Fran's arm, saying, "You're worrying me."

"It's nothing," Fran said with a sigh, freeing herself from

his hold. Arguing with the cloud made her profoundly unhappy. There was so much she didn't understand about it and their relationship. "Just having a slanging match with a cloud..."

"Good luck with that," Jakob retorted, grinning. "If you will hang around with such strange characters..."

I'm not strange, the cloud riposted. *No more than him.*

"Hey guys!" Fran exclaimed, ignoring the fact that Jakob couldn't hear the cloud. "We have urgent tasks to do." She looked around. With much of the smoke dispersed, she could now see the remains of the metal structure that had once supported the dome. Twisted girders pointed like sets of deformed fingers skywards. Here and there large panes of glass, or maybe it was plastic, hung precariously from broken supports.

What giant force could have wreaked such havoc? Despite the cloud suggesting they had not expected the collapse, she still suspected them. Who else would have the force to smash a giant dome that had weathered millennia in an inhospitable climate? If it were them, she'd have words with the head of the clouds next time they met. They hadn't given her the time they'd promised to let her fulfil her mission. Now she was literally having to salvage it from the ruins.

We did not destroy the dome, the cloud insisted, *although we knew that some day it would have to collapse. You'd probably call it a prophecy.*

If you didn't, who did?

Maybe you'd call it fate.

It was hardly an explanation. But Fran had no other. She shrugged and turned to go. It was then a thought struck her. Without one of girls along to guide her, she had no idea of the layout of the underground labyrinth. *Do you know your way around?* she asked the cloud.

Clouds live above ground, not under it, was its laconic response. *What's more, travelling underground in these circumstances is hardly wise.* Jakob must have spotted her glum expression because he asked, "What's up?"

"I have no idea where to look in all those underground

passages.”

His knowing grin was frankly annoying. What did he know she didn’t. “You might need this,” he said, pulling a folded piece of paper from his pocket. “Trixie made a rough map. She figured it might come in useful.”

The girl’s inability to read or write would explain why there were no labels, making the map hard to decipher. Fran did recognise the rounded shape of one part. “That must be the council chamber. I’ve been there. That’s a good place to begin.”

“Where are we?” Jakob asked, taking the map back from her and turning it round and round. “I can’t make head nor tail of this.” Of course, Trixie’s map depicted the underground, not the surface.

Fran surveyed the surroundings. Any familiar landmarks had been crushed by the fall of the dome. But what remained of the structure gave some indication where the centre must have been. “My guess,” Fran said, “is that the council chamber will be near the middle, over there.” She pointed in the direction of the centre.

It was one thing to know in which direction to go, but quite another to find access to the underground passageways, especially as the light was failing. Fran had been in such a hurry to get away, she’d completely overlooked that it would soon be dark. “Blast! I forgot to bring a torch.” Once again it was Jakob that saved the day, producing a tiny torch attached to his key ring.

“So what are we looking for?” he asked.

“A round metal plate on the ground, big enough to let someone down.”

They would never have found the entrance had it not been for the fact that it was night and the plate that covered it was cracked, letting light seep through from below. Trixie had marked entrances with crosses. If the one they’d found was the one marked closest to the council chamber they should only be a short walk away.

They’d just prized open the entrance and were about to

descend, when they were surrounded by a group of filthy youths most sporting cudgels and sticks, a few bearing flaming torches. Fran didn't recognise any of them. There must be several bands of wild youths roaming the area.

"On your knees!" the largest of the youths barked. "Hands on your heads."

"That's not a very polite way to greet people," Fran remarked, restraining Jakob who was bracing for a fight.

The youth raised his cudgel to hit her and was promptly blown some thirty feet through the air, landing awkwardly on a heap of rubble. As one, the whole group took several steps back, their faces terror-stricken. "Witch," several muttered.

The leader struggled to his feet, cussing and swearing as he did. Several times he stumbled and fell as the rocks shifted beneath him. His task was made all the more difficult that he seemed to have hurt his leg. "Grab them!" he shouted, limping forward. No one moved.

"I wouldn't, if I were you," Fran said. "Unless of course, you like getting hurt."

"This site is ours," the youth blustered. "We're not letting no filthy outsider pillage our place."

"Firstly," Fran retorted, wrinkling her nose, "if anyone's filthy here it's you."

The youth took a threatening step forward but was immediately shoved back by the cloud who sent him sprawling.

"Secondly," Fran continued. "This is not your site. It belongs to a group of girls who have lived here for centuries."

"They're all dead," he said with a dismissive wave of his hand. "Now it's ours." He stared greedily at the entrance to the underground passages. "Thanks for showing us the way in."

"If you'd been willing to help us rescue the survivors, we might have come to an agreement."

"I don't give a damn about no bloody survivors. They can rot as far as I'm concerned. This place is ours now."

His cocky, self-assurance irritated Fran. What gave him the right to do as he pleased? *Can you dump them somewhere far away where they can't do any harm?* Fran asked the cloud. *But not in my world. And don't kill them.* The only answer she got was a mental grin and the band of youths disappeared with just a vague echo of a startled squeal as they did.

"Remind me not to get on your bad side," Jakob said. It was meant to be a joke, but there was real fear in his voice.

Her thoughts were echoed by the cloud that spoke to her from far off, *When you wielded such power, it's difficult to have normal relationships.*

"Let's go do something useful," she said.

They knew they were close to the council chamber, but not a single passage in that direction was free. In fact, they could barely move away from the entrance. Judging from the chaos, that area had borne the brunt of whatever had caused the dome to collapse. Maybe the youth had been right, there were no survivors.

"How the hell are we supposed to find any survivors in this?" Jakob asked.

"I'll try calling," Fran said. *We've come to rescue you*, she said, *call out if you hear me.* She repeated the message several times, her thoughts as loud as she could make them, but got no answer. Fran didn't want to admit defeat, but if there was no response to her calls she had no idea how they could possibly find survivors in this chaos, if there were indeed any.

What do you want? a distant girl's voice asked, sounding none too friendly.

The bellicose tone was so unexpected it caused Fran to cringe. *A friend of Xristy's,* she replied, realising that giving her name would mean nothing, *come to help survivors.*

We don't need your help. Whoever it was was very angry. *Go away and stop interfering.*

Why are you so angry? Fran asked, astonished at the virulence. *We came to help not fight.*

How can you say that when it was you that caused the collapse of our world?

The flagrant injustice of the accusation had Fran struggling not to hit back. *You don't even know who I am,* Fran responded unable to keep the irritation from her voice.

Of course I know, shot back the girl. Having words spat mentally at her with such force was an unpleasant experience. She rubbed her temples to ease the emerging headache. *You're that meddling little friend of Xristy.* Fran guessed the girl must be a member of the council. *The one that brought down the clouds on us.*

The accusation had Fran worrying that the clouds had indeed been responsible for the destruction. *What makes you think the clouds did it?*

Have you seen the damage? Wreaking such havoc requires a great deal of force.

Fran had come to the same conclusion, although she'd dismissed it. *You have no proof,* she pointed out. *Only supposition.*

Who else could've done it? A measly bunch of boys? Come off it! Go home. You're not welcome. So saying, the girl broke off the communication such that it felt like a mental slap in the face.

"Phew!" Fran said, staggering. "That was nasty."

"Tell me," Jakob asked, steadying her.

"A snotty girl, probably one of their precious Council, blamed me for this disaster..."

"That's a bit rich!" Jakob exclaimed. "How could you possibly have done this?" He waved his arm, indicating the blocked passages in an all-encompassing gesture.

"Because I am known to consort with clouds and, according to her, they are the most likely architects of this apocalypse."

"So do we give up and return home?"

"She made it very clear I was not welcome."

"But what will you say to Trixie and the others?"

"The truth. That the Council chased us away."

"I still think we should visit the youths. Maybe they know what happened. And some of the girls might have taken refuge with them."

It seemed highly unlikely, given the hostility between the two. Fran was unwilling to make the detour. If no girls could be saved, she wanted to hurry home. She had misgivings about leaving them too long. Much could go wrong.

"Just a quick stop," he pleaded. "I'm sure we'll regret it if we don't."

Suspecting, on the contrary, she'd regret it if they did, she reluctantly instructed the cloud to transport them to the youths' camp.

A brooding silence greeted them in the wilderness that boarded the youth's ramshackle home. Even the incessant wind had stilled as if the world were holding its breath. Fran was thinking the place had never been so quiet when a sharp whistling rushed towards them. The next moment the cloud had flung her to the ground as an arrow flew inches above her head. Jakob dived after her.

As one they rolled behind a boulder just when a second arrow ricocheted off the rock and clattered to the ground. "I didn't know the youths had bows and arrows," she whispered.

"I don't think they do," Jakob replied, pointing round the rock to a giant cage half concealed by scrawny scrub and several large rocks. Shifting to get a better view, Fran saw a heap of youths, slumped and unmoving, enclosed within. Had that other band of youths taken them prisoner? They would have been ruthless enough, but Fran doubted they'd have the guile to pull it off.

Come out with your hands up, a familiar girl's voice said. It was the fury who'd spoken to her earlier.

Can you protect us from arrows? Fran asked the cloud.

Sure, was its answer.

"The cloud will protect us," Fran whispered to Jakob. Then, taking his hand, she called out, *Don't shoot. We're coming out.*

Three girls, protected by leather jerkins and what looked like sturdy skirts, trained bows and arrows on them. *On your knees,* one girl barked.

The déjà vu was striking. *The group of youths we met*

earlier said the same thing, Fran commented in an effort to appear relaxed and undaunted. She was tempted to threaten, but decided against it. Glancing around at the squalid encampment, she added, *You have little or no chance of surviving here. Those who wish may join us. We have lodgings, food and activities for everyone.*

Sure, the girl sneered. *And accept you as boss? No way! We'd never submit to a girl who has to bring a boy to defend her.*

Fran wondered how Jakob would react to being treated as a boy. *Jakob is no bodyguard,* she said. *He's a friend.* She smiled at him. It must be difficult being unable to follow such a key discussion. *I am not the boss of our community. We work together.*

Put him in the cage with the others, the haughty girl said to her colleagues, indicating Jakob.

Instead of trying to put down those who can do you no harm, Fran said, *you'd do well to send out search parties to rescue the survivors still trapped in the ruins.*

A waste of time, the girl said, a disdainful smile curled on her lips. *All those worth rescuing are already here.*

Surely not. Little differed these girls from the unfeeling youths they'd encountered earlier. *I dislike being forced to pass judgement,* Fran said, *but you just condemned yourselves to exile.* Turning her attention to the cloud she said, Could you dump them with the youths you carried away earlier? Oh, and leave their bows here.

34.

As the bows and arrows clattered to ground, no other girls dashed forward to grab them. Fran wondered if there really were any others. Just the few selfish, self-centred ones she'd sent packing. Wielding the cloud in the name of justice was both heady and disturbing. True, the girls' treatment of the youths had been vile and they'd threatened Jakob, but did that justify acting like a despot, eliminating those who were difficult to handle? The banished girls surely had a story to tell and she still didn't know why or how the dome had collapsed.

Jakob released her hand which she'd forgotten she was holding and turned to the prisoners. With the girls out of the way, it was time to set them loose. In the first light of dawn, the youths were beginning to stir, emerging from their stupeur and clamouring to be let out. Surely they hadn't just been asleep in a heap.

Once freed, the youths rounded on Fran, surrounding her in a tight circle, fists clenched, teeth bared. "Stop that immediately!" Jakob exclaimed, shoving back several very smelly youths who got too close. "Not all girls are as bad as those three who imprisoned you."

"Were's your leader?" Fran asked.

"Dead," one said. "The bastards shot him when he tried to resist."

"They treated us like cattle," another complained.

"Where have you sent them?" a third asked. "I hope they're

not coming back."

"They've been banished to a place where they can do no harm," Fran informed them, fervently hoping it was true. She had nightmarish visions of the girls and youths wherever the cloud had dumped them in a desperate combat to the death.

"What about you?" The smallest of the youths asked. "Are you going to take us prisoner?"

Finding a rock to sit on, Fran replied, "Why don't you sit down. I have a proposition to make. But before I do, maybe you can explain what happened. Why did the dome collapse?"

Her question was rewarded with blank stares. Several shrugged. Only one ventured an explanation, of sorts. "There was a big bang. The whole thing fell in, spewing smoke all around. When the dust began to settle, those three turned up." He pointed to the pile of bows and arrows.

Fran sighed. She might never know what happened. "Okay. Here's my proposition. You have no real shelter. You have little or no food. And you are easy targets for would-be attackers. I come from a place where there is plenty of food and shelter. My idea is to offer you a community in which to live where you'll be safe and have all you need."

"Sure. And we get locked up in cages like we did with that lot. Is that it?" the oldest of the youths spat. "We'd be your slaves?"

"No. You won't be locked up. Although there will be work. Everybody works, even I do."

"What sort of work?" he asked, his tone belligerent.

"There are animals to tend to, crops to harvest and, at the moment, a lot of construction work. We already have a number of buildings, but we need to convert them to suit our needs. And of course, there's cooking and cleaning, not to mention the many other tasks of every day life. We do all those things so we have food to eat, clothes to wear and a good place to live." She hesitated about mentioning their plan to learn together. Although they'd probably never set foot in a school, she didn't want to sour their impression by talking about teaching.

"All that is required of you is that you take an active part and live in peace with the others."

"Others?" the oldest queried, clearly suspicious.

"There are already a few boys living with us along with a number of young girls we rescued from here."

"No way! I ain't gonna live with no girls. They're animals," said an extremely skinny boy who'd been standing quietly at the back.

"I'm sure the girls would say the same of you," Fran said with a chuckle. "But that's the choice I'm offering you. Either you scrape out a meagre existence here till you die of hunger or exposure or get overrun and enslaved by others stronger than you. Or you come with us and take your chance with people different from you but who are prepared to work with you to make a worthwhile life."

As no one rushed to volunteer, she said, "I'll leave you to talk about it amongst yourself. If you want, you can ask Jakob to describe some of our plans." She glanced at Jakob who nodded. Getting up, she walked through the encampment in the direction of the shattered dome. Much of the smoke had dissipated but a haze continued to blur the contours of the disfigured girders. Reaching what once must have been the place where the youths had breached the dome, Fran halted.

Did the clouds have anything to do with this? she asked He'd already insisted they didn't, but she wanted confirmation.

The cloud didn't immediately answer, causing her to panic, thinking it had abandoned her, but then she felt it stir around her neck like a gentle breeze caressing her. *You should have more faith,* it whispered. *Remember, I'm a part of you and you of me.*

Well, other me, did the clouds do this? She pointed to a nearby girder than had been bent back on itself by some gigantic force.

You should ask them yourself.

Okay, take me to them, Fran said with trembling decisiveness. Confronting the clouds was never easy and she wasn't sure her solution of taking survivors to her world would meet their approval. The head of the clouds had asked her to put an end to their bickering. If her manoeuvre was successful, those on her farm would finally live peacefully together. She just hoped she hadn't exported their feuding to her world. There were enough problems with local bods without that.

No need, the cloud replied. *They're coming to you.*

Fran looked up to find a dense fog swirling around her, engulfing all in sight. And with it, an uncanny fear coursed through her veins making her breath catch in her throat as if she were about to suffocate. She gasped, struggling to force air into her lungs despite the awe that threatened to crush her.

It would seem you acted too late, a voice boomed all around her making the bones rattle in her body.

I disagree, Fran said, in trepidation. Contradicting the cloud was hardly wise. Her words were greeted by deep rumblings of discontent on all sides. *I've already got a number of the most promising girls to safety,* she pointed out, *and I'm in the process of rescuing some of the youths as well.*

At what cost? the cloud shot back.

I don't understand.

This place is in ruins.

I had nothing to do with that. Safeguarding this place was not part of our bargain.

Is that what you think?

Fran was struck silent, astounded at what seemed a unilateral shift in the terms of their agreement. There were clearly things she didn't understand.

Child, you have no idea, the cloud continued. *This dome was once a sacred temple. Surely you can't have imagined the girls built it? No. It's much older. The girls you met were once handmaidens of the temple. They were not allowed to live within the dome which was reserved for priests. Instead, they stayed in a small settlement just outside where those youths now live. They were charged with catering for the priests needs. When the priest first began contemplating leaving, a couple of the girls were invited in and instructed how to take the place of the priests. Much later when most of the priests had left, new girls were incorporated to help maintain the temple.*

His words confirmed what Trixie had told her.

The dome had a special property, it continued. *Anyone living in it did not age.*

I don't understand, Fran said. *If the dome granted everlasting youth, why ever did the priests leave?*

Thousands of years of religious devotion can become a little wearisome...

So now the dome was broken and some of the girls were in her world, what did that presage for them? She gasped, realising what that might mean. *Are the remaining girls going to shrivel up and die?* she asked, horrified.

No. They will simply get old like anyone else... except that getting old might be far more traumatic for them. Unlike the priests who left, the girls didn't chose to get old and they've never known anything other than eternal youth.

It struck Fran that the girls might not have known why they stayed forever young. *You hinted I was to blame for the downfall of the dome. Why?*

The temple was dedicated to the worship of clouds and, by association, all facets of the weather. That's why we are so attracted to this place. The girls mistakenly came to see us as the enemy when in fact it was their fellow citizens that were the threat. Long before the girls came on the scene, the priests had spoken out unsuccessfully against the progressive destruction of their planet. As the situation deteriorated, the priests came to believe that one day a person would come that would be both cloud and human. The advent of that person would bring back balance to the world and release them from their unending task, freeing them at last to live their lives. At that moment the dome would no longer be necessary and would cease to be a holy place. I doubt they imagined it would collapse.

Fran laughed nervously. *No. Surely not. I...* She couldn't follow through with the idea. It was just too absurd.

Yes, the cloud said. *You are the one. You are the real cloud catcher. Of course, being men, they expected a man or a boy. They might have been right if they'd stayed. But it was girls who watched over this place and so it is only fitting that a girl should come to release them from their guardianship.*

If I take away some of the youths and start a community in my world, what will become of this place? To be honest, she didn't really care, but she did worry about the clouds. *What will become of you?*

Don't worry about us. We'll be fine. Some of us might even migrate to your world. As for this place, the temple is finished, its power gone, its saviour come and gone. With it destroyed, there is little to sustain life here and should we leave, those people remaining will not survive.

The prospect seemed harsh but then it was the population that had rendered the place uninhabitable. Their choice had been made long ago, although they'd probably deny it. She thought of those rogue members of the Council. They might have had potential, but had preferred to cling to status and privilege, unable to change. She could not save everybody, especially those who refused to be saved.

Go, the cloud said, *but remember, make sure your world does not follow in the steps of this one.* The dense fog around her began to lift and, as it did, she heard the cloud say, *We'll come and visit you...*

Walking back through the encampment, she found the youths grouped around Jakob in heated discussion. Keeping to the shadows, she watched them argue. They bared their teeth and brandished clenched fists, pushing and shoving to get a word in. It was more of a brawl than an argument. In comparison, Porcupine, Scratch and Wriggle were harmless angels. She wondered if they could ever make something of this mob or if bringing them to the farm would cause the downfall of the whole project.

Stepping forward, she called for silence. At first they didn't comply, so engrossed were they in the battle of words. But silence came quick enough the moment she unleashed the cloud on them. "You have had ample time to discuss," she said, silencing the complaints with a wave of her hand that sent a mini-tornado swirling around them. "Those who want to join me should come and stand next to me. Those who refuse should leave. I wish you good luck. You're going to need it."

No one moved. She figured it was not doubt that made most of them hesitate but inertia. This might be the first time they'd ever had to decide about their future. "The way I am offering you is not easy. My world is very different from yours, but it is younger and provides more opportunities for those willing to take them. Here might be familiar, but from what I've heard, the future looks grim."

Still nobody moved. "I will count to five," she said. "At five I will leave with whoever has joined me. The rest of you will be stuck here. I will not come back to rescue you." Jakob moved to her side, but nobody else shifted. They seemed frozen in place. "One," she began. "Two. Three." It must be like a nightmare. Their expressions radiated terror but they were unable to move. "Four."

She turned to Jakob, "Are there any you recommend?" she asked in a whisper. He hesitated then shook his head.

Shove them, the cloud said. *Shake them out of their stupor.*

It was an odd idea, but why not. She moved over to the first youth and shoved him with all her force. He stumbled and fell, lying in the dirt where he'd fallen, showing no inclination to get up. She pushed the second who ended up lying next to the first. One after another, they sprawled on the ground in a growing heap.

The penultimate youth was one of the youngest and smallest. She went to push him, but he sidestepped and stood his ground staring at her. "Will you come?" she asked. He nodded. The final youth seemed quite out of place with his fine bones and an intelligent face. Where it not for his grubby appearance he could have been mistaken for a boy from her world. She didn't have to push him. Without the slightest hesitation, he said, "I'll come."

"Five," said Fran and the four of them left.

35.

Silence. After the racket in Xristy's world, the absence of sound was disturbing. True, it was early morning, but Fran had never heard the farm so quiet. Even the hens were speechless. Something was wrong.

You're right, the cloud said. *The farm is deserted. Where are all your people?*

"Something's amiss," Fran told Jakob who was shepherding the two new boys toward the barn. The door was ajar but when she pushed it open she found the place empty. The beds were deserted and blankets lay scattered on the floor. The medecine chest had been overturned and Trixie's tea formed a puddle around several smashed mugs.

Trixie, Fran called out. *Where are you?*

Of Fran, it's terrible, the girl replied. *They've locked us up under the ground in a small room without windows. They don't seem to care that Xristy's very ill.*

Can you find them? she asked the cloud who nodded mentally.

Trixie, get everyone together and make sure you are all holding hands. I'm coming to fetch you.

"I'm going to get the others," Fran told Jakob. "Barricade yourself in the house and let no one in. Give the boys something to eat, they must be starving and maybe a wash would do them good. But above all, keep yourself safe."

She noted Jakob's raised eyebrows at her string of orders,

but now was no time for justification. With no further ado she had the cloud transport her to the cell where the others were being held. Ignoring their startled reactions, she grabbed Trixie's hand, made sure all were linked and jumped back to the farm with everyone in tow.

Once Fran had freed herself from the hugs of thanks, she was about to ask the cloud to take her back to the cell when Jakob came in leading the two boys who looked clean but raw. The moment they saw the girls they crouched, ready to pounce. As for the girls they huddled behind Trixie whom they'd adopted as leader. From the sidelines Porcupine, Scratch and Wriggle watched perplexed.

"Stop that immediately," Fran exclaimed, placing herself between the opposing factions. As she spoke, she did something she'd never tried before, she projected her spoken words as thoughts to the girls, thus communicating with everybody. "This is not your world. You left that behind and I can assure you there will be no going back. Life there as you know it is over. Your future is here or nowhere. Leave your quarrels behind! They don't belong here. I promised opportunities. And you'll get them. But not if we fight amongst ourselves. As some of you have experienced, we have no shortage of enemies. I promise you they will not get the better of us, but we can only stop them if we're united."

Studying their faces, both boys and girls, she wasn't sure her speech had convinced them, but she had no time to argue. "I must leave for a moment," she told them.

Do you have to? Trixie asked. *I'm worried about Xristy.*

I'll be right back. What I have to do won't take anytime at all.

Okay. But hurry. I can't keep an eye on this lot and tend to Xristy.

"In my absence, Trixie and Jakob are in charge." She turned to the pair who nodded their agreement. "They'll tell you what to do and help you if there are problems. I'll be back shortly." And she was gone, the cloud responding immediately to her unspoken request.

The cell stood silent and empty, although a powerful stench of former inmates and human distress filled the air. With the cloud's help, Fran shifted beyond the door to the large hall that gave access to a number of cells. She checked each one. All were unoccupied. A flight of stairs led up to the ground floor. Quiet voices floated down, the night watch presumably. Half way up stood an electric panel with an array of meters and fuses. It seemed like an unwise place to put such a strategic object, but presumably the police thought a locked cabinet was protection enough. Good. It was just what she needed.

Can you fill the basement with water? she asked the cloud. *And let it overflow onto the ground floor?*

With pleasure, it replied. Hardly had the words been spoken than she felt it drawing water from the air and from nearby clouds till liquid gushed over the floor causing sundry objects to rise up and float away. For a moment she was caught in the shift from cloud to water. The sensation of coalescing and flowing out, formless, bound only by surrounding objects was alarming. Her sense of self began to drift away. Luckily, the cold water lapping around her knees brought her back to her senses. *We have to leave,* she told the cloud. *Will the water continue if you ferry me home?*

Don't you want to watch? the cloud asked gleefully, seemingly unaware of her dismay.

Not for the first time, she was disturbed by its unfeeling, nihilistic tendencies. *How?* she asked, struggling not to respond with anger. *If ever I'm seen, they won't hesitate to blame me.*

I can hold you suspend in the air above the building, like I did once above the farm. No one will know.

Fran was tempted to stay and gloat at the chaos they'd unleashed, as if she were being won over by the cloud's exuberance, but she was worried about what might happen at the farm, especially with Xristy. *No. Take me home.*

The tableau that awaited her was both hilarious and alarming. Porcupine and company held the two new boys suspended in midair, their arms and legs flailing, squealing like pigs awaiting slaughter. Across the room, Trixie was attempting to restrain the new girls who repeatedly tried to shove her in the direction of the boys, swearing at her silently in the most colourful language. Jakob was nowhere to be seen.

Noticing her, both girls and boys ceased immediately, a look of terror on their faces. *Where's Jakob?* she asked, ignoring them.

Trixie, who had a nasty gash on her cheek where someone had clawed her, tried to explain but she didn't have the words. There were so many things in this world she didn't understand. Turning to Porcupine, Fran repeated her question. "He got a phone call and had to leave." Nobody knew where.

Can you locate him? Fran asked the cloud.

I'll ask the clouds to look, it replied.

Trixie was trying unsuccessfully to staunch the blood that was seeping from the wound on her face. Fran opened the medicine cabinet, pulled out a wad of cottonwool and held under the tap. With it, she gently cleaned the wound. She was about to apply a cream from the cabinet when Trixie stopped her. *I don't need that,* she said, pulling a small jar from her pocket and opening it, filling the room with a pungent odour. She slid her finger inside and smeared some of the contents on the gash.

What do we do with them? Fran asked Trixie, fixing the new girls.

To think that after so many years they could act so irresponsibly at the sight of a couple of boys, Trixie said, sounding disgusted. *In olden times, they'd never have dared. There were rules. Everyone knew exactly what to do and what not to do it. So much so, they wouldn't have been able to even think of behaving like that.*

How about punishment? Fran asked, warming to the idea. She could understand why the clouds were sick of their squabbling.

Now's not the time. Trixie must have remembered something because lines of worry creased her face. *We have more important things to think about.* Taking hold of Fran's arm, she led her to the door.

Hold on a moment, Fran said, freeing herself. Turning back to the boys and girls who were cowering in separate corners of the kitchen, she addressed them all, "You are to make breakfast. Porcupine is in charge. If there's any trouble I'll send the troublemakers back to the ruins of your world." With which she turned on her heels and followed Trixie out of the room.

You're becoming a real boss, the cloud remarked.

I was never like that before I met you, she shot back.

As they climbed the stairs Trixie said, *Xristy is seriously ill and nothing I've tried helps. I put her in your room,*

Fran was totally unprepared for the horror that greeted her. Apparently Trixie had not foreseen such a turn of events either as she gasped mentally. Lying on her back lay a wizened old lady who vaguely resembled Xristy, her lush hair bleached a shocking white, dark blotches staining her once flawless skin, but the worst were the bulging, terror-stricken eyes that stared pleadingly at her.

Fran moved forward hesitantly, drawn and repulsed at once. Taking Xristy's hand in hers, she sat on the edge of the bed. Bony fingers curled around hers, chapped and icy cold, clinging tight, desperate.

Fran? Xristy queried, her voice an uncertain whisper.

My love, Fran replied, at a lost what to say.

My ... time ... has ... come, Xristy said, each word an immense effort that culminate in a violent fit of coughing.

Fran wanted so much to contradict her, to stave off the inevitable, but stark reality stared unblinkingly back.

It's ... been ... so ... long, Xristy managed before coughing overtook her again. For a long moment, she was unable to still the shudders that wracked her frail form till exhaustion put paid to her paroxysms. Fran had never heard a death rattle, but the noisy, laboured gasps that abruptly escaped Xristy's wrinkled mouth must surely be that. A sudden silence filled the room. It took her a moment to realise what had happened. The laboured breathing had ceased. Xristy was no more. A faint smile ghosted across her friend's parched lips as her eyes glazed over.

Oh no! Fran exclaimed, springing to her feet but there was nothing she could do. The two girls burst into tears, staring unseeing at the lifeless shell that had once been Xristy. Fran took hold of Trixie's hand, so warm and full of life after Xristy's, and pulled her into a hug, the two finding meagre confort in each other's arms. As Fran cried for a lost love that had not had the time to flourish, she couldn't help thinking that, after such a long life set against the backdrop of a constant struggle to survive, the end must have come as a relief. Was that why Xristy seemed to smile?

All those years finally caught up with her... Trixie said, stricken. *She'd been there the longest. Her and Narie. Much, much longer than the rest of us. So many years, I've lost count.*

As she gently freed herself from Trixie's embrace, a hideous thought nagged at Fran: were all the girls and maybe the boys condemned to such an atrocious decline and end? Had she doomed them by bringing them there? The prospect sent a shudder of revulsion and guilt through her.

Why are you so upset? the cloud asked. *The fall of the dome and with it the end of years of protection against the erosion of time were bound to have an effect.*

You don't understand, she shot back, annoyed at its lack of feeling. *If what your precious clouds told me is true, I am responsible for the fall of the shield those people have been hiding behind. That makes me responsible if they all die because of it.*

We triggered it, the cloud said. *You and I. By being together. But we had no say in the matter. Did you wake up one morning thinking you'd destroy the dome? No. Both of us were totally unaware of the impact our 'union' would have.*

His logic was as implacable as ever, but it was of little consolation. *Union?* Fran asked, only just managing to hold back a bitter bark of laughter. With Xristy's lifeless body spread out before her it would hardly have been appropriate. Union?

She'd given little thought to what united her to the cloud.

We should prepare her, Trixie said, putting an end to Fran's soul-searching.

Prepare? The word left Fran perplexed. How did they bury their dead in Trixie's world?

We only ever had one person die in all those years, Trixie said, *Narie. But I remember very clearly the instructions Xristy gave us, those that the priests had taught her. We need to build a pyre with a special sort of wood. I don't know if it grows here. Maybe we'll have to go back and fetch some.*

Fran shook her head. If the clouds were right, that world might no longer be habitable. *Can you draw the tree or its leaves?* she asked rummaging in her desk for some paper and a pencil. It reminded her of school! That seemed lightyears away. *Maybe we have your tree in the woods out back.* Trixie's sketch was clumsy, unaccustomed as she was to using a pen or pencil. But the leaf was recognisable, resembling an oak. *If that's what I think it is,* Fran said, *we have plenty of them.*

Good, Trixie said, her face set in grim determination. *Let's do this.*

36.

The other girls were devastated to learn of Xristy's passing. Tears in their eyes, they pressed Trixie and Fran to let them pay their last respects, but the two had agreed not to allow anyone to catch sight of the wizened figure. They were afraid the girls would grasp the significance of Xristy's demise and panic. To distract them, Trixie led them on a quest in search of the sacred wood.

It turned out to be an easy task. The trees surrounding the farm were mostly oaks. The challenge was finding wood that was dry. Trixie insisted the ceremony required it. What's more, they didn't want damp wood sending up a telltale column of smoke for the whole town to see.

Trixie and Fran were at a loss how to conceal the state of the body till Porcupine suggested building a coffin. "As a carpenter, I reckon we could manage quickly enough. There are some oak panels in the barn. We could use them and there's a circular saw..." when Fran agreed, he asked, a little embarrassed, "How big?"

Once the three youths had left, enlisting the help of the two boys from Xristy's world - would she ever cease to call it that? - her thoughts turned to Jakob. She'd had no news. *Heard anything about Jakob?* she asked the cloud. The moment she'd asked she could feel its discomfort. In the absence of other emotions, it stood out like sore thumb. *Well?* she insisted.

I didn't want to disturb you, you were so agitated, it began, unusually bashful.

Agitated? It was hardly the word she'd have used. When the cloud was reluctant to go on, she insisted. *The other clouds tell me,* it finally admitted, *he's in a dark, dank place under the ground and can't get out.*

Blast! Damn the town's people! It was surely them. Meddling idiots. But there was nothing she could do till the funeral was over. *Can your clouds watch over him and make sure he doesn't get hurt?* she asked.

Of course, was all it said.

They chose a large clearing in the forest and everyone chipped in to build the pyre according to precise instructions from Trixie. *The funeral would usually end with some form of frenzied love-making...* the girl told Fran, taking her apart so no one could hear. *The idea being to symbolically replace the lost one. In the circumstances, I'm not sure that would be a good idea.*

You bet! Fran wanted to say, cringing at the thought of a bacchanalian orgy spurred on by Xristy's aphrodisiac oil. Her father's condemnation would have been virulent. The hypocrisy of his imagined response irked her. That she could react like him was worrisome not only because she had no wish to think like him, but above all because it was just as hypocritical. What else had she been doing with Xristy if it hadn't been orgiastic?

Fran? Trixie said, calling her attention back to the moment. *We need to prepare Xristy.*

The body, which lay on Fran's bed, had been shroud in a white sheet to discourage inquisitive eyes. The coffin stood nearby perched on two trestles, the smell of newly cut wood rivalling with the scent of the flowers Trixie had strewn around the body.

Pulling back the sheet, Fran was horrified to see that death had not halted the decline. If anything, it had accelerated. Xristy was barely recognisable. She resembled a shrivelled mummy without the bandages to mask the decay. It was as if revengeful Time had clawed back the stolen years.

Trixie gasped in horror. *What a terrible price to pay for an endless life she didn't chose.*

Anger surged in Fran. No one deserved such a fate. All because Xristy had been condemned to a seemingly unending wait. And for what? For the end of her world. Had she known Fran was the one? She must have suspected after Fran's encounter with the cloud. How could she have known that the very coming she'd waited for so long would end in such horror? Gritting her teeth, Fran said, *Let's get this over with.*

The boys, who'd been waiting outside ready to carry the coffin, peered gingerly round the door when Fran called. If the situation hadn't been so grim, these young pall-bearers would have been comical as they hiked up the minuscule coffin. "Wow!" Porcupine whispered, eyebrows raised in surprise. "She's so light."

Fran winced and glanced at Trixie who looked away. "It's time," Fran said and she marched down the stairs hand in hand with Trixie, closely followed by the coffin. They filed across the hall heading for the back door which had been wedged open. Outside they were joined by the others who trailed behind, their eyes downcast, a temporary truce having been called between girls and boys. The path wound up and away from the house, penetrating ever deeper into the forest until it fanned out into the clearing.

In the centre lay a dense pile of interwoven oak branches that had been fashioned to resemble an altar. To Fran the scene conjured up some sort of Celtic burial right her father would have railed against. Him again! The coffin was heaved into place squarely in the middle while those present spread out to form a circle around the pyre. Despite a breeze rattling the leaves high above, there was an expectant silence in the clearing like an in-held breath.

Fran was acutely conscious of the cloud curled around her neck. Its presence heightening her senses such that she became aware of a host of other clouds forming ring after ring around the mourners, their anticipation palpable.

Porcupine lit a torch made of tightly wound twigs of oak which he handed to Trixie. She proceeded to circle the coffin three times before lowering the flame and kindling the pyre at the four cardinal points. Placing the remainder of the torch next to the coffin, she took several steps back as did everyone. The blaze was burning ever brighter.

Fran had attended several funerals with her parents - they'd been miserable affairs - but she had no idea how this other-worldly ceremony might play out. She didn't expect speeches and singing, as she knew it, was probably out of the question. But she was wrong. Softly at first, like a distant whisper that grew in strength, Trixie intoned a wordless mental lament. The other four girls added counterpoint, their combined voices soaring and gaining volume. It was as if all the girls, past and present, had joined them in their lament, a heavenly choir.

Fran was transfixed. A shudder of deep-felt sadness mingled with ripples of pleasure coursed through her. She just wished she could share what she heard and felt with those present who were deaf to such a wonder. *You can,* her cloud said, giving her a gentle mental push that rearranged her perceptions till the answer was obvious. She just took what she heard and relayed it further to those whose minds were normally closed to mental exchange, slipping past centuries of preconceived ideas, undermining mountains of scientific dogma, as she reached for a long-forgotten oneness.

The effect was instantaneous as a look of surprise and wonder lit up the faces of the boys of both worlds. The mind music had a magic of its own, driving all who listened to join in. Fran relayed the boys voices to the girls who sang on. With music flowing backwards and forwards through her, Fran's mind and body resonated in harmony, buoyed up by the addition of what sounded like a chorus of deep male voices. Had the spirits of the former priests joined them? The thought sent shivers down Fran's spine.

It's us clouds, her cloud whispered.

From time to time an acorn exploded with a resounding

crack sending a spray of sparks dancing upwards through the flames. The blaze burnt quickly, consuming the corpse till only a heap of smouldering embers lit the ecstatic faces of all present.

As the last strains of their singing died away, a discordant note made itself heard, as if the music had shielded them against the ugliness of the outside world. Strident cries shattered the beauty and serenity of the moment as an angry mob blundered through the trees chasing birds and wild animals in their wake.

A wave of fear swept through the mourners who shifted closer to Fran seeking shelter. Fran was not so much angry at this intrusion as weary at the persistence of these silly people. How on Earth could she get it into their thick skulls that they were barking at the moon?

Just give me the word... the cloud said, sounding gleeful at the thought of unleashing its fury on the meddling townsfolk.

With a flick of her hand she could have the cloud transport them to that no-man's-land where she'd already banished the intractable girls and boys of Xristy's world. But eliminating the idiots because they were a nuisance, however dangerously so, was no solution. *Surround them with a dense mist,* Fran ordered. *Confuse them and prevent them from reaching the clearing, but don't hurt them.*

She sensed the cloud would have preferred a much harsher response, so she said, *I'll talk to them.* Being privy to how she intended to do so went some way to mollifying the cloud.

Huddled together close to the dying embers, the group found themselves surrounded by a ring of mist so dense not even the trees could be seen. *Fear not,* Fran said, using her new-found ability to talk to them all. *The clouds will keep them at bay while I talk to our cumbersome neighbours.*

Would you like us to sing for them, Trixie asked. *I know a chant that could scare even the most fearless of women.*

... and men, one of the four new girls added.

Do, Fran said. *I'll relay it to them.*

I wouldn't do that if I were you, Trixie replied. *By relaying such music you won't be able to ward against it and it could make you sick with fear. Anyway, we have no need of a relay. Use your ability to protect yourself and the others.*

It won't kill them, will it? Fran asked, worried at Trixie's words. What other dangerous skills were these girls capable of?

No. But that concentration of fear might - how would you put it? - loosen their bowls.

Fran cringed at Trixie's clinical tone. The girl spoke as if such humiliation were commonplace. She asked the cloud to make sure the town's folk couldn't run away. They wouldn't be the only ones unable to get away. Surrounded as she and her friends were, they had no way to flee. *We're trapped. How the hell are we supposed to escape?* she asked.

No problem. I'll guide you once this is over, the cloud promised.

Fran explained to the boys what was about to happen, at least the little she understood, then she had them huddle close while Trixie and the girls did their work. Fran was supposed to protect them, although she had no idea how. The cloud offered no advice. She didn't even know how to protect herself. Luckily Trixie homed in on the intruders so that neither Fran nor the boys could hear whatever sounds were being used to torture them.

What they did hear were the screams and animal-like grunts that echoed all around. That in itself was a vocal nightmare that no amount of fingers jabbed in ears could block out. To make it worse, a strong stench of urine and excrement soon filled the air, as if they'd strayed into a giant latrine. It was Porcupine that had the idea of rekindling the fire with twigs and broken branches lying in the clearing. His hope was that the flames would lessen the stink. At least gathering wood and stoking the fire kept everyone busy.

Fran glanced at the girls who continued to chant, their eyes closed, their heads bowed. They must be exhausted, the ordeal was interminable. She wondered if she or any of them would ever be able to sleep soundly again. Then, abruptly, the chant stopped and the girls' eyes snapped open. The animal noises from the surrounding woods had ceased and the clouds were beginning to lift.

What happened? she asked the cloud, worried the townsfolk had finally managed to flee.

They were in such a sorry state, they couldn't have gone anywhere, the cloud said, trying to reassure her. *So we helped them get home.*

You did what? she exclaimed.

We shifted them to that underground room where your friend Jakob was. It was a bit of a squeeze. But we managed.

Fran was horrified. *What about Jakob?*

He's safe at the farm waiting for you.

37.

"I thought you might appreciate some tea," Jakob said with a grin, apparently unscathed by his stay in a cell.

"Are you alright?" she asked, hurrying to his side.

"I could ask you the same," he replied, studying her face. "You look like you've just seen a ghost."

Fran grimaced. "Worse."

"Did that stinking mob of snivelling townsfolk have anything to do with it?"

Fran groaned at the word stinking and surreptitiously sniffed her sleeve to ensure herself she hadn't brought the stench with her. "They tracked us into the forest."

"What were you doing there?" He clearly sounded as if doing so was a bad idea.

"Xristy passed away," Fran began, tears welling in her eyes as she pictured the flames licking round the coffin.

"I'm sorry to hear that," he replied, taking a step closer. "But why the forest?"

"We were giving her the last rites as practised by her people. A pyre and a magical chant."

She began to cry in earnest, not just for Xristy, but because of the horror they'd endured. Jakob took her in his arms and hugged her. She understood the gesture and appreciated his sollicitation, but it still felt misplaced. He must have sensed her unease because, to her relief, he released her and pulled back, saying, "You smell of woodsmoke."

She breathed a sigh of relief. The stink of latrines had not clung to her. "The pyre," she said by way of explanation, the image of the flames replaced by angry shouts followed by desperate cries for help. "Luckily the townsfolk arrived after the ceremony was over."

"I saw them briefly when the cloud dumped them in that prison. They looked haggard, their clothes ripped and besmeared with excrement." He looked appalled. "What on Earth happened to them?"

"The girls offered to scare them, to teach them a lesson," Fran said, shuddering at the memory. "It worked far better than I could have imagined."

Jakob groaned, shaking his head. "We can't go on like this," he said. "If this continues, we'll end up with out-and-out war."

"They were out for blood," Fran protested. "We were just defending ourselves." He hung his head to one side as if to say, you can't be serious. With hindsight, she had to admit their reaction might be seen as way over the top.

"Responding to aggression with more agression only breeds even more aggression."

He sounded like a vicar, although she could see his point, but in the moment hitting back had seemed like the only solution. "What do you suggest?"

"We call them the townsfolk, but in fact they're only a small part of those living in town. True, some of them have influential positions, but if we could win over the rest of the population we might stand a chance of prevailing without having to fight."

It was an appealing idea, but she could see no way of making it happen. She thought of the girls who'd shunned her at school. To be honest, she hadn't made much effort to befriend them. She passed in review her teachers, none of whom she'd ever got close to. As for the shopkeepers and other townsfolk, she'd kept contact to a minimum, preferring to spend her time on the farm with her trusty pony. "I have no contact with the other townsfolk."

"Maybe that has to change."

With all they had to do to transform the farm, Fran couldn't see how she'd find time to court the townspeople. "So how do I do that?"

"Make allies."

"With whom?"

"I have an idea..." When Fran said nothing, he continued. "The Judge."

It was true, the woman had taken a risk in defending Fran against the religious bigots. But that didn't mean the woman would continue to support Fran's cause. "What do you suggest?"

"Invite her here. Explain what we are trying to do. Let her meet the girls and boys. Gain her to our cause."

Fran spluttered at the thought of letting the boys and girls loose on the woman. She could picture them tearing each other apart. What a nightmare. "I can't see that working."

"Why ever not?"

"The kids'd just be at each other's throats."

"Let's ask Trixie," he suggested, turning to leave in search of her.

Fran couldn't help feeling miffed at him deferring to the younger girl, although it shouldn't have surprised her seeing their blossoming relationship.

When he returned, he had Trixie in tow, one arm casually slung around her shoulder.

At the surge of jealousy she felt, the cloud commented, *What do you expect? You wouldn't let him put his arm around you.*

She huffed mentally. He was right, but it was so unfair. How long would the spectre of her father continue to haunt her?

"This is going to be complicated," Jakob said. "Could you translate?"

"No need," Fran replied. "I'll just relay your words. You'll be able to hear each other."

"Since when have you been able to do that?"

"Since this afternoon. The cloud showed me."

Clever cloud, it crowed mockingly at which she gave it a mental shove.

So what do you wanna talk about? Trixie asked.

At the sound of Trixie's voice, a look of wonder and joy lit up Jakob's face. He was so moved he was at a loss for words. He just stared at the girl with love and admiration. Fran hadn't realised how much he missed not hearing Trixie. Acting as a conduit between the two it was hard not to feel the emotions of the pair. True, Trixie had a beautiful voice, all the girls did, a fact that probably had something to do with their long practice of mental singing.

"You had a question for her I believe," Fran reminded him.

He shook himself, trying to shrug off the magic of her voice that had him enthralled. "Yes," he finally said and explained what he had in mind to a captivated Trixie who seemed equally fascinated by his voice. Being able to hear both, Fran could sense the breath in his. It was reedy, like a wind instrument that contrasted with Trixie's bell-like tones. Jakob ended by saying, "Fran's afraid the kids'll fight..."

The way they've been behaving, that wouldn't surprise me. So we'd better make sure they don't.

How do you do that? Fran asked, more than sceptical.

In our world, everyone had a clearly allotted place. Each of us knew what was expected of us, Trixie said, her eyes fixed on some distant point in the past. *The priests dictated those roles, but here maybe people should chose their own in discussion with the others.*

Jakob was enthusiastic. Of course he would be. He'd probably go along with anything Trixie suggested. As for Fran, she was less convinced. She could see difficulties where tasks and competencies overlapped. More generally, she baulked at the rigidity. She cherished the freedom she had to do her thing without parents or others dictating her choices. That included being able to change her mind. Had not the strict adherence to roles hastened the downfall of the girls' world? *I'd prefer a system where people are free to adjust their roles as they and circumstances change.*

"I believe you are both correct," Jakob said. "Having clearly defined roles that individuals negotiate with the others makes sense of the community and gives place and recognition to each and everyone. Being able to discuss and modify those roles when necessary opens the way to change and growth."

Appreciating the clarity of his thoughts, Fran felt herself won over by his enthusiasm. She could picture the way forward as it unfolded in her mind. The image gave her confidence. "I reckon we could meet your judge once we've got this sorted."

Jakob went off to contact Judge Harriet Rainer leaving the two girls alone in the kitchen. Fran brewed more tea and they sat in silence at the table across from each other for a long thoughtful moment.

With all the nasty things that have happened, Fran finally said, *I'm beginning to wonder if we're not jinxed.*

Jinxed? Trixie asked.

Under a bad influence. Like spell. Or a curse.

We call it engramming, Trixie replied.

Fran had never heard the word. *What does that mean?*

It's the way thoughts and actions embed themselves in the walls, in objects, in everything around and continue to influence people long after the event. As the girl spoke, such was her self-assurance and the solidity of her knowledge, that Fran caught a glimpse of the real age of Trixie. *Under the dome,* Trixie pursued, *the rituals of the priests, their philosophy, their way of life left a mark on everything and that continued to influence us for hundreds of years after they'd gone. My guess is that something similar is happening here, although probably not on the same scale. Somebody has left a bad mark on this place and that is making things go wrong.*

The culprit was obvious enough. Her father. The thought that his past actions could continue to dictate her present and future was more than depressing. She'd suffered enough at his hands - literally - without him haunting not only her but her friends for the rest of their lives. *Is there no way to cleanse this place of his influence?*

His? Trixie asked.

My father, she replied, a bitter taste in her mouth. *He was a vile bloke.* She shuddered at the thought of all he'd subjected her to. When Trixie waited for her to say more, Fran gritted her teeth and kept silent not wishing to conjure up the nightmares.

We can rid this place of his influence, Trixie said. *That shouldn't be so difficult. But you're going to have to cast him out of yourself at the same time. That may be more complicated.*

Thanks for the positive suggestions, Fran thought, as she imagined wrestling with the man trying to get free. She'd been there before, in earnest, and lost, every time. *Why so?*

Because some victims find it hard to give up being victimised, even when the villain is long gone. The priests taught that.

Fran mulled over what Trixie had said. If they cleansed the farm of her father's influence, would she 're-infect' it by being so tied to him? *How do I get rid of his hold over me?*

Purifying this place might do the trick, if you were to do it yourself...

So what do we need?

There are three stages, Trixie began. *The first involves clearing out and, when ever possible, burning anything that reminds you of him.*

I've already chucked out much of what I associate with him.

You'll need to be very thorough if you really want to be rid of him.

That might take a while.

Good. Take your time. Remember this has been building up for years. While you're doing that, I'll take the two girls to help me prepare for later. Then we'll need to decide what we want from this place, room by room, including the barn, the stables, the vegetable patch, even the forest. It might be wise to involve everybody. After all, we'll all be living here.

Fran was perplexed. *What has deciding what we're going to do in the building to do with exorcising it?*

When you cleanse a building, you empty it of all the nasty influences. That creates a void into which the rot will come rushing back if you don't bar the way.

How do you achieve that?

By steeping the place in good intentions, filling it with your constructive plans for its future. I suggest you list your desires and wishes for each space, one at a time. Then, when the time comes, you can read out each list and pin it up in the corresponding place.

Fran could see how deciding people's roles in the community might go hand in hand with discussing future uses of the farm and how those fit with their desires for the future. That said, she still had no idea how the actual cleansing would be done. Surely not with soap and water. *Then what? A Spring Clean?*

Trixie didn't know the expression so Fran explained. The girl laughed at the idea of physically cleaning the place. *Cleaning would be a good idea,* she said, still smiling. *But the actual purification is done by wafting the smoke of burning sage in every corner. It's a powerful purifier.*

Fran knew sage could be used against infections, she'd even used it for her pony, but she hadn't heard of this use. *There's loads of sage out back, it's growing wild.*

Good. I'll go pick some. She got to her feet and was heading for the door when she turned back and said, *The cleansing takes a while to root out all that's accumulated over time, so we should plan a celebratory feast somewhere else while the sage does its work.*

Great. I'll get the boys to help clean out while you prepare the sage with the girls. Jakob should be back by then. We'll be able to call everyone together and work on conjuring up our future.

38.

"What about this?" Porcupine asked, dragging a heavy cardboard box from amid the dust-motes and cobwebs under the bed. They'd begun in her parents' bedroom. Fran had wanted to tackle the problem head on but couldn't face clearing out her father's study. That would be the worst. He might have beaten her whenever and where ever he liked, but it was always in his office that he'd grope at her, unheard and unseen. She dreaded going anywhere near the place. It was his kingdom, his alone. Her mother never ventured there. It was the sole door in the house that could be locked. Fran shuddered, vividly remembering the click of the key that announced another nightmare.

Staring at the box, Fran wondered how she'd missed it earlier. As Porcupine moved to open it, she feared it might contain another stash of her father's glossy magazines. "Leave it," she hastened to say. "I'll check it later." She couldn't risk the boy rummaging through the stuff. What if he were to be infected with the same foul craving that had had her father in its grip? "Shove it there," she said, pointing to a corner where a bedside lamp had once stood.

Opening her mother's wardrobe, Fran began ruthlessly tossing clothes into a tea-chest that Scratch and Wiggle held suspended between them by two solid thongs. It was quickly full, at which the two struggled away to empty it on the growing heap of trash that stood in the middle of the yard waiting to be burnt. No concealed sins lay hidden beneath her mother's clothes.

Crossing the room to her father's wardrobe, she prayed all it's dark secrets had been rooted out the first time she'd rummaged through his things. Handling his clothes was so distasteful she regretted not wearing rubber gloves. Removing shirts and trousers using only the tips of her fingers didn't alleviate the disgust. The lingering smell of him had her stomach lurching. She was tempted to ask the boys to take her place, but Trixie had insisted exorcising her father required her to do it.

Having found nothing of note, Fran began stripping the two beds. Once the sheets and covers were removed, several unfortunate stains were revealed that did nothing to settle her stomach. She was glad when the two boys from the other world staggered out with the mattresses between them.

They had barely reached the corridor with their load than there was a loud crash and a cry of pain went up. Hurrying after them, Fran found the two sprawled on the floor under the mattresses. At first she thought they were messing around and she was about to swear at them when one of the boys rolled from under the mattresses griping his ankle and groaning. It was Drew, the youngest. The other boy, Bruno, called for help, being stuck under a mattress.

Trixie, who'd just returned with an armful of sage, came sprinting up the stairs and knelt at Drew's side. *He's sprained his ankle,* she announced after a quick examination. She sent one of the girls accompanying her in search of her bag of medicines then turned to Fran, her expression grave. *I was afraid this might happen. Whatever nasty forces are lodged in this house they are trying to stop us driving them out. We need to be particularly careful.*

Once a salve was applied and Drew's ankle had been bound up, Scratch and Wriggle carried him downstairs and into the living room where they laid him on the sofa. Fran, Trixie and the others followed. *Can you relay my words?* Trixie asked. Fran nodded. *The house is aware we are wresting back control and it's putting up a fight,* Trixie began. *That's why Drew sprained his ankle.* Bruno, who had Porcupine to thank for freeing him, looked horrified. He must have realised it could just as well have been him.

Once we've finished properly purifying this place, we'll be okay, Trixie continued. *But in the meantime we need to take steps to protect ourselves.* Turning to a girl with a brightly coloured scarf wrapped around her head, she said, *Will you lead us in a chant to ward off malevolent forces, Ullie?*

"I hope it's nothing like what you sang in the forest," Bruno said, his recently broken voice cracking on the last word, making him sound all the more alarmed. "That was terrifying."

Don't worry. This chant won't make you ill, Ullie replied, her sing-song voice wrapping itself around them as she tugged off her scarf to reveal her hairless scalp. The sight took Fran's breath away. It was the first time she'd seen the girl's head uncovered. Not smooth as she might have expected but covered in tiny bumps and hollows granting it a character all its own that was astonishingly beautiful. It gave Fran hot flushes.

On the contrary, Ullie continued, oblivious to both Fran and the boys gawking at her, *it is designed to protect us. You boys should join in.* She looked from one to the next, fixing each boy until her penetrating eyes settled on Fran sending thrills up and down Fran's spine. The effect was almost as potent as Xristy's oil. Fran gripped the arms of her chair so as not to fling herself at the girl. A couple of the boys were even drooling. *It's important we all chant together,* Ullie concluded.

Her chant began softly, like a gentle breeze ruffling their hair only to be taken up by the other girls, forming a rich harmony that sent shivers through Fran's whole being. As Ullie sang, she moved around the room touching each person's brow, her index finger lingering on the space just above the bridge of the nose. That touch sent a bolt of music like electricity shooting through their bodies bringing with it an irresistible desire to sing.

When the chant drew to a close, a lingering stillness left each and everyone unwilling to break the silence. For a long moment, the group hung suspended, clinging on to the joy they'd just experienced. It was Trixie that finally spoke, releasing them from the thrall of the music. *I don't know about you, but all this singing has made me hungry.*

The girls headed to the kitchen to prepare the evening meal, enlisting Bruno and Drew to help. The singing seemed to have softened the two who were less antagonistic. Meanwhile, Porcupine, Scratch and Wriggle went to burn the heap of junk in the yard. Fran should have gone with them - had not Trixie insisted she be the prime mover in erasing her father's hold over the place? - but instead she seized the opportunity to confront the last remaining spoils of her father in his bedroom all on her own.

She sat in the middle of the empty room astride a chair with the unopened cardboard box at her feet. Suspended by a cord above her head, a naked bulb cast stark shadows on the scuffed floor. She'd just opened the box, revealing piles of neatly ordered papers, when Jakob strode into the room.

"Spring cleaning?" he asked.

"No. Purifying," Fran replied. "Or rather, exorcising." She explained Trixie's plan. "This stuff was hidden under his bed," she said picking up a well-used envelope resting on top of the papers.

"Would you prefer to do that on your own?" he asked.

Absently pulling a wad of photos from the envelope before replying, she gasped at the sight of herself naked, spreadeagled on her father's bed. Flicking through the first few images she felt shame and disgust surge inside her, quickly followed by rage. A red hot wind blustered around the room. "You'd better stay," she said between clenched teeth. "To make sure I don't do anything rash." He raised his eyebrows but didn't request an explanation.

She shoved the photos back into the envelope, unwilling to reveal her naked self to Jakob. It was not her depicted there, but rather her father's sordid image of her. How had he managed to get such photos? She had no recollection of being photographed. The pictures left her feeling tainted, tarnished, spoiled. They were a stain that would never wash off.

"It's that bad?" he asked, his face ceased in concern.

"Worse," she managed to say.

He must have realised it was photos, because he asked, "Are the negatives there?"

She reluctantly peered into the envelop, then nodded. Yes. They were. "That's a relief," Jakob said. "You don't want stray negatives of compromising photos popping up in the wrong places." He'd clearly guessed something of the content. Deciding he might as well see what her father was capable of, she held out the envelop. He declined, saying, "I don't need to see. From what you've told me, I can imagine."

The remainder of the papers in the box appeared relatively innocuous, so she let him sort through them while she went down to the yard, planing to burn the envelop on the bonfire. The boys were having a hard time kindling the fire as it had started to rain. Fran called on the cloud to stave off the downpour and fan the flames. With its help, the heap of papers and clothes and discarded furniture was soon ablaze, sending sparks soaring skywards above the flames.

She hesitated about tossing the envelop into the flames, fearful that half consumed photos would be scattered by the wind, leaving salacious evidence bare for all to see. *You should weigh it down,* the cloud suggested, its voice startling her. The cloud had been silent for a while. *How?* The cloud sent a gust of wind to stir a wooden vanity case that had stood on her mother's dresser. It lay at a distance from the fire waiting to be cast into the blaze.

Fran upended its contents into the flames causing brightly coloured spurts of flame to shoot upwards to the sounds of pops and cracks. She examined the box in the light of the flames. It was entirely made of wood and would surely burn easily. Retrieving the envelop from her pocket, she placed it in the box and closed and clasped the lid.

Fixing her attention solely on the box, she sent it arcing into the centre of the bonfire, thrusting with it all her disgust and shame at her father's abuse, all her pent up anger at not being able to get revenge, all the immense sadness over a marred childhood. The cloud must have added its thrust to hers, because the box burst into flames the moment it landed in the heart of the fire, burning an incandescent white as the pain and torture and loss were consumed.

Back in the empty room, she found Jakob had emptied the cardboard box, surrounding himself with numerous neat piles of papers and letters. "Found anything worth keeping?" she asked.

"Several things," he replied, stretching forward to pick up a small stack of papers. "It would seem your father had several brushes with the police. They were investigating repeated accusations of child abuse, but no charges were pressed. He was a well-known and respected public figure. The papers suggest the police accused the children of making it up."

So she hadn't been his sole victim. The news should have made her mad both at him and at the police, but she just felt deeply sad for the children whose lives he'd ruined.

"That ties in to the second discovery I've made. Your parents wanted to adopt a child." The news horrified her. It was like recruiting another victim. "Normally anyone suspected of abusing children," Jakob continued, "would automatically be barred from adopting, but the subsequent papers are missing. I don't know if this was before or after his difficulties with the police. I can only presume their efforts failed. I'll check in town tomorrow. Just to be sure."

Fran could see little point. What was done was done. Her parents hadn't been able to adopt a child. Thank heavens. "Did you manage to contact the judge?"

"Yes." He chuckled. "She was intrigued. I think she's taken a shine to you. She said she'd come the day after tomorrow. Can you be ready by then? I have to confirm."

Fran asked Trixie to explain the purification. The girl unashamedly straddled Jakob's knees going into the details of purifications while Jakob listened with wrapt attention. Fran closed her eyes letting herself be a conduit for their discussion while she drifted like an untethered boat floating freely on her own thoughts.

Is that what you humans call love? the cloud asked.

Love? Fran asked, startled at its voice surging in the middle of the background hum of conversation as it flowed back and forth through her mind.

Yes. They're acting like clouds. When she clearly didn't understand, it added, *Flowing into each other.*

Its description seemed obscene, but the moment the thought crossed her mind, the cloud responded. *No. Not that. Is that all you humans think of? Let me show you.*

Rather like the time it had enhanced her night vision, it now adjusted her eyes to reveal a swirling cloud of colours surrounding the two. *You call it an aura, I believe,* the cloud commented. She understood that these were invisible but vibrant parts of them that were interacting as they spoke. The cloud had been right, their respective auras were merging to form an iridescent whole that pulsed with life. The sight was so beautiful, it took Fran's breath away. She was so taken by what she saw, it interrupted the flow of their conversation which she had been unconsciously relaying.

"Hey!" Jakob exclaimed, as if waking from a dream.

What's up? Trixie asked, sounding worried.

Looking closely, she saw that their two auras had drawn apart and lost some of their radiance.

"Sorry," Fran said and she really was sorry to have put an end to such a beautiful display of affection. "I got distracted."

39.

It took them till late the next day to finish sorting through the farmhouse, the barn and the neighbouring outbuildings. No concealed nightmares surged up to plague Fran, but they did unearth a stock of gardening tools which must have belonged to her mother. Trixie was delighted and wouldn't stop talking about the gardens she planned to create. Porcupine and his friends were happy too. They discovered a stash of building equipment that looked new. Fran couldn't understand why her father, always so tight with his money, should've invested in so much stuff he never used.

Jakob arrived back in time for the evening meal. He'd slipped into town following a lead about a possible adoption by Fran's parents. He was clearly eager to share his findings, but Fran, who was busy preparing the evening meal with the girls, was in no hurry to hear. What did it concern her that her parents had failed in their attempt to adopt a child. That she might have had a sister or a brother to share her torture was no consolation whatsoever. It was only when the boys and girls, with the exception of Trixie, had retired to the barn that Jakob was able to talk.

"I went to the archives in town," Jakob said as the three of them sat around the kitchen table stringing together bundles of sage, "pretexting research for a case I was on. It wasn't easy. The archivist - a good friend of the mayor - kept sidling by to squint at what I was doing. Only when the slimy toad was called away for a moment was I able to find the papers I was looking for."

He pulled his bag from his shoulder and, opening it, drew out a wad of papers.

"You swiped them?" Fran exclaimed, astonished he'd stoop to stealing.

Jakob raised his hands in a sign of surrender. "Guilty." He grinned. "But they are surely safer here than in the hands of the mayor's crony."

Fran shook her head, although she had to admit he was right.

"The documents we found were legitimate," Jakob continued. "Your parents did file to adopt."

"That's not possible," Fran exclaimed. "I would know if they'd adopted a child."

"Of course you would," Jakob said. He pulled one of the documents from the wad and placed it on the table in front of her. "Unless of course that child was you."

Fran stared at him in disbelief, her mouth fallen open. "Me?" She glanced down at the paper, skimming for the name of the adopted child. And there it was. Her name, in black and white.

I don't understand, the cloud commented. *Why aren't you relieved? That monster was not your father.*

It's complicated, she replied, not sure she understood the wild mix of emotions she felt. Turning to Jakob, she said, "Does it mention who my parents were?"

"That sort of information is generally redacted."

Fran scanned the page to see if it identified her parents. The entry had not been blanked out. It simply said, parents unknown. Further down, the signature of the mayor sprawled across the page giving it the official seal, while the document had been witnessed by the priest and the head mistress. The same gang that hounded her now were in on her misery right from the start.

What does this mean? Trixie asked. *Can we continue to stay here?*

"Don't worry," Jakob said, running his fingers through the girl's hair. "The adoption papers are valid. Fran is the rightful heir."

Heir? Trixie asked.

"She becomes the owner of the farm if her adopted parents die or are mentally incapacitated," Jakob explained.

"If my mother..." Fran almost choked on the word, "were to recover, could she reclaim the farm?"

"Theoretically, yes," Jakob responded. "At least, her part of it, if three doctors certified she was no longer inapt."

Fran could see a nightmare scenario playing out. "I wouldn't put it past the townsfolk to get her released," she said. "Just to spite me."

"All the more reason to get the judge on our side," Jakob pointed out.

"So, is she coming?" Fran asked.

"Friday afternoon."

"This Friday?" Fran exclaimed, alarmed at how little time it left.

So soon! Trixie added.

"It's what we discussed, and anyway, if we wait," Jakob pointed out, "the townsfolk might act before we're ready."

"We'll need to do the purification tomorrow," Fran said, getting to her feet to pace the kitchen.

That's doable, Trixie said.

"...and while we wait for the sage to do its job," Fran continued, "gamble that we manage to agree on our common goals and who plays what role."

"Do you know any herb concoctions or any chants that focus people's attention when they work together?" Jakob asked Trixie. "We're going to need all the help we can get."

Yes. I know of just the remedy and the plants grow here. But I'll have to collect them now. She glanced apprehensively at the window, it was dark outside. *They must macerate all night. As for chants, I'll have to ask Ullie,* Trixie replied. *She's the specialist.*

"I'll come with you," Jakob offered. Trixie beamed and clasped his hand in hers.

Fran had no wish to get between the two who clearly longed for time alone, but she had to ask, "Will you be alright out there?"

I can keep watch, the cloud told Fran.

"The cloud has offered to keep an eye on you," Fran told the couple with a grin, "to make sure you don't do anything untoward."

I said no such thing, the cloud objected, rattling the windows in protest.

"I gather you misrepresented your cloud's words," Jakob said, raising his eyebrows.

I like him, the cloud said. *I think I might take up with him instead.*

"Off with the lot of you," Fran said, dismissing them with a wave of her hand. "I'll go talk to Ullie."

As Fran made her way to the barn, she wondered if she'd feel the absence of the cloud, imagining something akin to a hole in her inner self, but instead she was acutely aware of the link that connected them. She couldn't sense what it was doing, but, wherever it was, it remained bound to her.

In the barn, she found the whole group, boys and girls, huddled round a bed intent on something she couldn't see. A worried thought crossed her mind. Had they discovered some secret stash of her father's she'd overlooked? Blast the man! Would she ever be free of him? Apparently, burning his belongings had not sufficed.

Drawing closer she saw the object of their interest. It was indeed a relic she'd missed, a family heirloom, the ivory chess set that had belonged to her father and his father before. Not that her father ever played chess. She suspected he didn't know how. But that didn't prevent him cherishing the set as if it were a holy relic. Fran had never been allowed to go near it, let alone finger the pieces. One of the young ones must have stumbled on it and hidden it from her. Porcupine was trying to explain the moves in improvised sign language, a task made all the more difficult as the girls kept picking up the pieces to examine them.

"I see you've found my father's chess set," Fran said, causing several of them to jump in surprise while others struggled to conceal guilty looks. She'd completely forgotten he had such a set. Only on rare occasions had he taken it out to show a visitor. "So you know how to play?" she asked Porcupine.

He nodded enthusiastically. "Learnt at school. One of the few things I did learn."

School? Ullie asked, having heard the word relayed by Fran. Of course, those from Xristy's world would have no idea what school was.

Remind me to explain some other time, Fran said, taking the girl by the arm and leading her away. *We need to talk.* Ullie responded by slinging her arm around Fran's waist as if she'd been expecting Fran to come and fetch her.

Trixie suggested I talk to you, Fran said when they were alone. She struggled to avoid staring at the girl's bald head. Had she unconsciously sought to corner the girl when no one was around? If the cloud had been with her, it would've made some snarky remark about being morbidly fascinated by people skulls.

When Fran had finished her explanation, Ullie said, *You can touch it if you like,* gifting Fran a broad smile.

The invitation threw Fran completely. *Am I that obvious?* she asked, blushing.

Ullie nodded blowing her a kiss as they entered the empty kitchen. *And your cloud is not here to get in your way.*

You are aware when my cloud is with me? Fran asked, surprised at what the girl was capable of.

Instead of answering, Ullie took Fran's hand and placed it on the smooth skin that arced from ear to ear. The delicious feel of it sent shockwaves up her arm and down her spine. She sucked in a rapid breath and, leaning forward, kissed the shiny crown of Ullie's head. Fran should've known the girl would have rubbed the sacred oil into her scalp. She just had time to rush the girl upstairs to her bedroom before the frenzy set in.

So that was why you sent me on a wild goose chase, watching over people who didn't need me getting in their way, the cloud commented finding Fran naked, sprawled on her bed.

Fran instinctively pulled the covers over herself, disappointed to find Ullie was no longer with her. At the same time she was relieved. Had the girl been there, she probably wouldn't have been able to resist. The scent of the oil was still strong in her nostrils. And on her fingers, she realised, sniffing them.

I thought you two were supposed to be talking about our future, the cloud continued. *Or was that just an excuse?*

The cloud might not understand emotions very well, but it was getting adept at aping emotional displays it had witnessed. Judging from its tone, it sounded like an aggrieved grandmother disappointed with her grandchildren. Whenever had it ever seen a grandmother? The image was so incongruous Fran burst out laughing.

What have I done now? the cloud asked, genuinely confused at Fran's reaction. If Fran hadn't known better, she'd have said it was offended.

You sounded like a grumpy grandmother annoyed at her grandchildren for being naughty.

It seemed appropriate.

Well it could be, but you are neither a grandmother nor grumpy and I am certainly not your grandchild.

Well, at least I tried, the cloud said, attempting, and this time more appropriately, to sound like a pupil that had worked very hard but still failed an exam.

You did indeed, Fran replied, Genuinely impressed at its efforts. It was under no obligation to try to accommodate itself to her. *If I didn't have so many emergencies to deal with, I'd take you into a nearby town and we could watch people to identify and understand their emotions better. Unfortunately that's not possible.*

Don't worry, you have plenty of emotions for me to study. And as I'm with you, I have the advantage of knowing what thoughts go with them. Although the two don't always fit. Sometimes there aren't any thoughts at all. Like when you were rolling on the bed in the arms of that girl.

Fran baulked at the suggestion she'd been completely out of control, although, if she were honest, she had to admit that was indeed what had happened. *How long were you spying on me?*

Spying? How can I possibly spy on you? I'm a part of you and you're a part of me. We are together. Is that so hard to understand?

We're so different, Fran objected. *I find it hard, if not impossible, to see you as a part of me. It's so much easier to imagine you as separate. Anyway, we're not really one, because you can read my thoughts but I can't hear yours.*

There are good reasons why my thoughts are not accessible to you.

Fran huffed in frustration. *That's what you say, but you won't tell me why.* When it didn't venture further, she said, *I have a proposition. I'll teach you about emotions if you teach me to see the world from your point of view.*

Typical human, it retorted.

What do you expect? I am human. So what's human about that?

Always striving to achieve the impossible, the cloud added. *Human emotions are tightly bound to their bodies. As a cloud, I have no body, lest it be yours, so where does that leave me? What's more, human understanding is intimately interwoven with emotions. Without them, the meaning of the world, for humans, would fall apart. Yet the understanding we clouds have is all-comprehending and does not require emotions. Taking up your offer would be akin to striving for the unattainable.*

At least you get to try. I don't even get a chance.

That's not true, the cloud said, trotting out a good imitation of a misunderstood mother. It's way of toying with emotions was verging on disturbing. *I've given you several glimpses at how I see the world.*

Fran was incredulous. *When?*

You remember when I showed you your two friends and how their clouds mixed together with all those colours? And then there was the time when I showed you the television people at night from a long way off.

Fran remembered, although she hadn't thought of it that way. *So you can share your way of seeing the world.*

The frustration that whooshed through its mental sigh was almost realistic. *You win,* it muttered.

40.

Fran awoke to discover Ullie sprawled next to her with one arm laced around Fran's waist.

Morning, the cloud said, startling Fran. So much so, she jumped, causing Ullie to stir. The young girl let out a gentle moan then promptly slithered back into sleep.

If I were a man, the cloud continued, clearly in a talkative mood, *I might be jealous. Isn't that what human men feel in such circumstances. But, I'm not a man nor am I jealous. I wonder what a woman would feel.*

Jealousy too, probably, Fran replied. *But you are neither man nor woman.*

Thanks for reminding me! There was just enough humour in its voice to avoid it sounding seriously reproachful. *Did you actually sleep?* it asked.

The insinuation was not lost on Fran. Neither was the growing skill with which the cloud wielded not only emotions, but the subtlety of human conversation. *You should know,* she retorted. *I was asleep, but you were surely awake. Is not sleeping one of the human characteristic you haven't yet learnt to imitate?*

There's no need, it replied making a show of being surprised that she didn't know.

Who were you talking to? a sleepy voice asked. Ullie was awake.

The cloud, Fran replied, freeing herself from the girl's

embrace and getting to her feet. *It was making snarky remarks about finding you in bed with me.*

No I wasn't, the cloud shot back, but only to Fran.

Ignoring its rebuttal, Fran was tempted to climb back into bed, seeing Ullie lying there, invitingly uncovered - to hell with the cloud watching on - but she didn't get a chance. A knock sounded at the door and Trixie trotted in, closely followed by Jakob.

Big day, the girl began, taking several steps into the room before she noticed Ullie, at which her eyes lit up.

Jakob halted in the doorway, suspended in mid-motion a moment before recovering. His lips quirked in a smile, saying, "Modesty doesn't seen to be a virtue taught in the girls' world."

How about that for an interesting entanglement of emotions? the cloud commented, managing to sound even more matter-of-fact than Jakob.

"Why don't you folks see about some breakfast, while I find some clothes for Ullie," Fran said, relaying her words to the girls as well.

The smirk on both Trixie's and Jakob's faces, who'd shifted to stand hip to hip, said how much they doubted she'd really be looking for clothes. "Be gone with you, you mocking rabble!" Fran said, turning her back on them.

"That was quick!" Jakob observed a short while later when Fran entered the kitchen.

Don't tease, Trixie said, making Fran wonder how the girl knew what he'd said.

Being in this world is changing her... the cloud said cryptically. *And the others.*

A vision of Xristy's shrivelled form flashed through Fran's mind. She shuddered.

Not like that, the cloud added.

Will you quit reading my mind, Fran objected, annoyed, not so much at him doing it - his ability meant she didn't need to repeat her thoughts - as at not being able to read his thoughts herself.

I can't stop. It's part of who we are and the bond between us.

One by one, the others sauntered in from the barn, several yawning copiously, and took their places at the table while Trixie and Jakob served breakfast. Fran relayed conversations so that boys and girls could communicate. Doing so had become so second-nature, Fran was free to think her own thoughts and take part in the conversation.

She was relieved to see that the night spent with her had not resulted in any possessiveness on the part of Ullie who'd gone to sit with the other girls who were chatting animatedly amongst themselves.

Once the meal was over and the breakfast things cleared away, Fran got to her feet to address the group. All heads turned to look. "Today is an important day. Not only are we going to drive out what remains of the hostile presence in these walls, but we are also going to trace our future and each of you will chose your role in that." She paused to gauge their reactions. Above all there was interest, if not curiosity. "To help avoid us getting lost on the way, Trixie has prepared a special beverage and Ullie will lead us in a chant."

Fran had expected some bitter remedy but Trixie's tea was surprisingly delicious. As for the chant, it consisted of a simple round which all of them were able to sing. However, Ullie wove into the music a complex series of harmonies that were entrancing. Fran was encouraged to see that everyone enjoyed singing. She could imagine it being one of the solid pillars around which they could build a future.

"As part of ridding this place of the negative influences that have dug themselves in, we must replace them with our positive intentions for the future. That raises the question of what we as a group want to do here. It also questions each one of us about what role we want to play."

"You're asking us for our opinion?" Porcupine asked, sounding incredulous. "But this place belongs to you. Surely you have a better idea than any of us about what you want to do."

Fran had wanted to leave the others free to give their ideas before she shared hers. But Porcupine was right, this was her place. It was her project. She had to own it. "Young people like yourselves, me included, have great potential but that potential is frustrated by society. I want to create a place where young people can develop their potential and do great things. So maybe I should frame my initial question differently. What would you like to become? And, how do you see yourself contributing to the work needed for all of us to get there?"

"You've told us your vision for this place," Jakob said. "But what do you expect to do here?"

"I see myself as responsible for the overall management. But I also see myself journeying in search of other boys and girls to join us."

That search is very much akin to what both Xristy and Narie were involved in. Trixie said, sounding doubtful.

Fran couldn't help recalling that it was exactly that pursuit that had led to the demise of the two girls.

Shrugging off the despondent mood that had come over her, Trixie seemed excited at painting her future. *I know exactly what I want and what I would like this place to be. I want to develop my skills in healing and herbal craft and my ambition is for this farm to become a centre where people can come to be healed.*

I like that, Ullie said. *It fits quite well with what I had in mind. I want to continue developing my work with chanting and singing. It might be good if I could teach others how to sing and maybe some of my chanting could be of use in healing people.*

"It's alright for you lot," Bruno said, turning to confront Ullie and Trixie. "You've been trained for years in tasks you're good at. But what if we don't know what that is? I might be brilliant at something, but have no idea because I have never tried doing it, whatever it is."

"I agree," Wiggle said. "I might have trained in the building trade, but that doesn't mean that was what I want to do. If I had a choice, I might well do something quite different, but I've no idea what that could be."

"We're not like you," Scratch said, addressing Fran. "We're ordinary people. We have no special gifts. How can we possibly imagine doing extraordinary things like you?" Several people nodded in agreement.

There are all sorts of potential scenarios in which they could discover greatness, the cloud whispered in Fran's mind. *But those events have not yet happened and you're going to have to give that time to unfold.*

"I see the problem," Jakob said, jumping to the rescue. "Maybe, we should cater for basic needs first."

"What do you mean?" Bruno asked.

"Having food and clothes, cooking, washing, building a suitable home, tending the animals, collecting the eggs,..." Jakob replied, "There are many things we need to do just to be able to survive."

Drew, the small, silent boy from the other world surprised everyone by speaking up. "I've jotted down the list you made," he said, holding up a paper. As none of the boys or girls could read or write, Fran wondered how he'd learnt. It confirmed her suspicion he was probably not from the other world. "We could begin with that?" the boy concluded.

As he read out the list and people put down their names, Fran was disappointed. It had all seemed so easy. She'd traced out a path forward but she could see that wouldn't work.

Look, the cloud said. At its injunction. Fran's vision clouded then sharpened as she had the alarming impression her sight was being stretched, making it possible to see far into the distance although she could make out no details. *Not distance,* the cloud said. *Time.*

As she shifted forward through that vision, she knew, although she had no idea how, that she was following multiple threads that corresponded to Porcupine's possible future as he became clearly visible in different scenarios. She saw him tending to a sick cow. She saw him drafting architect's plans. She saw him playing chess in an international tournament.

There are many more like that, the cloud said, putting an

end to the vision, *an infinite number, in fact, although very few of them will ever materialise. Your job is not to force them to decide now when they have no idea where they're headed - that would collapse a host of possibilities - but to nurture their lives so that one such future can emerge. See yourself as a midwife that helps give birth to their future even if you cannot know in advance what that might be.*

Fran felt elated that such futures were possible and that she could play an active part in them. She wished she could see more, but she realised that knowing what might happen would not help guide people to an enriching future. She'd just be tempted to steer them towards one of the possibilities when it might turn out to be a bad choice. At the same time, she felt deflated at the realisation she'd got it so wrong.

Making mistakes is essential to learning, the cloud recited, playing the part of an irritating school teacher or a know-it-all priest.

"How about you?" Jakob asked, startling her from her reverie. "You're the only one who has not listed your responsibilities."

She was tempted to reply midwife, but that would require explanations she wasn't sure she could provide and attempting to do so would probably cast her as an interfering busybody. "I'll look after the overall management of the farm and the finances," she said, prosaically. "And I can help in the kitchen, in the gardens, in the stables and in many places."

That's great, Trixie said. *But we still need two things. An overall aim for this place to guide us in our decisions. We can always adjust it later. And our wishes for every room or space which we'll need to write down and pin up in each place.*

"I liked the aim you put forward, Fran," Jakob said. "If I remember rightly, you said: a place where young people can develop their potential and do great things."

Everyone agreed.

As for our wishes for each room, they can be simple, Trixie suggested. *For example, that this kitchen be a welcoming place for rich exchanges and a place we can always get good food.*

41.

The tiny bundles of dried sage they'd used to purify the place were all spent. Only the cinders remained and a lingering scent of sage to bear witness to the long ritual they'd just completed. Drew's hands were empty, the last of his little pieces of paper had been pinned up in the barn. To house and protect us and our future friends, it had read.

Stomachs were rumbling. They'd preferred to do the purification in one go and had not paused to eat at midday. They'd agreed not to return to the wood for a picnic after what happened with the townsfolk. It too would need a purification at sometime in the future. Instead, Fran, who was leading her pony on a rein, took them up to the ridge overlooking the town. As there was a light breeze, they opted for a sheltered spot surrounded by large rocks and spread a couple of tablecloths on the grass on which they laid out food and drink.

The meal had been prepared by Zandra. Apparently, she'd done most of the cooking for the girls in the other world. Using vegetables picked from the farm and herbs brought by Trixie from the other world, the girl had drummed up a feast. She'd been helped by Scratch, who apparently wanted to learn to cook.

In her saddle bags, Fran transported a cut of smoked ham wrapped in wax cloth to complete the meal. It dated from the year before when her father had still kept pigs. He'd slaughter them himself. Fran could still hear their desperate squeals. Fran's mother had been tasked with curing the ham. Unaccustomed as they were to eating meat, the girls from the other world preferred not to try. The boys, on the contrary, were delighted to have so much meat to themselves.

Easy does it, Trixie said, restraining Bruno's hand as he tried to stuff yet another slice of ham into his already-full mouth.

"Hey!" the boy objected, shaking his hand free.

You'll choke, she told him. *What's more, eating food like that is not good for you. How do you expect your stomach to digest all that stuff you're shovelling down your throat?*

Bruno ignored her warnings and defiantly pushed the slice into his mouth. With bulging cheeks, he grinned at her, but the girl wouldn't let herself be provoked.

"Trixie is right," Fran said, removing the rest of the ham from the makeshift table much to the annoyance of both Bruno and Drew. "I can understand why the sight of so much meat must be difficult to resist, especially when you've had next to nothing for years. But eating everything the moment it's available is not a good strategy. We need to keep something in reserve." It was partly her fault. She should never have brought so much. She'd naively expected restraint.

Typical human males, the cloud commented, sounding arrogant, as if it placed itself above such behaviour.

Fran wonder how it could be so sure, but she didn't bother to reply. "What's more," she said to Bruno and Drew, "as you now live with us, your health is our concern." Trixie nodded in agreement. "Should you become ill, who will do your work? Who will look after you?"

Fran returned the remains of the ham to her saddlebag and stood lost in thought as she petted her pony that was munching on grass some distance from the noisy group.

He's beautiful, a quiet female voice purred behind her. Fran turned to find Veth, the youngest of the girls from the other world, staring wide-eyed at the pony. *I've never seen anything like it. Do you think it would let me touch it?*

Hold out your hand, palm up, Fran said, doing just that to illustrate what she meant. The girl cautiously did as she was told. When the pony lurched forward to sniff her fingers, the girl snatched them out of reach, letting out a squeal as she did. The pony would have reared had Fran not had a tight hold on its rein.

"Gently does it," she whispered and, grasping Veth's hand, held it steady for the animal to smell. The pony eased out its tongue and licked the tips of the girl's fingers.

It tickles, the girl said with a giggle.

Now it knows you, Fran said, *it'll let you stroke it.*

Veth ran her fingers down the pony's neck causing it to whinny in pleasure and Fran to shiver in sympathy. Why were all the girls from the other world so damn cute? The girl leaned in, laid her head against the animals neck and the two stood in silent communion for a long moment while Fran watched on, fascinated. Something was passing between the two, although she couldn't detect what.

It likes you, Veth said, opening her eyes. *But it's not happy you don't take it out for a ride more often.*

The girl's words filled Fran with apprehension only to be replaced by wonder, quickly followed by doubt. *How the hell do you know that?*

The answer left no room for doubt. *I hear its thoughts.*

The feeling of loss at the news almost broke Fran. Her pony had been her only companion when everyone else was against her. Many a time she'd had to brave her father's wrath when she defended her pony. There were bruises on her backside to prove it. She'd spent hours with the pony roaming the countryside. She'd tell it about her woes, her doubts, her aspirations but never once had the animal spoken back. Now it conversed with this young girl at their first encounter. How could it flip allegiance so readily? She felt betrayed.

I told you being here was changing them, the cloud commented.

Its failure to address her hurt stung even more. In a fellow human being such a response would have seemed callous. The conviction that she was all alone assailed her, bringing tears to her eyes. She turned her back on Veth, not wanting the girl to see her distress. She needn't have bothered. The girl was entirely engrossed in silent conversation with the pony.

Don't be so upset, the cloud said. *Remember, you have me.*

Fran snorted. She was about to respond angrily that a cloud could never replace a pony, it at least had a warm body, but she managed to stop herself in time. Too late though, the thought had been thought and the cloud could hear every one of hers.

I don't hold it against you, it replied, sounding every bit the magnanimous old man. *Your thoughts are clouded by your emotions.*

If there'd been the slightest hint of gloating in his voice, Fran would have been furious, but his tone was level and free of emotions. The very absence of emotions was in itself irritating. Almost as if its lack of feelings made it superior. Cold, almost emotionless fury had been the trademark of her father. She'd had enough of superior men.

I'm not your father, the cloud reminded her.

Fran huffed and let her shoulders slump. No use revisiting old battles with new foes.

I'm not your foe either, the cloud corrected.

I know, Fran said wearily.

"We should be going," Jakob said, striding up at that moment. "The boys are getting restless."

"It's all that meat," Fran shot back, glaring at Jakob causing him to take a step back and raise his hands in surrender.

"What did I do?" he asked.

"Sorry," Fran said. "Not in a very good mood."

"Not because of that meat business, I hope?"

Fran shook her head. She wouldn't have known how to put it in words, even if she'd been willing to share it with him. "Men," she muttered.

"What have I done now?"

"You? Nothing." Fran shook her head. "I just lost a very close friend."

Jakob spun round on the spot, looking in every direction as if in search of the person who'd been lost.

"My pony," Fran said, nodding in the direction where the animal and Veth were drooling over each other.

Jakob burst out laughing, only to stop the moment he saw Fran's dark look. "Sorry."

He was a well-intentioned, sensitive man. It was unfair to beat him for the shortcomings of others. "I suppose it could be seen as funny." She nodded in the direction of Veth. "One minute she's terrified of the beast, the next she's talking mind-to-mind to it."

We're all learning new tricks, Jakob said mind-to-mind, a broad grin on his face.

"How the hell did you manage that?" Fran asked. Another of her advantages had just gone up in smoke.

"Trixie tried to teach me, but it didn't work very well. In the end, I think it was you that taught me."

"Me?"

"Yeah. By constantly relaying the girls' words, I reckon that gave me a feel for such conversation and made it much easier."

Told you so, the cloud said. This time it really did sound like it was gloating.

"Has anyone else learnt?" Fran asked. If any of the boys had, that would put an end to their claim they were nothing out of the ordinary

"Dunno. Haven't had a chance to ask."

Veth, can you bring the pony down to the stables? Fran asked. *We're going back now.*

Sure. The girl's reply was almost a whinny.

Fran had no time to contemplate the transformation the girl was undergoing as she had to help pack up the picnic and carry the hampers down to the farm. Once back in the house, she had to begin tidying up in preparation for the judge's visit.

As she went about her work, she decided to test each of the boys, unbeknown to them. She was intrigued. How many had spontaneously developed the ability to speak mind-to-mind? To her surprise, both Bruno and Drew had. As for the three apprentices from her world, they heard her voice but were unable to reply. Maybe they lacked the incentive that Trixie was for Jakob. Or maybe there were genetic factors that explained their inability. If they didn't learn, Fran worried the three might end up ostracised as the only ones who couldn't speak mind-to-mind.

You could try teaching them, the cloud suggested. When Fran responded with scepticism, the cloud replied, *Your relaying the girls' thoughts already gave them the ability to hear, even if they can't talk. Maybe you can shift them a step further.*

Fran took Porcupine aside and led him into the sitting room, pretexting the need to light a fire. Once a log was ablaze in the grate, she invited him to take a seat. *Porcupine?* she said, mind-to-mind, causing him to look up, startled.

"Yes?" he replied, uncertain.

Speak your thoughts to me, she encouraged.

He shook his head, bemused. "I dunno. Hearing voices in my head always struck me as spooky."

You're in the wrong place, she thought, unable to suppress a smile. *You're surrounded by people who talk mind-to-mind?*

Porcupine cast an anxious glance around, but they were alone. "When I was younger," he said, almost in a whisper, "I couldn't shake the feeling I was different, odd, peculiar. Making friends was all the more difficult because of it. Being alone, I talked to myself a lot. I even imagined voices talking back. The more it happened, the more I worried I was going mad."

Let me reassure you, Fran said. *If hearing voices in your head means you are mad, then all of us are. Almost everybody here can talk mind-to-mind. That's why it's important you and your two friends learn. So you're not left out.*

"That'd be nothing new," he said sourly. "We know something about being left out."

We're all outsiders, Fran said, hoping to reassure him. He looked sceptical. *We talked earlier about our mission. We could have said we're out to make something good of being an outsider. The stance might be uncomfortable, but if you can get over bemoaning your bad luck, being an outsider offers a refreshingly new perspective on things. It can be challenging, but it's also creative. We should welcome it.*

The way you put it, he said, unaware he'd slipped into mind-to-mind communication, *we're all outsiders. That makes no sense. Someone has to be on the inside for there to be an outside.*

You're right, but now you're very definitely on the outside, my friend...

A grin spread across his face as it dawned on him what had happened. *Well I'm blowed!* was all he said.

Come on, Fran said, getting to her feet, *let's go convince your friends to learn.*

42.

The afternoon of Friday September 27th had arrived and Judge Harriet Rainer was due at any moment. Jakob had driven into town to fetch her. Fran would have liked to prep the boys and girls in the hope they'd make no blunders, but, for all her preparations, it was very difficult to predict how the young would react to the old woman or her to them. Seen from the outside, they must appear a weird bunch.

Veth had trotted off to tend to the pony. Since she'd learnt to talk to the animal she rarely left it and had begun adopting mannerisms that reminded Fran of her pony. Zandra and Scratch were in the kitchen, baking for afternoon tea with Yssel laying the table which she adorned with flowers. Trixie was with Wiggle in the greenhouse checking on the herbs they'd brought from the other world. Ullie had joined them, wanting to see if her chanting could help plants grow. That left Porcupine, who'd taught Bruno and Drew to use a tape measure so they could help him draft plans for the construction in the barn.

Jakob and Fran had spent the greater part of the morning discussing ways to present the group, but, despite wise interjections from the cloud, many points remained unclear, notably how to explain the girls' inability to hear and speak, not to mention their startling appearance with their bald heads. On one thing Fran was categoric. The girls were forbidden to use their oil. The frenzy of two fornicating policemen was still fresh in her mind.

Trixie, who'd been communicating with Jakob mind-to-mind as he accompanied the judge, came to warn Fran the woman was not alone. *She's accompanied by a young clerk who works as her assistant,* she said. *Her name's Mindy.*

Trixie must've warned everyone, because an eager delegation stood aligned on the front steps waiting to greet the judge and her assistant. Fran was unsure they grasped the importance of the visit, especially the boys. She'd tried to explain, but local politics was far too illogical for people who were completely unused to bent truth and blatant corruption. Standing there on the steps they looked like a school outing in a totalitarian state forced to greet an official visitor. That unnatural impression was reinforced by Ullie's soft chanting that went unheard by either the judge or her assistant. The girl was easing the tension that accompanied the visit.

Mindy turned out to be much younger that Fran had imagined. She could well have been the judge's granddaughter. She had the same intelligent expression and the all-seeing eyes of the older woman although she lacked the self-assurance that age and experience brought. The judge presented the girl as her assistant and discreetly leaned on her as they walked the short distance to the entrance to the house.

"We could walk round to the back and meet in the garden, if the stairs are a nuisance," Fran said.

"That's considerate of you," the judge said. "I hate to admit it, but my arthritis is playing me up these days."

Zandra, Scratch and Yssel hurried off to set up the tea things in the garden. The others crowded round as Fran introduced them. "Trixie here," Fran said, "is a specialist in herbal cures. Maybe she knows of a natural remedy that can ease your pain."

When Trixie just smiled but didn't answer the judge's greeting, the woman looked questioningly at Fran.

"Apart from myself, none of the girls living here can either hear or speak," she explained.

"That's terrible," the judge exclaimed. "How do you manage?"

It was the very question Fran had been hoping to avoid. "We've developed other ways of communicating." As if to illustrate her point, Fran relayed the words of Trixie. "Trixie says she'll make you a tea with a plant that should help ease the pain. She wants to know if your assistant would like to help her."

The judge turned to her assistant, who shook her head. "You might need me," the girl insisted.

"If that's alright with you," Fran said to the judge, aware she was taking a risk, "you can lean on me while your assistant goes with Trixie."

This is one of those confusing human moments full of contradictory emotions, the cloud pointed out.

How useful to know, Fran shot back, dryly.

"Go. You spend far too much time looking after me," the judge said. Relinquishing the girl's hold on her, she tended her arm to Fran who took it.

Mindy pursed her lips, her stance stubborn as if Fran were stealing her role, but Trixie slung an arm round her shoulder and led her away.

No tricks, Fran warned.

Me? Never!

Jakob must've heard Trixie's reply, because he was struggling to conceal a grin.

Are they all conspiring to get me into trouble? Fran asked the cloud.

It didn't reply, clearly recognising a rhetorical question when it saw one.

Fran led the judge at the head of a slow procession that wended its way solemnly around the main building. The garden out back had been neglected by her parents who never invited people. Any entertaining her father did was done by him alone in his lodge on the other side of town. Trixie had trimmed the roses and cut back the bushes, freeing a space that the others had worked to clear. It had been part of their purification drive.

Zandra and her two helpers had managed, in such a short

lapse of time, to layout a delicious high tea on trestle tables festooned with flowers. An array of tiny cakes, embellished with a fruit or nut or flower, formed the centrepiece alongside a selection of lightly baked vegetables each with its own dip. In a particularly thoughtful gesture, an armchair, bolstered with colourful cushions, had been set at the head of the table for the old judge to get the weight off her legs.

"You needn't have gone to so much trouble," the judge said, admiring the table.

"On the contrary, the young people have enjoyed honouring your presence. It gave them a welcome pretext to show off their skills." Fran called Zandra over, presenting her as responsible for the culinary delights.

The judge was at a loss how to communicate her pleasure at the food without words. In the end she clasped the girl's hand in hers and held it for a long moment as she stared into the girl's eyes. If she hadn't known better, Fran would have said the two were communicating mind-to-mind. It was only when the judge relinquished her hand that Fran heard Zandra say, *You're welcome.*

Those few words spoken mind-to-mind had Fran's stomach summersaulting in alarm. It was just the sort of gaffe she'd been afraid of. But to her surprise, the judge didn't seem to notice. Had she mistakenly believed Zandra had spoken out loud? Whatever, the judge accepted the cake Zandra offered as if nothing had happened. Fran glanced at Jakob who was staring at the judge with an intensity bordering on rude. She kicked him in the shins under the table, saying mind-to-mind, *Stop staring.*

"You realise that some of the townsfolk are set on shutting down this place," the judge said. "They seem to think you're practising some form of devil worship."

"Yes. I've noticed. I think they're misguided," was Fran's reply. "Although I suppose such a reaction is to be expected, given our vocation as a centre that welcomes misfits and outcasts. What their Bible calls the people left by the roadside."

"One of the problems with such a project is communication.

You have to ensure the local people understand."

Fran was readying herself to point to how some influential people in town were bent on preventing any communication, but she didn't get a chance. Mindy came rushing up, her cheeks flushed, her eyes wild and sweat pearling on her brow. What had Trixie done to the poor girl? Surely not that satanic oil.

"This place is awesome!" Mindy exclaimed, waving her arms to encompass the jumble of buildings. "Did you know they have a whole greenhouse full of healing plants? And there's a barn they're going to convert into living quarters. But the most extraordinary thing is how they talk." There was no stopping the girl. She was so excited by her discoveries, she was oblivious to the alarmed stares of all those around the table.

Luckily Trixie arrived bearing a steaming jug, a timely distraction. Fran's relief was short lived. *Your herbal tea,* Trixie said, pouring a cup for the judge, who once again appeared undaunted by the mind-to-mind communication. Fran could only guess Jakob must have informed Trixie of the judge's reaction. She couldn't believe the girl would deliberately sabotage their plans.

The judge's attention had turned to Mindy who was bouncing up and down in a way that hardly fit her role as assistant to a judge. "Remember what the doctor said about getting over excited," the old woman said, placing a firm hand on the girl's forearm. "Why don't you go with Trixie. Maybe she has a plant that can help you calm down."

"Is she ill?" Fran asked the moment the girl with out of earshot. She was probably overstepping the mark, but she had to ask.

"Ever since her parents died in a car accident a few years back, she's been..." she hesitated over the word, "...unstable, hyperactive the doctors call it."

"I'll have to ask Trixie - she's our specialist - but maybe we can do something for her," Fran said.

The old woman gave Fran a watery smile. Gone was all the strength and self-assurance that had characterised Judge Rainer when they first met in court. She looked tired, exhausted even, unable to confront the difficulties that assailed her. "Caring for my granddaughter has been both an immense pleasure and an enormous challenge, although I must admit I have no idea how to help her further. She has sudden violent outbursts. She lashes out at all around, only to sink into depression for days in a row. The doctors prescribed pills, but they only make a vegetable of her. I can't bear to see that. She used to be such a lively, intelligent girl."

Ullie, who'd been sitting next to them listening to their conversation relayed by Fran, said, *Maybe one of my chants could help. Do you want me to try?*

Fran wasn't sure how far she could push the judge. Maybe mind-to-mind singing would be too much. *Call Trixie and get her to bring the girl back,* Fran said to Ullie. *I'll sound out the judge to see if she'd be okay with that.*

The judge, who'd been watching Fran closely, asked, "What did you say to her?"

How observant. "You're an astonishing woman," Fran said, giving free reign to her intuition rather than bowing to caution.

"I don't know about that. I just try to be open to new things. But you folks really put that to a test."

"Sorry."

"Don't apologise," she said, patting the back of Fran's hand. "It does me good. So what do you propose for my granddaughter?"

Fran briefly explained what Ullie was capable of and suggested they try one of her chants to see if it could help Mindy.

"It's hard to imagine how someone without a voice could possibly sing," the judge said, addressing Ullie directly.

We don't think of ourselves as being voiceless, Ullie replied. *On the contrary, voice is extremely important to us. We just don't take it for granted like you talking folks seem to.*

Ullie's words left the judge thoughtful as they waited for Mindy to return. Trixie must have found a remedy because the girl was noticeably calmer. She sat next to her grandmother and, slinging an arm round her waist, leaned her head on the old woman's shoulder, her eyes closed.

If you are moved to sing, Ullie said, getting to her feet, *that's quite normal. Our music has that effect on people. Don't fight the urge. Feel free to sing along. Our music has no words and no set pattern, but it does have intention. In that it resembles what you call prayer. In this case, our intention is to aid Mindy. Like the music itself, we have no preconceived idea of a path that might follow, just the overarching intention to come to her aid.*

The girl took a deep breath and a soft whispering sound like a breeze in the trees swirled around them inviting everyone to close their eyes, to lean back and let go. As it rose in pitch, it split up and took on different forms, each rising and falling like a flock of birds, together but separate. More and more voices joined them, some deep and masculine, others rich and comforting in the middle ground, while yet others were perched high above, intoning a celestial melody.

And through it all, the singing was punctuated by Mindy's gasps as the girl sobbed almost inaudibly, no doubt reliving the loss of her parents and the despair of finding herself alone. The more Ullie's chant progressed, the more the tones became warmer till they cradled the gathered group in comforting, nurturing arms. No one wanted it to end, but end it must, leaving a lingering feeling of loss mingled with a sense of peace that had the world aglow.

"Thank you," Mindy whispered, her tear-streaked face radiant.

43.

"You do realise," Judge Harriet said as she stood alone with Fran and Jakob on the front steps to the farmhouse, "if my granddaughter stays any length of time with you, as she so ardently wishes to do, I will no longer be able to take such an active part in your defence. Her presence here would lay me open to accusations of vested interests." She shook her head. Seeing her granddaughter so much better had brought a smile to her lips but, at her words, the look of weariness had caught up with her. "I came here with the firm intention of assisting you in your plans. Instead, you have generously helped me, making any assistance I might offer nigh on impossible."

"We are happy to contribute to the wellbeing of your granddaughter. That is far more important than any petty legal threat levelled at us by fanatics," Fran said. "If you still wish to help us, I'm sure you'll find other ways."

"Talking about offering help," the judge replied, "you should set up a foundation so people can donate money to your cause."

"Yes," Jakob said. "I'd thought of that."

"For the moment, money is no problem," Fran said. "And if ever you were pondering making a financial contribution, there's absolutely no obligation. Helping you and your granddaughter was a pleasure." By way of farewell, Fran hugged the old women, who, in the space of an afternoon, had become a grandmother to them all.

"Take care," Harriet said over her shoulder as she followed

Jakob to his car.

"See you soon," Fran called after her.

You took a risk there, Fran said to Trixie who came down behind her on the steps.

Not so much of a risk, Trixie replied, gifting Fran a kiss on the back of her neck that sent shivers down her spine. *Once I realised Mindy could talk mind-to-mind, it seemed a good bet that her grandmother could do the same or at least the sight of it would not throw her.*

Well, your gamble paid off, Fran said. *I don't think things could've gone better. Although I've no idea how that will play out.*

Having her granddaughter here might turn out to be a liability. If something goes wrong and the girl has an attack we will certainly be blamed.

True. But she's in capable hands with you and Ullie.

I've been thinking about what that woman said of our need to communicate with the local population, Trixie said. *Do you think we could win them over with our ability to heal, rather like we did with her?*

Fran'd had a similar idea, but she'd dismissed it, imagining the townsfolk accusing them of witchcraft or the local doctors trying to chase them out of town as quacks. *We need to know if there are people in town willing to call on us for help,* she said. And if there are legal reasons why we couldn't do so, she thought to herself, filing the question away to ask Jakob.

What if you disguise it as something else? the cloud asked.

What do you mean? Fran asked.

Concerts. Surely they couldn't object to that. You who like telling stories, you could do so accompanied by Ullie's music. With a little help you might be able to tell stories that have a similar effect to Ullie's chanting. After the concert, you could sell tiny snacks and drinks using Trixie's herbs. You could propose singing lessons or cooking courses or storytelling classes to those who particularly like what you do.

Fran relayed its suggestions to Trixie who was enthusiastic

and immediately went in search of Ullie to set things in motion.

What did you mean about storytelling? Fran asked the cloud.

In simple terms, what Ullie does is add intention to the emotion of music. It is not so much the music that has the impact, although it helps, but the intention that weaves itself into the music. Now storytelling is different. The cloud was in full professorial mode. *Words bear both meaning and emotion. But there are ways in which you can add intention above and beyond them. In addition, you can use the story itself to open your listeners to the underlying intention. Ullie would be the best person to teach you about intention and I can give you some ideas about storytelling. Who do you think whispers all those stories to the wind?*

When Fran finally made it to her bedroom, she discovered Ullie waiting for her under the covers. Girls from the other world generally didn't wear clothes in bed but the temperature in Fran's corner of the world was much fresher than in their home. The girl had donned a pair of Fran's pyjamas and had wrapped a colourful silk scarf around her neck.

Fran's room was particularly cold, being exposed to the easterly wind. There was a fireplace but, as far back as she could remember, it'd never been used even in the harshest of winters. Another of her father's miserly achievements. Explaining to Ullie what she planned, Fran returned to the kitchen and fetched a basket with kindling, several logs and a box of matches.

The fire was a nice touch, Ullie said, running her fingers down Fran's spine, *but you realise I could've warmed you up in no time.* As if to underline her point, Ullie reached for the small bottle of oil sitting on the bedside table. Fran held up a hand to stop her, saying, *Can we make love without outside help for once?*

Ullie looked perplexed. *I don't understand. It's infinitely better with the oil.* A look of betrayal flitted across her face only to be replaced by a furrowed her brow. *Does it make you ill?*

No. It's not that. The moment that stuff takes over, it brings on such a frenzy I lose myself completely. Sure. It's great. I can't deny it leaves me satiated. But I don't remember a thing. I want us to be together for once without being out of our minds. I want to remember how it feels to run my fingers over your body, to feel you move me in ways only you can.

Fran had never seen Ullie look so stricken. *I've never done it without the oil,* the girl admitted. *I don't even know if I can.*

Sure you can, Fran replied, taking the girl's hands in hers and kissing the tips of her fingers as she held her gaze. It seemed odd to take the lead when it had always been Ullie or Xristy that had been the initiator of their lovemaking. But Fran pursued, spurred on by a heady feeling of breaking new ground. Tugging Ullie closer, she slid a hand round the girl's waist and, sensing a rising wave of urgency, clasped a wad of pyjamas in the small of Ullie's back and crushed their two bodies together. Their lips met and passion had them in its grip.

Unlike with the oil, where frenzy blinded her with a deluge of sensations, she was acutely conscious of their every move, their every touch, her every sensation. The smooth surface of Ullie's hairless scalp. The intoxicating scent of sweat that lurked in every fold of her skin. The opulent curve of her buttocks or the tiny depression in the small of her back. Even the softness of the sheets or the scent of woodsmoke in the air took on a sensuality that had her body shuddering with pleasure.

As Fran lay on the bed, entwined in Ullie's arms, a deep sense of peace settled over her. It was not just satisfaction. She felt complete for the first time, as if she'd been fractured, broken, cut off from herself, without realising it. Now she was whole. The sensation intrigued her. She wanted to explore this new-found oneness, but sleep stole up on her and spirited her away.

When Fran awoke to a quiet Saturday morning, memories of the night came flooding back that should have filled her with pleasure but instead she couldn't shake an inexplicable foreboding. Something was wrong. Ullie was no longer with her, but that was normal. The girl had a habit of slipping away before dawn, as if she had no wish to flaunt their intimacy, a fact that Fran appreciated.

She strained to hear, but all was still. Turning to the cloud, meaning to send it to check, a rush of fear engulfed her. How had she not noticed? It was gone. Normally, when it was off somewhere, a link remained, a constant reminder they were joined, but now she could sense no such link although she didn't feel torn or incomplete. Could it have slipped away, abandoning her without her noticing? She imagined herself alone, evoking a feeling of solitude that had a sharp bite to it, like an icy-cold wind. Shivering, she sprang from her bed, hastily dressed and hurried downstairs.

A disgruntled trio sat around an empty kitchen table staring blankly into space.

"Where's everybody?" Fran asked.

"Dunno," Porcupine replied, emerging from his torpor. "All gone. Including Mindy."

"Mindy?" Fran exclaimed. It might make sense for all the girls from the other world to disappear, but Mindy was not one of them.

"Maybe it's some woman's thing," Scratch mused, sounding miffed at being excluded.

Fran dismissed the suggestion with a huff. "Then why didn't they tell me?" she asked, her frustration mounting.

"Where's Jakob?" Wriggle asked. "Has he gone with them?"

"No. He drove home late last night," Porcupine said.

"Alone?" Fran asked. To the best of her knowledge Jakob had never slept with Trixie, but their relationship seemed headed in that direction.

"Alone," Porcupine insisted, clearly grasping her allusion.

"Well, make yourself some breakfast," Fran said gruffly, turning to leave. "I'm going in search of them."

All three rose as one and took a step after her. Like clockwork soldiers, you'd have said they'd rehearsed the move. "I don't want to stay here alone," Scratch mumbled. "It's spooky with them gone."

"Me neither," Wriggle echoed.

"We'll help you look," Porcupine added as all three trotted

after Fran into the hall. "Can't you send your cloud after them?"

She shot him a pained look.

"Gone too?" Porcupine asked, evidently unhappy at the news.

She nodded.

"What a mess," he replied.

They searched the farm, but found only the two boys from the other world who were fast asleep. What troubled Fran most was the absence of the cloud. Imitating how it would have done, she let her awareness drift outwards, roaming the land close to the farm. She encountered no familiar presence. In fact, she found no one. She couldn't believe the cloud would have left her for anything other than an emergency. Yet, searching back over the recent past she could find no sign of an imminent problem. Ullie, who was finely attuned to the underlying forces in the world, had said nothing.

The only plausible explanation - and it required an enormous stretch of the imagination - was that she'd inadvertently slipped into one of those parallel universes the cloud had shown her. Surely that wasn't possible. They were supposed to be potential scenarios, not realities. What's more, those possibilities branched forward from the present. There was no going back.

"Hey look," Porcupine called out from across the barn. He pointed to an empty space in a corner that meant nothing to Fran. "The rucksacks," he explained. "They've gone." Turning to Scratch he sent him to look in the larder. Wriggle was to check on the girls' wardrobe. When the two reported back, it was clear the girls had gone off taking clothes and food with them.

All three turned to look at Fran. "I'll see if I can trace them," Fran said.

"Without the cloud?" Porcupine said, sounding dubious.

"Apparently I can do things the cloud did, even when it's not with me."

Fran leaned against the barn wall and closed her eyes. Sending out her awareness as she'd often felt the cloud do, she stretched ever further away from the farm, up beyond the forest, beyond the ridge where they'd picnicked and over into a small sheltered valley where there was a neglected Celtic ring of stones. It was there she found them.

Using another of the cloud's tricks, she homed in on them, magnifying her sight till she was able to see quite clearly. Each girl stood erect and proud, flanking a giant stone. Fran could not hear them, but she guessed from the intense expression on their faces they were singing. It would be wrong to interrupt. She'd have to wait, but she had to inform the boys. They'd be worried. She didn't want to hurry back for fear she might not be able to return. Who knew if she'd continue being able to ape the cloud's abilities? So she spoke directly into their heads informing them she'd found the girls.

I'll stay for a while, she told the boys. *Go make us a good breakfast. I'll be starving when I come back.*

Fran searched for Mindy, eager to ensure the girl was safe. She needn't have worried. The judge's granddaughter was taking part as if she'd been doing so all her life. Her face was radiant, her expression ecstatic.

Rising higher above the circle, Fran looked down and was amazed to see the whole landscape crisscrossed with a web of glowing lines which flowed into and around the circle as if it were some sort of hub in a giant network. Whatever the girls were doing, it was feeding energy into the network making it glow brighter for miles around. Hardly had she wondered what it could be than the answer came as if whispered by some personal fountain of knowledge. Ley lines. Immense conduits that circled the globe channelling the earth's energy. The meaning of the girls' ritual suddenly became clear. They were the handmaidens, channeling the Earth's energy, tending to it, coaxing it, replenishing it.

As she hovered high above, surrounded by clouds, she felt the energy flowing through her, pulsing in time with the girls' song. The emotion was so intense, it brought tears to her eyes and as it did, she felt the clouds around her cry with her threatening to dowse the ceremony below with their rain. She mentally dried her eyes, managing to stop them just in time.

The ritual had come to an end and the girls were moving away towards an area where they'd spread out a picnic. Reassured that they were in no danger, Fran opted not to interrupt, returning, instead, to the farm and a welcome breakfast.

44.

So you're up, Trixie said as she traipsed into the kitchen followed by a gaggle of girls bearing rucksacks. *Ullie told us there was no way she could wake you at four this morning.*

True, Ullie said, joining them. *She was so soundly asleep I had to lay my head on her chest to check her heart was still beating.* She shot Trixie a meaningful grin.

Were you afraid all those excesses last night had got the better of her? Trixie joked.

Four? Fran asked, ignoring their jibes. *Why on Earth were you up so early?* She decided it would be better to pretend she didn't know. People might not be comfortable if they learnt she'd inherited some of the cloud's gifts.

It was Mindy that replied. *It was wonderful,* the girl said, jumping up and down in her excitement. So much for keeping her calm. *It's a real shame you weren't there.*

So what were you doing that pleased our young friend so much? Fran asked Trixie and Ullie.

Straightening out your world, Trixie replied, clearly in a playful mood.

We might have rid the farm of its ghosts the other day, Ullie added, *but something else was wrong, a deeper malaise in the Earth itself. Checking, I uncovered a problem with the flow of energy. I've no idea what you folks have been up to, but it takes a concerted effort over a long period to damage the world to that extent.*

We don't know if it was done deliberately, or if it just developed over time, like a creeping sickness, Trixie said, *but we've fixed it for now. But we'll have to keep an eye on it.*

Couldn't you have done that at a more reasonable hour? Fran asked.

Sunrise is the best time to do such work, Ullie replied.

You realise you scared me, Fran said.

How come? Trixie asked.

I awoke to find you girls gone. The boys had no idea where you were. I searched everywhere... I know it makes no sense, but I was afraid you'd returned to your world... Tears welled in her eyes.

Ullie pulled Fran into her arms and hugged her. *Silly billy. As if we'd abandon you!*

Couldn't you have sent your cloud to find us? Trixie asked.

Fran made a face. *I would have, if I knew where it was.*

Trixie looked shocked. *It's gone?*

Well, it's not here, Fran confirmed.

But you don't seem any different, Ullie protested, squinting at her to get a better look. *I reckon I'd notice the difference if the cloud was not with you. Together, you and the cloud have a presence like no one else.*

I can assure you, it's not answering my calls and I can't feel the link to it anymore.

It's almost as if it has become an integral part of you, Ullie speculated.

The idea was far from welcome. First of all, she'd got used to the cloud being separate, a compagnon, someone she could confide in or ask advice of. But then, more importantly, she wasn't sure she liked the idea of the cloud actually being her. What would that make her? She'd be completely different from the person she'd thought she was. A stranger. But remembering what had happened that morning when she went in search of the girls and how she'd flown with the clouds and stopped them raining, Fran wondered if Ullie wasn't right.

Maybe our righting the energy fields helped you integrate

the cloud better, Trixie mused.

Or maybe it was the exquisite love-making yesterday evening that pushed you over the edge, Ullie said, playfully teasing. *The intensity was too much for the cloud and drove it deep inside you till it became a part of you.*

You flatter yourself, Fran shot back. To which Ullie replied with a coy smile.

There's one way to know if you've become the cloud, Trixie said. *Can you do any of the things only the cloud could do?*

Fran wasn't ready to admit she'd already done so. Instead she asked, *What do you suggest?*

One of the first things that impressed me about the cloud, Trixie replied, *was the way it rattled the windows when it didn't agree.*

Ullie chuckled. *That scared me too.*

Fran was surprised they chose such an innocuous activity, but then they probably had no idea what the cloud was capable of. She turned her attention to the windows and tried to make them rattle. To her disappointment nothing happened. The cloud had disagreed with her, Trixie had said. How could she disagree with herself? It was comical. She must be going about it wrong. What would the cloud have done? It wouldn't try to rattle the windows. No. It would stir up the wind outside. The moment she thought it, she knew exactly what to do and was rewarded with the windows in the kitchen rattling violently.

Most of the girls, who hadn't been paying attention to Fran's conversation, jumped in surprise. *No need to panic,* Trixie said, *it's just Fran playing a practical joke.*

We should celebrate, Ullie said, turning back to Fran.

Fran was not eager to broadcast the fact that she had some of the powers of a cloud. She was concerned the young people would shun her if they knew.

"Celebrate what?" Jakob asked, entering the kitchen at that moment.

Both Trixie and Ullie turned to Fran, leaving her to answer. "The girls have managed to further heal this place and make the energy more positive."

"Great!" Jakob said. "I have good news too. I bumped into the judge this morning. I told her about your idea of holding a concert. She was enthusiastic and suggested you build a small hall where such concerts and possible courses could take place. If you agree, she said she'd drop by this afternoon with an architect she knows. I believe she'd be willing to finance it."

Fran was busy discussing a possible site for the concert hall with Ullie and Trixie when the car pulled up and Judge Rainer stepped out. She was accompanied by a disheveled man with the beginnings of a beard and a severe-looking young woman dressed in a suit. The woman, who was toting a briefcase, greeted Fran with a hint of a stiff bow when the judge presented her as Miss Gertrude Schmidt, the architect. Her unsmiling expression did little to endear her to Fran who took an instant dislike to the woman. The judge went on to explain that Miss Schmidt was the person she'd mentioned to Jakob.

Stan Blithe was the name of the man, who turned out to be a doctor. He gifted Fran a broad smile that went some way to counteract the bad impression his colleague had created. Dr Blithe's casual appearance and his informal manner hardly fit Fran's nightmarish experience of doctors. Another legacy left by her father. Why had Stan come? Was he the woman's partner? Or her doctor? Fran was stuck with her questions because no explanation was forthcoming.

"So where do you plan to stick this building?" Miss Schmidt asked.

The tone of the woman's question struck Fran as unnecessarily aggressive, although the judge showed no sign of being shocked. "Here," Fran replied, pointing to a series of poles they'd planted in the ground.

"That won't do at all," the woman shot back. "The orientation is completely wrong."

Orientation was one topic the girls had debated at length. Trixie and Ullie had pointed out the energy lines at that point left no other choice. Having cast a bird's eye view on the scene,

Fran could see they were right. The future building would nestle snuggly between key lines of force. What's more, placing it there would considerably enhance the uplifting feel of the place, a bit like some older churches. But the woman insisted.

What a monster! Ullie exclaimed. *How can anyone be so blind yet so sure?*

Fran was tempted to challenge Miss Schmidt, asking her what made her so sure, but instead she asked, "What are the criteria for your refusal?"

"Access is difficult," the woman replied. "But above all, it needs to run north-south, in line with all other buildings in the area. You won't get planning permission, if you suggest anything else."

"I'll leave you to survey the site," Fran said, taking the judge by the arm and leading her away. The doctor followed. Trixie and Ullie headed from the kitchen. "We have other matters to discuss," Fran said over her shoulder.

If the redness of her face and her pinched lips were anything to go by, the woman was furious, but apparently found no acceptable reason to object. She stomped off across the field, doing her best to appear in deep contemplation of the lay of the land.

"Well done," the doctor said when they were out of earshot. At Fran's astonished glance, he added, "I found that very rude of her. After all, you are the owner of the place. She doesn't seem to realise what her rightful place is."

The judge chuckled. "I wouldn't have put it quite like that, but I agree. She does come across as very rigid in her beliefs."

"Have you worked with her before?" Fran asked, wondering if the woman had hidden merits.

"No. Never. An acquaintance recommended her."

"So you have no objections to me telling her we've decided to use somebody else?"

"You really are something," the judge said with a chuckle. "No, I haven't, but I'll let you tell her."

"Thanks." Fran made a face at the judge which only made

her chuckle all the more. "And while we're being direct," Fran said to the doctor, "why are you here?"

The judge burst out laughing to the surprise of both Fran and the doctor. "That really is my fault," the judge said. "My thinking went as follows. You want to work in the field of healing. That's the heavily guarded reserve of the medical profession. You're likely to run into trouble with them. Now I realise you don't need the help of a doctor. In fact, most doctors would get in your way. But if you have a sympathetic doctor who cautions your work that might help stave off or at least delay attempts to stop you."

"And do you think, Dr Blythe, you'd be the man for the job?" Fran asked.

"I have no idea," the doctor replied. "I gather you have unconventional methods, but I have no idea what they are."

"You'd have to talk to Trixie and Ullie about that, but talking to them might be something of an eye-opener."

"Ear opener," the judge corrected.

"I don't understand," said the doctor said, looking from one to the other, perplexed.

"Neither girl can speak or hear in the way you or I are doing." Fran said. "I'll let you hear for yourself." So saying, Fran called the two girls who were in the kitchen helping prepare a snack for everybody.

While they were waiting for the two to arrive, Fran turned her attention to the architect who was nowhere to be seen. She wasn't sure she could call on her cloud nature and spy on the architect while she remained with the judge and the doctor. But something had to be done. She felt uneasy letting the woman roam freely. "I just have to check on something," she said and hurried away into one of the near-by outbuildings.

Once she was hidden from sight, she let her presence soar up and zoom across the fields in search of the architect. She was surprised to find the woman snooping around the barn. Unable to intervene directly, she called on the clouds and had them dowse the woman in a sudden icy shower. The sense of control over nature's elements was so inebriating, she had to struggle not to conjure up a full-blown storm. When the woman persisted in her attempts to enter the barn, Fran drummed up a violent wind that drove the architect into a nearby thorn bush. The more Miss Schmidt struggled, the more she got entangled.

As Fran emerged from the outbuildings, Jakob drove up and stopped in front of the farm. Getting out, he glanced around as if in search of someone then asked, "What have you done with the architect?" Trixie must have told him something.

"She was with us only a short while ago," the judge replied, casting about but finding nothing. "Is she all right?"

Jacob didn't need to reply, because the woman came staggering along the track from the barn, wailing, her clothes drenched, her skin lacerated with a host of tiny bloody gashes. "Everything they say about this place is true," she screamed. "It's hell on Earth." She grovelled in front of the judge and the doctor begging them to take her away but both were so shocked, they stood unresponding.

Ullie? Fran asked. *Can you do anything for her?*

Ullie wasted no time. She began singing immediately.

Turning to the doctor, Fran said, "To alleviate Miss Schmidt's suffering Ullie is using song. You can't hear because she's communicating mind-to-mind." Fran switched to mind-to-mind speak, saying, *Like I'm doing now.* The man gasped but said nothing. *To give you a glimpse into our healing methods, I'll help you hear her song.*

A frown of concentration wrinkled the man's brow as Fran began relaying Ullie's chant, but his expression quickly relaxed as a smile spread across his face. His attention was focussed on the architect who had ceased her wailing. Sinking to the ground, she sat crosslegged on the grass, her head in her hands, rocking gently back and forth as Trixie applied unguent to the many scratches.

"Impressive," the doctor muttered.

45.

"How is she?" the judge asked.

"Asleep," the doctor replied from the doorway. "Something's wrong with her brain according to the girls. When you can't converse normally, it's difficult to understand, but I don't think they mean she's mad. I can't tell without a thorough examination, but her erratic behaviour could be due to a tumour or something similar."

"That'd be awful," Fran said.

"She did complain of headaches in the car," the judge added.

"True, but I put that down to migraines," the doctor said, joining them at the fireside. "If it's a tumour, I don't hold out much hope that singing will magic it away."

His scepticism annoyed her, but Fran was sceptical too. She knew so little of the girls' healing abilities and all her upbringing and education pointed to costly surgical interventions as the only path to partial recovery.

The conversation turned to the new concert hall. "I'd prefer a more intimate atmosphere," Fran insisted when the doctor began sketching grandiose schemes. "Fifty people. No more. We need to get a feel for the audience and they have to be immersed in the world of sound we are creating."

"With a small audience," Jacob said, seemingly preoccupied - he'd been quiet for quite a while - "it'll be easier to keep an eye out for troublemakers."

"Do you really think that'll be necessary?" the doctor asked.

"Unfortunately, yes. I'm surprised we haven't had more trouble. That there has been no riposte since the last debacle in the woods is a bad sign."

Doctor Blithe was eager for more details, but the judge, no doubt sensing Fran's discomfort, steered the conversation elsewhere. Listening to them talk about how to promote the future concerts, Fran struggled to stave off nightmarish memories of scenes in the wood.

Fran? Trixie called out from a distance. *We need to intervene urgently if we are to save that woman.* She explained that the woman's condition had seriously deteriorated and briefly described what they planned to do. *I'd let that doctor take part, but he wouldn't be able to see our work with the lines of force. And anyway, I'm not sure we can trust him.*

I think it'd be okay, Fran replied. *As for the seeing, I can help. I'll show them the energy lines.*

Wow! Trixie exclaimed. *You've been keeping secrets.* And, with a mental grin, she was gone.

Interrupting the conversation, Fran said, "Miss Schmidt has taken a turn for the worse."

"We should rush her to hospital," the doctor said, springing to his feet.

"Before we resort to that," Fran said, "the girls propose using an ancient procedure to cure her."

"We have no time to mess about," the doctor interjected. "This is serious. Minutes could mean life or death."

"If you want to cooperate with us," Fran replied, "you need to have some faith in our abilities." Trixie had sounded confident and Fran wasn't going to admit she had her own doubts.

"I'm sorry," the doctor said, "but years of training and experience are screaming at me not to trust you."

"If you call an ambulance," Fran replied, "by the time it gets here, Ullie and Trixie will have done their work. If you feel more comfortable doing so, call an ambulance, but do accept the girls' invitation to watch. I suspect you'll learn something."

The doctor seemed torn by indecision, but Fran didn't have

to wait long. "Okay," he said, huffing out a breath of frustration. "Let's go." He headed for the stairs, no doubt meaning to return to the room where the young woman had been, but Fran stopped him.

"Not there," she said. "She's been moved." Fran led the doctor, followed by Jakob helping the judge, out of the house and down the drive to the site where the concert hall was to be built. Luckily the weather was clement.

"In choosing this site, the heightened level of energy was our main criteria. Now we are going to use that energy to heal the person who was so sure we'd chosen the wrong spot." Fran wasn't sure where she got the ideas from. They seemed to spring to mind spontaneously when she needed them. Like a knowledgeable voice in her head. The answers were just there.

The group walked in thoughtful silence till they reached the place where the architect lay unconscious on an improvised stretcher. Around her in a circle stood all the boys and girls of the community. Fran was pleased to see Porcupine and his two friends amongst them. Even Mindy was taking part. Fran hung back, indicating the doctor and the others should do the same. Some foresightful individual had laid out a row of chairs. Once they were seated, Fran said, switching to mind-to-mind speak, *I'm going to show you the energy field from above. It might be less confusing if you close your eyes.*

She gave them a bird's eye view of the farm. Much to her satisfaction, she was able to depict not only the land but also the energy networks rather like one of those mixed maps. All three spectators, including Jakob, gasped at the sight but she didn't let herself be distracted. She was about to explain what each line meant, but paused to wonder how she'd come to know so much. A moment earlier she'd been unaware of it. Yet the knowledge was crystal clear. She could only suppose that being part cloud had given her access to it.

Focusing on a smaller area around the reclined woman revealed a tight knot of glowing lines curving around her body like a cocoon. They could clearly see its energy was being enhanced by the singing. As Fran homed in on the woman, a shift in perspective rendered the tumour in her brain visible as a dark, shadowy mass. *What you're seeing,* she said, *is not the tumour itself, but the signature of its negative energy.* The combined effect of the energy lines and the chanting was evident. The mass was shrinking, but desperately slowly.

With a shock, Fran realised their efforts would not be enough. Her impression was confirmed by Ullie who cried out, *We're losing her.* The chanting faltered and in that pause she heard the doctor groan, clearly aware of what was happening. *Keep chanting,* Trixie instructed and the music took up again with renewed determination.

Fran knew, although she couldn't say how, that more energy was needed and that she would have to bend the lay lines so they went through the architect. Without hesitating she applied force to the lines, compelling them ever closer till a thick wad coursed through the architect's body and her brain. But it was not enough. One much larger line resisted, like some fat sow lounging in self-satisfaction. She leaned on it with the full force of her intent and it slowly bent and curved until it joined the others flowing through the architect's body.

The tumour fought back, swelling even further, but the immense force of the energy lines was too strong. Like a tsunami, it shattered the tumour, scattering the dark mass in tiny fragments that were immediately swept away. As if in echo of what had happened the chant shifted key, becoming warmer, more colourful, more relaxed and gratifying.

Fran relinquished her hold on the three spectators who gingerly opened their eyes as if unsure what they might see. She herself felt drained and remained seated with her eyes half-closed, trying to recuperate. She didn't feel up to answering questions. Luckily, the others left her alone. The judge spoke in urgent whispers to Jakob, both of whom seemed shaken. The doctor went to examine the architect, who slept on, unaware of the drama she'd been the principal actor in. As he did, he struck up a conversation with Ullie.

"However did you learn to do that?" he asked, unable to conceal his awe. Fran automatically conveying his words to Ullie and Trixie.

We never needed to accomplish such complex healing where I came from, Ullie said. *Us girls never fell ill. But the priests instructed me at length on how to heal many an illness. Healing this woman turned out much more difficult than I anticipated. Without the Cloud Catcher's help we would never have succeeded.*

"Cloud Catcher?" Stan asked, perplexed.

It's the true name of Fran, Trixie replied, dodging what promised to be an awkward line of enquiry.

At the mention of her name, everyone turned to look at Fran who was still struggling to get up the energy to stand. *Poor thing,* Ullie said, hurrying to her side. *She's exhausted.* She snaked an arm around Fran, pulled her into a hug and covered her face with tiny kisses. *She's worked a miracle, no wonder she's worn out.* Fran felt better immediately, suspecting the young girl of feeding her energy, but she couldn't be bothered to check. She was content to let herself be kissed.

"Talking of miracles," Stan said, running his thumb along the architect's arm. "Look at this skin. It's completely healed."

Trixie put a term to the doctor's adulation, asking Porcupine and Wiggle to carry the woman inside. *She should rest and she'll need warmth and nourishment,* she said. *Talking of food,* she added, *I'm famished.* Everyone agreed. It was well past lunch time and they were all hungry. Zandra and Scratch hurried off to prepare a meal, embarking Mindy to help.

"That's another miracle," the judge said, watching her granddaughter walk away. "She seems so happy and self-assured."

She's doing well, Trixie said. *Life with us seems to suit her.*

"That's your granddaughter," Stan exclaimed. "I wouldn't have recognised her. She'd changed so much."

"If you work with us," Fran said, having recovered enough to join the others, "you might end up unrecognisable too. Do you want to take that risk?"

"You bet I do!" the man exclaimed. "I have so much to learn."

Fran didn't want to dampen his enthusiasm, but he had to know there were things he might never be able to do. "You might find that some of what we do can't be learnt," Fran cautioned, "but we will willingly teach you what we can and you no doubt have things to teach us."

"All we need now," the judge said, leaning on Jakob's arm as they headed for the house, "is an architect."

"I reckon you'll find we've got one of those too," Jakob said, "thanks to Fran, Trixie, Ullie and the others."

It was towards the end of their improvised meal that the architect joined them, her step unsteady, her face pale but her eyes bright. "My apologies," she began, "I don't know what came over me." The ordeal had transformed her voice which had lost its cutting edge, becoming mellower and more engaging.

"You had a malaise," Fran said, not wanting to go into details. "But you look much better. How do you feel?"

"Marvellous." She sounded surprised at her own answer. "That dreadful headache has gone. I'd almost forgotten what it was like to be able to hear my own thoughts. The thumping in my head had been my constant companion for months. It's amazing. I feel like a different person."

Trixie cleared her a place at the table - the judge and the doctor making room between them - but the architect preferred to sit next to Ullie, saying, "This place feels better."

You must be starving, Ullie said, beaming as she served her.

The woman shook her head. "I'm normally a big eater, as if I were constantly empty, but now it's like I feasted only a short while ago."

Good. Follow your instincts. Don't feel obliged to eat, Ullie said.

"Fran spoke of a malaise," the architect said, leaning across the table towards the doctor. "But what was wrong with me, doctor?"

Stan glanced at the judge, then at Fran, as if asking how much he should say. "You had a tumour."

"A what?"

"A brain tumour," he replied. "A very large one. But now it's gone."

"You shouldn't joke about such things."

"I'm not joking," the doctor said. "If it weren't for these young people," he gestured to all those sitting around the table, "and in particular Ullie and Fran, you'd be dead now."

The young woman stared at him wide-eyed, her mouth fallen open.

"It must be hard to believe," Fran said. "You wake up refreshed after what seems like a long siesta only to be told that you have been rid of a tumour that was threatening your life and about which you knew nothing."

Tears sprang to the young woman's eyes and she put her head in her hands. "But I did know," she wailed. "I saw the surgeon only yesterday. He said he should operate as soon as possible, although he gave me little chance of surviving. Coming here was my last outing before the operation. And I made such a mess of it."

The room was completely silent, everyone suspended on her reaction. When nothing further came, Ullie leaned over and took the young woman in her arms and hugged her.

"Thank you," the girl said, addressing everyone. "I can feel it's gone - there's none of the pressure in my head like something was trying to force it's way out. The screaming headaches have gone too - but I have no idea how you did it and I'm not sure I want to know. For me, it will remain a mystery."

"I understand your reluctance to delve into what must've been a shocking experience," the doctor said, "but you need to know something about how you were saved, if only because I believe it will have a strong impact on your future as an architecture."

"Architect?" she said, uncomprehending. "I don't see the connection."

It was Fran that explained. "To heal you, Ullie used chants, a special form of singing that, combined with the energy of the Earth, can work miracles. You have to know the energy of the Earth takes the form of lines that criss-cross its surface. It was those lines I think Stan was referring to. They are particularly strong at the place where we plan to build the concert hall, so it was there Ullie chose to heal you."

"The very place I, in my blindness, rejected," the architect recalled. "So much for years of expert training." She paused as if contemplating her past behaviour. "Could you teach me to see those lines?"

"I can certainly show you," Fran said. "Whether you will be able to see them for yourself is another matter."

46.

A strident bell rang out across the farm, sending birds that had settled on the roof scattering in every direction.

"Not again!" Fran exclaimed as she hurried out of the house and down the drive. For the third time that week someone had tried to set fire to the stock of wood destined for the new building. She could have called on the clouds to dowse the fire, but she didn't want to soak the wood. Doing so would delay the construction.

Porcupine, whose turn it was to keep an eye on the building site, had the blaze under control, spraying the flames with a fire extinguisher. The arsonists had not been very successful, having failed to delay the work. In fact, the building was ahead of schedule thanks to Miss Schmidt's masterful management. The foundations had been laid, the lower section of the walls made of brick was complete. Now it was the turn of the carpenters to get to work. The architect had had the foresight to order fire-resistant wood, a fact their fire-wielding enemies were apparently unaware of.

The arsonists had been reported, but the police were in no hurry to apprehend them. It was to be expected. The head of the police was a member of the sect that opposed Fran and her friends and was probably behind the attacks. Jakob had lodged a formal complaint and Judge Rainer was doing her best to see it got attention. But neither held out much hope.

"I don't get it," Scratch complained as they returned to the house. "Why ever do they persist in trying to destroy us?"

"If there's such a thing as 'social genes', they must have got theirs royally screwed up," Porcupine said. "Couldn't we 'heal' them like we did the architect?"

If bad behaviour has its roots in physical illness, like with the architect, we might be able to intervene, Trixie said. *But I doubt we would have much impact on rigid belief systems. They are inward looking and defend themselves against all outside influence.*

"We have police and law courts for such people," Jakob said. "Punishment or the threat of it are supposed to be a deterrent."

"Doesn't work very well," Wriggle muttered, "especially if the police are twisted."

"There must be some way we can bring them to justice," Fran said, just as frustrated as the boys. "Can't we set a trap for the head of the police?"

"That's a risky gambit," Jakob said. "We could end up caught in our own trap."

"Well at least we should give it some thought," Porcupine said. "Not being able to do anything is unbearable. I'd like to pay that bloke back for what he did to us and to all of you."

No more was said until later that evening when Porcupine dragged in a bedraggled youth who was struggling desperately to get free. He had the youth under control although, judging by Porcupine's black eye, it hadn't been easy. "I've caught one of our fire mongers," he said. "I suspect he might have an interesting story to tell." So saying, he shoved the youth forward. The moment the boy was free he made to run for the door, but a howling wind drove him against a wall and pinned him there.

"You hungry?" Fran asked, coming to stand in front of the youth.

The would-be arsonist, who must have been the same age as Porcupine but was less solidly built, glanced hungrily over Fran's shoulder, taking in the remains of their evening meal only to shake his head.

"Shame," Fran said, "the stew was particularly delicious.

So, apparently you have a story to tell us."

"I ain't got nothing to say," he replied.

"Let me guess," Fran said, glancing at Porcupine, hoping he'd forgive her for pinching his story. "You're a petty criminal. You have no work and your family have disowned you. The police pick you up and threaten to take you to court. You're too young to go to prison, but you could be sent to borstal. The idea terrifies you. You've heard what life is like in there. So when the police offer you a deal, you jump at it. All you have to do is cause us some aggro. Easy peasy. Now you've got caught again and you're wondering what nightmare we hold in store for you. Back to the police? To court? Or to a punishment of our own making? Am I right?"

Her question was greeted with a sullen silence.

"In fact we'll do none of those things," Fran continued. "We're going to give you a choice. Either you can go free or you can stay with us. Of course, if you go, the police are sure to catch you again. I imagine they won't be very happy with you. But I'm sure they'll find a good use for you. Something criminal, no doubt. Something that will make you more and more dependant on them. As for the alternative, you'll have to work hard but you won't be in prison or borstal and we'll protect you from the police."

"I chose freedom," the boy blurted out.

"I'm sure you do," Fran replied. "But which choice leads to freedom? To help you make up your mind, I'll let you talk to Porcupine and his friends for an hour. They might have some advice for you." She turned to Porcupine, who was grinning. She grinned back. "Don't beat the brains out of him, we have no use for brainless individuals."

An hour later no one was grinning. All four youths looked unhappy.

"I've chosen to leave," the youth said. "But I have one question."

"Go ahead."

"If I change my mind, can I come back?"

"That depends if you intend to join us or set fire to us," Fran said.

"Join you," was his reply and he turned and walked out.

"I'm sorry," Porcupine said later as they were clearing away the dishes. "I thought we'd be able to convince him. But he kept coming back to the other boys caught by the police and, even though we told him we'd try to stop the police, he didn't believe us."

"I'm not convinced you failed," Fran said. "He did ask about changing his mind. There's hope yet."

"Well, we'll know if they come back and try to set fire to the place again," Scratch said ruefully.

What surprises me, Ullie said, *is that we purified the house and realigned the energy fields in the area but bad things continue to happen. This place is strange.*

"Maybe you just can't rid the world of evil so easily," Porcupine suggested.

Although she wished they could, Fran was inclined to agree. "It might be akin to wanting day but not night," Fran mused. "I'm not talking about that boy earlier. He and his fellows are a nuisance, but they're not a danger. But there are those who really are a danger. Like the head of the police or that priest or the neighbouring farmer. We can't just eliminate them. Maybe we have to learn to live with them."

"I always said you should be a lawyer," Jakob said.

"I always thought lawyers were passionate about punishing people," Porcupine said.

"That's not quite true," Jakob said. "But justice is about making sure those who are guilty get punished."

"To be honest," Porcupine shot back, "punishment doesn't work well. Many of those who are in prison become even worse criminals."

"But it's supposed to be a deterrent…" Jakob protested.

"Do you really think hardened criminals are deterred?" Porcupine asked. "They do their best to avoid getting caught but if they are put in prison they use their time to network with future associates."

"I agree," Jakob conceded. "But the fact that you and your two friends are here, even if you probably never would've become hardened criminals, is proof that something can be done. I think you need to thank Fran for that."

It was the tingling at the tips of her toes that awoke Fran. Thinking it was a bad case of pins and needles, she tried to flex her toes but instead of going away it spread to the tips of her fingers. Next to her, Ullie slept profoundly. The bedside clock said 4:30. Fran crawled out of bed and slung a shawl around her shoulders. The tingling had stopped but something was calling to her and it was insistent.

Clouds, of course. She'd asked them to warn her if anyone approached the farm. Hastily getting dressed, she toyed with the idea of waking some of the boys. But in the end decided to go alone, knowing that her cloud-side would provide ample protection.

With her excellent night vision it was easy to spot the group of four youths creeping up the drive. A whispered voice off to one side startled her. "Sorry. I didn't mean to frighten you," Porcupine whispered, as he stepped out to join her. "I thought they'd be back."

"Let's go see what they want," Fran said.

"Shouldn't we get the others?" Porcupine asked.

"Nah. We can handle this."

The youths must've heard them because they'd halted in their tracks and seemed ready to flee. "How can we help you gentlemen?" Fran asked.

"You said I could change my mind," a familiar voice said.

"I did indeed. And I meant it."

"Well, before I do, I'd like you to meet my friends. They're in the same spot as me. Is that okay?"

"Sure. But keep the noise down, it's too early to wake everybody."

Seated around the kitchen table, Fran studied their faces

while Porcupine brewed some tea. The youth had brought three friends. A few months ago, if she'd seen such a gang heading her way, she'd have crossed the road or turned round and hurried away. Their faces were hard, their hair filthy and their looks grim. All were staring at her, although she didn't sense aggression, at least not directed at her. More like curiosity.

"So you want to join us?" she asked.

"No," the youth said, surprising her. "We've come to ask for help."

"And how do you expect me to help?" Fran asked.

The youth glanced around the room as if checking no one was listening. "We want you to help us get rid of the head of police."

"I don't go in for murder," Fran said, her voice steely.

"Not murder!" the youth said, taken aback that she should think such a thing. "No. We want you to help us put him behind bars."

"How do you expect me to do that."

The youth reached into his jacket and pulled out a small packet wrapped in oilskin and began unfolding it. "He's been doing dirty deals with key folk in town for years. And we've found proof that he was doing it." He extracted a notebook from the packet and handed it to Fran.

Fran gingerly opened the notebook to the first page. Traced with hand drawn lines, the page was divided up into a series of columns. Each had an inscription at the top. Date. Name. Sum. Transaction. Follow-up. Next to the first date was the name of the priest, the sum of a thousand pounds and under transaction she read, deliver one willing girl, age fourteen. She glanced down the list. Many of the names were familiar. Friends of her father. Mostly from their sect. Even the headmistress had ordered a girl for a modest price to be paid in four instalments. The more she read, the more it was clear the man traded not just in children, but in anything and everything illegal. Every detail had been carefully noted in neat schoolboy script.

Bile rose in her throat as Fran struggled not to throw up.

She snapped the book shut and hastily laid it on the table as if holding it a moment longer would wear off on her. "However did you get this?" she asked, her voice shaky with emotion.

"He's an arrogant sod. He was sure no one could get into his office. But we did. He hadn't even bothered to lock the drawer it was in."

"He's going to be one very scared man," Fran said. "What will he do when he finds it gone?"

"Explode, most likely," the youth said, "and kill everyone in sight."

"Do you think he'll know it was you?" Fran asked.

"He'll figure it out sooner or later."

"Then we'll have to act quickly," Fran said. "Will you entrust that book with me? I have to show it to someone."

The youth nodded, although he looked scared. All of them did. They'd taken a great risk.

"I really appreciate your courage," she said, spontaneously clasping his hand in hers. "Porcupine will show you a place to hide - the old barn," she said to Porcupine as an aside, "and provide you with food and drink for a couple of days as well as blankets. I'll tell you as soon as I know anything. In the mean time, I'll teach you how to send me silent messages without anyone knowing." The youths' eyes lit up at the prospect. "Just in case. But whatever you do, do not come out till I say. Is that okay?"

The three nodded, although their worried expressions spoke of their doubts.

"We have as much interest in ridding the world of those people as you," she said, hoping her words would reassure them. Mind-to-mind she spoke just to Porcupine. *Visit them regularly. They're frightened and will need all the support they can get. It wouldn't do to have them panic and make a run for it.*

47.

Fran decided not to tell anyone about the three boys and the book, for the moment at least. The fewer people who knew, the less likely the secret would leak out. She instructed Porcupine to keep quiet. There was only one person who had to know and that was Jakob. She took him aside and asked him to join her as she walked her pony. Her request clearly intrigued him, but he asked no questions.

It was quite a while since she'd seen her pony, let alone ventured out with it. Veth had taken her place and watched over the animal like a jealous lover. Of course, the girl insisted on accompanying them. It took considerable ruse to separate her from the pony. Even then it wasn't easy. The pony shied away from Fran as if she were a stranger. The unfaithfulness of the creature left her feeling hurt and disappointed. To think it had been her closest friend and ally for years. Now it was probably complaining bitterly to Veth. For once she was glad she couldn't hear its thoughts.

"So what's up?" Jakob asked once they were out of earshot.

She told him about the book and the boys.

"Is it in a safe place?" he asked.

She pulled the book from her inside pocket and handed it to him.

He stared in disbelief. "That's hardly a safe place."

"I know, but you need to see it."

"True."

"I thought we'd show it to Judge Rainer, she'll know what to do."

He flipped through the pages. "Good Lord! This is immense! It'll take an army of police to round up this lot. There's no way we can deal with this locally."

"We need to hurry," Fran said. "We don't want the head of the police getting his hands on those three or coming in search of the book."

"Where are they?"

"In the old barn."

"We should get them away from here. This is the first place he's likely to look."

Fran! a voice called out in Fran's head. It was Trixie.

What's up?

I think we might've found the cause of the bad luck, Trixie said.

Is it urgent? Fran asked. She didn't want anything to get in the way of dealing with the notebook and the police.

I believe it is, Trixie replied.

Okay, Fran said. *We'll meet you in the stables in twenty minutes.*

"That was Trixie," Fran told Jacob. "She reckons she's found the source of our ill fortune."

"Can't it wait?"

"That's what I asked. But she's sure it's important. So let's find out."

Trixie was waiting for them in the stables with Ullie and, of course, Veth. Handing one delighted pony to a just-as-delighted Veth, Fran led the others away from the stables. *Where?* Fran asked, not wanting to waste words.

You're snappy all of a sudden, Ullie remarked. *No greetings. No kiss. No thank you. No congratulations.*

Sorry. There are big things afoot, but I can't tell you about them yet, Fran replied.

In the hayloft over the barn, Trixie said.

There was very little hay in the loft. The farm didn't really needed it. A large part of the space was given over to stocking junk accumulated over the years. Fran groaned when she saw the heaps of disused clothes, overflowing boxes, discarded picture frames, broken furniture and other useless trinkets. It would take them years to find anything in there.

Where now? Fran asked.

Ullie closed her eyes and there was a long pause while she concentrated. *Over there,* she said pointing to a particularly precarious mound of rubbish. *I can't pinpoint it any closer,* she said. *Maybe you can try your method.*

It was Fran's turn to close her eyes, soaring above them. Looking down, she shifted her sight so she could see the lines of energy, but there was nothing out of the ordinary about them. She shared what she was seeing with the others along with her frustration.

Try to home in on the centre, Trixie said. *My guess is it's there. Remember the way you examined the tumour. See if you can't look at the pile like that.*

Trixie's suggestion made sense, but Fran had no idea how she'd done it. Sensing her difficulty, Trixie said, *Try looking at it as a person.* It didn't help. She still had no idea. If only the cloud had been with her, she could've asked. As if replying to her own thought, she heard herself say, 'Try asking all the same'. So she did, and although she got no answer, the answer was obvious. Her vision shifted and there was the object plain to see like a dark shadow lurking beneath the floorboards.

We have to shift this junk. It's underneath, Fran told everybody.

Many of the discarded objects evoked memories, not all of them pleasant, but Fran ignored them, intent on reaching whatever was concealed beneath. They finally uncovered the floorboards as the light was fast fading. None of them had a torch, but Jakob had a lighter. By its feeble flame they could just make out that one of the floorboards was loose. Apprehensive about what they'd discover, Fran tugged at the floorboard till it came away revealing a wooden box below.

A sinking feeling of dread stole over Fran as she reached in and lifted it out. She could hardly ask the others to look away, but she was afraid of what they might see. The box was not locked and the lid opened easily revealing a small notebook, another one. Underneath was a faded buff envelope exactly like the one she'd found hidden in her father's bedroom.

Attentive as ever to her feelings, Jakob suggested they look away while Fran examined the contents of the envelope. He handed her the lighter. What she uncovered was profoundly shocking, but she was relieved to find she figured in none of the photos. Her father must have kept images of her for his private collection, the one she'd burnt. The head of police might have traded in a variety of illegal goods, but her father, true to form, had one singular obsession that was in evidence in every photo. He'd even gone so far as to number each photo and jot down protagonists' names on the back.

Almost all the adults in the pictures were people she knew. Some figured in the chief of police's notebook. To her surprise, her mother was present in several, like some steely matron marshalling the children. Fran had always thought the woman ignorant of her husband's perverse pursuits. How wrong could you get?

Pocketing the envelope, Fran picked up the notebook and several folded sheets of paper fell out, an account statement. The bank mentioned on the letterhead was not one she knew. She had to read the total at the bottom of the last page several times, it was preposterously large. To her relief, it would seem he'd kept his dirty money separate from his other savings. Having to pay back his criminal earnings with the money she needed for the farm would have been a terrible blow.

Flicking through the pages of the notebook, she discovered long lists of names. Opposite each were dates, sums of money and references to numbers on the photos. It took her a moment to understand. Apparently, her father had been in the business of blackmail. All of a sudden everything made sense. The mayor, the headmistress, the farmer, the priest, and all the others were terrified their crimes would come to light and desperately sought to recuperate and eliminate the proof.

"Blackmail," Fran said to Jakob. "No wonder they so desperately wanted to get their hands on the farm."

Taking the notebook, Jakob flipped through. "I suspect your father's role was not limited to blackmail. He provided the children for the head of the police's customers." He pointed to a list of children with names, addresses and ages at the back of the book. There were even sinister annotations about suitability. "Are the photos further proof of their crimes?"

Fran nodded, unable to rid herself of feeling soiled and abused. A wave of disgust and anger surged in her. It was so strong she was unable to retain it. Her stomach heaved and she spewed her dinner across the floor, splattering the now-empty box.

The two girls helping her to her feet, Trixie handed Fran a handkerchief and Ullie offered her a flask of warm tea. Her mouth wiped, the tea was sweet and soothing. The meagre flame that was their only light abruptly went out. The fuel was spent. To escape the smell of vomit, they had to feel their way in the dark. Several times someone overturned an unseen heap of rubbish sending up such a clatter it was a wonder no one came running.

Once at ground level, Jakob said, "I'll call the judge. If she can come this evening, would that be okay with you?"

"The sooner, the better," Fran replied, handing him both notebooks, the bank statement and the buff envelope. "Better make copies if you can."

In minutes Jakob returned saying he was off to fetch the judge and would be back as soon as possible.

The girls had barely reached the house, than a violent hammering at the front door had them alarmed. The sight of five policemen in tight formation about a civilian on the doorstep had Fran terrified. Her nightmare had begun. To make it worse, Jakob wasn't there. *Whatever they want,* Fran said to the girls, *we need to stall them till Jakob and the judge get back.*

"Good evening gentlemen, what can I do for you?" Fran asked.

"I am a Bailiff," the man in the grey suit said. "It's my task to deliver an order of eviction."

"Eviction? Who are you evicting?"

"You and everyone else in this farm."

"And how do you justify that?" Fran asked, having some difficulty containing her anger.

"I have a court order."

"Why don't you come inside," Fran said. "It can get quite cold in the evenings at this time of the year." She pushed open the door and gestured for them to enter. It was clear from their faces that they hadn't expected such a greeting and hesitated as if it were a trap. Little did they know. Unheard by the men, Ullie was already chanting as were most of the other girls. *Block your ears to it,* Trixie said, *it's soporific and we don't want you falling sleep.*

To her surprise, Fran found herself alone with the men in the kitchen. Everyone was keeping well out of the way, but before she left, Zandra had strategically placed a couple of bowls of chocolates on the table and there were also cups and a pot of tea. She imagined them laced with some potent drug, but she knew better than to offer anything to eat or drink. They'd surely be suspicious. Instead, she ignored the things on the table, hoping Ullie would add hunger to the sleeping effect of the chant.

"So let me see this court order," Fran said.

The Bailiff was reluctant. She even wondered if it might be a fake. It probably was. Not that she could tell. "Surely you are not going to turf us out without me being able to read it first."

When he handed over the paper, she took a seat at the table and indicated they should join her. Only the bailiff sat down. The policemen remained standing rigidly behind him. Several times she caught a policeman looking longingly at the chocolates but they continued to resist.

Fran took her time reading the document, pausing every now and then to ask a question about a particular word, pretending she didn't understand. Although the chant wasn't sending them to sleep, it's certainly was having a calming affect. They no longer seemed so aggressive. The bailiff's answers to her questions were almost cordial. Luckily the text was long and full of legalese. As she read it, she felt a bit like Scheherazade in A Thousand and One Nights, trying to stave off the fatal moment.

Glancing at the clock over the stove she saw she'd been reading for nearly half an hour and several of the policemen were beginning to wilt. Little of the text was left so if they didn't fall asleep soon, she was going to have to find another strategy. Hearing a car drive up outside, she was relieved to think Jakob had finally arrived. But, to her dismay, Trixie informed her it was the head of the police.

48.

"You're too late," Fran said, struggling not to show her fear with the head of police towering over her, his eyes boring into her, his mouth twisted in sheer hate. To make things worse he'd brought a dog and a dog handler with him. No doubt hoping both to intimidate and sniff out the notebook. The animal, which was straining at its leash, growled threateningly, its teeth bared, its mouth drooling as if it hadn't eaten for weeks. "What you're looking for is no longer here. It's in the hands of the justice."

The man roared and hurled himself at Fran. She stepped back, preparing to use the cloud to fling him across the room when, much to her relief, several of his colleagues grabbed him and held him back. Revealing her abilities in front of the police would hardly have been wise.

"What's got into you?" one policeman asked. "Pull yourself together. You can't behave like that."

Lashing out in every direction, the head of police managed to break free several times, but more and more policemen joined the fray, till he was at the centre of a scrum of men in uniform.

"Let me go!" he screamed. "How dare you! I'm your superior."

"Do you think we don't know what you've been up?" one of the older policemen said, using the man's handcuffs to secure him. "Talk of your disgusting trade has been oozing through the dark corners of town for ages, getting us all a bad name. You'd never have been able to get away with it if there weren't so many key people under your thumb."

"You should've been locked up ages ago," another said.

"Let him go," a voice barked. All heads turned to see who'd spoken. There in the doorway stood a policeman, a gun in hand trained at Fran. "If you don't, I'll shoot the girl." Judging from the grim determination on his face, it wasn't an empty threat.

There was a moment's hesitation, then one of the policeman produced a bunch of keys from his pocket and unlocked the handcuffs, releasing the head of police. The man took a step in Fran's direction. She braced herself, sure he was going to hit her, but instead he spat at her with all his pent up fury. She dived under the kitchen table, narrowly missing the gob of spittle which soared over her shoulder. Several policemen pounced on the head of police while others cornered the man with the gun. A shot was fired. There was a scream. Then silence.

When Fran ventured from under the table, she found the policemen kneeling around one of theirs lying wounded on the floor. The head of police and his accomplice were nowhere to be seen. *Trixie,* Fran called out, mind-to-mind. *We need your help. Someone's been shot.* Trixie must've been waiting next door because she burst into the room immediately. While everyone was preoccupied by her treatment of the wounded policeman, Fran made the most of the distraction to remove the chocolates. It wouldn't do to have policemen poisoned now they were on the right side.

It was only once she'd poured the contents of the teapot down the sink and rinced it that Fran noticed the Bailiff was missing too. Fran wanted to call Jakob to warn him, but she'd never used mind-to-mind communication with him over such a distance. At the third attempt she managed to get through.

What's up? he asked. *We're almost there.*

Fran explained what had happened, adding that apparently the head of police, his accomplice and the Bailiff had taken all three police cars, stranding the other policemen at the farm with no means of communication.

Don't worry, Jakob said. *We're with the county police and*

Trixie informed Fran the wound was only a graze and that the policeman's life was in no danger. With the help of two of his colleagues, they carried him through into the sitting room and laid him down on a couch. Meanwhile Zandra was sliding a tray of scones into the oven and Scratch was busy making tea.

"I've managed to get through to the county police," Fran said, grateful no one wanted to know how she'd managed what they couldn't. "They'll be here soon. So you might as well take a seat and enjoy some of Zandra's delicious scones while you wait for them to arrive."

"We've even got some home-made jam," Scratch said.

One of the policeman must've recognised him, because he asked, "Aren't you one of those three youths that hung around the station doing the head of police's dirty work?"

"Yes," Scratch replied, surprising the policeman with his self-assurance. "He blackmailed us into doing his bidding. But we escaped. We've been very lucky that Fran here, and her friends, agreed to take us in. As you can see," he said, full of pride, "I'm learning to cook."

In the sitting room, the wounded policeman had regained consciousness and was trying to engage Trixie in conversation. He was eager to thank her. Fran explained that none of the girls could either talk or hear. "They were born like that. But I will relay your thanks."

The whole group of young people joined them for tea. The moment Veth caught sight of the dog, she went boldly up to it and began petting it, much to the alarm of the dog handler who expected the animal to growl at her. "She's got a way with animals," Fran explained. "Of course, you might just find it difficult to get your dog back." Fran chuckled. "By the way, don't waste your time trying to talk to her, she's deaf and dumb."

Hearing her, one of the policemen asked, "What is this place?"

"I suppose you could call it a refuge for young people who've had a difficult time in life," Fran explained. "Together we're working on making life better, not just for ourselves but for others around us."

"We're building a concert hall," Porcupine said. "Gertrude Schmidt is our architect. I can show you the plans, if you're interested. There are also to be rooms where we can receive those who need advice or help with health or diet. We're working with a local doctor. Stan Blithe. Maybe you know him."

Several policemen were staring at Porcupine in surprise if not admiration. He'd no doubt changed immensely since they'd seen him lounging around the police station. "Well," one policeman said, voicing everybody's thoughts, "this place has certainly done you a world of good."

That was Jakob's cue to enter, closely followed by Judge Rainer and a woman who turned out to be an inspector from the County constabulary. She was seconded by a group of policemen, policewomen and plainclothes detectives who began taking down statements.

"We'll need to put more scones in the oven," Fran said, greeting the inspector.

"That's kind of you," the woman replied. "But I'd rather hear your version of the story. Not here though. Can you show me where you found the notebook and the photos?"

"I'm sorry about the mess," Fran said, wrinkling her nose at the stench as she negotiated her way across the hay loft. "The sight of those photos turned my stomach."

"I understand," the woman said. "They sickened me too. I gather you suffered at the hands of your father. You don't have to discuss it now, but we're going to have to talk about that at some time. Tell me," she asked, surveying the chaos in the loft, "how did you manage to find those photos?"

"It's a bit difficult to explain," Fran said. "We've been beset by difficulties. We wondered if there wasn't some sort of dark shadow hanging over the farm. So we set out to cleanse the place. Imagine it a bit like a cleaning lady's form of exorcism." The woman smiled at the image. "We managed to rid the farm of most of the nasty influences, but we could sense that something rotten remained.”

Fran wondered how to explain what they’d done. Better to use images. “Do you know what a dowsing rod is?” Fran asked. When the woman nodded, Fran continued. “Imagine having something like an internal dowsing rod that allows you to feel negative and positive energy. One of us has developed such an ability and we used that to locate the source of dark energy...”

“Yes, I’ve heard about such things,” the inspector said. “I could use someone with that sort of ability from time to time, if ever you’re interested.”

Fran ignored the offer and gestured to the piles of rubbish on either side of the box. “As you can see, it was hidden under an enormous heap of junk. When I found the box beneath the floorboards, I feared the worst. Days earlier, when we were ‘cleansing’ the place, I stumbled on a similar envelope... full of photos.”

The inspector inclined her head, an unspoken question in her eyes.

“Me... little ...without any clothes on.” Fran paused, struggling with her emotions as she recalled the degrading photos. “I burnt the lot.”

There was no accusation in the woman’s expression, only suffering and sympathy.

“So I was afraid this was more of the same.”

“And you found the notebook in the same box?”

“Yes. Along with the bank statement.”

“Excuse me for asking, but did you know anything about these activities prior to finding these photos?”

“Yes. That other notebook, the one the boys stole from the head of police, made it clear what they were up to.”

The woman nodded. “I mean, when you were younger.”

“Ah...” Fran sucked in a shuddery breath. “My father forced me to do things with him, but there was never anyone else present. I was his personal plaything. If my father and mother did such things with other children, I was never around to see. He does have a hunting lodge in the woods on the other side of town. He often met people there. Maybe that's where they went."

"I'll have the place checked."

"What are you going to do now?" Fran asked.

"Once we've caught the three who fled, we'll round up all those mentioned in the notebooks. They will be tried and hopefully convicted."

Fran hesitated to mention it, sure it was her paranoia, but she had to ask. "Will we be safe?"

"Safe?" It was not so much a question as a careful weighing-up of the word.

"Because of us, because of me, many of the most influential people in town will be behind bars. Won't they seek revenge?"

"You are not responsible for their crimes."

"No. I know. But will they see it like that? If I hadn't..."

The inspector held up her hand for Fran to stop. "We can organise the trial so you don't have to appear publicly. We do have a witness protection programme, but in your case that won't work. I imagine you have no intention of leaving the farm or disappearing."

Fran shook her head. From being a prison, a constant source of misery, the farm and her project had become the centre of her life. She couldn't abandon it or her young friends. "If anything," Fran said, "our conversation has made me realise that we need to reconsider the security of the farm."

The inspector glanced around the loft shining her torch in every direction. "Do you think there's anything more?" she asked.

Fran didn't immediately understand what she meant. When she did, she said, "I'll check." The moment she said so, she realised she'd revealed that it was her that could search in such an unusual manner. She sighed. What was done, was done. She closed her eyes and searched every corner of the loft. "At a casual sweep, there doesn't seem to be anything more. At least, not that shows up some dark threatening mass."

"One last question," the inspector said. "How did you learn

you had this ability?"

Fran took a good look at the inspector's face, distorted as it was by the sifting torch light. There was kindness and concern in it alongside a no-nonsense, steely efficiency. Fran had the impression the woman could become an ally if not a friend. Yet she was reluctant to reveal too much of her tale. "It's a long story. Maybe, when all this is over, we will find time to sit down and talk about it."

49.

Fran had managed to wrench her pony from the grips of Veth and was on an early morning ride along the ridge above the town. It seemed ages since she last ventured out on her own. It was only an impression, but so much had happened in so little time. She'd become accustomed to being surrounded by others and enjoyed it, but now she was alone, she realised how much their presence dampened her sense of self and the world. She became acutely aware of the clouds shifting languorously above and the response of the cloud within her that wanted to soar and join them.

When the call of the clouds became ever more insistent, Fran halted her pony, closed her eyes and let herself rise up to join them. She was jostled on all sides. It was the clouds' way of greeting her. *Someone wants to see you. Someone. Wants. To see you. See. You.* All echoed the same message over and over. And Fran knew, although she had no idea how, that the 'someone' was important.

Daughter, you've been neglecting us, a voice boomed behind her.

Spinning round in mid air, Fran was delighted to discover what she had once called 'old grandfather cloud'. But now it looked different. Or rather she was looking at it differently. Her sight was not focused on the swirling mass that most people saw when they looked at a cloud, but rather its deeper essence that gave it life and intelligence.

You might have accepted your cloud nature, it said, *and for that I rejoice, but you keep ignoring the messages we as clouds receive, the messages the world sends us.* Sensing that its words left her perplexed, it added, *You need to learn to be in tune with both your natures at the same time. If you were, you'd realise that this world is suffering and that if you people continue in the way you do, it will end up as devoid of life as that other world you originally came from.*

Came? Fran exclaimed, latching on to the revelation the cloud's words had let slip. *I came from the other world?*

I suppose your knowing doesn't matter now the other world is gone. You are the daughter of the most important cloud that watched over the temple and the head of the handmaidens. When your father was exiled for consorting with a human and the priests threatened to throw your mother out for being with child, she came to this world to give birth and had you adopted.

She dumped me! Fran shouted with a thunderous rumble that would have made even the biggest of clouds proud. Below, sensing her pony uneasy at the threat of a storm, she reined in the lightning and thunder claps.

Human motivations can be hard to fathom, the cloud said, *but I suspect your mother was trying to protect you. Staying in the temple would have been out of the question and, given the state of the rest of the world, as a baby you would not have survived outside. Neither would your mother.*

She could at least have chosen better parents, Fran thought.

Handmaidens are not oracles, the cloud replied, in that irritating way clouds had of responding to unspoken thoughts. *As you have discovered, they are more of healers. The idea of a healing centre is good. Young people in this world have potential. Fostering that is a worthy challenge. But you must also look to the health of the world and set an example how people can avoid trampling and poisoning it.*

I might have been brought up on a farm, Fran replied, *but I know precious little about ecology.*

That's your human side talking. Listen to the cloud in you. It knows all you need to know.

Thanks. The human side of her felt she was being lectured, but her cloud side knew it to be true. *Will I see you again?*

Maybe. But you don't need to see me to talk to me. We clouds are all connected. Learn to use that connection.

With his words still ringing in her ears, their meaning sent thoughts racing in every direction. So she was a daughter of the temple, a girl of the other world, a cloud catcher. More than that, she was a child of a human and a cloud. No wonder she'd felt out of place in this world. Yet, over the years, it had become her world and the world she came from was no more.

As Fran re-integrated her body, the pony under her shifted nervously, the skittish animal seeking reassurance. She stroked its neck and whispered words mind-to-mind. When that seemed to do the trick, Fran wondered if she would soon be able to rival Veth, but the animal still refused to talk to her.

Back in the farm, she asked to see the plans for the new concert hall and persuaded the architect to make important changes. Luckily the woman was all for ecological solutions and welcomed Fran's modifications. Fran then toured the farm with Jakob and Porcupine discussing more sustainable solutions. Although the cloud side of Fran knew what was needed, she had no idea of the technical solutions available. Jakob knew an expert from the university in a nearby town who was delighted to share her knowledge.

Throughout the day, Fran concentrated on being aware of both her human and her cloud nature. For the most part, she was successful. The knowledge and insight that came from her cloud connections proved to be particularly useful when it came to grasping their place in the world but also with healing. The biggest challenge came when she slipped under the sheets with Ullie. Their lovemaking was a celebration of their bodies that couldn't have been farther from the apparent ethereal nature of a cloud. For the duration, Fran abandoned herself entirely to her human body and let the cloud slumber.

Narie was my mother, Fran told Trixie as they sat at the kitchen table sharing a muesli. It was shocking news to break over breakfast, but Fran had to share it with someone and who better than her best friend from the other world, Trixie.

The girl stared at her in disbelief. *That's not possible,* she exclaimed. *Narie died a long while ago.*

I know, but time flows differently in the two worlds. Her cloud side assured her this was true. The flood of information that surfaced was overwhelming. Fran had to turn her attention away, not to be distracted by a lengthy explanation that threatened to turn into a university-level physics lesson.

The news of Narie must have touched Trixie deeply because she stirred the remains of her muesli, staring absently across the kitchen. *How did you learn she was your mother? Are you sure?*

The clouds told me and clouds can't lie. Narie took a fancy to the cloud responsible for the temple and I was born of their union.

I never knew, none of us did, Trixie said. *I've no idea how she hid it. It would have caused a uproar. Getting pregnant is supposed to be impossible. That's the price we girls paid for being handmaidens. We may never have seen a pregnancy, but we'd recognise the signs sure enough if we saw them.*

Narie often travelled to other worlds, Fran pointed out. *Apparently she came here to have her baby.* Fran wonder if she might find some trace of her mother's stay. She must surely have gone to a maternity to give birth. There'd be records. *The cloud told me she gave me up for adoption, but it made no mention of where I was born.*

She was often gone for long stretches. In her absence, Xristy would deputise for her. But it was never the same. Narie was like a mother, although she was barely older than us, in appearance at least. In realty, of course, she'd been the first handmaiden and had been there much longer.

Fran tried to envisage her mother as head handmaiden but all she could conjure up was Xristy. Xristy the lover, not a mother. Fran was about to ask Trixie to describe Narie but a sleepy bunch of youngsters traipsed into the kitchen in search of breakfast.

When Trixie told Jakob the news later in the morning as the three went down to talk to the builders, his first question was, "How come you can hear and speak if you're from that other world temple?"

Fran had no idea.

Maybe living here made the difference, Trixie suggested.

Fran wasn't convinced, but she had no time to answer. They'd reached the building site. She was surprised to discover the walls and windows were already installed and a small crane was manoeuvring sections of the roof into place under the watchful eye of the architect.

"Hi, Gertrude," Fran greeted the architect. "It's looking good."

"It is indeed. I was afraid we'd be delayed by the solar solar panels, but I managed to find a supplier not far from here who had enough in stock."

A car drove up and stopped some distance away. Fran shuddered, fearing it meant trouble. Maybe some of the head of police's accomplices had managed to slip the net. Then, to her relief, the inspector stepped out and beckoned to her. Apologising to the architect, Fran walked down the drive, meeting the inspector half way.

"Sorry to disturb," the woman said, "but..." She didn't get any farther because a shot rang out and the inspector flung herself forward, knocking Fran to the ground, her body shielding Fran. A second shot rang out and a cry of pain pierced the air, followed by a tense silence.

Fran shifted to see what was going on, but the inspector pressed her down, whispering, "Keep still."

"It's all clear," a voice called out from the inspector's car. "I got him."

The inspector cautiously lifted her head to survey the scene before clambering to her feet and offering Fran a helping hand. "Are you alright?" she asked.

"I'm okay," Fran replied, still trembling.

"I came to warn you the ringleader was still at large," the inspector said, linking arms with Fran and leading her in the direction of the car, "apparently only just in time." Turning to the driver, a policeman in uniform, she asked, "Where is he?"

"In the bushes, over there." The man pointed down the slope to the right into scrub that lined the drive.

"Call an ambulance," she told the man. "You stay here," she ordered Fran, adding, "I'll check on him." Gun in hand, she headed off into the bushes.

The man offered Fran a safe seat in the car, but she refused.

"He's dead," the inspector announced, joining them. "Good shot."

Fran was surprised at the sting of her regret. The man would never be called to account for all the lives he'd marred. At least, not in this world. "It's a shame," she said.

Both the policeman and the inspector looked at her in surprise. Their reaction made sense. The man had just tried to kill her. How could his death be a shame? He didn't need to die, her cloud side said. "I would have preferred he be tried and found guilty, for all those he made suffer, that they see justice done."

The inspector nodded. "Yes. We all have a thirst for justice."

A crazy idea suddenly struck Fran. She had no inkling if it would work, but she had to try. "Where was he hit?" she asked.

"In the chest."

"Show me the body," Fran insisted.

"You don't want to see," the inspector said, shaking her head as if Fran were driven by some morbid curiosity. "It's not pretty."

Fran had no time to spare. If she had the slightest chance of bringing the man back, it had to be immediately. "Show me, quick," Fran insisted. Both stared at her as if she'd gone mad. There was no point trying to explain. They wouldn't believe her. When neither moved, Fran strode off in the direction the inspector had come from, a dense mist rising to cloak her. She heard the woman calling after her, but paid no attention.

The inspector was right. It wasn't a pretty sight. Blood was splattered everywhere. Her stomach heaved and she almost threw up, but, at the thought of all the victims, she steeled herself to proceed. You're gonna have to help me, she told her cloud side. By way of answer, she expected to be flooded with a detailed anatomy lesson but all she got was silence.

She leaned closer to get a better look, holding her nose as she did. It would take painstaking work to piece him together. She swore. She had no idea where to start or what to do. Give up, a part of her insisted. It didn't need to be perfect, she replied. How could it be? Judging from the mass of blood, the man must have been torn apart by the impact. Even if she managed to bring him back, he'd be severely handicapped and probably wouldn't survive. At least he'd make it to the trial. That was all that mattered.

Around the man's neck hung a medallion. It was familiar. She'd seen one on her father. Other male members of their church sported one too. A mark of fraternity, of complicity. Brothers in sin. Fascinated, she reached out to examine it, but the moment her finger came close to the man's skin a sharp crack resonated in the air and a flash arced from the tip of her finger to the man like a miniature bolt of lightening. Fran recoiled as if struck by an electric discharge. To her amazement, the man cried out and opened his eyes, his stare homing in on her, a look of sheer hatred. It was like being repeatedly slapped in the face.

She recoiled, leaving him clasping his chest as he writhed on the ground. Obeying an instinct, she ran, finding refuge in a large clump of bushes, the thick veil of mist lifting as if on command. The inspector and the policeman must have heard the cry because they arrived at a run. From behind her bush, Fran watched, terrified, afraid she'd be accused of black magic, of raising the dead. Was that not what had happened? The cloud in her had answered her call and shocked the man into life.

"I could have sworn he was dead," the inspector said, searching in every direction for an explanation.

50.

The sound of the approaching ambulance siren greeted Fran as she made her unsteady way out onto the drive and headed for the police car. Neither the inspector nor the policeman were in sight. When the ambulance pulled up next to her, she directed the men into the scrub. They reappeared shortly afterwards bearing the wounded man on a stretcher, closely followed by the inspector and the policeman. The latter accompanied the criminal into the ambulance leaving the inspector to drive herself back.

"What did you do?" the inspector asked, once the two were alone.

Fran struggled to think up a convincing lie, but finally replied, "I've no idea. It was like static electricity. From my finger to him. The shock must have revived him because he cried out. It hurt me too."

The inspector stared at Fran's unscathed finger, clearly sceptical "Why didn't you call us?"

"The man gave me such a murderous look, I was terrified."

"Remind me never to get on your bad side," she paused, "or even shake hands." It was meant as a joke, but the inspector looked grim. "Tell me one last thing," the woman said. "Why did you rush off in search of the man?"

"I was upset that all his victims would go without justice. I hoped to find he'd survived to stand trial."

The inspector nodded several times, thoughtfully. "I

understand. One of the greatest frustrations of my job is when those who are clearly guilty get off scot-free." She stared off into the distance as if passing in revue a series of similar events.

"You realise that such extreme cases of men's violence against women and girls are just the tip of the iceberg," she continued. "I understand you want nothing to do with it. You've been sullied and hurt personally all your young life. You want it gone. But the roots of the violence are everywhere. Rather than ducking out of the way in the hope it will not return, you should consider standing up and speaking out."

"It's tempting," Fran said. "Clearly the perpetrators of such violence have to be unmasked, but I'm not convinced mass finger-pointing is the answer." The inspector shook her head but didn't interrupt. "I know that's not what you meant. But there must be another way. Three of the boys who joined our little community were once petty criminals. They tried to attack us - it was the former head of police that sent them - but we took them in. That has transformed their lives. I'd rather stand up and trumpet that sort of outcome."

"I salute your foresight. What you are doing is exemplary," the inspector said. "But I don't think it will be enough. We have to address male violence against girls and women at its roots in the way our society is organised, in the language we use and in every aspect of our daily lives..."

The woman didn't get any further because Trixie came running up and flung her arms around Fran in a desperate hug. *Are you alright?* the girl asked. *We heard shots and shouts. We hid in the new building, afraid to come out.*

The inspector stood back, watching. It must have been obvious some sort of exchange was passing between them, but all the woman said was, "Someday you'll have to tell me what's going on here. But, in the mean time, I have work to do."

The woman held out her hand to say goodbye, but Fran pulled her into a hug. It was risky, maybe being an inspector made easy-going behaviour out of the question, but Fran liked the woman. She would certainly be a good ally, if not a friend.

I promise I'll tell you, Fran said mind-to-mind, before drawing back and turning away, paying no heed to the inspector's gasp.

"That wasn't very wise," Jakob commented when he heard what she'd done. "She's a police inspector."

Fran was tempted to tease him. He could be stubbornly rigid when it came to policing and the law. A consequence, maybe, of his training. "Are you talking about bringing back monsters from the dead," Fran asked, washing the lunch things, "or whispering sweet nothings in a fellow woman's ear?"

"You know what I mean," he replied, taking the plate from her and drying it.

"It was you that said we would need allies."

"Yes. But you don't have to tell your allies all your secrets."

"Come and have a look," Porcupine said, bursting into the kitchen. "The roof's complete and they've almost finished fitting the solar panels."

Fran snatched the two sandwiches she'd prepared for Gertrude - the woman had skipped lunch to survey work on the site - and followed Porcupine out, glad of an excuse to escape Jakob's browbeating.

Fran was pleased the panels were going up. They'd long discussed how to heat the place. At first she'd favoured wood pellets, thinking it was an ecological solution, but they'd turned out to cause too much pollution. In the end, following the advice of the expert, they opted for a combination of solar panels, geothermal sources and a wind turbine higher up the hill. The installation Gertrude had designed was big enough to provide energy and heat for not only the new hall but also the house and the farm once they'd been renovated.

It would soon be mid-October and the weather would turn. They'd need heating for the girls and some of the boys who had no experience with cold and rain. In the other world, if anything it had been too hot and it never rained. The plan was to camp in the new building while work progressed on the farm. That was partly why they'd had a kitchen installed. If the winter wasn't too severe and the work went according to schedule, they hoped to move back into the farm next spring.

Trixie was already at the new building with Ullie. They were discussing how to consecrate the place. Fran was a little surprised. She'd always thought consecration was reserved for churches. When she questioned the idea, Ullie replied, *We want this to be a place of physical and spiritual health. In a similar way to the purification of the farm, we need to invest the new building with our good intentions for its future. That'll be our consecration.*

The idea of imprinting their will on the building rather than leaving the task to a hypothetical all-powerful being appealed to her. *Should we do it when we hold the inaugural concert?* Fran asked.

No, Trixie replied. *This concerns us and only us. Even if all those who attend are our supporters, it is not for them to say. It is our collective intentions that have to be woven into the fabric of the new building.*

A screech of tyres interrupted their discussion as a car swerved to a halt in front of the building, almost knocking over Fran, and the headmistress burst from the vehicle screaming, her nun's habit swirling angrily about her. Close behind came an outside broadcast van. A camera crew tumbled out and immediately began filming.

"You horrible child," the headmistress spat, so enraged she was unaware she was being filmed. "You're trying to poison our lives with your lies. How dare you? We are the pillars of society." She raised her fist and was about to strike Fran but Porcupine grabbed her arm and pulled her back.

"Get your filthy hands off me!" she exclaimed, struggling unsuccessfully to get free.

"I did nothing to you," Fran said, squaring off in front of the woman. "It was you that took advantage of those children. I've seen the photos. You abused them. If anyone was poison, it was you. You poisoned those kids lives. For ever. And why? For a moment's pleasure. If you and your accomplices are pillars of society then society needs a deep purge."

A police car drew to a halt behind the other vehicles and the inspector strode out closely followed by several policewomen. "We'll take over from here," the inspector told Porcupine. "Thanks for your help."

When the headmistress had been led away, the inspector turned to Fran asking, "You all right?"

Fran nodded, adding, "Am I going to have to confront every one of them?"

The inspector shook her head. "You shouldn't have had to speak to this one either. Someone tipped her off and she dashed here."

"Inspector?" It was the same journalist who'd cornered Fran during the night. "Why are you arresting these good people? Has there been some sort of conspiracy? Is it a putsch?"

"Now is not the time," the inspector said. "We are in the middle of a complex investigation. You will be informed in due course." Turning to Fran, she added in a whisper, "You don't have to talk to these people if you don't want to." And she left.

Shifting her attention to Fran, the journalist renewed her questioning. "Were you part of this ring? I gather your father was involved. Did he use you to entice other children?"

The woman's questions made Fran furious but it was useless to answer back. She'd already experienced how these people twisted her words. If she were to speak her mind, she'd have to stop them filming. Easy enough. A sharp electric discharge, like a mini lightning strike hit the camera and sent up a puff of smoke closely followed by a cry of alarm as the cameraman let his equipment clatter to the ground.

Distracted by the antics of the cameraman, it took several taps on the journalist's shoulder to get her attention. "You're no better than those who molest young children," Fran said. Her accusations shocked the woman, but Fran, in her anger, gave the journalist no chance to respond. "Why? Because your questions imply that I was a perpetrator rather than a victim. By so saying, you condone the abuse by accusing the abused. Such behaviour, especially on the part of someone from the media, only further perpetuates the violence against women and children."

"That's utter nonsense," the woman blustered.

"Think about it," Fran said. "You're going to have plenty of time on your hands."

"What are you talking about?"

"If I were you, I'd hurry home," Fran said, sensing the clouds racing to respond to her call. "There's a storm brewing and it's going to be really bad. You wouldn't want to get stuck out in it."

The woman looked up at the sky. Not a cloud was in sight. She spluttered in disbelief. "Are you threatening me!"

"No," Fran replied, her anger bubbling over as a clap of thunder rolled around the surrounding hills and a dark cloud abruptly obscured the sun. "Just suggesting." Her words, spoken through gritted teeth, came out more like a hiss.

A strong gust of wind buffeted the television crew as they dashed for the shelter of their van. When they didn't drive off, a furious wind rocked their vehicle, almost overturning it. Their response was immediate. The motor burst into life and the van careened off down the hill, its roar quickly lost in the claps of thunder.

Fran didn't want the storm to damage the new building they'd so painstakingly constructed, but she had great difficulty reining in her anger. Already water from the downpour was cascading off the roof and down the road, racing after the van like a vengeful torrent.

That that woman had dared suggest Fran had aided and abetted her father in his filthy trade was too much. Every time she replayed the woman's words in her head, a violence crash of thunder burst from the thick blanket of clouds now roiling in the sky and the rain redoubled its efforts to flood all in its path.

Breath deeply, Trixie said at her side. At the girl's words, Fran became aware how laboured her breathing was. On her other side, Ullie took her hand and began chanting softly. All three were soaked but the wet clothes did nothing to dampen Fran's anger. For a brief moment she was tempted to turn it against the girls for treating her like a patient, but the thought of her dear friends carried off by angry waters stemmed her fury and the storm abated.

What was that about? Trixie asked when the rain ceased and a ray of sunshine pierced the clouds.

I was so angry, Fran replied, taking the towel Ullie had fetched from within the building. Having rubbed her hair and dried her face, she wrapped it around her shoulders. *That woman...* The word sparked a renewed surge of anger and a bitingly cold wind swirled around them. *...accused me of being an accomplice in those heinous crimes against children.*

I don't understand, Trixie said, also wrapped in a towel one of the girls had brought down from the house. *How could she say that? You were a victim.*

Fran paused to collect her thoughts. It was not an easy thing to explain. *You will not know this, coming as you do from another world, but there's a widely accepted attitude in society here towards women and girls, but also children in general, that sees them as inferior, as second class, as less intelligent, as worth less, as expendable. That is why they so frequently get abased, assaulted, abused, because mistreating the inferior is the right and privilege of the superior.*

Fran could feel her anger rising again. She took a deep breath and calmed the wind swirling around them. *And whenever some brave person speaks out against that abuse, those around point an accusing finger at the abused, saying her behaviour caused the abuse. By that slight of hand, the abuser becomes the abused and his guilt is absolved.*

51.

"Well, at least we know it keeps out the rain," the architect chuckled, dodging the drips as she emerged from the new building.

It took Fran a moment to grasp what the woman was talking about. Her mind was still grappling with Trixie's question.

"I'm glad we managed to get the last of the solar panels in place before the downpour began," the woman continued. "Now all that remains are the fixtures and fittings."

"We'll be in in a short while," Fran said. "I'm looking forward to seeing the interior."

That's terrible, Trixie said when the girls were alone, clearly still preoccupied by their earlier discussion. *Is there no way we can change it?*

The inspector had been right, Fran ardently wanted the problem gone. She wanted to hear no more about it. But what good did it do to lock those people away if the rot persisted in society? If everyone was tacitly involved, any hope of eliminating the problem was a sheer pipe dream.

I don't think there's a simple remedy, Fran said. *It would be great if we had some powerful ritual to set things right, like we did when we purified the farm. But the distinction between what is seen as superior and what is deemed inferior is deeply rooted in society.* She couldn't shake the suspicion that in some way such a distinction was necessary if not useful. Although not when it led to violence, abuse or oppression. *For a start, it's embedded in language. It's woven in ways of teaching and learning and working. It's ingrained in people's identities, in the very structure of society.*

You sound defeated before you even start, Ullie said. *That's not like you.*

Maybe I've been living here too long, Fran replied. It was a sobering thought. Had she unwittingly adopted the limits and bad habits the people of this world took for granted?

Perhaps you should step out of it for a moment, Ullie suggested.

I can't leave now! Fran said, alarmed. Were they trying to get rid of her? As Narie's daughter she was next in line as head of the girls. Maybe they wanted her gone. She halted, acutely aware she stood at the edge of a delusional precipice. How stupid! There was no more temple to be head of.

I didn't mean literally, Ullie corrected, fling an arm around Fran and hugging her.

Well, at least we can set a good example, Trixie said.

Like the followers of Jesus before they became Christians, a society built on community, solidarity and a quest for transcendence Fran thought, but the reference to Christianity would mean nothing to these girls.

That said, Ullie continued, *we could try to come up with a series of rituals. The Earth's energy has a wide ranging impact on people. Even if it doesn't entirely eliminate the problem, it might help.*

Well done, Fran said. *Between you, you've already come up with two strategies. A community to set an example and a ritual to improve the Earth's energy. But I suspect more will be needed.*

Being an example is all very well, Trixie said, *but people have to see you if they are to follow your example.*

You have to venture out into the world and tell people, Ullie added.

The suggestion smacked of missionary work which didn't appeal to Fran at all. She'd had enough of being forced to accept others' beliefs at school and at home. She said so to the girls.

Being an example, Trixie responded, *isn't about ramming your beliefs down someone's throat, but rather by being exemplary in what you do.*

Part of the problem, Fran mused, *is that nobody is talking about it.* She thought of the TV journalist. *Well that's not strictly true. But many of those talking, especially in the media, are making things worse. They twist information and confuse people. Those who do speak up about their experience of abuse are called into question as attention-seekers, liars, or profiteers.*

"Are you coming?" Porcupine asked, leaning out of one of the new windows. "You should see this, it's really great."

A strong smell of wood greeted Fran as she stepped inside. The whole interior was wood-panelled. "It's been treated with a special flame retardant," Porcupine informed her. "We'll need to give it a fresh coat about once every two years."

Passing through a large hall which was to serve as vestibule and cloakroom, they walked into the main concert hall. A few parts of the floor were not yet complete. "We're laying down the floorboards now they've finished installing the underfloor heating," Porcupine explained. An army of carpenters on hands and knees were busy making swift work of the remaining floor.

Fran knew from the plans that there was to be no raised stage. They didn't want the people singing to be higher than those participating. As for the acoustics, the architect had insisted on getting them right, even if the girls' performance was mind-to-mind. "You never know when you might want to hold a traditional concert," she'd said.

"The smaller rooms are finished. Let me show you," Porcupine said.

They may have called the place a concert hall, but in reality more than half the space was taken up by little cubicles that would be used to receive patients. They'd had a separate entrance built for patients round the back, with its own reception and parking space. It was in those rooms they planned to live while they waited till the rest of the farm was renovated. There were also one or two larger rooms that could be used for meetings or meals and then there was the kitchen. Zandra had overseen the work, insisting it fit the needs of a growing community like theirs as well as being suitable for receptions in the concert hall. And finally there were a number of toilets and bathrooms.

Opening a door, Trixie led them into a surprisingly large room which had row upon row of shelves lining the walls. In the middle were work benches and lines of cord hung like so many washing lines from the ceiling. *This is the pharmacy,* she said. *Most of our stock of herbal teas, simples and unguents will be kept here and we'll also be able to dry herbs and prepare various potions and creams.*

"Isn't it wonderful," Wiggle said, sticking his head round the door, a grin on his face. "I'm really looking forward to working here."

To think he'd seen himself as ordinary and futureless. He'd travelled far from the days when he was a petty criminal exploited by the police. Remembering that failed assault on their greenhouse, Fran said, *It would be good to have a secret reserve elsewhere, if ever this place gets attacked. We wouldn't want all our supplies wiped out.*

"We've catered for that," Porcupine said. "Follow me."

He led them to the rear of the pharmacy, unlocking and pulling open what looked like the door to a large cupboard. "Come inside," he said, ushering them in. "It won't work with the door open." Once closed, he pressed one of the floor boards and a trapdoor clicked open revealing a flight of stairs.

"That wasn't in the plans," Fran exclaimed.

"No. It was my idea," Porcupine said. "We've been attacked so often, it seemed important to have a safe place to shelter that could also house emergency supplies."

"I wondered why they were digging such deep foundations," Fran said.

"We tried to mask it," Porcupine replied. "It's meant to be a secret."

"Can we go down?" Fran asked, intrigued.

"Better not," Porcupine replied. "It's not finished yet."

Stepping out of the cupboard they met the architect. "I see you're getting a guided tour from one of our best workers," Gertrude said.

Fran wondered if she was being ironic. It was the sort of question the cloud would have voiced. She had no time to ponder her doubts because the woman clarified.

"He's asked me to take him on as apprentice architect," she said with a chuckle. "It's not how we normally do things, but he's really good so I've promised to give it a try once we begin work on the farm."

Seeing him beaming, Fran remembered the cloud's words. People's futures were indeed difficult to predict.

The consecration of the new building was planned for three days later, but they had to put it off for three more days, partly because work inside was not quite finished, but mainly because of the trial.

The local police station had been gutted when water had mysteriously flooded the basement and the place had caught fire. The large number of suspects in what had become known as the trial of the Bent Bourgeoisie meant that temporary prison facilities had to be found nearby. For that reason, the procedure had been expedited. True to her word, the inspector had made sure the cross-questioning of both Fran and the other children took place in closed sessions.

As was to be expected the lawyer for the defence attempted to discredit Fran by making her responsible for the misdemeanours of the adults. Being accused had Fran's blood boil. "How dare you?" she shot back, shaking with rage. It was all she could do to rein in her cloud-side that wanted to smash everything in the courtroom.

"There is clear photographic evidence that these people abused children," she went on. "And you know that. Yet you stand there trying to turn the tables and argue that it is the victims that are the abusers. You should be ashamed of yourself. If anything, you yourself should join the accused on the bench because your discourse condones and encourages their behaviour."

Waiting till Fran had finished, the judge reprimanded her for the angry outburst, but agreed that the defence lawyer was out of line. Turning to him, she reminded him that this was not a trial of the victims and that he should refrain from baseless accusations.

Despite all the precautions taken to shield her, the experience was traumatic and Fran slept badly. The worst part was hearing the stories of the other victims. She spent a considerable amount of time with them as they had to wait to bear witness. A few were angry with her because her father had recruited them. But most realised she too had been a victim and welcomed having someone willing to listen to them.

It was during those long periods of forced waiting, talking to the young boys and girls, that Fran had the idea of drafting a book about their experience. More immediately, she enlisted their help in the inauguration. Not all were willing to participate, but those that were she invited to the farm. It had taken some persuasion on the part of judge Rainer and the inspector to convince parents to let their children attend. Naturally they were extremely wary after all that had happened. The inaugural event was set for a week after the consecration, giving them time to rehearse.

Finally, it was on Friday, October 11th that they gathered in the new building to begin the consecration. Trixie had wanted to decorate the hall with flowers but in that season few were to be had. Instead, she used pinecones and stones and twisted branches as well as large sheets of paper on which, thanks to Drew's skills in calligraphy, were depicted the key words that captured the essence of their new space in celebration of the potential of the young. Health. Joy. Community. Equality. Empowerment...

Everyone accompanied Ullie in a rich chant created specially for the new building, then Fran called on each of those present in alphabetical order asking them to state their name and what they were. Bruno security and accountancy, Drew calligrapher and writer, Jakob lawyer and protector of the weak and those in need of help, Mindy singer and musician, Porcupine carpenter, builder and architect, Scratch electrician and cook, Trixie healer and herbalist, Ullie singer, healer and teacher, Veth friend of animals, Wiggle plumber, herbalist and chemist, Yssel administrator, Zandra cook and caterer. When everybody was named, she pronounced her own name. Fran, Cloud Catcher, daughter of Narie and the Temple of Clouds, bridge between the worlds. Her words were followed by a pregnant silence. They had come a long way since they last discussed what their future might be.

52.

"Here," Jakob said, tossing the newspaper on the kitchen table where it landed with an ominous thud. "You might be interested in this."

Bent Bourgeoisie Trial - Judgement Day, the headline read. Jakob's grim expression augured nothing good. What if the blighters were set free? How could she protect her little community with those good-for-nothings at large and bent on vengeance? She tried to reassure herself. From what she'd seen, all indicated the culprits would be locked away for a long time. How could it be otherwise? The evidence was stacked against them. Yet such thoughts did not allay her fears.

And there it was. Suspects released after judge reluctantly pronounces a mistrial. The defence had successfully argued that the expedited procedure potentially led to serious injustice. Further down the page the head of police, the headmistress and the mayor were crowing in an interview about being vindicated. They threatened to take Fran to court, blaming her for them being wrongly accused.

The inspector however reminded the journalist that the decision did not disculpate the suspects. It indicated only that, due to difficult circumstances, the procedure had been flawed. The crown prosecution would press for a re-trial. In the interim they were seeking an injunction to prevent the suspects from exercising their professions as that could put young people at serious risk. An additional injunction would be sought to prevent them from approaching Francesca McKenzie, prime-mover in their arrests.

What's wrong? Trixie asked.

Fran let Jakob explain. She was too down-hearted to talk.

That's terrible, Ullie exclaimed. *Your justice system is really weird.*

"Doesn't surprise me in slightest," Porcupine said. "How could you possibly expect creeps like that to get punished? They're above the law."

"Nobody's above the law," Jakob intoned, although not with his usual conviction.

Wouldn't happen if clouds were in charge, the cloud-side of Fran chipped in.

So what would you do? Fran asked her other half, annoyed at anyone and everyone. *Eliminate them, I suppose.*

S'not my fault they were released, it shot back.

A perfidious thought sprang to mind, no doubt emanating from the cloud. How about holding her own trial?

Fran immediately dismissed the idea. *Anyone can't just try the accused. Special people are appointed to do that, in a place dedicated for the purpose with its own set of rules and procedures.*

The riposte was quick to come. *They say the same about schools. But neither teachers nor schools are needed to learn. In fact, you probably learn better without them.*

That said, the parallel was flawed and the idea wouldn't work. Finding abusers guilty might bring satisfaction, but it would have no more legitimacy than if you awarded yourself a university degree.

You alright? Trixie asked. *You've gone alarmingly quiet.*

I was arguing with my cloud-self. It suggested we hold our own trial.

"That wouldn't work..." Jakob began.

Fran sighed. "I know. I told it."

I'm not so sure, Trixie said. *We have all the people concerned at the inaugural concert. A number of victims will participate, along with many local dignitaries - those not involved in the scandal. Only the perpetrators would be lacking.*

"How could that possibly help?" Jakob objected. "Convoking those criminals would be like inviting a blood bath."

Fran shuddered, imagining how the children would feel being confronted with their abusers. She couldn't possibly subject them to that. What's more, the parents would never allow it.

Your penal system is based on punishment as dissuasion, her cloud-self thought. *For the moment they've been spared that. They even claim they've been vindicated. What you need is a public admission of guilt.*

We can't force them, Fran pointed out. *That wouldn't count. They have to be seen to do so willingly.*

Not everything that happens can be seen, the cloud said slyly.

Fran relayed the cloud's ideas. None liked the plan. They saw it as a long-shot that could go terribly wrong. Especially Jakob who considered it a mockery of justice. But all had to agree that admitting guilt publicly - if it worked - would unequivocally expose the crimes and the criminals without further harming the children. With considerable misgiving they agreed to take the risk, even Jakob who'd been its most vocal opponent.

Preparing was going to take a lot of work. The invitations had already been sent and the children's choir rehearsals programmed. Apart from readying the 'mock trial' - Jakob persisted in calling it a mockery of a trial - only the question of the media remained. After the fiasco of the trial, local and possibly even national media might be eager to cover the event.

"I want to be sure they can't misrepresent what happens," Fran said. It was tempting to put the media on trial too, but turning on them wouldn't help. The admissions of guilt required widespread coverage if their plan was to work. There had to be no room for media moguls to twist the news to suit their thirst for sensation.

"I'll see if Judge Rainer can help reining in the media," Jakob said.

Fran was relieved he offered to help. She'd been afraid his continuing opposition might cause their scheme to flounder. "Do you intend to tell her what we plan?" she asked.

Jakob shook his head. "What we have in mind challenges courts as the unique place where trials of such gravity can legitimately take place. I can hardly see a judge agreeing to that."

Fran wasn't so sure, but she said nothing. After much hesitation, she took the judge and the inspector into her confidence, explaining what they planned. She expected objections, but they heard her out and even made suggestions. Fran declined the offer of armed plainclothes police in the audience and insisted the inspector come unarmed.

Zandra and Scratch had prepared an impressive buffet in a conference room only a door away. Trixie and Yssel had decorated the concert hall making it resemble a clearing in a forest using saplings planted in large pots. The boys had collected dried oak leaves and acorns which lay strewn on the floor bringing not just the colour but also a scent of Autumn. Veth had even coaxed a number of birds to flit from branch to branch, occasionally breaking into song. She stood vigilant nearby whispering mind-to-mind to assuage the birds' fear of humans.

Drew's calligraphy was prominently displayed hanging like mobiles from branches turning in a faint breeze Fran had conjured up. They depicted the key words that underscored their community: empowerment, equality, health, learning, nature, balance, ecology, justice,...

Rows of foldable chairs, their backs to the entrance, had been set for the audience. The children's choir, along with Ullie who was to lead the singing, were seated around the audience on three sides. Ullie was already chanting mind-to-mind, bringing calm and confidence to the children who were both excited and daunted. An upright piano had been installed next to Ullie on which Mindy was to accompany the choir. Opposite the entrance, two rows of empty chairs had been set up side-by-side facing the audience with the word 'Reserved' written on them.

The media were not allowed near the building. Fran didn't want them turning the event into a show. However, an acquaintance of Jakob's who ran an independent, outside-broadcast company was discreetly filming and the video was being fed to the media.

Some fifty people were expected, including parents of the children, their teachers and local dignitaries. Fran was waiting for them at the entrance, flanked by Jakob and Trixie. The first to arrive were Judge Rainer and the police inspector. In their wake came Stan Blithe, the doctor, and Gertrude, their architect. They were closely followed by small groups of parents and teachers chatting quietly amongst themselves. As they greeted Fran, some briefly bemoaned the outcome of the trial, before entering the hall.

Behind her she could hear the gasps of surprise and appreciation at the decoration. But she had no time to listen as a steady flow of dignitaries began arriving. There was shaking of hands and exchange of civilities as each was presented to Fran by Judge Rainer acting as a benevolent intermediary. Fran found most distant and wary as if they were afraid of her. Trixie who smiled at each one winningly was, unbeknown to them, using one of Ullie's chants to unknot tension and encourage confidence.

Once everyone was inside, Fran spoke briefly to Bruno who was in charge of security and on the look out for rogue media. As for the abusers, they'd come. She'd made sure of that. The cloud had done a good job.

With one last glance down the road, Fran turned, entered the hall and pulled the doors shut behind her. As she walked down the aisle separating the audience in two, a silence fell, broken only by the occasional tweeting of birds and the unheard mind-to-mind singing of Ullie.

"This evening we are gathered to celebrate the inauguration of our new concert hall. We had planned a joyful event with music and food, followed by a guided visit to the health centre next door and a presentation of the ecological aspects of the building, but the outcome of the Bent Bourgeoisie Trial weighs heavily on many of us and no doubt you too. We will not forego the music led by Ullie accompanied by Mindy on the piano with the children's choir. Nor will we decline to savour the delicious buffet Zandra and Scratch have prepared for you. And a glimpse into our work on health is still programmed along with insight into the ecological considerations that guided the architecture of the building. But we insist on beginning by honouring those children who were the victims of abuse, some of whom are singing for you tonight."

One more thing remained to be clarified. "Concerned that what we are about to do would be misrepresented by the media, we have asked a trusted independent company specialised in retransmissions to document the event. They have been given strict instructions not to show the faces of the children nor of you as audience. Their coverage is being broadcast live to the local cable network and made available to the media."

Fran paused, letting her eyes roam the audience. "So let's begin by evoking the names of all those who were abused."

A tense silence gained the hall at Fran's announcement only to be swept away as the choir stood as one and began solemnly reciting the names, including their own. Bill. Frida. Angela. Thomas. Anita. Beth. Princess. Tammy. Rina. John. Amber. Tricha... The list went on and on. Listening to it was unbearable, all the more so that it was being relayed mind-to-mind not only by Ullie, but by all the members of the community. Like an immense chorus chanting the names one at a time, they penetrated deep into the minds of all those present.

When the list finally came to an end, Fran spoke again. "For a victim of abuse, it may seem illogical to say so, but it is hard not to feel guilt. As a child, everything conspires to convince you you are to blame. How could your teacher, your headmistress, your brother, your father, the mayor, the priest, and all the others possibly be guilty? It is unthinkable."

"As a child, you take on much more blame than adults realise. No need for crooked lawyers, inconsiderate media or society in general to point the finger. That guilt and doubt stay with you throughout your life. However misguided and unjust the feelings may be, guilt and anger are almost always the legacy of the victim of abuse."

Mindy struck up several notes on the piano and the choir began singing a wordless song with Ullie and the others underscoring the emotions of the moment in their accompaniment. Glancing round, Fran saw that several of the audience had tears in their eyes. Many others were moved.

When the music ceased Fran asked Mindy to take the children to a room at the back of the building. "Zandra has prepared a delicious snack specially for you," she told them. "We'll call you back to sing later."

The moment they were out of the room, the front doors flew open and a gust of wind blew in, bringing with it the head of police who sat slumped in a wheelchair, his policeman accomplice pushing him over the threshold. The pair were closely followed by the mayor, the priest, the headmistress and all the others accused of abuse. Seeing them there where the children had just been was shocking.

Fran had considered having them enter naked. After all, had not these people stripped the kids and exposed photos and videos of them for all to see? But revenge was not what she was after. Above all, she wanted the truth to be known. Shouts of protest went up. Adults sprang to their feet. Ullie was doing overtime putting a cap on fear and indignation.

"Please be seated," Fran said, calling on all the authority of a grandfather cloud. The audience reluctantly sat and the buzz of conversation gradually died down. Looking lost and embarrassed, the crowd of miscreants were obliged by an unseen force to sit on the vacant chairs facing the audience. All shifted uncomfortably as they stared belligerently at those watching. Next to them the head of police was parked, clutching his bandaged chest.

"The wish to get rid of these people is almost irresistible," Fran said. "Have they not ruined the lives of countless children? If only we could wave a wand and watch them disappear and all our woes with them. Yet elimination is no solution. Violence against women and children is deeply rooted in society and doing away with these miserable specimens will not weed out the rot. All the same, we need some form of closure." She nodded towards the sorry band of former dignitaries. "The mistrial has temporarily robbed us of that. But we have an opportunity to remedy that shortcoming tonight."

Turning to face the abusers, Fran continued, "You treated your victims as objects to be used, abused and cast aside. Unfortunately, we cannot confront you with your victims. That would only perpetuate the violence you initiated. But, we can confront you with the names of your victims. Tonight, we are generously giving each of you a chance to publicly own up to and regret the abuse you committed."

The looks that greeted her words were hard and unrepentant. Little did they know that each of their victims' names she pronounced would be driven deep into their minds by Ullie, breaking through all barriers of self-justification and denial.

The headmistress was first. At the mention of her victims' names, she broke down and cried, clutching her crucifix to her chest. "I'm sorry," she wailed. "So sorry."

Fran had expected the priest and the mayor to hold out, but they too were deeply affected and sobbed, pleading to be spared, as if they'd been abused themselves. Only the head of police resisted, refusing to recoil at the mention of his victims, impervious to Ullie's onslaught.

A squad of police, stern in their uniforms, came for the abusers who got unsteadily to their feet and were led, shuffling, heads bowed, eyes downcast, to the door. Only the former head of police remained, abandoned by his accomplice and all his criminal associates.

"You orchestrated this," Fran accused, waving a hand over the seats left vacant be the abusers. "It was your lucrative business, peddling children to twisted adults."

"Not without the complicity of your father," the man replied, his voice little more than a rattle as he struggled to breathe.

"That vermin," Fran exclaimed, utter contempt in her voice. "I was his favourite victim. Yes. He was guilty. But you can't offload your blame on him. He was your henchman, but you were the instigator, the ringleader."

The man sat there, a wizened figure who, despite knowing his days were likely numbered, stared directly into her eyes in an attempt to intimidate, as if to say, 'So what?'

The audience hung suspended at their silent exchange, no doubt wondering who would give. For all his diminished state, the man was as hard as flint. Fran was at a loss. What could you do with someone so stubbornly unrepentant, even in the face of death? It seemed likely that, despite their efforts, he would not admit his guilt.

Epilogue

A violent clap of thunder exploded outside, shaking the whole edifice. The lights went out and the walls glowed an unearthly blue. *Enough,* grandfather cloud roared, his voice reverberating round the hall. Several of the more religious people made the sign of the cross. Many others, clasping hands over their ears, moaned in terror.

The front doors flew open and a bolt of lightening streaked down the aisle, causing a wave of panic as people dived out of the way. The former head of police had just the time to open his mouth to scream when the lightening struck him in the chest, ripping wide his unhealed wound and bowling him over several times before his corpse came to rest against the wall with an unimpressive thud.

The audience froze in a weird tableau of shock, caught mid-flight, lit only by the emergency lighting. Stepping out of a side door, Bruno and Porcupine righted the wheelchair and heaved the body onto it, then wheeled the smoking remains solemnly down the aisle and out into the hall. A gust of wind followed, chasing the stench of burnt flesh after them.

When the doors clicked closed and the lights spluttered on, Fran said softly, "Please be seated," as if addressing frightened children. Bewildered, they obeyed. "Close your eyes," she added. "It will help."

At the back of the hall, unnoticed, Trixie had wheeled in a burning brazier on which she threw herbs. The specially crafted incense wouldn't erase the memory of the shocking scene, but it would blunt the sharp edges and make it more bearable.

Ullie chanted, as did the other girls, curling their voices round the minds of those present, instilling a semblance of peace. When the terror had subsided and the tension eased, Mindy led the children back into the room and, once she was seated at her piano, the choir began to sing accompanied by the boys on drums and fifes.

Their lilting song was gay and full of life, raising the spirits of all who heard. Fran recognised the ancient tongue of the temple even if she couldn't comprehend the words. It was as if it were destined for her and her alone. It filled her with joy. As for the audience, the song might have been alien, but it swayed them all the same.

The ancient song of the Cloud Catcher, the rumbling voice of grandfather cloud said in Fran's head. *Your song.* All trace of anger was gone from its voice, replaced by the benevolence she had glimpsed in their earlier encounters.

When the audience stood to applaud, Zandra and Scratch opened the double doors to the buffet. Time to eat and chat about the inauguration before the planned visit. Accounts differed. "It was as if God intervened," one murmured in reverence. "More like a freak storm," a more sensible voice insisted. "There's always the broadcast," a third put in, seeking certainty. "You'd be so lucky," a man added, dashing their hopes. "Apparently the electrical failure interrupted the recording at the key moment." Little by little talk turned to other things.

Fran followed the discussions from a distance, remaining alone in the now-empty concert hall, wishing her cloud could still curl around her neck to comfort her. The outcome of the evening had shaken her to the core and she was exhausted. As she drew in a shaky breath, she felt a faint breeze ruffle her hair and a presence wrapped itself around her neck, immense and powerful yet considerate and caring.

Well done, grandfather cloud said, *Fran the Cloud Catcher, daughter of Narie, child of the clouds, bridge between worlds…*

Annexes

386   Alan McCluskey

Thanks

I'd like to express my thanks to the unknown girl on horseback met on one of my many solitary walks in the countryside during the pandemic. We exchanged only brief words of greeting, yet her troubled but endearing smile set this story in motion. Gratitude is also due to the multitude of clouds that accompanied me on my walks and opened my eyes to the very nature of clouds. In addition, thanks go to Elisabeth Pastor whose passion for the depiction of the Annunciation drew my attention to the encounter between flesh and spirit that gave birth to a life born to save the world, echoing the union of cloud and girl that underpins The Cloud Catcher. Thanks also to Joelle Chautems, as stimulating as ever, whose recent conference on purification inspired several scenes in the story. Particular thanks go to Ginger Dawn Harman for her sound advice about abuse and for clarifying the point of view of victims.

The photo I used for the cover was taken during a monumental storm while out on one of my walks, the very walks during which the large part of this story was dictated. One last thing. There was a glitch in the software I used to write this novel. Whenever I dictated direct speech, it inverted the inverted commas at the end of the sentence. Spotting them was a dyslexic writer's nightmare. If any managed to slip through, my apologies.

Alan McCluskey, Saint.-Blaise, June 2021

The author
Alan McCluskey

One of his former pupils once confessed, with typical candour and ambiguity, that Alan McCluskey had taught her the creative value of madness. His work, whether as a teacher or a video artist or a company director or a scientist or a novel writer, has always been marked by a need to question the obvious, adopting what he calls the Martian perspective in which the self-evident is not taken for granted. He has brought that questioning perspective, along with a passion for images and what they can reveal, to novel writing, together with a long-standing fascination for the dream world and the magic of fantasy.

For information about Alan McCluskey, his books, short stories and artwork, see:
Secret Paths: https://secret-paths.com
Facebook: https://www.facebook.com/Secret.Paths

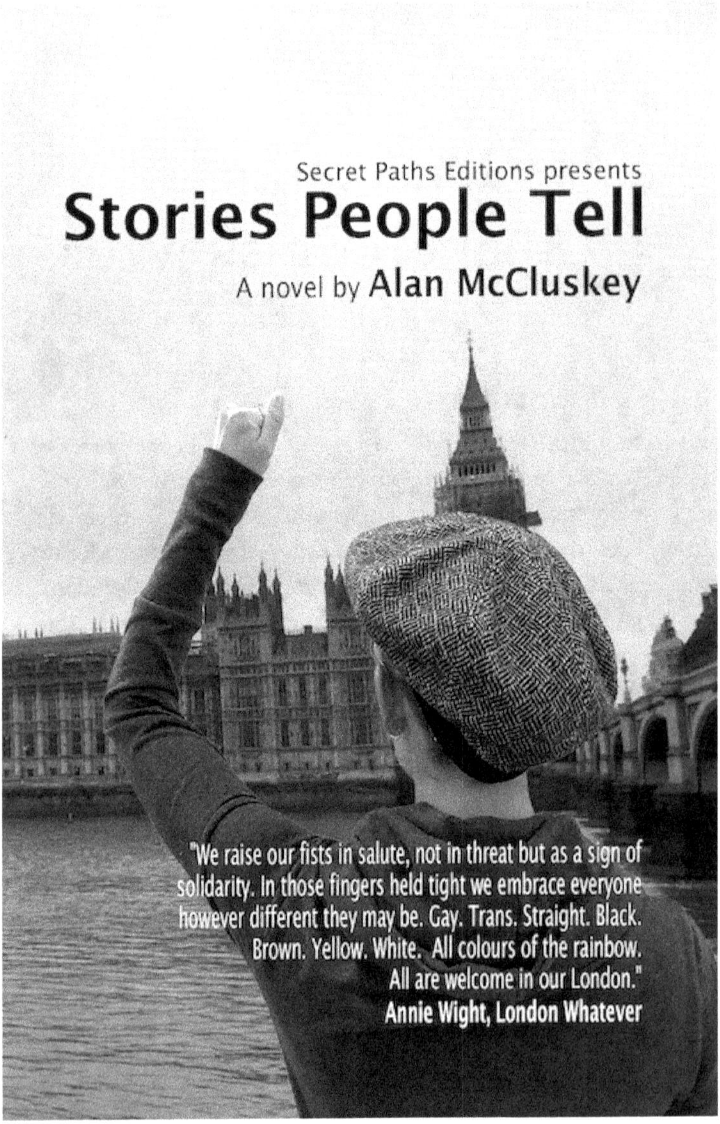

Secret Paths Editions presents
Stories People Tell
A novel by Alan McCluskey
"We raise our fists in salute, not in threat but as a sign of
solidarity. In those fingers held tight we embrace everyone
however different they may be. Gay. Trans. Straight. Black.
Brown. Yellow. White. All colours of the rainbow.
All are welcome in our London."
Annie Wight, London Whatever

Stories People Tell

by Alan McCluskey

Stories People Tell is a tale about Annie Wight, a shy schoolgirl who, despite sustained, cruel treatment and personal doubts, blossoms into a major voice in the grassroots movement 'London Whatever' celebrating gender diversity while struggling to end violence against women and care for the weak and marginalised.

Annie wasn't expecting to stumble on love or notoriety when she got swept up in 'London Whatever'. Nor could she have known that, right from the outset, she would become the number one target of Nolan Kard, the homophobic Lord Mayor of London. who was campaigning to 'Keep London Straight'. She bore the brunt of attacks from his rogue police, not to mention from a sinister gang of ghost-writers, the nightmare of all Kard's enemies.

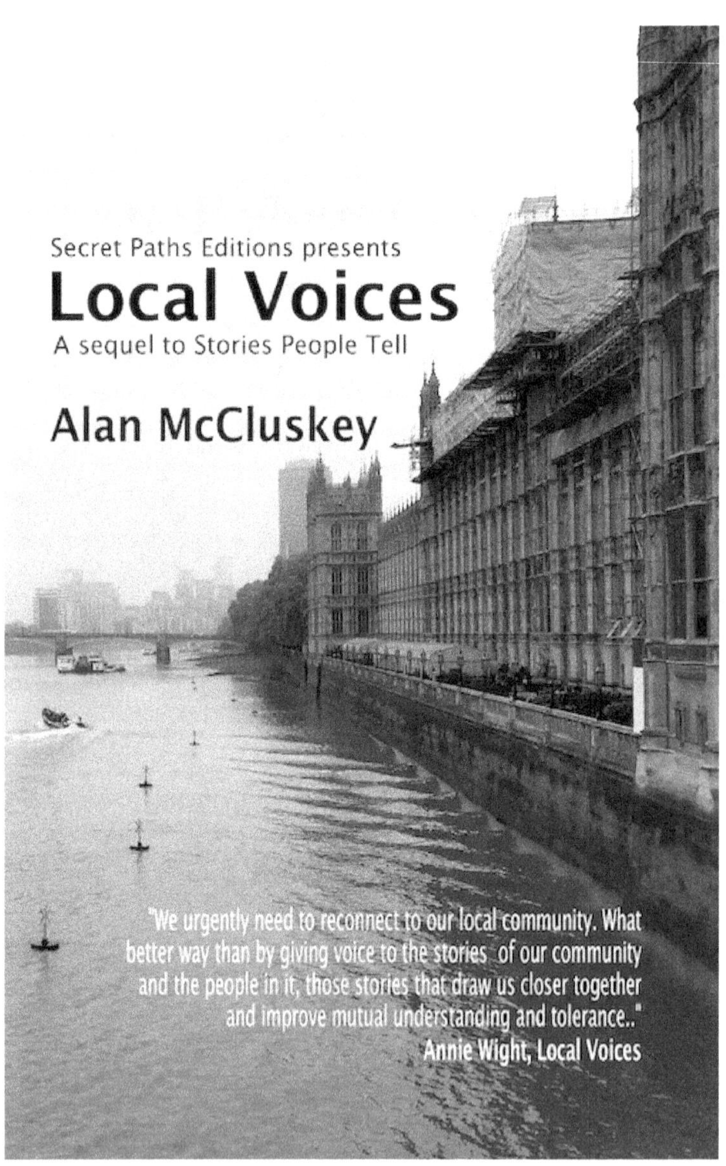

Secret Paths Editions presents
Local Voices
A sequel to Stories People Tell
Alan McCluskey
"We urgently need to reconnect to our local community. What better way than by giving voice to the stories of our community and the people in it, those stories that draw us closer together and improve mutual understanding and tolerance.."
Annie Wight, Local Voices

Local Voices
A sequel to Stories People Tell

by Alan McCluskey

In her campaign to re-assert and strengthen the role of women at the heart of hearthside healthcare, seventeen-year-old Annie Wight finds herself pitted against Health England, a conservative think-tank backed by pharmaceutical giants and private healthcare providers. Pretexting the defence of the National Health Service, they stop at nothing to stamp out Annie's efforts. They target not just her but those close to her, wreaking havoc in friendships and affairs of the heart. As part of her response, Annie launches a project to share the stories of those that never figure in the spotlight. By celebrating local voices, the project fights against isolation and disempowerment.

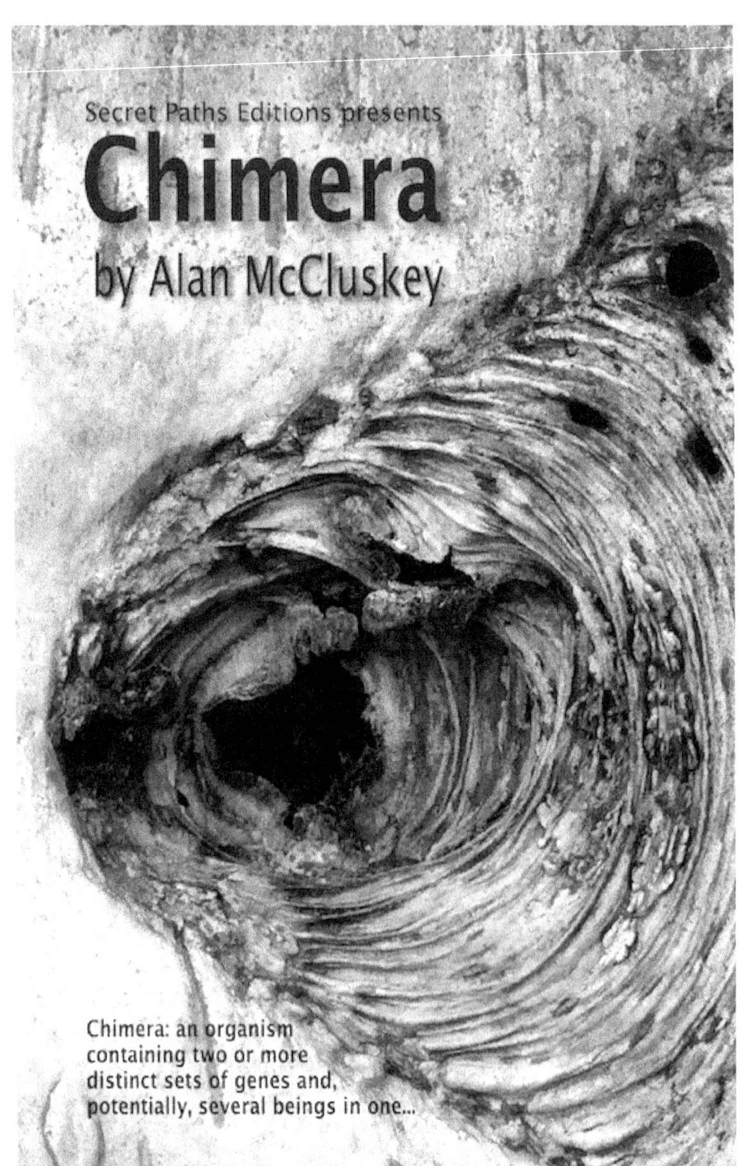

Secret Paths Editions presents
Chimera
by Alan McCluskey
Chimera: an organism
containing two or more
distinct sets of genes and,
potentially, several beings in one...

Chimera

by Alan McCluskey

A chimera is an organism containing two or more distinct sets of genes and, potentially, several beings in one. Sami and Sam are a chimera, two people in one, a girl and a boy, a leader and healer of people sharing a body with a brilliant but autistic child.

Sam talking to himself on discovering he is one half of a chimera...
:: not being able to speak, to move - such was the price I had to pay - to cut out the chaos and confusion from a world run wild - a raw satisfaction - being barricaded in my head these past twelve years - all for nothing - that blasted girl has ruined everything
  surging out of nowhere - pirating my body - bridging the gap between me and the others - letting chaos rush in - beguiling everyone with her codswallop - not me - I'm not impressed - some say she's destined to be our saviour - as if the block-head could save a fly - I just want her gone

Sami's first ever words to her teacher and her father...
"I … need … to explain. Words come with … difficulty. I must … be brief. Sam and I are a … chimera ... there are two of us... Sam is the boy you know. New things terrify him. He cannot speak … out loud. He stumbles. He falls. I am new. I just awoke. I am a girl. I play piano I talk. I walk. As for that violence you just saw, that was Sam trying to kick me out"

Boy & Girl

Alan McCluskey

Boy & Girl
by Alan McCluskey

When Peter awakes in the head of a girl, he is both delighted and alarmed that his secret yearnings have become reality. Very quickly, however, his error is apparent; this girl is not him. Kaitling –that's her name – is twelve years old, like Peter. She's the daughter of a magician, a prominent figure in another world. Boy and girl travel back and forth from each other's minds, but have little time to get acquainted before Kaitling's island is overrun by warrior priests and she has to flee. At home, a conflict erupts in Peter's family forcing him to take refuge at a friend's place. Meanwhile at school, a haughty new girl goads him about his girlishness and, spitting in his face, vows to rid the earth of people like him. The stage seems set for a desperate struggle to survive, but will ingenuity and youthful fervour be enough against folly and fanaticism?

Boy & Girl Saga Book 2
In Search of Lost Girls
2020 edition
Alan McCluskey

In Search of Lost Girls
by Alan McCluskey

If you listen carefully you can just hear the mournful tolling of a convent bell over the shuffle of girls' feet as they traipse to Mass, nursing bruises and numbing despair. No one cares. No one is there to stem the torrent of injustice and abuse. They are lost and forgotten. In another world, the walls of the cathedral still reverberate to the sound of angelic singing as the mourners make their way to the exit, heads bowed, voices hushed. If only they knew that those girls who delighted them with their music were really boys in disguise, sanctity would flee in the face of raging indignation. The scene is set. The author picks up his pen with trembling fingers and begins to write. Time to tear Kate and Peter apart. The thought of making her life hell has him dribbling in anticipation. He ought to know better. Things rarely turn out as an author expects.

We Girls

by Alan McCluskey

Peter is beset by an existential choice, retain his androgynous ambiguity or say goodbye to his girlish self. Circumstances, however, force both him and Kate to take up other challenges. By straddling the line between child and adult, between carefree creativity and weighty responsibility, between play and work, they find imaginative ways to confront far-reaching problems on which adults persistently turn a blind eye.

The Storyteller's Quest ~ Book One
The Reaches
Alan McCluskey

The Reaches
The Storyteller's Quest Book One

by Alan McCluskey

The quiet town of Avan with its port, its provincial university and its conservative seafaring folk would hardly be the place you'd expect to run into an adventure and frankly neither Brent nor Sally nor Keira were going out of their way to have one. At least nothing more than the occasional torrid love affair and the awkward self-questioning typical of many young adults like themselves. Sally was finishing her studies in the Theosophy Department of the University hoping to become Professor Rafter's assistant, Keira, Sally's best friend and lover, was a young librarian who occasionally sang in a popular folk group and Brent was a would-be writer who couldn't quite get his act together and who spent hours wandering the streets and lanes of the town in search of inspiration. Yet unbeknown to them forces had long been at work that would throw them together in a series of adventures that were going to tax them to the extreme forcing them to develop abilities that went way beyond what would seem possible. Their journey would take them from the real world to the realm of dreams and on to another world called the Reaches that at first sight looked deceptively like their own.

The Storyteller's Quest ~ Book Two
The Keeper's Daughter
Alan McCluskey

The Keeper's Daughter
The Storyteller's Quest Book Two

by Alan McCluskey

It wasn't Brent's fault if he was stuck in the form of an owl, at least he didn't think it was as he sat on a branch preening. The threads of his stories had become inextricably muddled in his owlish head. To think that he'd once prided himself on being a storyteller. His stories had become adventures and some of those had become nightmares, and now he was stuck with them. He'd flown in search of his friend and lover, Mia. She'd been dragged off by a band of thugs just when it was time to return to their world. Only Sally, their mutual friend and lover, had made it back to their hometown of Avan. Hearing her story, despite the dangers she'd had to face, her friends suggested Sally teach them to travel to the Dream Realm and beyond to the Reaches. The idea appealed to everybody. Not that Sally knew how to get back to the Reaches, but the idea of a 'dream class' as they called it pleased her and, above all, she wanted to return to the world where her newly-found half-sister lived and where her two friends had so abruptly disappeared.

The Storyteller's Quest ~ Book Three
The Starless Square
Alan McCluskey

The Starless Square
The Storyteller's Quest Book Three
by Alan McCluskey

A weekend of joyous festivities! Such was the Theosophy department's response to a group of fanatics bent on destroying their reputation and having them shut down. Theosophy? Professor Rafter, head of the department, called it "the study of our direct relationship with that which is beyond and above the normal range of human experience". He could just as well have been describing the adventures of the group of young friends who had been called back from their travels in another world to defend their department with their new-found abilities. But how could entrancing singing or breath-taking storytelling or exquisite cooking possibly stand a chance when pitted against the evil black cloud that threatened to obscure the Starless Square?